MAMMON

MAMMON

J.B. THOMAS

RANDOM HOUSE AUSTRALIA

A Random House book
Published by Random House Australia Pty Ltd
Level 3, 100 Pacific Highway, North Sydney NSW 2060
www.randomhouse.com.au

First published by Random House Australia in 2011

Addresses for companies within the Random House Group can be found at
www.randomhouse.com.au/offices.

National Library of Australia
Cataloguing-in-Publication Entry

Author: Thomas, J.B., 1971–
Title: Mammon / J.B. Thomas
ISBN 978 1 74275 074 3 (pbk)
Target Audience: For secondary school age
Dewey Number: A823.4

Cover design by Mathematics, www.xy-1.com
Cover images by iStockphoto
Internal design by Midland Typesetters
Author photo by Lloyd on Admiral
Typeset in Adobe Garamond 12/15.5pt by Midland Typesetters, Australia
Printed in Australia by Griffin Press, an accredited ISO AS/NZS 14001:2004
Environmental Management System printer

10 9 8 7 6 5 4 3 2 1

The paper this book is printed on is certified against the
Forest Stewardship Council® Standards. Griffin Press holds
FSC chain of custody certification SGS-COC-005088. FSC
promotes environmentally responsible, socially beneficial and
economically viable management of the world's forests.

FSC
www.fsc.org
MIX
Paper from
responsible sources
FSC® C009448

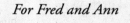

For Fred and Ann

Prologue

IT WAS NEARLY DAWN. The sun seemed to hang behind the earth, teasing a fine gold line along the horizon. Soon it would burst through and punish the city with another day of wracking heat.

But in a darkened alley, an unnatural frost was on the move, creeping up grimy walls, chasing flies away from rubbish bins, sweeping over rats hiding in gutters.

And finally, touching the lips of a sleeping boy.

He snored; his chin dipping with each breath, nudging his collarbone. A blond fringe hung over one eye. He wore a dusky blue t-shirt. A rip had ruined the elite logo and a clump of sweaty chest hair poked through. One hand rested on his filthy jeans, in the other lay a worn snapshot of a little girl perched on a swing.

His grey canvas backpack lay on its side, surrounded by an unopened pack of chilli noodles, loose banknotes and three empty cans of pre-mix bourbon.

The frost was now a cloud around his lips, staining his breath. He coughed; icy flecks floated into the air. As he opened his eyes lazily, he noticed the snapshot and sighed. Too much to think about. He jumped, startled by noise from above. Shadows flitted along those walls beyond which bakers yelled sharp, foreign words and cinnamon scents lingered.

With a groan, the boy bent his head. Bittersweet pain hit him with the stretching. A rumbling in his gut made the boy smile in the direction of the shouting as he pictured himself climbing up those stone stairs one more time into an oak-lined room, where the air was drenched with vanilla; imagined sliding into a soft red booth, could almost feel his tongue tingle with coffee and hot, sugary bread.

He kicked the empty cans away, his stomach turning at the morning-after stench.

He glanced sideways tiredly. With a jolt, he jumped up. 'You found me!'

Leaning casually against a wall, with curled fingers pressed thoughtfully against his lips, the visitor watched. His dark, neatly trimmed hair sat evenly above a fresh linen collar. He tapped his foot lightly; the dark leather of his shoe seemed to repel the dust.

At first the boy was shocked and then silently admiring. He shook his head in wonder. *Amazing. Not a drip of sweat. So composed. So calm. In this heat.*

He shook his head a second time – as if to banish a clouding in his mind.

No. He wouldn't be blindsided now. There was something very wrong here.

The man radiated frost.

'Sleep well?' The man watched his own fingers stretching; absorbed by the interchanging of muscle, bone and flesh; his dark eyes glittered with a fascination that was intense, yet fleeting.

'Yeah.' He tried to pass off a casual shrug. *Run. Now.*

'Why did you leave?'

The boy fought a swelling in his throat. Nervous sparks raced along his spine, his neck hairs stood rigid. A month ago he'd seen the violence that now simmered beneath those harsh eyes, that latent anger. He felt its potential. The axeman pacing in the shadows, the shark waiting to strike. 'It's in my nature to move around.'

Why aren't you running?

'To live like this?' The man eased off the wall, pausing to smooth his tie with elegant strokes. 'You look miserable, Jeremy. All you had to do was try. *Really* try – and you'd have succeeded.'

Don't be fooled. Run! The swelling worsened, trapping air in his throat. Claustrophobia hit. Rooftops conspired to close him in.

He closed his eyes. *But I can't run forever.*

Grinding his teeth together, the boy glanced up and gave the man a firm stare. 'Look, this thing you want me to do. Why do you want it so badly? I'm not so sure I want to do it at all –'

'Jeremy, if you can open the gateway for me, you'll know unimaginable power.' The man stressed the last word. With clenched fists he began a slow, rehearsed walk, his eyes always on the boy's face, eyes that narrowed now, searching, analysing, probing for a key.

'Hmm. You think you're just like everyone else, don't you?'

'I am.'

'No. You have the gift, my son.' He was whispering now, reverently. 'To bend space and time . . . to *your* will.' His dark eyes flashed.

'Secrets of the universe.'

The man nodded at the photograph and raised his eyebrows. 'You might be able to change your own history.'

Tightness hit Jeremy's throat again, but from tears not terror. Could he really have them back? Lulu, safely curled up in his palm was, in truth, alone in the dark with a ton of earth trapping her. He remembered Dad, demolished by guilt, his head blown apart by the thunder. The rank stench of blood spilling onto carpet. Mum, mad-eyed, feverishly cleaning the wound, pleading with him not to give up; not to leave her alone.

Her shattering descent into madness.

Two junked-up years, stumbling around from one cesspit to another until rough voices would come; meaty fists yanking his hair and thrashing him against walls.

Jeremy looked up at his mentor – the unlikely friend who'd brought him to a new, privileged life. Cars, women, clothes. Toys that had distracted him from the questions he should have asked: *What do you really want, and why, oh why, do you sweat icicles?*

'Try again for me.' The man's voice soothed him, encouraging.

No! You can't do it! Run! Now!

But his eyes flickered to his sister's face. Sighing, he slid the picture into his pocket. In his peripheral vision he saw the man's head nod sharply. 'Yes. Son, you can do this.'

His palms sweated with fearful anticipation. He'd been here before.

The man licked his lips, as if tasting a triumph to come.

Hovering near Jeremy's face, a white dot quickly grew into a small sphere.

'That's it!' The man stepped excitedly towards the boy. But his smile soon fell. The rift was not growing. The man lunged forward. 'Give it everything you have! Everything!'

The rift shook – a volcano on the verge of eruption – restrained power needing a final spark; an elusive catalyst by which it would explode into life.

But Jeremy slumped, pressing his hands against tired knees. 'Can't.'

'No,' the man said, slowly. 'You can't, can you.'

Then, the air fell silent. Jeremy could hear the man's teeth grind together.

Panting, he looked into the man's face. He'd seen this look before, from men who would sell their own children to win the game. 'I just can't do it.' The statement was reckless, Jeremy knew that – but it was courageous, nonetheless. It was the type of courage that comes when there's nothing to lose. It was a relief, at last, to tell the truth. Time to throw the cards on the table. Coughing, Jeremy glanced up. 'Anyway, there's something very wrong . . . about you.' He curled his lip with distaste. 'Screw you.'

A loud crack and Jeremy was airborne, only realising he'd been thrown after crashing on a stack of pallets. Trying to move, he gasped and gave a sharp cry of pain; he'd been impaled by a wooden stake – from which now trickled a stream of blood.

'Screw me? Screw you! You know what your problem is, boy? You're afraid!

'And now, useless to me.'

The man's face froze, lifeless. No spark in those dark eyes.

Jeremy felt his limbs sag. All his energy seemed to seep out.

A black cloud began to rise from the back of the man's head. A horde of rats ran from their gutter.

A smashing sound and then bricks tumbled, dust puffed into the air. Coughing, Jeremy saw the slash marks of claws on the damaged wall. The dark shape moved forward.

A warm stickiness streamed down his leg.

Wincing, he hugged his side. A primal rumbling filled the air and the stickiness streamed some more. Overhead, windows shook. Rhythmic jolts of pain hit as the beast came closer; the alley trembled. A series of low snaps sounded; each slab cracked as though under a great weight. Even in the midst of the fury, Jeremy shook his head in awe. 'How . . .' he gasped. 'What are you?'

The Shadow Wolf roared, shattering the air, leaving Jeremy's eyes burning, watering. His hands flew to his ears. Surely they must be bleeding. Frost numbed his cheeks. He squeezed his eyes shut, willing his body to fly away as the thundering pounded his face again.

'Coward! Do you know how long I've waited?'

Something clamped his ankles, cutting in, and then he was hanging. The walls spun, closing in on him. He flew against one – in a surreal instant he saw the dent left behind and the glistening of blood.

Then, no more.

The Shadow Wolf raged on, smashing the boy from wall to wall. Its roaring was low and terrible.

But soon, it tired. Jeremy's body flew one last time – landing with a squelching sound on a bed of splintered glass and brick dust. A contemptuous growl – for every time this being was freed from its human host, it rejoiced in the unrestrained power – then the cloud began barrelling into the back of the man's head.

Cold eyes opened. Only the small streak of light gave hint to the life force once again animating the flesh.

Reaching into the smooth coolness of his suit pocket, the man slowly drew out a handkerchief, working the silky fabric into a neat triangle and patting the frost from his face.

With the barest flick of his wrist, he tossed the handkerchief and watched it flutter away, intrigued by the white folds struggling in the warm wind like a dying dove. It went on to tumble past the remains of the runaway boy – but by then the man was walking into the new day.

'Master.' The elderly servant smiled and bowed. His Lord had just done the impossible: assumed his real form. Sustained it in Earth's atmosphere. Incredible.

The man slid into the car, smoothed his tie and slid on a pair of mirrored shades. He tapped his clean, neat fingernails against his knee.

The old man limped to the driver's door. Groaning, he slid onto the seat.

'Halphas.'

'My Lord?'

'I am disappointed. Take me home.'

'Yes, Master.' Halphas pressed the ignition button. The engine roared, startling a group of pigeons that hopped away from the kerb.

Still, the voice called from the back seat. 'Halphas.'

The old man felt a burning at the back of his neck. 'My Lord?'

'Tonight I will name my new apprentices. They will help us find the next Ferryman.'

'Who have you chosen, Master?'

Halphas glanced in the rear vision mirror, but Master was staring out of the window now, observing the City's early morning activity with insatiable interest.

His City.

In the alley, a pale-faced man, speckled with flour and sweat, slowly sank onto a stone step, wondering how a boy could have been beaten to death by nothing more than air.

PART ONE

ONE

AT THE EDGE of a lonely continent, between a broad desert and stormy sea, lay Border City.

To the west, seabirds congregated on top of rocky towers that had prised their way up from the ocean floor. Barrelling waves tore against cliff faces.

To the south, mist-drenched forests spread for miles.

To the east, a row of stony-faced mountains guarded the City from the desert's brutal sands.

To the north: the Wasteland. Plundered, abandoned, ignored.

And there, in the middle of it all, stood the great mirrored towers, where the sophisticated few met for coffee on the waterfront or strolled through glass-lined colonnades. In Cold River's tranquil bays, white hulls bobbed and noise was restricted to refined laughter, or the swoop of a pelican's wing.

But when the sun pulled away, the City showed another face. The River: grey, choppy and barren. Soft, respectable tones – sunset against polished glass and steel – gave way to vulgar neon, flesh and fear.

It was here that the next Ferryman was born.

* * *

'Okay, Year Elevens. Let's break down the question: how does Plato use the Allegory of the Cave to illustrate how man can believe in a false reality?' The teacher glanced around the room and laughed. 'Come on, you guys! It's not that bad!'

A groan rumbled through the class. 'Oh, miss! You must be joking! It's so hot!'

The teacher smiled. 'I know.' She leaned back on her desk, tapping her fingers against the wood. 'But just imagine how the prisoners felt next to the fires in Plato's Cave.'

Outside, parched leaves hung from weary branches. Birds stalked the ground for puddles, their angry caws cutting the stagnant air. Clouds bulged, threatening rain.

Students slumped across desks, throwing woeful stares in her direction.

'Come on, people! We've been through this!' She sighed. 'Just try. That's all I ask. Start by highlighting the keywords.'

Grace's head felt heavy – like the monsoonal grey that passed as the sky. Absently, she coloured in the words that she hoped were key to the question. Her stomach clenched and churned. She'd felt uneasy for days.

Tomorrow, she might feel better. It was just the heat.

She drew a hairtie from her pocket and scooped up her long, dark curls into a messy bun. She could feel the leering stares of two boys in the next row. Grace didn't want to look at them. But of course, she did. One of them, a tall, blond guy, made an obscene gesture with his tongue and two fingers. His friend laughed.

Grace scowled. 'Get lost, you pig.'

Her cheeks burned as she reached for her water bottle. It tipped. Lazily, she watched it fall to the floor. Everything seemed to be in slow motion today. As she leaned down and grabbed the bottle, a small crack in the nearby window glinted, catching her eye.

It glowed strangely in the afternoon's grey light. But more – it was moving. Spreading like humid breath on cold glass, swallowing up her reflection.

Frost.

Her eyes narrowed. She touched her finger against the pane. It was cold, even though it was a 38-degree day.

A shadow fell across the window. It was the Tyler boy, Jesse. Trudging; his hands in the pockets of his black sweat-shirt, hooded.

Moisture in her mouth: a telltale watering. She was going to be sick. Nerves twisted her stomach. Her fingers tightened around the bottle.

Jesse Tyler stared straight at her.

She knew this boy; knew the family. A mean, gritty history. Not the breeding ground for happy assimilation into adult life.

His eyes burned at her with a cold fury. *What are you looking at?* She heard him, although she could swear his lips hadn't moved.

The bottle gave an audible crack.

There was something there with him.

On his back.

A shadow – clinging to his body like a parasite.

Then she connected with Jesse's mind. The sensation was like falling in a dream, she felt as if she were tumbling out of control; she saw his life . . . heard a man's voice – hard and unforgiving. A drunken stench. A leather belt, burning lines into his back.

She wasn't breathing.

Jesse spoke again – a low, rumbling echo.

It couldn't be real.

She could faint. Heart hammering, she closed her eyes and pleaded for it to go away.

Abruptly as it had begun, the shaking stopped. Grace opened her eyes to an empty window, but the world was still a blur; the fallout still lingering in her stomach.

A few feet away, her teacher stood clasping a paper. 'Grace, what's the problem?'

She stared at her fingertip, still damp from the frost that was receding from the glass. Something bounced off her back and drew a flurry of laughter.

'Brian and Adrian!' The teacher's voice boomed. 'Not the kind of behaviour I expect in a senior class!'

Grace gagged. Her mouth bulged with bitter stickiness.

Away from the teacher's call, the mocking murmurs, the cluster of catty giggles – she clutched her bag and let her legs race her to the bathroom, mouth forced closed by tight fingers, only to lose the contents of her stomach all over the basin.

* * *

JOE PEERED OVER the engine, wrench in hand. Sweat trickled along his stubble. He stood back, ignoring the row of droplets that sat on his hairline. 'Okay.' He looked at his teacher. 'Then, I replaced the brake pads.'

'Right. And after that?'

'You can see that I've replaced the spark plugs. Um, what else . . . I checked the timing and that's okay.'

'And that's it?'

'Oh, there was a crack in the hose so I replaced it.'

'Excellent, Joe.' The man scrawled rough notes on a clipboard. 'Don't rest on your laurels just yet, but I think you're going to graduate top of the Year 12 automotive class.'

Joe wiped the sweat from his forehead and nodded. 'Thanks, sir.'

'And you know what that means. Guaranteed placement. Have you given any thought to where you'd like to work?'

'With bikes, sir. I don't care where, just with bikes.' Tossing the wrench onto a trolley, Joe began winding up a rubber hose. Behind the sink was a large window and the teacher's desk. Joe caught his reflection: a mass of brown curls that begged for a cut; a shockingly white smile against sun-cooked skin.

'Hey, Callahan.'

A boy lounged against the sink. His work shirt was open, revealing a white singlet and several silver chains. He examined his fingernails with a casual, arrogant air.

Joe threw him a careless glance. 'Enzo.'

'How's Grace?'

Joe turned on the tap and grabbed a yellow bar. Without glancing up he began scrubbing his hands. 'Aren't you supposed to be working on your car?'

Leaning back, the other boy crossed his legs and tilted his face towards Joe. 'I was thinking . . .' His eyes sparkled through his curly fringe. 'I might ask her out.'

Joe looked him up and down but kept scrubbing. 'Not your type, Enzo.'

The boy scowled. 'Think I'm not good enough for her?'

Joe shrugged. 'I wouldn't let you near my sister.'

Leaning in closer, Enzo swept a glance around the room. 'Is she playing in the school concert? Some of us guys thought we'd go and watch.'

Joe flicked on the hot tap.

Enzo's voice dropped to a whisper. 'I heard that she's a real firestarter. Is it true about her and Dylan James?'

A sudden crack. Enzo staggered, hand pressed against his cheek where Joe's fist had left a heavy mark.

Enzo backed away, hands raised. 'Okay, Joe. Okay.' Joe's eyes now seemed laced with red, deep with threat.

In the abrupt quiet of the workshop, tension tinged the air. Joe stalked back to his engine, his chest moving in hard breaths while the injured boy retreated to the corner of the room. The silence was only broken by the teacher's heavy footsteps. 'Right! Joe and Enzo! With me, now!'

* * *

GRACE AVOIDED HER mother's laser stare by watching the purple ripples of her bedroom ceiling; ripples that seemed to move in the shadows of the dying sun. But then, it was an illusion. Wasn't it? Her gaze wandered over familiar objects. Comforting. Her music books piled against the wall. Her pink feather boa – the matching silk gown lay in wait for the upcoming dance, hanging between t-shirts and jeans. High-cut tops and sensible skirts, courtesy of Mum's overbearing demand for modesty since Grace's figure had begun to swell into an hourglass. It made her feel self-conscious among her skinnier friends and inspired a range of X-rated nicknames among the boys; names she'd rather not have known.

Of course, her best friend, Allie, had given her a much nicer pet name – Peaches 'n' Cream – on account of Grace's clear, smooth skin.

Her gaze fell on a picture of herself and Allie at a water park last year. Careless, joyful faces. Grace had just turned seventeen; Allie only had three months of life left.

Grief fades over time, but guilt can last forever. A fresh spear hit when Grace thought about the nickname she'd given Allie. She used to call her a Jesus freak, that she had blind faith. Allie never let on that Grace's words hurt her. Now she knew they did.

But then again, God hadn't stopped her killer from climbing into the driver's seat and crawling from pub to pub, until his car slammed into Allie crossing at the green pedestrian light.

Enough. Grace tore her eyes away from the picture, and for the thousandth time, she forced away the guilt, boxing it up and kicking it out into space where it couldn't hurt her.

She turned her attention to her work in progress: a collage of various impressionist images crawling steadily up her wall. Dark, depressing pictures. What was wrong with her?

Her mother took the thermometer between her fingers. 'Well, you don't have a fever. That's good. But I don't think you need all these layers.' She pinched the hem of the quilt and pulled it back.

'No!' Grace yanked the quilt up to her chin. Racking shivers travelled along her limbs.

Her mother looked closely into Grace's green eyes. 'Honey, tell me what's going on. Is it a boy?'

Her mother's voice soothed her – like the only safe harbour in a violent, storm-swept ocean – but there was something else in the air. An unfriendly wind prickled her skin then passed on, leaving a cold sensation behind. Something new and terrifying was out there.

Oh, if only she could tell Mum. Grace sat up, edging towards the wall and hugging her legs to her chest. Even her own room looked surreal, like the walls could change, burst into something else. She mistrusted her own mind, her own eyes. 'No, Mum. It's nothing. I just don't feel well.'

'I'll be the judge of that.' Her mother spoke crisply, but she couldn't quell her worry over her daughter's strangled silence. She reached up and stroked Grace's fringe out of her eyes.

'Has anything strange happened, dear?'

'No, Mum.' Grace shivered at her mother's cool touch. Her heart still jolted occasionally. Little aftershocks.

She remembered the thing on his back . . . clinging to him, like a parasite.

'You're not going to tell me?'

Grace shook her head. 'It's nothing, really.'

Her mother kissed her forehead. 'Well, all right then. Go to sleep. You'll feel better tomorrow.'

As her bedroom door closed, Grace pulled the blankets over her head, curling up against the wall. When she shut her eyes, the shadow hung there, watching, waiting.

TWO

FIRST LIGHT. DAWN'S glow touched the curtains and eventually broke in, bathing the room in gold-white tones.

And so came the knocking, the gentle entry into the room; Mum, starchy-fresh in her work uniform, dark hair smoothed into a tidy bun. 'Morning, honey.' She swept the curtains aside and turned, hands on hips. 'Well, you look a whole lot better.'

Breakfast was punctuated by her mother's efficient steps around the kitchen, the rustling of bills and the tapping of calculator buttons. 'Right,' Mum muttered, rubbing her forehead as she tallied the amount due. Her eyes drifted up to the calendar, and she bit her fingernail. Payday was still a week away.

Grace just stared into her cereal, swirling the pieces with a spoon.

Her mother looked over. 'You'll never finish it at that rate.'

The spoon scraped against the bottom, Grace's fingers squeezed tightly around the handle. A sudden breathlessness hit. She closed her eyes and tried to push the image of Jesse Tyler's shadow from her mind.

Mum shook her head as she got up from the bench, folded up the bills and slipped them into her bag. 'You have to go to school, sweetheart. Unless there's something else that you're not telling me about.'

Joe snorted. 'She's faking it.' He grabbed a bottle of chilli sauce and shook it, drowning the fried eggs in red, sticky liquid.

Mum grimaced. 'Yuck, Joseph. How can you ruin those beautiful eggs?'

Joe shoved a runny square into his mouth. Absently, Grace watched the yolk dribble down his chin.

A voice piped out of the television. *And in society news, Vanquish Industries owner and CEO, Mammon Jones, must be celebrating this morning after his horse, Pegasus, took first place at the Midsummer Cup.*

Images splashed across the screen: a handsome, dark-haired man walking with a purposeful stride, smiling behind mirrored sunglasses and sitting in a nightclub, flanked by glamorous women.

'Rich bastard,' Joe muttered.

Mum smiled. 'And if you were that wealthy, Joseph, I can't imagine that you wouldn't have a string of gorgeous girls following you about.'

'Mum, priorities. First you get the bikes, then you get the fame – and then you get the women.' Joe put down his fork and pulled his phone from his pocket.

The newsreader continued. *Jones, who recently split with aristocratic supermodel Sophie Gaines, has a personal fortune of $50 billion with interests in banking, military technology and media networks. He has been dubbed the father of the City's economic revival, with major banks reporting a record profit and mining interests being bought by overseas investors.'*

'It'd be nice if some of that profit would come our way,' said Mum. She glanced at Grace's backpack near the front door. 'Don't you have orchestra practice after school today?'

'Oh . . . yeah.' Grace stood up. The room began to spin.

'Finish your breakfast.'

'I'm not hungry, Mum.' Her mouth tasted bitter again. She swallowed hard, wincing at the dull ache in her throat. She put the bowl in the dishwasher and headed for the stairs.

'Don't forget to brush your teeth!' Her mother glanced out the window at the grass, strewn with brown leaves – then looked back at her son, who was muttering, engrossed with the game on his phone. Mum rolled her eyes. 'You'll have to be up early tomorrow if you want to get the garden done before Dad gets back.'

'Aw, Mum!'

'You are *not* going to argue with me.'

'You know it wasn't my fault.' Joe scowled. A rush of heat hit his face. Deep down, he was itching to have another swing at Enzo – indeed, at all the scum who spread the rumours about Grace. 'He provoked me.'

Mum adjusted her watch. 'I know, but you do have to learn to control your temper. You never see your father flying off the handle like that, do you?'

11

Joe looked up at her. Sighing, he put his phone away. 'Yeah, I know.'

'I'm working in the emergency ward today, so I might have to do some overtime. Which means you're going to have to bring Grace home after her music practice.' Mum watched Grace plod back into the kitchen, violin case in tow.

Joe grimaced. 'You're not bringing that thing.'

'Of course I am!'

Mum folded her arms. 'Why shouldn't she?'

'She's always whining at me to pull over 'cause she thinks she's gonna drop it.'

'I can manage it.' Frowning, Grace slung the case over her shoulder. 'You wear the backpack.'

Joe eyed the pink bag distastefully. 'No way.'

Mum glared at Joe. 'Remember, you need to wait after school for Grace to finish practice. Joseph! You are not to forget her again. And no speeding!' She handed Grace a helmet and kissed her on the cheek.

* * *

As always, Grace found the accompaniment soothing. The piano's gentle undertones; clarinet and oboe striking harmonious, lengthy notes, an exquisite breathing out. But her violin spoke of a lonely journey; the music seemed to reflect the madness of yesterday. She wondered: had the composer seen strange things too?

The tempo slowed again in the lead-up to the key change and eventual build towards the crescendo.

She dropped the bow, a wild, sudden heartbeat thumping

in her chest. Jesse Tyler was walking past the music room. Horrified, she stared.

He walked on.

She had to know if the shadow was real.

'Grace!'

'I need the bathroom, miss,' she choked, and she was running, violin abandoned on her chair.

Keeping a sensible distance, she followed the boy, climbing over the waist-high chain fence that bordered the school, passing the red brick of the public bathrooms and their musty scent. Ahead, next to a rusty climbing frame, a girl waited. Jesse stopped and began to turn. Heart still pounding, Grace fell back to the safety of the red wall. No footsteps sounded. Breath still held, she peered around the corner.

Jesse Tyler scowled. 'Where's Tom?'

Grace stared. It was really there. The shadow clung to the boy like scum on a pond's surface.

It was real.

It had eyes – dark hollows that watched her. Then they looked to Jesse and he nodded – like the shadow said something.

He was possessed.

The girl lifted her chin. 'He asked me to come.' She trembled.

Could she see that thing on his shoulder?

'Hmm.' Jesse stared at the girl. 'Okay. Gimme the money.' He thrust out one hand, the other fishing through his pocket, scooping out a small, white bag.

'You're twenny short. What's Tom playin' at?' He snatched the money and stared hard at the girl, but she was looking over his shoulder, her face tight, tense. 'Whatsa matter?' Scowling, he followed the girl's stare, his own eyes narrowing angrily.

'Oi!' With gritted teeth, he shoved the bag back in his pocket.

Grace took a backward step.

The girl tapped Jesse's shoulder. 'Hey! The stuff!'

He shoved her away; she stumbled back, tripping on the metal frame. The boy started coming towards Grace.

The anger washed over her like fire, needling her skin, growing stronger with each step he took.

Yet she felt so cold. Shivers ran down her legs. He reached her. She retreated; he quickly closed the gap. 'What you doin' here?'

Then he stopped. 'Oh, it's you.' He grinned, lips parting to show a row of grimy teeth. 'I saw you yesterday. Grovelling about on the floor. Why the hell did you follow me here?'

'Who says I followed you?'

'You're Grace Callahan. I know you.' He leaned in close and winked. 'You've been around, haven't ya?'

Anger overtook the fear. 'Shut up, you scum.'

'You stupid bitch! Calling *me* scum!'

He smelled of violence . . . as if there could be such a smell. His face covered in sweat . . . or was it frost? She blinked.

Her legs felt paralysed.

'I'm not scared of you!' Oh, but that thing on his back. She stared past him at the climbing frame and a smear of blood left behind by the girl. For once she wished Joe was here.

Jesse was so close now, his breath staining the air with cigarettes and curry. She closed her eyes. If she looked too closely at the darkness around him, she'd faint.

'Not so mouthy now? I can smell the fear off ya.'

The tremor spread to her ankles. She shouldn't have followed him. *Joe, where are you?*

Her mouth wouldn't work. *Get away from me.* She squeezed her eyes shut.

Get away!

He winced. 'Stop it!'

Grace's eyes flew open. She watched him roll his head from side to side, shaking it as though something was rattling around inside, tormenting him. Like a dog shaking a mouse to death. The shadow shook, too, but stayed fast. Glued to him.

Grace felt her bottom lip sagging. A squeak escaped her throat. In her head, the words came tumbling. *Go away! Go away! Go away!*

'Aargh! Get out of my head!'

'Grace!'

She glanced over her shoulder. Joe was running across, his eyes promising violence. But as he neared, he slowed to a walk, his mouth wide, eyes large. 'What *is* that . . .?'

Grace's heart drummed hard. Joe could see it too.

'Oi! Jesse!'

All three glanced across; on the other side of the basketball courts, an older boy stood. 'Get your arse home.'

Grace edged over to her brother, gripping his arm. 'Joe –'

Jesse backed away, eyes darting between this strange girl and her brother. 'Yeah, yeah. Comin'.' Jesse flipped his hood over his head and swaggered into the distance.

Grace and Joe watched as the two figures spoke briefly. The older boy glanced over.

He had a shadow too – but darker, stronger.

A soft wind blew across Grace's face, cooling her clammy skin. She turned around. 'Joe?'

He grabbed her arm. 'Come on.'

'Did you see it?' He saw it. She knew he did.

'Come on!'

She yanked her arm back. 'Don't drag me.'

'It's time to go home.'

'My violin . . .'

'Hurry up!' He shoved her towards the music room.

She crept in, past the woodwind section, and shoved the violin into the case as delicately as she could. 'Grace!' The conductor held up a hand. 'What's going on?'

Grace slung the strap around her back and grabbed her backpack. 'Sorry, miss. I have to go home. My mum called.'

'All right, but make sure you practise. The concert is only two weeks away!'

'Yep.'

She could feel Joe's impatient glare from the doorway, intensifying as she approached the bike. 'Come on!' Snatching her backpack, he slung it over his shoulder.

'You saw it, didn't you?'

'Get on the bike, Grace.'

She swung her leg over the seat. 'How did you know where I was?'

'I heard you screaming! Surprised the whole neighbour-hood didn't hear you.' He kick-started the engine, revving it, the spluttering soon settling into a steady hum.

'I didn't scream!'

'Yes you did!' The bike sped through the front gates, tyres squealing as Joe opened up the throttle.

* * *

'WHAT WERE YOU doing down there, anyway?' Joe grabbed a tennis ball from his bedside table and started lobbing it against the wall.

'Joe, that was Jesse Tyler, right?'

'Yeah. The oldest brother did eight years for armed robbery. Just got out. The other one, Travis, got expelled last year, d'you remember?'

Grace watched the ball bounce in a triangular pattern. 'What did Jesse look like to you?'

He shrugged, looking out the window. 'Oh, bit weird.'

She watched a drip of sweat snake down his neck. 'Like what?'

'Just weird. Who cares?' His hands shook.

She narrowed her eyes. 'I know you saw it.'

The ball bounced harder.

'Answer me!' Swooping in, she snatched the ball.

'Give it to me!' He lunged for it; she hid the ball behind her back. 'Uh, uh!' She wagged her finger. 'Tell me what you saw!'

Too quickly for her to react, Joe grabbed her left hand and pinned it down, wrenching the ball away. 'Ow!' She rubbed her hand.

The bouncing resumed.

Indignant, Grace got to her feet. 'If it's nothing, why did you rush home?'

Joe caught the ball, squeezing it hard. 'Look. You embarrassed me and yourself. I was working on the engine and you dragged me away from it, screaming like that.'

'I didn't scream.'

He scowled. 'Get out, Grace.'

'I didn't scream! Why won't you listen to me?'

'Get *out*!' Jumping to his feet, he flew across the room and dug his fingers into her arm, dragging her.

'Ow! You're hurting me!'

He slung her across the hallway, her shoulder grazing the wall.

'Ow!'

He slammed the door. Startled, Grace jumped. Her throat clenched, she swallowed hard. She leaned closer to the door. 'Just admit it, Joe. You saw the shadow. You heard me in your head. And it's freaking you out!'

* * *

GRACE TOOK A sip of juice, mingling it with the leftover custard taste from dessert. She put the glass down on her bedside table and gazed out at the night sky. She rubbed her shoulder, still tender from when Joe had shoved her out of his room.

'Joe heard me. So did that boy.' Shivering, she kicked off her slippers as the shadow floated through her mind. 'But why? What *is* it? Why couldn't we see it before?'

The heat still hung in the air, although a very light

wind whistled through the trees. Dinner had been quiet, uncomfortable, with Mum casting concerned glances between her two children.

Grace turned, folded her arms and stared at the wall.

Joe.

Joe?

Joe!

Reliably, a hard kick to the wall confirmed it. 'Grace, *shut up!*'

'Ha!' She peered around the doorway and then darted into Joe's room, shutting the door behind her. Still in his school clothes he lay on his side, arms folded, staring at the wall. An amber glow from the bedside table shone against his wall, which was papered with hot rods. A small ant colony had taken up residence in the dregs of a cola can. Socks, shirts and shoes were strewn about.

She grimaced. 'You're such a slob.'

He grunted. 'Stop yelling through the wall. I thought you stopped that game years ago.'

'So,' she said, drawing a triumphant breath, 'you heard me again.'

'You yell so *loud*. What the hell?'

At least he wasn't angry anymore. She sank onto his bed and tapped her fingertips on the bedframe. 'I wasn't yelling, Joe.'

Groaning, he buried his face in the pillow. 'Oh, God. You *were*.'

Am I yelling now?

He sat upright, wild-eyed. 'Stop it, Grace!'

She shrugged. 'If I was only yelling, why would you freak out so much?'

'You're being weird.'

She waited for his eyes to meet hers again. *I'm not yelling, Joe.*

'Don't,' he gasped, holding up a warning hand. His voice came slow and heavy. 'I don't know what trick you're playing, but stop it.'

'There's no trick.'

He stared. 'Your lips didn't move.'

Grace nodded. 'The thing is, I can't tell if you can hear me unless you say so.'

He shook his head rapidly. 'Na. This is bull.'

She could tell his heart was pounding.

'Go to bed, Grace.'

'But Joe –'

'I'm going to sleep now.' He curled away, nose to the wall again. Absently, she rubbed the fabric of the bedsheet between her fingers, staring at his back. With a deep sigh, she rose and plodded back to her own bedroom.

* * *

THE DREAM STARTED like it always did – she was walking past the river. The first change she noticed was the strange light that surrounded the City. It was ashen . . . burned. She stood, caught by the scene around her: voices yelling, engines screaming, the smell of exhaust fouling the air.

She looked to her left; Joe looked back.

With a strange smile, he lifted his hands. A black circle appeared above him, rippled by lightning. It exploded in a cascade of brilliant white, releasing trails – black slivers of murky fog that swam through the night air.

She staggered backwards, holding her arms out as Joe stared at her, his eyes shining with a strange glow. His face, hair and body became invisible – everything fading into a dull grey against the brutal fire shining in his eyes.

He wasn't Joe anymore.

She beat her way out of the dream, clawing, crying – returning to consciousness, screaming in the darkness, breathing fast, hot tears gushing down her face.

THREE

THE BONAPARTE CLUB – Mammon's favourite haunt in Border City – was crowded with politicians, merchants and other people of consequence. Halphas walked across the foyer – an oak-lined room where burgundy curtains billowed around arch windows that overlooked a terrace garden. A bust of Julius Caesar graced the inner wall; overflowing lily arrangements lent a light touch to the mahogany reception tables.

In the main dining area, the sunset gave a soft glow to the linen and glassware on the untouched tables. It was the aperitif hour. The elegant strains of a string quartet filled the air. Silent waiters moved among the crowd. This was a place where the rich did not wish to see them.

And Halphas knew they most certainly wouldn't want to see *him*.

But he definitely felt the prickling attention of the four young demons – Master's new Anointed Ones. His apprentices. Former scholars of business, politics and law, they'd fallen away from their studies and under Mammon's spell. All too easily seduced by his lifestyle.

Master had given these four the best gift of all.

Invisibility. These four could appear to the Sighted as ordinary humans. They could hide their true faces, their essences.

Just like Master.

It was as if Mammon intended to create younger versions of himself and shape them as he saw fit.

Andras, gifted with the power to influence, persuade and divide, stepped closer to Mammon and gave Halphas a critical stare. Halphas looked the young demon over: from the glossy shoes and black silk suit to the fresh linen collar, slick hair and whiff of subtle cologne, Andras had moulded himself into a perfect little clone.

The nerve of him. The nerve of them all! Upstarts, still possessing that aura of youth. Insolent pups. Halphas quietly seethed.

The other apprentices stood nearby. Haures, the shape-shifter, was enjoying an obscene amount of male attention. Flashing a smile, she slid her fingertips through waves of ruby hair that cascaded over her pale, bare shoulders. With each stroke, the strands shone like fire. For Halphas, everything else started to melt away – except the urge to stroke her hair and press his mouth against her luminous skin.

Haures caught his stare. 'Hello, Halphas!' She gave him a teasing smile and fluttered a Japanese fan in front of her face.

Halphas looked away. Dirty succubus.

The mind-reader Andromalius was pacing, ear pressed to a phone, cigarette in hand. 'I know what you're doing,' he hissed. 'Do not try to lie to me.' He drew a puff and pressed his fingers against his forehead, shoving aside his blond fringe. 'I'll be at the docks myself, and if I see anything missing from the shipment . . . What? You don't like your cut? Consider yourself fortunate. The boss isn't usually that generous.'

The conjurer Zagan was staring at a vase. Halphas smirked at the young demon's choice of attire: jeans, rugby jumper and brilliant white runners. Topped by a shorn head, the young demon looked criminally rough, given the fine company in this club.

Zagan tilted his head, closed his dark eyes. The vase lifted off and floated above the stand. Halphas brushed past. 'You're terribly underdressed, young man.'

The young demon opened his eyes with a start, lunged forward and caught the vase. 'Watch where you're walking, *old* man!'

Andromalius flicked his cigarette on the floor and stared at Halphas through pinched blue eyes. 'You're late, Halphas. You know he doesn't like to wait.'

How dare she try to tell him about Master. Halphas strode on, mimicking Mammon's effortless glide but lamenting the ache in his knees.

He recognised Master's companions as Senator Julian Ellis and Anton Van Beuren. Both men owed their fortune to Master, in one form or the other. They were red-cheeked and overly friendly; Master listened to their stories in a comfortable human stance: hands in pockets, smiling occasionally.

* * *

Mammon glanced lazily at Senator Ellis's wife. His eyes lingered on her neckline, where ruffles of purple satin blended into the shiny black curls that spilled over her tanned shoulders. A pleasing sight. His gaze trailed up her neck and face; with each centimetre he seemed to be marking his territory.

She gasped, pulse quickening. Her hand rushed up to touch her throat.

Smiling, Mammon took an appetiser from a floating tray: a square of lamb garnished with an asparagus spear. 'The problem with your staff, Van Beuren, is that they don't know their place. You tell me they're all unionised. Well, I'm telling you that you can sack them all without fear of union reprisals, then replenish your workforce with a more compliant host of workers. Just ask, and it will be done.'

Halphas coughed – not to attract his master's attention, but rather to clear the dusty phlegm that had gathered near his windpipe. 'Ready to set sail, Master?'

'You're late.' Mammon finished his wine. 'Well, gentlemen, the hour has come and gone. I bid you goodnight.'

He settled an expectant stare on the Senator's wife.

The Senator, whose eyes had dulled with the weight of acceptance, nodded, voice husky with regret. 'Go on, Maria.'

'Goodnight, Julian.' She took Mammon's arm; her pulse visibly pounding in her neck as he guided her into the sultry night.

* * *

Halphas peeked into the rearview mirror and shook his head. Women. By the time they'd reached Mammon's yacht, Maria Ellis was giggling and letting Master kiss her neck. His eyes drifted across to the four apprentices seated in the back. With a quiet chuckle, he pictured her reaction if she found out just whom she was keeping company with.

As they boarded the yacht, the staff were assembled in a neat, white row. Efficient, silent, obedient – just the way Master liked them. The chief steward gave him a servile nod. 'Sir. Wonderful to have you aboard again.'

Mammon guided the Senator's wife towards the stairs that led to the upper deck. 'Show the lady to my stateroom and make her comfortable.' He stretched his arms and nodded at the captain. 'Let's get to sea.'

The engine rumbled; several deckhands moved around the yacht, casting off the ropes. Above the bridge, a vast spotlight radiated across the water, bouncing off the smaller vessels that scurried aside, making way for the dark blue leviathan that was thundering away from the pier.

The yacht pierced through the waves, its mammoth hull merging with the blackened waters of the late evening. In the distance, the lights of Border City were a neon blur; above, a heavy moon hung in the velvet sky, its reflection catching the waves.

* * *

THE SMELL OF roasted garlic and prawns filtered through the cabin, creating a dull ache in Halphas's stomach. His eyes wandered to the clock: it was eight-thirty. He glanced at the chambermaid, whose arms were beginning to sag under the weight of Mammon's shirts. 'No, not that one!'

Halphas reached over and yanked a dark grey garment from the pile. 'Where's Master's ivory silk shirt?'

Wide-eyed, the maid shook her head. 'I don't know, sir. I don't remember seeing it. I'm sorry, sir!'

'Rubbish. It's on this boat. I told laundry to bring it aboard. Fetch the boy to me.'

The maid pressed an intercom button. 'Bess, can you send William up to the boss's stateroom? Thanks.'

She released the button and staggered forward. 'May I lay the shirts down, sir?'

'And let them get rumpled and dirty? Absolutely not. Stay where you are.'

A light tapping and a tall, slender boy entered the room. The maid gave him a sympathetic smile. Poor lad. First time to sea and he was about to get a kicking.

Halphas eyed the boy. 'Where is the ivory silk shirt that was brought aboard?'

William bit his lip. 'I don't know.'

'You brought the clothing yourself. I remember showing it to you, telling you it was one of Master's favourites, urging you to take care with it. Master wants to wear it tonight. So, I repeat, where is the shirt?'

'What brand was it? Maybe I can remember . . .' the boy stammered.

Halphas sneered. 'It was no brand – Master's clothes are all tailored! Now, I ask you for the last time – where is the shirt?'

'I don't think we have it.'

'What do you mean by that?'

'I mean . . .' William cast a nervous look at the maid. 'I think it's ruined.'

'What?' Halphas wore a look of horror. 'Where is it?'

'I'll show you, sir.'

They made their way downstairs to the bowels of the yacht and the cramped service areas. The smell of pine filled the air as they passed a kitchen hand squeezing out a mop. Then they entered the oppressive moisture of the laundry, where a row of neatly dressed women folded tablecloths and napkins. No heads were raised on Halphas's entry. He shoved William through the door; the boy tripped and caught his balance on a benchtop.

'Show me,' Halphas hissed.

With a forlorn limp, William moved across to a row of wastepaper bins. Silently, he reached in and fished out a crumpled piece of fabric.

Halphas snatched the garment and held it up. Patched across the fine fabric in the centre was an iron stain. Several small holes punctured the fabric. He turned and gave the boy a long, piercing stare. 'You don't iron this, you idiot!' With the destroyed shirt in one hand, he grabbed William and shoved him towards the door. 'You're going to account for this yourself, with Master.'

Mammon was waiting in his dressing room when Halphas pushed the boy through the door.

'Why aren't my clothes laid out, Halphas?' Mammon stood in front of a full-length mirror. The carpet was soaked; he'd folded a towel around his waist and now stood, dripping, gazing at his reflection. He'd chosen well this time. A worthy vessel. Dark hair played across his forehead in a gentle wave. Skin that glowed with an olive warmth meant that he never looked tired or ill. A panther-like sensuality, a sexual confidence that simultaneously frightened and aroused those around him. Of course, it was his Shadow, his glorious essence that gave the body such alluring energy.

His eyes drifted to the old man, watching him in the mirror with a tense expression. To the boy, to the ruined shirt. 'What's this?'

Halphas shoved William forward. 'This boy burned your shirt, Master. The fool tried to iron it.'

'Did he?' Mammon drew a deep breath. 'And do I have another like it?' He took a handful of pomade and smoothed back his hair.

Halphas nudged the boy. 'Answer him.'

'No, sir,' William stammered.

'Mmm. That's disappointing!' Mammon walked over and patted the boy's shoulder. 'You need to learn how to do your job better, son.'

William held his breath; his heart pounded. He let Mammon walk him out onto the deck. 'I'm sorry, sir. It was an accident.'

Halphas waited, his eyes glinting with the anticipation.

'Mmm.' Mammon drew back and regarded the boy. 'Well, would you be careful in future?'

William breathed out. 'Yes, sir. Of course.'

Mammon smiled. 'Of course you would.' He lunged forward and grabbed the boy by the throat, yanking him off his feet, carrying him towards the railing. William kicked his legs; a futile, pointless act – infantile. Below, the dark waters lay in wait.

'Please, sir! Please don't!'

Mammon jutted out his chin, bared his teeth. 'I liked

that shirt.' He lifted the boy higher and threw him out into the air.

There was a brief silence, then William crashed into the water. Halphas watched the boy's head emerge and his panicked eyes snap left and right. The old man looked to the horizon, and he knew what William was thinking: there was no land in sight. The sun was disappearing behind the earth; sea and sky merging in a suffocating blackness.

The boy would never see home again. Within minutes he would be gulping water; the waves being so high and all. Without emotion, Halphas watched the boy become a dot in the distance.

Mammon drew a deep breath and rolled his neck from side to side. 'God, I love the sea air.' He turned and made his way back into the stateroom. 'Find me another shirt, Halphas.'

FOUR

IN THE CALM of early morning, Joe was flying.

He passed a dying star, its brilliant shards of purple light beaming out from the fiery core.

He felt the tingle of ice particles, a ring that orbited a lonely world. Voices cried from that space, calling to him.

Mercy.

The dark bubble that carried him couldn't shut out those voices. They rose from the planet's core in dark, murky waves. He turned away, tormented by the collective agony.

A tunnel lay ahead. Made of thunderclouds, moving, illuminated against the blackness of space by ripples of lightning that charged up and down curved walls.

He floated at its entrance. It would take him to eternity, but he wasn't ready to go there yet.

And so, he woke.

Opening his eyes, he stared ahead. The light in his room seemed strange. His limbs felt jump-started, as though electricity had coursed through them, shocking him back to the real world.

Joe blinked again.

Something dark and shadowy hung above. He squinted. Yes, it was something black but shimmery. It sat strangely against the pure, fresh light of dawn.

He shot up, sitting rigidly. Gasping.

A sphere with grey clouds as wide as the ceiling. Every few seconds, lightning rippled up and down its walls.

He laughed. He was still dreaming.

He sat, just staring at it as the room became lighter. The house began to hum with the whistle of the kettle, the clunk of pipes in the bathroom – but the sphere remained.

Was it waiting . . . for him?

Joe lifted a finger to touch the edge of the cloud. Just air. What did he expect, though? He pulled himself up on to his knees, staring up in awe. 'What the hell is it?' Again, his finger brushed the circle's edge. It was like touching dust motes sitting on rays of light. He lowered his finger; the cloud wobbled and expanded like clay on a potter's wheel, spinning, contorting, growing.

What if it grew into something uncontrollable? Sharply pulling his hand away, he ducked his head sideways. The ceiling was still up there, on the other side.

He jumped, startled by two loud knocks. 'Joe! Time to get up!'

'Okay, Mum!' He crept around the edge of the bed, almost on tiptoe, investigating the strange entity.

Inside the sphere: darkness. Like camping in the country beneath overcast skies. An endless, gloomy path, lit up only by the slivers of lightning that danced along the walls.

Walls! How could it have walls? It wasn't even solid! He rolled a tennis ball between his fingers like a giant worry bead. No way was he putting his head in there.

He stared into the black depths for a few seconds – and then threw the ball.

It was sucked into the sphere. Joe gasped. 'That was fast.' Eyes still pinned on the swirling clouds, he leaned back and fumbled around his desk until his fingers touched the computer mouse; his eyes darted back and forth as he waited for the screen to warm up.

'Okay.'

He lifted the webcam, holding it at the sphere's edge. 'Here goes.' Slowly, he pushed the camera through the cloud, peering sideways to watch the screen.

A loud screech and the camera was jolted from his grasp. Sparks charged up and down his spine. On shaky legs, he backed away and stood against the wall. Joe watched the cloud as it hung there, as unassuming as before.

Except it had eaten his camera.

The computer screen revealed nothing but static.

He crept over, crouched before the monitor and pressed play.

At first it was just darkness. Then – and he guessed the camera spun wildly at this moment – an eyeless creature, bony, teeth bared, swam through the blackness, claws extended. At first it moved with such speed it resembled a milky smudge. The thing observed the camera passively but then lunged, the mouth stretching impossibly wide. The last thing the camera saw was a row of long, sharp teeth.

Then, static.

He was sitting down. He didn't remember sitting down. Trembling, he clicked the mouse again. The face resembled nothing he'd seen on earth or within the ocean depths; it wasn't a horror-movie monster, nor comic-book creature feature. Eyeless cavities, a body of chalky bone. What seemed to be a massive ribcage. Long jaws, like the snout of a hound dog if all its flesh and blood were stripped away. Epic teeth.

His chest ached from his relentless pounding heart. What was that thing? Where did it come from? Any minute now it might decide to take a chunk out of him.

Time for it to go.

When he turned back, the sphere was gone.

* * *

GRACE SAVOURED THE RICH, sweet smell of tea and jam-smothered toast.

Her mother poured a cup of tea and pushed it towards her daughter with a bemused smile. 'Sleep okay, honey?' Grace warmed her hands against the cup. She felt groggy from oversleep. 'Did it rain overnight, Mum?'

'No, not yet. But it'll come soon. I can smell it.'

A tousled head of dark curly hair moved past the window that overlooked the back garden.

'What's Joe doing?'

Delicately, Mum picked crumbs off her plate. 'I told your brother to get started on the garden.'

Grace watched the crumbs disappear. 'When's Dad back?'

'Around four.' Mum sipped her tea.

'Have you told him about Joe getting in trouble?'

'No, not yet. We can talk properly when Dad gets home.'

Grace gulped her tea, flinching as the hot liquid scalded her throat. She padded over to the sink and rinsed her cup.

'Not hungry?'

'Not really.'

Her mother smiled and frowned at the same time. 'You still won't tell me what's wrong?'

Grace hesitated, her mind weighing it up. It would be good to spill her worries out. But . . . no. Joe had seen that boy, and he was in denial. Nobody would believe her. 'I'm okay, Mum. Honest.' With a forced smile, Grace made her way upstairs for a shower, feeling like a coward.

* * *

JOE CURSED AS another gust of wind barrelled through the leaves, scattering them over the grass again. 'Damn it!' Flailing uselessly, he tried to flatten the leaves only to be undermined by another gust. 'Oh, come on now! This is getting stupid!'

He peered upwards. Mum had gone to pick up Dad, Grace was probably in her room. Nobody could see him in the backyard. Now would be a good time.

Again, his fingertips began to tingle.

Curiosity overcame fear.

And there were leaves to get rid of, anyway.

'Okay.'

He threw another glance at the house, took a breath and focused on imagining the cloud.

Perhaps he needed to say something, like a spell. He opened his mouth – but the air in front of him had already changed, darkening, like a mini thunderstorm.

In the afternoon light, the sphere seemed even more surreal. He gazed at it, well aware that thing was in there.

'Let's give it something to eat.'

Quickly, he raked up a clump of leaves and shunted them inside the sphere. Shovel after shovel went inside until his arms ached.

'Wait a minute . . . why am I working so hard?' Extending a forefinger, Joe pulled on the bottom edge of the cloud; obligingly, the sphere expanded, nearly touching his feet.

Joe grinned. 'Much better.' He held the shovel close to the edge, watching leaves pick up and fly into the hole like a sharp wind had got behind them.

Laughing maniacally – the situation was crazy, after all – too late he noticed the sudden pressure on his neck. With a pop, his chain was gone – Celtic cross and all.

'Crap!' Throwing down the shovel, Joe gazed into the hole. Within the hovering, wispy leaves he saw the silver links and cross also floating. But too far to reach in . . .

He couldn't lose it. Mum would kill him.

But that thing was in there.

Too bad. Steeling himself with a deep, calming breath, he stepped inside.

As he took tiny steps forward, he struggled to adjust to the sensation. Sure, he was walking on something, but it didn't feel as though there was anything there.

He glanced back. Thankfully, he could still see the windswept yard. 'Okay.' Joe reached forward and snatched the chain, taking its links tightly between his fingers.

The skin on his neck began to prickle: a warning.

He froze.

The bone creature hovered, staring at him just like it had at the camera, claws outstretched evenly on each side.

Joe closed his eyes, breath trapped in his throat, heart hammering. *Well, I guess this is it*, he thought to himself.

But silence followed. He slowly opened his eyes. Pure darkness lay ahead, punctuated, of course, by the flashes of lightning – but no more leaves, no monster.

With a light feeling in his limbs and nerves pooling in his gut, Joe turned and walked quickly back out of the sphere's entrance. His feet touched the grass. He heard a car pull up in the distance.

Again, the sphere appeared to be resting, waiting.

He scratched his neck. A tunnel on the inside, but a sphere on the outside. He shook his head. Too weird.

Grace's voice broke the silence. 'Joe! Dad's back!'

He stared at the sphere. *Go away, now*, he willed. The clouds subsided into nothing. He ran his chain links through trembling fingers.

'It's mine to control.'

* * *

'HI, DAD.' GRACE let her father pull her into a tight hug. He smelled of aftershave with a hint of motor oil. Like Joe, he needed a trim – his dark fringe bounced into his eyes. Grace smiled. 'You look as if you've been living wild for six months.'

Her father pulled a mock expression of hurt. 'Wow, thanks a lot, honey. Anyway, how are you?'

Grace pulled back, avoiding his eyes. 'I'm fine, Dad.' She felt the burn of her mother's stare. 'I've already told Mum that.'

'Mmm,' her father said, narrowing his eyes. 'Something's up.'

'Honestly, Dad. I'm fine.' What else could she say? 'Stop going on about it.'

Stretching his arms out, her father yawned. 'Okay, okay!' He gave her a curious glance as he headed towards the kitchen.

Grace flopped on to the couch and pressed a button on the remote control. From the kitchen, the sound of cups and saucers clacking against each other nearly drowned out the TV. Her mother pressed a teabag to her nose, inhaling appreciatively. Mum's happiness was like a vapour, thick in the air. Dad was home. It was good for everybody.

Joe wandered in.

'Hey, buddy!' Dad looked up and grinned. 'Got some sun, I see!'

'Hi, Dad.' Joe leaned down and embraced his father briefly. 'Want to have a look at the bike?' His eyes twinkled.

'Give your dad a chance to have a cuppa, Joe.' His mother sank into her chair and smiled at her husband, who squeezed her hand.

'It's okay, Suse. I'll run up for a quick shower and we can all have some tea in the garage while we admire Joe's work.' He smiled at Joe. 'And we can have a chat too, son.'

'Sounds good, Dad.'

His father got up and moved slowly through the living

area, pausing to blow Grace a kiss. Smiling, she caught it and pressed against her cheek.

Slowly, Joe walked over to the window and stared into the back garden as the kettle whistled away. Oh, yeah. They were gonna talk, all right.

* * *

'BIKE'S LOOKING GOOD, son.' Joe watched as his father moved around to look at the other side. 'You've been doing a great job, keeping it up.'

'Thanks, Dad.'

'So . . .' his father began to wipe the fuel tank with circular strokes. 'What's been up at school?'

Joe's face dropped. 'Mum told you.'

His father took a deep breath. 'Yep. Things like this, I need to know.'

Joe picked up a wrench and tapped it against his open hand. 'You would've done the same thing.'

'No, not these days. Okay, okay, so I cracked a few heads when I was your age. If he'd said something like that about Aunt Diana, then I would've found it hard not to smack him. You and I – we share a short fuse. But you've got to learn to control it. Don't repeat my mistakes.'

'It's not that easy.'

'I know. But revenge is a bad idea. It leads to consequences that you might not have thought of. Trust me, son.'

They stared at the bike for a few seconds.

'Dad, there's something I need to tell you.'

With a smile, his father stood back to appreciate the shine off the fuel tank. 'I'm all ears.'

Joe hesitated. His father looked over. 'What's the matter?'

'Oh, it's weird. I had this dream. I was in space, and . . .'

'What, son?'

Joe gazed at his father's face. How could he explain it? 'When I woke up, it was like the dream was still going on.' He shoved his hands into his pockets. 'Even though I was awake.'

'Mmm.' His father examined his fingernails. 'That's happened to me after a double shift. You're probably just a bit tired.' He stood up. 'Now, what'd you do with my tool kit?'

'No, Dad. I saw something.'

Dad raised his eyebrows. 'Oh. What was it?'

Joe hesitated – his dad wasn't going to believe it. 'It might be easier if I just show you.' He handed his father the wrench, savouring the excited anticipation, the now-familiar tingle in his fingers.

'O-kay.' Grinning, his father leaned against the work-bench, running his fingers back and forth over the metal rim.

Dad watched expectantly – but his smile soon dropped.

His eyes became wide with horror as the room turned dark, and clouds gathered, forming a sphere. In the middle of his garage. He flinched as a bolt of lightning ran down the side.

Joe grinned. 'I think I'm a wizard, Dad!'

Dad dropped the wrench. 'Oh, *no*.'

From the doorway came his wife's scream.

FIVE

TREMBLING, DAD WAVED his hand through the air. 'Close it! Now!'

With a pounding heart, Joe stared into the swirling cloud, willing it to disappear. Why was Dad so upset? He glanced at the doorway where his mother stood, a wide-eyed Grace beside her. Mum seemed – angry? Around her feet, shards of china lay next to spoiled sandwiches.

'Oh, no. Not him. Not my son!'

A sweat droplet slid down Joe's forehead. He blinked it out of his eyes. 'What's the matter?'

Grace stared into the space where the strange cloud had been. 'What *was* that, Joe?'

Dad grabbed Joe's shoulders, his eyes searing. 'Son, you must promise me that you will never do that again.'

Joe buckled against his father's grip. 'Why, Dad?'

'*Don't question me!* Just promise!'

'Okay, okay! Stop shaking me!'

Dad's fingers had turned white. Grimacing, he dropped his hands. 'You don't understand, son.' He ran his fingers through his hair, breathing hard. 'You don't know what you've just done.'

Not the reaction Joe had expected. 'I thought you could explain what it is.' Was that *fear* in Dad's eyes?

A sudden pressure – Mum's fingers on his arm; the sway of forced movement. 'Get inside.'

'Dad . . .'

'Now!'

Grace jumped; Mum's voice cracked through the garage like a gunshot. Trailing behind Joe and Mum, she glanced back. 'Go on, Grace,' Dad said. 'With your mother.'

Mum pointed to the sofa. 'Sit.' Grace tumbled on to the chair; Joe followed.

In the garage, Grace had felt her mother shaking, seen tears in her eyes, but now Mum was focused. The controlled intensity of a coach at half-time. Dad stood nearby, arms folded, jaw tight.

'Right. Joe, how many rifts have you opened?'

He blinked. 'You mean the sphere, Mum?'

'Yes.'

'Three.' Joe's heart pounded.

Dad cut in. 'When did it first happen?'

'Yesterday.' Joe ran his fingers over the sofa. They still tingled from the power.

'Where were you?'

'In my room.'

'The second time?'

Joe coughed. 'The garden.'

'Outside?' Dad frowned. 'That was very dangerous, Joe.'

'Why?'

'You must never do that again.'

'Why not, Dad?'

Mum turned her sights on Grace. 'What about you? Have you seen anything strange?'

'Y-yeah.'

'Such as?'

'A . . . boy. But he was weird.'

'What kind of weird?'

'Just weird . . . I can't explain it!'

'Try!'

'I don't know how to, Mum.'

Her mother kneeled, took Grace's shoulders between firm hands. 'Tell me everything, honey. Now.'

Grace pressed her fingers against her temples, rubbing away a sudden, darting pain. 'It – wasn't there all the time. The shadow, I mean. At first I thought I was seeing things. But it was there, it was real. It was a monster.'

Mum swapped a glance with Dad. 'When was this, Grace?'

'Yesterday . . . and the day before.'

'Did you see him, Joe?'

'Yeah. At school. Out the back, selling drugs. I heard Grace calling –'

'Too close for comfort.' Mum stood and began walking the room.

'We should call Diana now, Suse.' Dad glanced at the telephone.

Grace watched her mother pace. 'Why call Aunt Diana?'

'No, don't call her just yet.' Mum looked at Grace. 'Is there anything else that's happened? Anything at all?'

'Oh, not really.'

'What?' Mum pressed. 'Tell me.'

Grace sighed. 'Just that – Joe can hear me when I'm calling him.' She pointed to her forehead. 'In here.'

Mum gave Dad another tense look. She kept pacing, her hands clenched.

'Sit down, Suse.' Dad tapped the sofa next to him; Mum stopped and sat down.

She gave Dad a pleading look. 'There's so much they need to know. I thought they were both too old for anything to emerge now, but I was wrong.'

Dad squeezed her hand. 'But we were right to give them a normal childhood. We talked about this, Suse.' Dad's voice was low and gentle as he looked at his son. 'I mean: a Ferryman. Of all things. Who would have guessed?'

Joe's eyes narrowed. 'What are you talking about?'

'In the old days, Joe, your people – or people with your skill – were known as Ferrymen,' said Dad. 'You have the power to move between worlds. That sphere, as you call it, is actually a dimensional rift.'

Joe's eyes went wide. Grace stared. 'Dimensional?' Images of strange alien life, born of the stars, came crawling through her mind.

'This gift has been passed down to your brother from a very old line of highly skilled mercenaries, known as the *sarsareh*. People who have the Sight, who can see the truth around them when most of the world can't. Your mum and I worked for an organisation founded on the *sarsareh* tradition. Your Aunt Diana is still a part of it. But we quit when you were born, Joe, and came out to the suburbs. We knew it was the right thing to do. It would have been no life for children.'

He raised a finger. 'You've both had a good, normal upbringing, and there was no guarantee either of you would be gifted. We didn't think this would happen. Gifts usually emerge at a younger age.' Dad started to shake his head. 'Oh, you are yet to grasp who you are, son. Your kind is so rare. Your gift, so powerful.'

Dad glanced between his children. 'This will be very hard for you both to accept, but you must try. The reason why that boy looked so strange to you, Grace – and to you too, Joe – was because . . . well, there's no other way to put it. He's a demon.'

'What?' Grace shot up, sitting upright on the sofa. 'Whoa, whoa! What are you talking about?' Joe's face mirrored what she knew hers must look like: pale skin, open mouth, frightened eyes. Her breath was coming tight and rapid.

'But th-they look like people,' Joe said.

'Yes – but the shadow they give out is pure demon energy. It's something they generate themselves. They *are* the demons. They *become* the demons through their own moral decline. They're not possessed, they just *are*.'

Dad squeezed Grace's hand. 'Don't be afraid, honey. I promise we won't let anything happen to you. It's been a few years, but we haven't forgotten our training.'

Grace stared at her father's eyes. 'Training?'

'Special operations. Contract work.'

'You're talking about . . . you used to be mercenaries?' Joe's mouth dropped open. 'That's friggin' awesome!'

'It's not all fun and games, Joseph'. Mum gave him a sharp look.

'Sorry.'

Grace felt numb. This had been going on all this time. Mum and Dad had been hiding things from them. She gave her mother a hard stare. 'So, can you still see them?'

'Yes. But I try not to go looking for them.'

'Well, why did you stop fighting? Don't you want to?' Grace's voice shook with anger. It couldn't be true. It wasn't. There was no way it could be.

Her mother leaned forward, palms open on her knees. 'Of course I do. But we knew the only way to keep you both safe was to quit our old jobs.' Her eyes fell on Joe. 'But your brother changes all that.'

* * *

DESPITE HIS EXCITEMENT, Halphas walked a steady pace along the upper deck, passing through the double doors into the saloon. A smoky ether hung in the air, filling him with a sudden stab of nostalgia: the scent reminded him of the opium dens of old London. Cascades of golden silk draped the walls. Candelabra shone gaslight rays through the mist. The crack of billiard balls, the jostling laughter. Young men lounged on leather sofas, sucked on cigars.

Cream chiffon swayed in the breeze, women were strewn around the room like exotic flowers. They came in many varieties; Master preferred it that way.

Halphas stared, but his eyes did not undress them.

Instead, he noted the small signs of nervousness. Twitching fingers. Gleaming sweat on arched eyebrows. Eyes darting around the room. Trembling legs, rustling the satin of a fine dress.

The room pulsed with anticipation. They all felt it, knew it. It was the energy that Master gave out.

Yet Halphas was tired.

Against a large window that spanned the starboard wall, silhouetted against the sunlight, stood Mammon, hands in pockets, staring out across the water.

'Master,' Halphas said. 'I've seen a Sign!'

Mammon turned and gave him a sharp stare. 'Are you sure?'

'Yes, Master! In this very city.'

Halphas fought an urge to shrink: even behind his sunglasses, Master's eyes were searing. 'Are you *absolutely* sure, Halphas?'

'You have no reason to doubt it, my Lord. I've tracked the Sign to the City's northwest. I have people monitoring the house now.'

Mammon stared at him. 'The suburbs?' He curled his lip. 'How unpleasant. I do hope this isn't another disappointment.'

Halphas tensed. The billiards game had ended; he felt an insolent gaze burning in his direction. Then, predictably, Andras slithered his way to Master's side. He folded his arms and regarded Halphas with a cool stare. Halphas ran his own gaze over Andras's clothes – the upstart looked as though he'd just emerged from a menswear catalogue. What a good little clone he was.

Halphas turned his eyes to Mammon. 'The signal is very strong, Master. Only thirty seconds this morning, and yet – so very powerful. It was easy to tune in and find him. The boy lives with his parents and sister. He's been outside working on a motorcycle all morning, so my people have been able to watch him for some time. Seems like an ordinary teenage lad.'

Halphas drew a breath and smiled. This was his moment of glory. Using his unearthly intuition, he'd tracked another Ferryman in just days. These apprentices could not offer Master anything close to this.

Mammon slid his sunglasses into his shirt pocket. 'Well, what do you suggest now, Halphas?'

The old servant scratched his ear. 'There's a problem.' Despite himself, he stared at the floor, Master's expectant gaze burning into his forehead. 'The house is protected.'

'That won't stop us,' said Andras.

Halphas threw him a triumphant glance. 'Our kind can't cross a Line of Protection.' He raised his eyebrows as Andras's smile fell. 'Or didn't you know that?'

'It still won't stop us,' Andras said. He turned to Mammon. 'Master, I can sort this.'

'Mmm.' Mammon's lips twitched. 'We need to draw the boy out. But carefully.' He paced for a few moments, then he turned to Halphas with a lifted finger. 'Dig into the family's background. It's not normal for a suburban house to have a Line of Protection.'

Halphas bowed his head. 'I have already made extensive enquiries, Master. I have been told by a reliable source that the Line was there years before the family moved in. After watching the family, I believe that they are not aware of its presence. A mere coincidence.'

'Master, let me help,' Andras said. 'It will be far more discreet than using any of your military resources.'

Mammon pressed his fingertip to his lips. 'It has to be done right.'

'It will be.'

'Well, fill me in on the plan.' Mammon placed his hand on Andras's shoulder and led him on a slow walk towards the deck. He threw a last glance over his shoulder. 'Turn the boat around, Halphas.'

The old servant gritted his teeth as he made his way from the room. Master blamed him for the last failure. And now Andras was taking control with a thrown-together plan. Why did Master indulge these young ones so recklessly?

* * *

GRACE DROPPED HER book onto her bedside table and sat up, letting her legs swing over the edge of her bed. She stretched. Pale afternoon light streamed in through the gap in her curtains; new rain pattered on her window. Yawning, she slid on her slippers and shuffled towards the window to pick up her watch. Three-thirty.

A rumbling shook the walls. She peered down. There was Joe, leaning over the bike, revving the engine in sustained bursts. Grace glanced at the sky: surely he wasn't thinking of riding in this? Even as plump raindrops splashed on to his hair, he seemed oblivious, tuned in to the bike's steady vibrations.

* * *

49

ACROSS THE ROAD, behind the safety of a tinted bedroom window, Halphas shifted in his chair, his fingers clenched. Even at this distance, the Line of Protection around the boy's home set off a painful stinging in his skin.

Andromalius watched the upper window where a woman had stood, minutes earlier. He closed his eyes and concentrated on the minds inside the house.

Halphas watched the young girl appear in another window. He wondered how her tender skin would react to the attentions of a sharp blade.

Mammon's gaze never left Joe.

Andromalius opened his eyes. 'The father's trying to reach someone on the phone.' He threw a concerned glance at Mammon. 'I can't tell who. Could be trouble. We might get some unwanted company.' He paused slightly. 'Shouldn't we get moving?' He threw a careless glance towards the homeowner, sprawled in the hallway. 'This one might wake up and become a nuisance.'

Mammon shook his head. 'Then we put him to sleep again. And we don't need to worry about whoever the father is calling.' He gave Halphas a hard look. 'Do we?'

The old servant shook his head. 'No, Master. They're just an ordinary family.'

Zagan folded his arms and leaned against the wall. 'Why don't we just kill the family and force Joe to come with us?'

Mammon gave him a scathing stare. 'A Ferryman won't be taken like that, you fool. I didn't get this far in life by being rash and impulsive. We're going to lure Joe in, carefully.' He pinched his thumb and forefinger together. 'Today, we plant a seed of desire in him.' He nodded with a confident smile. 'He'll come to us – sooner, rather than later.'

Footsteps pounded up the stairs. A tall, very thin man with a dark beard entered the room. He wore a red-checkered shirt and black leather jacket, emblazoned with a logo for the Northern Raiders motorcycle club.

Haures screwed up her nose at the man's tangy scent.

'You're late,' said Andras, without looking at the newcomer.

The biker shoved his hands in his pockets and gave Andras a shrug. 'I had to head into the City first. Mike needed me to do a job there.'

Slowly, Andras turned and gave the man a dark stare. 'From now on, you follow our orders first.'

'Keys, please.' Haures thrust out her palm.

The biker stared, jaw open. Such hair . . . it floated around her face like waves of fire. And those lips . . . fighting against the temptation to lean over and kiss her, he handed Haures a set of keys. 'All yours, pretty lady.'

She threw Andromalius a smile before disappearing out the door.

The biker turned back to Andras. 'Shouldn't she be wearing leathers?'

The young demon stared out into the street. 'That won't be necessary.'

* * *

GRACE SIGHED AND made for her bedroom door. Moving into the hallway, she glimpsed her father sitting on his bed, phone in hand.

'Are you okay, Dad?'

He smiled. 'Yes, honey.'

'Where's Mum?'

'Taking a shower. She's made you a cup of tea.'

'Okay.' She jumped in fright as a clap of thunder shook the walls. A heavy lashing of sound above told her the rain had begun in earnest. Soon it would flood the back garden and flush pools of fresh water over the pavers.

Usually, she liked the rain.

But today, it meant sitting inside for cups of tea and talking. Making plans, mostly. Before all this weirdness started, she would have looked forward to a Saturday afternoon with Dad and Mum: watching movies, eating fish and chips, snuggling up in a blanket against a sudden cold snap. But today felt laced with a sense of uncertainty, as if tomorrow would bring great change.

What would that change be?

* * *

JOE SQUINTED, LIFTING his hand to shield against the fierce glare from the road. Something had happened. A telltale thud; the sound of an engine idling in mid air. It could only be one thing. He walked towards the glare. A shape came into view: a rider, lying on the tarmac. Joe shook his head. The wet must've gotten to this poor bastard. He kneeled over the rider, pulled the viser up. 'You okay, dude?'

He caught his breath as a pair of deep green eyes gazed up at him. Velvet skin and rich, moist lips. Strands of brilliant red hair poking through the side of her helmet.

'Whoa.' Joe gulped. 'Sorry. I thought you were a guy.' He glanced back at her right leg, bent at a painful angle. 'I'm gonna help you to the kerb, okay?'

She nodded. 'Thank you.' Her voice was a warm, husky whisper. He ached to hear more. 'What's your name?' He slid his hands under the woman's shoulders and began to drag her to the kerb.

* * *

GRACE MADE HER way across the living room and pressed herself against the window, wiping away the fog, straining to make out the movement in the distance. At the sound of squealing tyres she'd almost tripped down the last two steps in her rush. Now she saw the source: a rider, lying on the far verge; Joe bent over her. A downed motorbike.

To the right, the hill's abrupt descent and treacherous curves had caught speeding drivers before. It was easy to see what had happened.

* * *

THE RIDER LOOKED up at Joe with a grateful smile. 'My name is Serena.'

She was beautiful. Joe smiled. 'Well, Serena, you'll need to see a doctor. Your leg . . .'

'Can you take me?'

'I can come with you in the ambulance.' His eyes focused on those delectable lips.

She gasped. 'No!'

'What's wrong?'

She blushed. 'It sounds silly, but . . .'

'Tell me,' Joe whispered, stroking her hand.

'I don't like paramedics or ambulances. My sister was killed in a car accident, and –'

Joe squeezed her palm. 'Okay. Don't worry. I'll take you.' He stood up and turned towards the road to pick up her bike.

In the distance, Mammon stroked his chin. 'She's doing very well.'

Andras nodded. 'She just has to get him away from here, and we'll be on our way, Master.'

* * *

AT HOME, GRACE watched Joe help the rider to the kerb.

Her father appeared at her shoulder, phone still in hand. He peered out the window. 'What's going on?' His jaw dropped. 'That's not *Joe* out there, is it?'

'Yeah,' Grace said.

'Damn it!' Dad lunged past and pushed the wire door open. 'I told him!'

A low, rumbling roar approached, accompanied by twin beams of light. The truck bore heavily down the hill, gathering speed as it descended. The driver, whose head had lolled more than once on this journey, rubbed his eyes and yawned. Not too far now.

Grace pushed through the door and stood next to her father. 'What's wrong, Dad?'

'Joseph!' Dad roared, waving his arm. 'Get over here, now!' Cursing, he headed towards the kerb, shooting tense looks around the neighbourhood.

Joe squinted at his father. 'What?' His voice barely carried in the intensifying downpour. A fresh boom of thunder sounded. Something moved in the corner of his eyes; glancing sideways, he saw the truck bearing down on him. His feet felt glued to the ground.

'Joe!' Grace's heartbeat tore through her chest as she watched the truck rush towards him. She broke into a run – but tripped as her foot slid into a deep, uneven dip in the grass. She shrieked as pain exploded in her ankle.

Through droopy eyelids the truck driver peered at the boy on the road. Recognition came too late. 'Oh, no!'

Clouds of grey smoke plumed as brakes locked, the trailer swinging sideways. All Joe could see was a black sheet of metal coming at him, the jackknifing trailer spanning the entire width of road. Even if he moved now . . .

Mammon took a step forward and raised his arm.

Joe watched, stunned as the truck slowed . . . like a giant, shadowy hand had slammed against it; shockwaves rippled through the trailer – folding steel as easily as a paper fan. He ducked but twisted his neck to stare up into the underbelly of the trailer as it spun and soared; a terrified, sweaty face stared down at him from the cabin. Then the whole rig tumbled to the ground, smashing into shards of metal and glass that spilled across the road.

SIX

'WELL DONE, MASTER,' said Andras.

Sparks of residual energy filled the room as Mammon lowered his arm and watched the boy stumbling around on the road, his face white with shock. He could taste it now – the nearness of the boy, this new Ferryman. 'You were too slow there, Zagan.'

The young demon swallowed hard. 'I'm sorry, Master.'

Joe stood up slowly, the tremble in his fingers too strong to even grasp the handlebars of Serena's bike. He could only stare at the destroyed truck, watch the neighbours emerge in a flurry of voices. And Serena – where had she gone?

He turned to see his father's grim face. Silently, Dad seized Joe's arm and hurried the staggering boy across the road. He shoved Joe towards the door. 'Inside! Now!' He waited until Joe was safely inside and then looked down at his daughter. 'Get up, Grace.'

'I've sprained my ankle.' She was rocking back and forth, holding her foot.

Dad reached down and slid his hands under Grace's armpits, lifting her.

Blinking back tears, Grace let Dad guide her through the front door, where Mum stood wrapped in a robe, the blood drained from her face. She had Joe in a tight hug. Joe drew away and turned to look at his father.

Dad reached out and grabbed Joe, pulling him into a swift, crushing embrace and then held him at arm's length. 'What did I tell you about going outside, son?' His eyes were harsh.

'But there was an accident . . .'

I don't care! You don't leave the property!' Dad shook Joe. 'Out there – on the road – you weren't protected. Anyone could've got you.'

Joe gasped, wrenching himself away. 'But no-one did.'

Dad shook his head. With a hiss, he jerked forward, pulling Joe to the window. 'You don't get it. The EMF only runs so far.' Deep below, a series of electromagnetic cables formed a protective barrier around the house. 'I told you this last night.'

Joe stared out at the yard. 'I didn't think, Dad.'

'No, you didn't.'

Grace felt herself sway. The shock – the near miss with the truck and the pain in her ankle was overwhelming. 'Mum,' she whimpered.

Her mother glanced down at the injured ankle, then she turned and headed into the kitchen.

Joe stood at the window, arms folded. 'I don't even know if the driver is alive.' He watched the crowd gather, tried to ignore the creeping chill that was clinging to the back of his neck; the cold sweat lining his back. What just happened? Against all laws of gravity . . . who or what could do that? He tensed his fingers, still trembling.

Dad picked up the phone and pressed it to his ear. He waited for a bit before throwing it down. 'For God's sake, Diana! Where are you?'

He stalked into the kitchen. His wife, bent over a first-aid box, looked up with frightened eyes. She rose and reached out for him with a trembling whisper. 'Danny.'

His eyes clouded over. 'I don't want to face it, Suse. I can't.'

'I'm scared for Joe.'

'So am I.' He squeezed her shoulders, his breath coming in shudders.

She began shaking her head. 'If anything happens to him . . .' Tears emerged. She blinked them away and glanced in the direction of her children.

'Don't let them see you upset,' her husband said. 'Come on. I'll pack, you stay here with the kids. I'll keep trying Diana. The sooner we get her, the sooner we'll know they're both safe.'

* * *

GRACE WATCHED ANXIOUSLY as Mum swept back in with bandages and an icepack. Dad had walked past and given her a small smile. Mum pulled over a low stool, lifted Grace's leg and started to wrap the bandage around her daughter's ankle. Grace gazed at Mum's face; a safety pin was clenched in between her mother's teeth. 'What's going on?'

Mum removed the pin from her mouth. 'We're going to fix your ankle.' She looked up at Joe. 'Come away from the window now. It wasn't your fault, son.'

Joe grunted. 'Tell that to the driver's family.' He turned around. 'Come on, Mum. Something's going on here.'

Mum continued bandaging the ankle in silence. She peered at the ceiling. Upstairs, her husband was rummaging through wardrobes for suitcases. By this time tomorrow, they'd be in the south.

'We're going away for a few days, kids,' Mum said suddenly.

Grace grimaced as Mum tightened the bandage. 'Where are we going?'

'To stay with your aunt. No, keep your ankle elevated. You'll feel better in a few hours.'

* * *

HAURES RACED UP the stairs and into the bedroom. 'What the hell went wrong? Damn it!'

She froze. At the window, the boss's shoulders were tense, his fists clenched. She backed away and sank onto the bed.

Mammon looked at Andras. 'We need to act now.'

'Yes, Master. I've got men ready to go.' Andras glanced at the biker. 'You can leave.' He pulled his phone from his pocket.

'Don't you care about your girl here? She busted her leg . . .' The biker did a double take as Haures stretched out both legs on the bed. He scratched his head, eyes drifting to Andras. 'Look, uh . . . I don't know what game you people are playing here, but I want compensation for my bike.' He pressed his lips together and squared his shoulders.

Andras shook his head. 'Get out.' He flicked through his contacts, searching for a number.

'No dice. I let your bitch crash my Harley. Now pay me.'

Haures stood up, scowling. 'Did this maggot just say what I think he did?' She then threw Andromalius an incredulous grin.

The biker turned to the quiet man standing near the window. Surely he'd be reasonable? But, to be sure, he walked over to the man and poked him in the chest. 'I want my bike replaced, and payment . . .'

Mammon lifted the man into the air; squeezing iron fingers against his throat. A satisfying crack sounded as the spinal cord ruptured.

With a grunt, Mammon kicked the body into the hallway.

Haures gave him a grateful smile. 'Thank you, Master.'

Andras pressed the phone to his ear, his eyes pinned on the boss's stony face. 'What about the family?'

Mammon folded his arms and stared at the house. 'We need to take everything away from the boy. Kill the parents and the sister. And then I will become Joe's rock.'

* * *

GRACE WATCHED JOE pace back and forth in front of the window. 'Sit down, Joe!'

Joe spun around, his face grey. 'The driver's dead. I saw the ambulance take him away.'

Mum swooped in, pulling him into a hug. 'It's not your fault. It was an accident.'

60

'I feel sick.' Joe stepped away and gazed out of the window.

Grace craned her neck to look. The scene was eerily calm and clear; all wreckage tidied up. Dusk had long fallen, brown and murky compared to the pinky haze of last night. The sound of the doorbell echoed in her memory; visitors ranging from concerned neighbours to a policeman seeking information – Mum had turned them all away with a firm tone. 'Joe can provide a statement tomorrow.'

Of course, by then he'd be safely tucked away in his new home.

Dad came thudding down the stairs, dragging three suitcases behind him. Propping them against the wall, he nodded at Mum. 'That's everything we'll need for now. Diana will be here in an hour.'

Mum took a deep breath and rubbed her eyes. 'Thank heavens. Now we just have to wait.'

Joe looked at her. 'Can't we just drive ourselves?'

'No. It's not safe.' Dad walked back to the dining room table and opened a small wooden chest. Slowly, he drew out two strange-looking guns. Mum got up and walked over to him, lifted one of the guns and examined it. She and Dad exchanged mutters.

Grace tried to sit up. 'What are those for?'

Joe crossed the room to stand next to his father. 'It's a taser,' he said.

'That's right, son.'

Mum turned around, gun in hand. 'They're special weapons, Grace. For demons.'

'You think we'll need them?' Grace laughed as a stab of hysteria took hold. The absurdity of it all. Plus the fact that she was virtually a cripple. How could she hope to do anything? 'What can we do to defend ourselves? Just sit here?'

Mum put down the gun and sat next to Grace. 'You won't.' She reached back and unclasped her necklace. 'It's time for you to have this.' She dropped her pendant into Grace's hand: a sliver of amber wood lined in gold.

'Grandma gave you this.'

'No, she didn't.' Mum drew the pendant and put it around Grace's neck. 'All *sarsareh* wear one of these. It's very special; so look after it.'

Grace's fingers tingled when she touched the pendant. What effect would it have on a demon? Hopefully she wouldn't have to find out.

'Here, son,' said Dad. 'You get one too.'

Joe reached under his t-shirt and pulled out his Celtic cross. 'I don't need another chain, Dad. I've got this one.'

His father nodded before leaning forward to string a pendant around Joe's neck.

Grace looked at her father. 'Will these protect us?'

'No, honey. It's not like that. The pendants are more symbolic than anything.'

'Oh.' A new wave of fear hit at his words.

'Don't worry, Grace. We're protected here. No demon can get across our EMF line.' Dad took a deep breath and smiled. 'All we have to do now is wait for Diana and her team.' He took Mum's hand and squeezed it.

Grace and Joe waited; speechless, nervous. Dad guarded the window; Mum checked her watch every few minutes. 'Oh, Diana – please hurry,' she whispered.

But then, with a soft click, the power went out, and the house fell into silent, vulnerable darkness.

SEVEN

'DANNY!'

'Downstairs! Quick!'

'Move! Now!' Grace felt herself dragged through swamping darkness, adrenaline numbing away the pain; Joe's heavy steps behind her. Ahead, a small light led the way. Grace squinted – the silver reflection told her it was a phone. 'Just keep walking.'

'Suse – your gunlight.'

A small click, and something brighter lit the way. The shadowy party made their way to the rear of the house.

'Dad . . .?'

'It's all right, honey. Keep walking.'

She heard the click of a door handle, and then she was being led again, step by careful step, slowly descending into the sweet, musty air of the cellar. Beneath a small window, which allowed dim light through, she could identify the outlines of Mum's pickling jars, standing in rows, and a lumpy shape poking its head up: a sewing machine, layered in swirls of fabric.

So they would hide here. Fine. She reached out, trembling hands searching for the soft comfort of the old armchair. She needed to rest her foot: the stabbing pain had started again.

A clunky creak filled the air, then a slam. Grace stiffened. 'What's going on?'

'Come on.' Dad's fingers pressed into her forearm. He led her a few steps away from the window light. 'Step down, one leg first.'

Grace stared down into the unfamiliar void. 'What is this, Dad?'

'Just climb down.'

'Are you serious? What's down there? You can't expect me to –'

Dad's voice was hard. 'You never needed to know about it. Now, move.'

'But my ankle!'

'Do it!'

Grace winced, lowering her good ankle until she touched wood, then she gently brought her other foot down. 'Okay . . .' Looking up, she gazed at Dad's face, silhouetted by the glow from Mum's gunlight pointed unnervingly in her direction. Even so, she felt the calm emanating from her father's eyes.

'Good girl. There are eight rungs. One at a time, honey.'

'I've got it.' Grasping the wooden sides, she stepped down again on her bad foot, wincing. Okay. Six to go. She felt the ladder give, lurching to the right as Joe climbed on.

'Okay, son?'

'All good, Dad. If Grace can just move her arse.'

She was on the final rung now. Joe's impatience hit her in waves; he was practically stepping on her. In her haste to get to the bottom, her foot swung past the last rung and hit hard ground.

She'd misjudged the distance – now her ankle felt as though a giant had stepped on it. Gasping, she hopped on her good foot, holding her sore ankle. A heavy click, and a hum filled the air. Steadying herself against a cold, rough surface, she glanced up at the cold light spreading across a ceiling that seemed to bear down on her.

'Okay.' Mum swept over, pulling a plastic chair behind her. 'Sit down, Grace.'

Dad shoved the ladder against a wall, yanked open the fuse box and snapped a switch. 'Okay. EMF's back on.'

'They had plenty of time to get inside, Daniel.'

'I know. They won't get in here, though.'

From her seat, Grace watched the intermittent flicker of the fluorescent light, humming and buzzing as though it were zapping flies. A bunker. That's what this place seemed like.

'Why won't they get in here, Dad?' Joe folded his arms tight, leaned against the wall and swallowed hard. He cast a wary look around the room.

Grimacing, Dad snapped his phone shut. 'Damn. No signal.' He rubbed his forehead. 'God. We've done every-thing we were trained not to.'

From the centre of the room, Mum threw Dad a tense look. 'Stop it. We did the best we could. We'll just have to wait, Danny. She told you it would be an hour – and that was how long ago?'

He sighed. 'An hour, Suse.' He began to pace around the cramped room.

'Everything will be fine, Danny.' Mum looked at her children: pale, terrified, vulnerable – and her fingers tightened around the gun.

Grace's eyes searched the room: over the grey walls, along the stubbly cement floor and up to the anaemic light, flickering and buzzing. 'Why couldn't we just stay in the cellar, Dad?'

'This room is armoured, Grace.'

'What does that mean?'

'Demon-proof. In more ways than one. This room is a cage. Look at the walls.' He strode over to the fuse box and pulled a switch; the room fell into darkness again.

'See?'

Grace peered at the walls, where a foreign script was splashed in luminescent blue paint. 'What does it say?'

'They're incantations. But that's not all.' Another click; the dreary glow crept through the room again as the fluoro lit up. Dad nodded at her, his hand still on the switch. 'The part you can't see is the virtual cage that this room is. EMF-protected. Demons can't get in here.'

'What do we do now, Dad?'

'We sit and wait, son.'

* * *

MAMMON RUBBED HIS palms together. 'Soon. Very soon.' He gave Halphas a rare grin.

The old man returned the smile. A cloud was lifting overhead. Soon – very soon, indeed. Master was bound to reward him for this.

Andras frowned as an unwelcome rumbling hit his pocket. He fished out his phone. 'What?'

'They've gone into the ground,' the voice responded. 'Past the cellar. There's a trapdoor, but it's deadlocked. We can't break it.'

Andras peered sideways; Mammon was staring at the sky, watching the darkness crawl towards the horizon. Andras turned away and hissed into the phone. 'Listen, you bug! Draw them out. Do what you have to!'

'Okay, sir.'

'Remember – *do not* let the boy come to harm.'

'Consider it done.'

Halphas's skin began to tingle. 'The Line of Protection has been re-activated.'

'I know. But it won't bother the humans, will it?'

For the first time, Halphas felt his demonhood a handicap, rather than a gift. He watched as one of the men struck a lighter, which brought a yellow glow to the house. 'Get it right, damn you,' he muttered to himself.

* * *

'How long now, Dad?'

'Half an hour, honey. Won't be long.' Dad lowered his watch, giving Grace another reassuring smile. Mum tilted her head towards the ceiling. She gasped. 'Danny!' Her eyes narrowed. 'Can you smell that?'

'I can see it, Mum!' Joe pointed to the trapdoor, where tendrils of smoke were gathering around its edges. Grace tensed on her chair, her fingers ached from holding the edges so tightly.

'Here.' Mum ripped open a cupboard door and snatched out wads of blue cloth. She rushed over to a small metal sink and flicked a tap, which brought out a gush of water.

'Hold this against your mouth.' Mum pressed a cool, wet square to Grace's lips. 'Now, get down on the ground.' Grace bent her knees, steadying herself with one hand to sit next to Joe. She crossed her injured ankle over her knee and stared at Mum, who held a cloth to her own mouth, exchanging urgent stares with Dad. He glanced upward; she nodded. The tendrils had gathered to form a grey cloud. 'There's an extinguisher in the cellar – if we can get that far.'

'Doesn't feel as though there's enough heat for the fire to be in the cellar. No, it's further up. Someone's trying to smoke us out.'

'Here.' Mum threw Dad a pair of goggles.

'Cover your mouth, Joe.' Dad bent over a long metal chest, shoved tight against the wall. Yanking the lid open, he drew out a rifle and peered inside the magazine.

Joe held out his hands. 'Yeah! Gimme . . .'

Dad shot him a warning look. 'Only if you need to use it, son.'

Joe nodded. He motioned to the rifle. 'Hand it over, Dad.'

Holding the rifle ready in front of his chest, Joe stood. 'Come on, Dad! Let's go upstairs!'

Dad sighed. 'Son. Listen to me now. You can't afford to be reckless. Stay here. Protect yourself. Protect Grace.' Dad nodded. 'No matter what happens. Remember who and what you are – you can't take stupid risks.'

'*This* isn't stupid, Dad!'

'Joe! For once, do as you're told!'

Joe slumped. 'Okay, Dad.' He pocketed the bullets and threw Grace a look. 'Don't you think she should have a gun, too?'

Grace's head began to spin; the taste of smoke in the air made her heart beat faster with panic. She couldn't be trapped here with fire raging above. 'Mum, let us go up with you. Please.'

Mum stroked Grace's hair back from her forehead, tucking loose strands behind her ears. 'You need to stay here.'

Grace took shuddering breaths, blinked aching eyes, gulped air – as fresh tears burned. Mum's hands were comfortingly warm against her cheeks.

'Honey. Promise me you'll try to stay calm while we're up there.'

'I don't want you to go!'

'Promise me.'

Mum didn't normally speak like this. Or hold her like this.

'I will, Mum.'

'Good girl.'

Joe kicked at the wall. Time was getting away, and he couldn't stop it. He speared his fingers through his hair. 'This isn't right! I want to go with you!'

Dad's hand gripped his shoulder. 'No. Stay here. Guard Grace.'

Joe paced uselessly; with a hard thump he banged his fist against the wall.

'Son. Don't do that. Sit down.'

Joe pointed up. 'No! I'm going with you!' He lunged towards the ladder; but Mum swerved in front of him, taking his shoulders. Firmly, she pressed him against the wall.

'Son, we told you to sit down, and that's what you'll do.'

Joe drew in a sharp breath, staring past Mum's shoulders. He could charge up there now . . .

'Do what your mother says, son.'

Joe sighed. He sank to the ground, arms folded. The rifle lay by his side. 'This isn't right.'

Smoke had turned the sickly fluoro into a brownish grey. Mum threw Dad an urgent look. 'We have to get moving.' Dad nodded. Together they began to climb the ladder with calm, purposeful steps.

'Be careful! *Please!*'

'Dad and I know what we're doing, Grace. Stay calm!'

As they disappeared into the smoke, Joe grabbed the ladder and slid it across the floor, resting it against the wall – all the while his gaze pinned on the hole above, where smoke had begun to escape, leaving a black spot in the ceiling.

Struggling to swallow, Grace's throat was dry and tight. What was coming to kill them?

Joe's fingers tightened around the gun. His heart drummed uncontrollably, adrenaline giving his mouth a bitter taste. He glanced at Grace, who was also staring into the open trapdoor. 'We should've gone with them.'

She nodded. 'I know.' In the distance, a door slammed.

'Calm yourself. They'll be fine. Everything will be fine,' Grace tried to convince herself.

Who was she kidding? Even now, as residual smoke stung her eyes, and her throat clenched with a rush of tears, it was the heavy cloud of emotion that hit her hardest: her parents' fear, doubt and false confidence.

Dread washed over her in waves. She knew what was going to happen, and there was nothing she could do to stop it.

EIGHT

HER MIND WAS torturing her. In her imagination, the world that was this little underground room vanished and she pictured the violence that was going on above. Mum and Dad dead on the ground. The sound of savage footsteps. Hard voices, murderous hands that would reach down into this place to kill her and Joe.

She drilled her fingers into her temples, trying to squeeze the horrors out. Holding her breath until it was all over, she huddled in the corner. She drew her knees to her chest and took a deep, shuddering breath.

A series of shots boomed above. Her eyes flew open. Sparks flashed in the distant darkness. She could smell smoke. Grace's chest grew tight, her fingers gripping the wall's bristly edges as her eyes wildly scanned the ceiling. What if it collapsed? The fire could spread. The thunder's echo left a strange buzzing sound. It was awful – nothing good could come of this.

And there was Joe, alert, watching the ceiling, ready to kill.

Grace closed her eyes, rocking slightly. She hoped more than anything that Mum and Dad were okay. And that it was the bad guys she saw.

After all, good guys always win – don't they?

She caught her breath: above, voices grew louder. Joe tensed up, aimed the rifle at the hole.

A shuffling sound above. Joe squinted. 'Who is it?'

Fingers slid around the edges. A white face, startlingly pale against the engulfing darkness, peered down. 'It's me, Diana!'

Joe dragged the ladder across, settling it beneath the trapdoor. 'Where are Mum and Dad?'

'Hold on!' A pair of black boots settled on the top rung, descending quickly to reveal a short, black-clothed woman with cropped dark hair and vivid blue eyes. Diana Callahan jumped off the last rung but then stopped, abruptly, and took stock of the situation.

Wedged into the corner was her niece, knees curled up to her chest, peering sideways; her nephew stood soldier-like, rifle cocked, eyes hard. 'What's happened?'

'Are you both all right?'

'Where are Mum and Dad?'

'Put down the gun, Joseph. Grace, come here.'

Joe lay the gun down. Tension was spreading through his stomach, a bitter taste seeping into his mouth. He saw the look on Diana's face; the truth was creeping towards him now.

'Where are they?'

He heard the tremor in his voice, knew the futility of the question. Even as his aunt moved towards him, hands outstretched, he resisted, wanting to reject the kindness in her eyes, to destroy it so this wasn't real. Not Dad. Not Mum. No.

'No – no they're not. No they're *not*!'

She clasped his shoulders. 'I'm sorry, Joe.'

'It's not true!'

'If we'd got here just five minutes earlier . . . there were too many of them.'

'Shut up! Don't you tell me that!'

'She's right, Joe.' Grace watched a tear form in Joe's eyes. Shocked since the moment she saw Diana's face, she couldn't cry now if she wanted to. A numb calm had taken hold, as if she was watching the whole thing from the outside.

'I want to see them!' Joe shoved past Diana and jumped at the ladder, taking two rungs at a time, plunging ahead through the now-lit cellar; behind, Diana helped lift Grace.

'I hurt my ankle.'

Grace heard her own voice: dim, distant, disconnected. She hobbled across the cellar floor and up to the sound of low voices, mingling. She felt Diana's hand on her back. 'Best if you sit down in the living room, dear.'

Grace shook her head. 'No. I want to see them too.'

In a slow, surreal walk through the house, she saw them everywhere: men and women dressed in black, military-style clothes. She passed a small group standing around a laptop in the kitchen.

There were people outside too, dark, anonymous sentries, guns in hand.

Calm and clear, her mind had shifted gear, into a place where the horror couldn't reach her.

From the garage, Joe's voice filled the air. 'No! Leave me alone!'

Grace ran through the garage door. Ahead, two paramedics were dragging her wriggling, red-faced brother out of the garage – and a third stood poised with a white sheet.

Mum lay closest, one arm sprawled over her chest, the other flung out to the side – the taser gun nearby. Staring upwards, Mum had a strange glass-like look in her eyes.

She couldn't see Dad's eyes, but saw the blood instead. And then . . . closest to the outer door, lay three other bodies.

She wandered closer.

A pair of hands grasped her arms, gliding her backwards and into a room filled with busy solemnity.

She sat, watching, the numbing protection of shock taking her deep into the netherworld. She couldn't even feel her ankle anymore.

Joe glared at her. 'What's wrong with you? Why are you so calm?!' The fire in his eyes burned harder. He jumped up and pointed at the garage. 'I could've done something!'

Diana came over. 'Sit down, Joe.'

'Let me up!'

'You can't do anything now, Joe!'

'Let me go! I have to do something!'

'Listen to me.' Diana grabbed Joe's shoulders, forcing his attention. She stared at him, unshrinking despite the blistering rage in his eyes. 'You will have your chance. I promise you.'

Joe shook his head. 'I won't. It's too late. They're gone . . . I could've stopped it.' The tears came, diluting the rage in his eyes to a dull, watery red. He slumped back on the chair and pressed his face into his hands.

'Diana?' A girl with short red hair leaned over. 'The ambulance is here.'

'Thanks, Maya.' Diana stood up and straightened her jacket while observing the window, where the ambulance stood, red lights flashing. Two young men descended from the cabin; each wore a green tunic and dark pants.

'Are we taking anyone into custody?'

'No, Maya. The ambulance is simply here to send a message. Two messages, actually. One to the public, who expect to see an ambulance whenever there's a tragedy. They can't see the incantations. To them, it's a normal ambulance. Makes for a good cover. Helps settle things back to normal quickly.' Diana scanned the neighbourhood. 'Secondly, to any ghoulies who are watching – it's a reminder that we don't mess around, and that we have the means to drag them to hell, so to speak.'

Maya shook her head. 'But this wasn't demon activity.'

'I think it was. We just need to find out who did this.'

'The neighbours are very curious.'

'Of course they are. I'll deal with them. But first,' she said, checking her wristwatch, 'we need to get these two moving.'

* * *

MAMMON WATCHED THE ambulance pull into the yard, his face tense with anger.

'You didn't do your homework, Halphas.'

The old man wound his fingers together and drew a deep, settling breath. 'Perhaps if I'd had more time, Master.' He bit his lip against the retort that was bursting to get out: it's your fault, Mammon. You were in such a rush, weren't you?

'I apologise, Master.'

'I've heard enough from you now, Halphas. Andras –'

The young demon fetched an armchair and placed it next to the window. Mammon sat; his dark eyes rolled back and his Shadow essence soon spilled out of the body into the air.

* * *

'I CAN WALK okay. It doesn't hurt.'

'Never mind.' Diana slung her arm under Grace's back. 'Tread lightly.' She swung a glance backwards; Joe was trudging behind, flanked by her stern-faced team. Diana bit her lip. The poor kid. He was never going to be able to take a step anywhere without one of them watching his back.

Grace squinted – something bulky was ahead, but she couldn't tell what. As they drew closer, her eyes focused on the outline of a van; black and shiny, nearly invisible next to the red flashing lights. Diana reached in front of her and yanked open a sliding door.

She helped Grace into the van, lifting her ankle onto the bench seat. 'Keep your leg up. We'll be moving in a minute.' She watched as Joe climbed in.

Grace stared out into the street, where Diana made her way across to the crowd.

* * *

76

MAMMON PACED ACROSS the yard, twisting his facial features until they took on a comforting, reassuring expression. The paramedic's body felt unpleasant – squat and flabby. Not the calibre of vessel he was accustomed to.

Stopping a few feet short of the van, the paramedic shoved his hands into his pockets and nodded at the mercenary. 'Hi.'

Maya responded with a sharp nod. 'Dawkins.'

The paramedic glanced towards Joe. 'This boy needs treatment.'

The girl grinned. 'Not the type you normally dish out, Dawkins.'

The paramedic gave her a patient smile. 'It doesn't take much to see he's in shock. At least let me give him some water and some aspirin, hmm?'

'The girl has a sprained ankle.'

'I'll bring her some aspirin too.'

Maya sighed. 'Okay, but make it quick. We'll be on the move soon.'

The paramedic stepped in closer and led Joe away. 'Come with me, son.' He flung open the ambulance's rear doors, wincing as the energy prickled his skin. To the human eye, this was a normal ambulance: white paint, red cross, blazing sirens. But the infernal scripting lashed all over the paintwork would have put a lesser demon on his back by now.

He gritted his teeth and reached into a plastic first-aid box. 'Sit down, lad.' He fished out two tablets and peered around for a water source, catching Joe's eye in the process. The boy's jaw was tight, his eyes flashing. Inwardly, the paramedic smiled. A small wave of hope rose inside of him. Already, the signs of anger were showing. Very encouraging.

* * *

HALPHAS SMILED, OBSERVING Mammon move about the ambulance. By now, the incantations must have been burning into his flesh. With begrudging admiration, he watched. Taking the body of one of *them*, undetected. Pure brilliance.

* * *

DIANA HELD UP a badge. 'I'm from central police. We are moving members of the family to protective custody. You all need to go home, now. We'll be in touch with some of you for witness statements in due course.'

Diana swept a firm, reassuring gaze around the crowd. Gradually, the people turned and made their way back into their homes.

* * *

THE PARAMEDIC WATCHED Joe gulp the water. 'You must be feeling pretty bad right now.'

Joe scowled. 'Yeah, you think?' He crushed the cup and threw it away.

'If that had happened to my parents, I would want revenge.' The paramedic gave him an earnest stare.

Joe breathed a deep, shuddering gulp. 'I do.'

'You should. But . . .' The paramedic lowered his voice to a whisper, throwing a cautionary glance around. '*They* won't let you.'

'What do you mean?'

'All I can say is, if you want this problem dealt with, don't involve your aunt. Or any of them. They are systematic people and they follow certain rules. I've been in this business a long time, and I can tell you they choose their targets for certain purposes. No revenge jobs.'

'I don't know,' Joe muttered, his eyes dim.

The paramedic reached into his pocket and slid a small white card into Joe's hand. 'Here. This is a very exclusive, special contact. When you're ready, give him a call.' He leaned closer. 'I promise you, Joe, that *he* will find the one who killed your parents. Then you can take your revenge.'

The paramedic smiled and gave him a firm pat on the back. 'You're still in shock. Take it easy – rest. Just don't lose that card.'

Diana turned and walked towards them. The paramedic was now taking Joe's temperature.

'I was thinking that we should get this lad to hospital for a check-up.'

'That's not the place he needs to be right now, Dawkins.' She laid a hand on Joe's arm. 'Thanks for your concern.'

'He's suffering from shock. He could use a sedative. Let me take him for a proper examination.' The paramedic reached out and took Joe's other arm; the confused boy glancing from side to side.

Diana gave the man a long stare. 'You're looking awfully sweaty, Dawkins. Perhaps you're the one who could use a check-up.'

The paramedic reached into his pocket and wiped the frost from his forehead. He would grind the insignificant woman into dust.

All in good time. But the boy! So near, yet so far. An angry hiss escaped his lips as he watched the Ferryman walk away.

With a final glance around, Diana closed the door and the van disappeared into the darkness.

NINE

'EVEN THOUGH I knew Daniel for forty-three years as my little brother, I can't seem to think of him in any other state than paired with Susanna. They were a unit.' Diana smiled across the congregation, shivering in the small, stone chapel, but her eyes kept flickering back to Grace and Joe.

'Their relationship was something special – a love that the great poets would have written about. The mission had gone wrong, Susanna was injured – she couldn't walk, and my brother carried her to safety. He knew she was the one that moment. He even told her, that very night, that if she wanted him to, he would take her away.

'And so it was. He did take her away, with their infant son, into the safety of suburban anonymity.' Diana clutched the lectern. 'Unfortunately, they didn't travel quite far enough.

'They were loving parents, who wanted their children to be free – so very much.'

The mourners stood; their murmuring gave way to the

rise of choral music. Celtic songs of lamentation. The two coffins began their lonely descent. Grace looked out the window — to a cliff face, where white waves continued their timeless ebb and flow. And so it was. Life just went on. Relentlessly. She swallowed, trying to kill the bitterness inside.

She still hadn't cried. Couldn't.

Solemn light shone through the myriad colours of stained glass.

Joe's face was downcast, his eyes filtering out all contact from others. He wouldn't cry in front of these people now.

* * *

WIND LASHED THE cliff's grassy crags, sending ripples through the grass before whistling its way along the muddy earth and whipping at Grace's ankles. She rubbed her hands up and down her arms; goosebumps had spread in a regular pattern beneath the thin sleeves. The air gusted, sweeping along stark walls, billowing into the courtyard, where a lone willow thrashed.

It was quiet outside the chapel. Minutes before, mourners had spilled out, showering her in sympathy. Strangers, mourning her parents in this strange place.

So this was Renfield. Her new home.

The journey here was a blurred memory: driving south, past the neon glow that bounced off the City's towers, their reflection fragmented against the River's bleak surface. Rumbling across a railway line and into the outlands, where the undesirables of Border City had been pushed away to live in government-issue weatherboard houses.

Into the smothering blanket of the night. Three hours later, thundering along a tree-lined road, where all light was swallowed up save the two steady beams at the front and the white-cold headlights behind. The moon bobbing along the treetops, surrounded by a midnight-blue sky that was punctured with thousands of stars. A strange calm in an unfamiliar forest.

Another world.

A training ground for demon hunters. Allegedly, Mum and Dad had spent years living somewhere like this. Was it possible? Had they really been part of a mercenary squad, running around the grounds at dawn? Fighting hand-to-hand in a training simulation? Jumping – armed with rifles – into a helicopter and flying away on some mission?

Impossible.

Every night since arriving here, she'd curled up in bed, trying to adapt to the abrupt silence that fell at night; the hallways a brutally dark void compared to the warm yellow light of home that would filter from the living room as her parents drank tea and watched the late news.

'I won't introduce you to any of the other recruits just yet,' Diana had said. 'You and Joe need to rest and take time to think about your future. You can join up and train with us, or we can send you to a secure location.'

Run away and hide – for how long? The rest of her life? Grace peered out at the ocean and the trio of rocky towers that stood just off the coast. Skyscrapers of jagged stone and moss. They seemed to have sprung out of the ocean, or even forced their way up in a mutinous earth shift. Wave caps rushed the shoreline before they were sucked back out to sea.

Joe stood at the edge of the trees, his face turned into the wind, eyes closed.

Grace stepped over a rock boundary and squelched her way over through the spitting rain. She stopped, wrapped her arms tighter around herself and stared at the moss climbing up the towers.

Joe shoved his hands into his pockets. 'I was supposed to go to Raven Point with Dad today.' He scratched his chin. 'I'll have to go riding by myself now.'

She glanced across. 'Someone will go with you.'

'Don't try to make it better, Grace. You always do that.'

She frowned. 'As if I could, Joe. I know what you're thinking –'

'No, you don't.' He held up a hand.

'Yes, I do. You're blaming yourself.'

'How would you feel, if you were me? I mean, think about it, Grace! I got this gift – this ability – and I didn't even use it!'

'Stop blaming yourself!'

'I could've saved them. I didn't even think about opening a rift! We could have got out that way! Why was I so stupid?' He lunged forward, kicking a small rock into the air. It soared over the cliff edge and disappeared. 'You're acting like it doesn't matter!'

Grace ran her fingers through her hair. 'I'm not accepting this . . . I'm not going to forget about what has happened. Diana told us to make a choice. I've made mine.'

Her eyes glimmered with anger. 'I want revenge.'

PART TWO

TEN

GRACE LAY ON top of her bed, on the undisturbed sheets and cover, still tucked into the wooden frame. She glanced out into the grey dawn and the stately bricks of the Residence. During the week that had passed since the funeral, strangers had carted in her old room, piece by piece.

Her cherrywood dressing table and stool, lined in purple velvet. Her gaze ran over the small family photos stuck to the mirror's edge.

Her heart swelled with grief.

The matching bookcase with Mum's old china cups, the ancient books. Their splintered, cracked spines wedged in rows between guardian-angel teddy bears in pink and blue.

Her feather boa, and the dress she'd never get to wear.

They'd even brought her art collage, peeled off the wall in careful fragments.

Diana was building a life for Grace in this room, pulling together chunks of her old world in an attempt to build comfort, familiarity.

The furniture didn't look right here.

She pressed her fingertips together, watching the skin turn white as the blood drained away. Enough of this room, now. Time to move.

'Rest,' Diana had said. 'Take time to grieve.'

Rest? How could she? Where was she? This place was a universe away from her sunny home. Compared to the peace of her mother's house, the sure feeling of contentment – no, it went further than that – *safety* – the knowledge that Mum would make all things right.

No wonder Mum had been so protective. Often the worried look in her eye, exchanging glances with Dad. The hushed conversations behind their bedroom door.

Voices rumbled outside. People were on the move, their shouts competing with the omnipresent, thudding music.

Three short beeps sounded. Grace reached for her bedside drawer and the small pink phone Mum had bought her just a month before. The SMS read: 'As a valued customer of Horizon phone network, you are entitled to two VIP tickets to Riverside Music Festival. TONIGHT ONLY. Quote number 6940 at the festival gate.'

She sighed, pressed 'Opt Out' and put the phone down.

* * *

Diana made her way across the driveway towards where Grace and Joe stood. She took a moment to study their faces. 'Looks as though you haven't changed your minds. Still want to join up?'

They nodded.

'You know that if you do, you will have to assume the roles of mercenaries, soldiers. We're not part of the mainstream army, but we do have that kind of structure as a private military company. Are you both prepared to take orders from us, even if you don't agree with them?'

'Yeah,' said Joe. Grace nodded. 'Absolutely.' Anything – for Mum and Dad.

'Well, I can't imagine that Danny and Susanna told you about how things work around here.'

'No,' said Grace. 'Not really. We didn't have time.'

Diana pressed a fingertip to her lips. 'Last night I stayed up thinking of how to introduce you to it all. A crash course in modern demonology.' She took a deep breath, clasping her fingers. 'I could talk and talk, but I didn't think you'd dig that. Or, I could just show you.

'So, follow me.'

Crunching their way along the driveway, the group moved towards the forest. Grace squinted and lifted her hand to shade her eyes against the sudden break of sunlight through the trees.

'You have probably seen some of the old movies about demon possession,' said Diana. 'Well, if only our job were that simple – stab a demon with seven holy daggers, compel them to leave by chanting incantations.'

She chuckled. 'The modern demon is far more difficult to catch – and even harder to destroy.'

Passing a blue picket fence with a 'Pesticide-free zone' sign, Diana paused. 'Oh, that's our organic veggie garden. Sarah is the instigator of that little project. You'll meet her.'

She walked on. 'So, where do demons come from? It's horribly simple. No possession, no intervention from hell. It happens when a person reaches a critical point, and he or she starts to manifest, or *grow* the demon energy until it becomes an irrevocable part of them.

'Oh, see the clock tower?' She pointed to the left. 'That's our Operations Building, where all the weapons and tactical training go on. Very high tech. We have a flight centre and medical bay as well, down there.'

Grace glanced at the tower. 'How much flying is involved?'

'Quite a bit,' said Diana, smiling. 'Are you a nervous flyer?'

Grace shrugged. 'I wouldn't know.' Mum and Dad couldn't afford to take them on holidays. She bit her lip. Where was she with her money, when they were struggling?

'Anyway,' Diana said, 'as I was starting to explain to you, these humans are responsible for their own degeneration. There can only be so many wrong decisions, so many immoral choices before, inevitably, they degenerate, lose the best part of their humanity. What's left? Our darker sides. The worst aspects of humanity. Rage, violence, lust, greed. Acted upon in unspeakable ways. So, that's why we exist; that's why the *sarsareh* do what we do.'

They progressed further into the forest, their feet now crunching on shards of bark, shed by the ghostly giants that stood all around them. Grace veered around the knee-high ferns that carpeted the forest floor. 'Where are we going?'

'Look ahead.' Diana pointed; Grace and Joe peered through the mass of trees at the giant, grey monstrosity that loomed there. As they moved closer, the sun disappeared behind it, bringing the huge wall into clearer view.

Joe frowned. 'What the hell is it?'

'This way.' Breaking through the last line of trees, Diana let them towards a curve in the wall.

Gazing up, Grace noticed the razor wire that ran along the top of the wall. 'Is this . . . a *prison?*'

Diana punched in a code and waited. A bearded face appeared in the window. He leaned into a microphone. 'Morning, Diana.'

'Hello, Brutus.'

The guard gave Grace and Joe a once-over. 'Fresh meat?'

Diana grinned. 'My niece and nephew.'

'Go on through.' He turned away; the door swung open. They moved through the guardhouse, where Brutus and another guard stood behind a glass barricade. Behind them was a wall of surveillance monitors with blinking monotone images.

Grace squinted, trying to make out those images.

'Come on,' said Diana.

Proceeding through another door, they moved out into a courtyard. The door closed, echoed off the walls like thunder.

No colour, no sound. Around the sparse courtyard sat three storeys of concrete, topped by a corrugated iron roof and the obligatory razor wire. No windows. Diana led them towards a white door, strangely stuck within the concrete. Through long windows of frosted glass, Grace could see the dull light within. She struggled to draw air. The whole place felt . . . sticky. As if they'd stepped into a different climate zone.

Grace pictured the Residence, with the ocean air that brought the scent of roses through windows that glowed amber at night. Cool, yet welcoming. Could this really be on the same grounds?

'It's our secure facility,' Diana said. 'Where we bring the bad guys. Consider it a jail . . . for demons.'

'Oh.' Grace pulled her jumper tighter around her. Her gut began to burn as the nausea rose. She sucked in a breath of stale air, folded her arms and stared at the pavers. The place felt so dead, so resistant to life that weeds dared not grow.

They moved on through the door and into a cramped reception area. Staff, all dressed in hospital tunics, sat behind a long window and stared at computer screens.

Through another door into a large recreation room. A suffocating cleanliness. Everything was slathered in white paint.

Standing out against the pale visage were a number of guards, covered in black from head to toe; faces obscured by balaclavas and black goggles. Each stood rigid, alert; each one held a rifle to their chest.

The guard standing nearest turned his head a fraction. Through the mask, she could feel vigilant eyes penetrating. She caught her breath at the sudden feeling of angry suspicion that overwhelmed her.

Diana touched her arm. 'It's all right, Grace. They're here for our protection.' She stopped at a water cooler, grabbed a cup and began to fill it.

'Here they are!' A voice boomed across the room. A slim, middle-aged man with short dark hair, glasses and a friendly smile crossed the room with long, confident strides. He wore a light blue polo shirt and beige pants. Behind him were two other adults, wearing white tunics and matching trousers, both with short hair and unsmiling faces.

All three wore the same pendant as Grace. She reached up and grasped her pendant, a twinge of sadness at the memory of Mum's fingers securing it around her neck.

'Hello.' The bespectacled man smiled and nodded. He shook her hand; Grace noted the roughness of his palm and his educated yet friendly accent. 'My name is Lucius Penbury.'

'Lucius is the boss,' said Diana. 'And yours, *if* you decide to join.' She gestured towards the silent man nearby. 'Marcus, his brother.'

Marcus didn't smile but looked out through calculating grey eyes. Harsh, thin lips sat below a perfectly trimmed moustache. He had curly blond hair, was taller than his brother and wore an air of superiority. A study in opposites. Grace shook his hand. His palm was soft, his nails manicured.

'Hello,' Marcus said. 'You can address me as Doctor Penbury. I'm sorry to meet you under such unfortunate circumstances. This is my subordinate, Agatha.'

'Hello. Welcome to Renfield.' The woman, petite yet muscular with short black hair, spoke in a strong Scottish accent. Grace folded her arms, trying to ignore the distinct feeling of depression, almost hopelessness, that seemed to radiate from the pair.

Something moved in her peripheral vision. She glanced sideways; the nervous tumbling in her stomach returned.

Each of the guards had turned, as though to acknowledge Marcus's presence. Watching him. Guarding him.

Diana cleared her throat. 'Marcus and Agatha run this facility.' She handed Grace a cup of water. 'Joe, want a drink?'

A new voice cut in from across the room. 'It's actually an asylum.'

'What?' Grace shot her aunt a look.

Red patches darkened Marcus's cheeks. 'You speak when you are asked to, Cassandra.'

'Oh well, I've started now. Might as well go on.' Two people crossed the room: a woman with beady eyes and long black braids framing her face, and a guy with dreadlocks who looked as though he could be her brother.

The woman gave the guards a derisive glance before swishing across to stand next to Diana.

Grace found it hard to place her accent. American? Canadian?

'I'm Cassie.' The woman leaned forward and pulled Grace into a hug.

Grace stiffened. 'Hi.'

Cassie paused before smiling at the frowning Joe. She lifted her hands defensively. 'Don't worry. I won't force a hug on you.' Cassie pointed her thumb at her companion. 'This is my brother, Calvin. We run the shelters in the City's east. Cal's just started.'

Calvin winked. 'Hi.'

The siblings were flashes of colour in a bland world; both wore colourful cotton shirts with cargo pants and sneakers.

Grace looked at Diana. 'Asylum?'

'Psychiatric research and rehabilitation,' Diana said. 'Nothing to worry about.'

Marcus pressed his palms together. 'Some demons, when they are just starting to degenerate, can be rehabilitated. Through psychotherapy and other means.'

Cassie coughed. 'But the success rate is very low, isn't it, Marcus? As our investigation will reveal.'

Marcus gave her a flat stare. 'Why don't you tell these two about *your* work?'

Agatha snorted. 'Yes, I'm sure they'll be impressed, in light of their recent history.'

Cassie looked at Grace and Joe. 'Our shelters are proper rehabilitation centres.' She threw Marcus a smile. 'Unlike our friends here, we practise non-violence. Our goal is to generate understanding and compassion for these beings. Demonhood is a sickness. Not an evil.'

Joe glanced between the colourful pair. 'What . . . you actually feel sorry for demons?'

Grace scowled. 'That's ridiculous!'

Calvin peered at her. 'We don't take part in the torture.'

The cup wobbled in Grace's hand. 'You'd feel differently if your family were killed.'

'I didn't mean anything by that.' Cal's gaze flicked from the angry girl to her brother. 'Sorry.'

'All right.' Diana placed her hand on Grace's shoulder. 'Calm down, relax.'

Cassie coughed and then glanced at her brother. 'Well, time for us to go. Nice to meet you both.' Slowly, she and Calvin walked towards the exit.

Diana watched them leave. 'We have different ways of looking at the problem, but we all have the same goal in mind.'

'Why don't you just kill them?' Joe said, cocking his fingers like a gun.

'That would be easy, wouldn't it?' Diana smiled. 'If we do that, the dark energy stays here, on Earth, and will quickly reattach itself, making another demon even stronger.'

Grace looked around. 'So, you just bring them here? Then what?'

'The dark energy must be expelled and cleansed.' Marcus's voice was tight.

'What happens to the person?' Grace pressed.

'The body cannot survive the expulsion.' Marcus looked at Joe. 'Of course, now that Joe is here, we will not need to go through this long, arduous process.' His eyes glittered as he looked at Diana. 'Have you explained what the *sarsareh* do?'

Diana lifted her hand. 'All in good time.'

Marcus grunted. 'Your aunt is protecting you, Joe. But you will come to realise that you are a revelation.' He gave Diana an innocent shrug. 'It's the truth.'

Joe looked up. 'Yeah?'

'Oh, yes.' Lucius smiled. 'You'll revolutionise our work.'

Breathing deeply, Diana struggled to control the quiver in her voice. 'They must be allowed to think things over first!' She glanced between Grace and Joe. 'So many scenarios we haven't considered. To begin with, one day you may come across someone you once knew as a school friend, or a neighbour. Someone who is now a demon. How will you handle that?'

Joe shrugged. 'Dunno.'

'You haven't had time to think it through. To come to grips with what we're dealing with here.'

'Well, let's show them, then.' Marcus walked across to the water cooler and drew himself a glass. He took a swig and looked at the two newcomers. 'There are three simple rules. Do not interact with the inmates. Stay behind the yellow line. Move when I tell you to. Understood?'

Agatha ducked into an office and picked up a satchel. She put it over her shoulder and jogged to catch up with Marcus, who was leading the group towards at a set of dark blue double doors, which were framed in a silver metallic line. Grace followed, shooting one guard a wary look as she passed. Even though he was staring straight ahead, she was sure his eyes were following her.

Marcus pushed the doors open. 'Remember: don't make eye contact with any of them. If you feel strange, tell me.'

Grace peered down a long, brightly lit hallway. Plastic walls flanked them on both sides. Cubes for cells, again, whitewashed, each with a chair, bed, and bathroom area. And, once again dispersed at even intervals: the men in black. 'No bars?'

'No need. That stuff's stronger than steel.' Diana nodded to a guard, who was pacing the corridor. He held some kind of remote control device that had a large red button in the middle.

She felt the nausea rise in her stomach, the cold needling along her spine . . . In hope of some distraction, she glanced at the numbers posted outside each cell. 'Level Fourteen?' She threw Diana a curious look.

Agatha stepped forward. 'That refers to the Stone Scale of Evil. It's how we categorise the various demons we come into contact with. Level Fourteen demons are easy to apprehend. We have quite a few of them here.'

Grace stole a glance into each cell as they moved along. For all the world, the inmates could have been human. Slumped on beds or in chairs. Looking away, non-confrontational – yet, the Shadows were watching . . .

'This level of demon is certainly psychopathic but out for themselves, to gain some benefit, usually financial. The most famous Level Fourteen demons in history were Herman and Paul Petrillo, who started the Philadelphia Poison Ring. Murdered over one hundred people – all in the name of greed.'

With every few steps, the air of madness grew thicker.

'What's the highest level?'

'Twenty-two.'

Grace felt her spine tingle. 'Do you have anyone . . . of that level?'

'Yes,' Agatha said. 'But, one step at a time. Ever heard of Charles Manson? Leader of a cult known as the Manson Family. Under his instruction, the cult members carried out a number of vicious murders. He was Level Fifteen.'

They moved past another row of cells. 'These are our Level Fifteens. Our most famous inmate here was arrested for a shooting spree in a suburban shopping centre.' Agatha rolled her eyes. 'He claimed he was unfairly dismissed by his boss.'

Lucius shook his head. 'They love to make excuses.'

'Right. Here we are. Level Sixteen. Telepathic. The most

famous Level Sixteen in history is Myra Hindley, who murdered children in the north of England decades ago. But, unfortunately, we have our own version here. She helped her husband kill four young women.'

Grace could feel the demon looking at her. She could see the frosty breath coming from the demon's mouth; could feel its chill climbing the walls. Despite the warning, she turned and met the inmate's gaze. The eyes seemed to radiate a wave of dark energy that hit her, bringing a cramp to her stomach and a burning sensation in her eyes. And the voice . . . the hissing, growling that seemed to echo inside her mind. She doubled over, clutching her stomach. 'She wants to kill me,' she whispered.

Agatha waved one of the remote control devices at the inmate. 'Face down!'

With a hiss, the demon lowered her head.

'We warned you. Do not make eye contact with them.' Agatha slid the device back into her pocket.

Diana put her arm around her niece. 'Do you want to leave?'

Grace straightened up and took a deep breath. 'No.' She moved forward. 'Keep going.'

'Level Seventeen. Keep your eyes averted. This inmate confessed to eight murders but is suspected of having committed three times that many. To most people, especially women, he was attractive, charismatic.' Agatha paused. 'You must realise that when you apprehend a demon, any UnSighted who witnesses the act will protest strongly.' She put on a simpering voice. 'He's really a nice guy. He had a hard childhood.' She shook her head.

The demon lifted his head and looked at Joe with a violent glint in his eye. Joe gave him the finger.

Diana turned and swatted his hand away. 'It's no joke, Joseph!'

They stopped and Marcus punched a code into a security system.

The door seemed to open with a burst of air, as if a vacuum seal had been opened.

'You're about to meet the Hannibal Lecter of Renfield,' said Marcus.

Grace felt the tension hit her immediately. A sinister power lay within these walls.

This cell was medieval compared to the others. A hovel, barely the size of Grace's old bathroom. Walls were coated in slime, criss-crossed steel bars separated the inmate from the visitors. Above, a grimy light flickered intermittently. There was a damp, stale taste in the air.

'This one is Level Nineteen,' Agatha said.

Marcus smiled at the inmate. 'Hello, Raymond.'

Even though this was a demon – the Shadow clinging to his body told her that – Grace couldn't get past the pale, dishevelled young man whose orange tunic and pants were far too big, giving him a childlike, comical appearance. His sullen eyes were fixed on the wall, his fingers laced together on his lap.

'He seems harmless.'

Marcus stepped closer to the cell. 'That's what makes him such an effective killer.'

Grace stared at the doctor. Marcus almost sounded as though he admired him.

'Does he talk?' Joe stepped forward and tapped on the cell wall.

'Don't antagonise him.' Diana moved forward and pulled Joe's hand away from the plastic.

Grace looked back at Raymond. He was staring right back at her, his expression neither sad nor angry. Just blank. But she felt herself become very drowsy, very quickly. A rapid onset of sleep – like the needle they gave her when she had her appendix out.

And she wasn't in the asylum anymore. She was alone with him in a house she didn't recognise. It was similar to Gran's cottage but creepy. Gloomy, coated with dust. Raymond was leading her towards a dark brown door. Every few seconds he shot her a look of anticipation.

Grace could smell something cooking – roast meat.

Raymond led her down a staircase into a small, damp room, dimly lit. He led her across to a large, white chest freezer. With a hiss, the door opened. Raymond pointed inside. *See?*

Inside the freezer, row upon row of meat joints. Wrapped in plastic.

That's the scent from the kitchen. You noticed it, didn't you? And I didn't need a gun, or even chloroform. As you can see, I haven't got much in the way of muscle. But I can win them this way. He tapped his head, hard, and then nodded at the frozen joints. *This guy was six foot two and about twice my body weight.*

Grace staggered back, her foot brushing against something hard. She looked down: there was an axe, embedded in a chopping block; its metal stained dark red.

Her head hit brick, and she was in the asylum again.

The demon had her trapped in his stare. Grace shook her head rapidly to waken her body from the anaesthetic effect of the trance, the echo of his voice inside her mind.

Raymond's gaze was serious, matter-of-fact – even sympathetic. *You said I was harmless. I thought you should know the truth.*

'Get out of my head!' Her scream bounced off the walls. Startled, Agatha slammed the red button on her remote. Raymond's hands flew up to the collar around his neck.

Shaking, Grace looked over at Agatha. She'd come alive doing this, her eyes shining, jaw clenched. She held the button until the demon finally collapsed, arms and legs limp.

'Fry him some more,' Joe growled.

Agatha shook her head. 'He's restrained now.'

Joe put his arm around Grace. 'It's okay, sis. You're safe.'

'Take it easy,' said Diana. 'Just breathe.' She turned to Agatha. 'Shouldn't you have been watching things more closely?'

Agatha put the remote into her pocket. 'New recruits need to experience this kind of thing so they know what to expect.'

Grace trembled. 'I was somewhere else . . .'

'Yes,' Marcus said. 'That's how he does it.'

Grace gazed at the cell. The walls seemed translucent, lined with frost. 'Why do they do that? 'She pointed to the icy sheen.

'We don't know where it comes from,' said Diana. 'But our best guess is this: when demons are on the attack, they seem to draw all the energy out of the air. Notice how cold it has become in here?'

Grace exhaled and watched her breath form a cloud. That was true. Jesse Tyler was angry and then he seemed to sweat this stuff. What he was doing the first time she saw him?

'Raymond seemed almost friendly,' Grace whispered. 'Almost as if he cared about me; that he wanted to warn me about his nature.'

'Classic psychopath,' Lucius said. 'He'll act like your friend and even come across as intelligent and insightful. Then he'll sink his axe into your skull.'

'Agatha,' said Marcus, 'access Raymond's history for me.'

The woman fished into her satchel and drew out a computer tablet. Frowning, she began scrolling through files until she reached Raymond's record. She passed the tablet to Marcus.

'Look at this.' Marcus gestured for Grace and Joe to come closer. They peered into the screen and at a mug shot of a dishevelled, wild-eyed face.

'This is Raymond's rap sheet. He murdered twelve people, most of whom were young boys, and froze their body parts.' He leaned closer. 'Then ate them.'

Grace shuddered. 'I know. He showed me.'

'Dirty cannibal,' Joe said.

'He's a copycat killer. A great admirer of Jeffrey Dahmer, the American serial killer.'

Grace gulped. 'He can't get out of here, can he?'

'Raymond is scheduled for expulsion, Grace.' Marcus looked at his watch. 'Three days from now, he'll be dead.'

'Why three days?'

'That's how long it takes. Expulsion of demon energy is no small matter. Even after physical death, the energy lingers.'

He gave Joe a pointed look. 'Of course, opening a rift would be an instantaneous expulsion. Far more efficient.'

Joe nodded. 'Hell, yeah.'

'Come on,' Diana said. She put her arm around Grace and led her back up the hallway. 'I think the kids have seen enough for now, Marcus. On to brighter things.'

Grace moved along the corridor, trying to ignore the feeling of dread rising in her stomach. 'Are there others like him out there?'

Diana patted her back. 'If there are, we'll catch them.'

ELEVEN

GRACE DREW IN deep breaths of fresh air as the group stepped outside the wall. Instantly, she felt her mood lift at leaving that place and its creepy inhabitants behind.

Diana looked at her watch. 'Sarah's going to meet us in about five minutes, and she can take over from there.'

Grace looked at her aunt. 'When did this problem start? I mean, people becoming demonic?'

Diana sighed. 'No-one can be sure . . . our great writers have recorded the worst times in history – when we fell into our darkest days. Times like these have become known as Scourges.' She clasped her hands. 'Some have a theory that a cosmic phenomenon, like the order of the planets, inspires the uprising of a Scourge and also gives some demons their special powers. They've made definite links with demon uprisings. But we can't measure it, can't predict the next outbreak. Even when it subsides, a Scourge will never truly disappear. Always, in some deep recess of our collective consciousness lies an echo of what has been. Waiting for an opportunity to rise up again.'

'Are we in a Scourge now?'

Diana gave Grace a wry smile. 'I believe so.'

Joe lifted his head. 'But now I'm here.' The burn had begun in his gut – a desire to hunt down his parents' killers. Even now, his fingertips were tingling with anticipation, the paramedic's card ever-present in his pocket.

Lucius smiled. 'Yes, you are.'

Diana narrowed her eyes. 'I'm not in a hurry to see you out in the field, Joe.'

A tall, fair-haired girl walked towards the group. Her hair was short and neat, her eyes dazzling in the sunlight. She was tall, nearly the same height as Joe, who'd zoomed up in the past year to six feet two. She wore sky-blue cargo pants, a white t-shirt and yellow sneakers. A black embroidered eye sat on her sleeve. Her look was fresh – like she'd stepped out of an advertisement for laundry detergent.

'Hi.' She smiled. 'I'm Sarah Sanderson.'

Joe coughed and ran his fingers through his hair. He stole a glance at Grace; she raised her eyebrows with a small smile.

'Hi,' said Grace.

Joe reached out his hand. 'Nice to meet you, Sarah.'

Sarah gave Diana a friendly nod. 'Are they ready to go?'

'That's if they're still interested.' Diana glanced between her niece and nephew, and then sighed. 'Okay, then. Guess if you're still gung-ho after our little tour here, there's no stopping you. Fine. You can start your training today.'

'Bye, then,' Sarah said. She smiled at the newcomers. 'Shall we?'

DIANA WATCHED THE trio disappear into the forest. 'I don't want Grace and Joe pushed into anything they're not ready for. Am I understood?'

'Relax, Diana.'

'No, Lucius. I will not risk him like this. The minute he goes into the outside world, they'll be after him. To finish what they started with his parents. Or worse . . .'

'Fair enough,' Lucius said. 'We will keep him under protection and work on perfecting his skill.'

'And securing his loyalty,' added Marcus.

'Joe must not be allowed to leave the premises,' said Diana. 'The incident with the truck was demonic intervention on a high level. Whoever this demon is, I don't think he'll be willing to let Joe slip away a second time. We must be vigilant and remember that someone's trying to get to him.' Diana took a deep breath and stared at her intertwined fingers.

'If we only knew who.'

* * *

'WE'VE GOT COMBAT training first up.' Sarah led Grace and Joe through the main passageway that separated the sleeping quarters from a large recreation room. The limestone walls were coated with posters. A drinks fridge and cluster of red, padded chairs took up the corner, where a giant TV and games console sat. Matching striped sofas were wedged against the wall, all to make room for the pool table that stood in the centre of the room.

'Cool,' said Joe.

'Who pays for all this?' said Grace.

'Marcus raises the funds to keep this place running. From "concerned benefactors", as he puts it. It's funny, we're stuck in practically the most isolated place on Earth, yet little old Renfield has a worldwide reputation for excellence in training and combat. Even though we've only been going for two years.'

'Who gives him the money?' Grace asked.

'People who have been affected by demon activity and want justice.'

Grace nodded at the crest on Sarah's t-shirt sleeve. 'Is that some kind of um . . .?'

Sarah nodded. 'It marks me out as a telepath. We only wear these while training, never on missions. The mercs have their own crests, as do the engineers.'

'Can you read minds?'

'No,' Sarah gave Joe a half-smile. 'I can plant ideas in others' minds, that's all.' She scratched her head. 'I don't really use my gift much – I work in research and development instead, and sometimes I work with the communications systems.' She cleared her throat and shot a glance between Grace and Joe. 'What did you guys think of the asylum?'

Grace shuddered. 'Those guards are creepy.'

Joe smirked. 'Without their guns, they'd be pussies.'

Sarah gave him a doubtful look. 'Not really. Marcus picks the cream of the mercenary crop to join his guard, so they're pretty good.' She shrugged. 'Most of the time they just stand there with guns. It's a waste of talent, really. Nobody gets out of those cells – ever.'

They approached a group of boys sitting at a table. Grace noticed each of them wore a triangle insignia on their sleeve.

A guy who appeared to be in his early twenties looked up. His eyes, warm and brown, radiated a deep intelligence. His skin, smooth and even, was a light shade of caramel, and his hair a mass of tight, fair curls.

'Hi, Sarah.'

Sarah grinned. 'Hey, Seth. This is Grace and Joe Callahan.'

Seth stood up and nodded. 'I know. Your reputations precede you. Settling in okay?' He fell into step with them.

'Reputations?' Grace shook her head. 'We haven't done anything.'

'That's not what we've heard.'

The group walked on.

'Seth's part of the engineering core. Their crest represents Pythagoras. They're learning to design weapons and communications systems and fly choppers. The very technology that the grunts . . . I mean, mercs, rely on.'

Seth clasped his hands behind his back, lifted his chin and put on an English accent. 'Actually, I'm in charge of the core.' He looked down his nose at them before bursting into a bright grin.

Sarah shook her head. 'Crap acting, buddy. You can't even *pretend* to be an arsehole.' She punched his arm.

'Oh.' Seth put on a mock pout. He threw Grace a grin and winked.

Grace tore her eyes away to give Sarah a questioning look. 'Who are you imitating?'

'Malcolm, Sarah's brother,' said Seth.

'Stepbrother.' Sarah waggled her finger. 'He thinks he's better than everyone else.'

'Definitely not an engineer,' Seth added. 'Certainly not skilled enough to be a telepath.'

'Ah,' said Sarah, 'you flatter us.'

Seth lowered his voice. 'Although, Daddy's the head honcho, isn't he? Malcolm probably thinks he's going to inherit power, like this is some kind of monarchy.'

Grace looked at him. 'Lucius is Malcolm's father?'

'No, Marcus is.'

'Oh,' said Grace. 'I thought Lucius was in charge of us.'

'He's supposed to be.' Seth sighed. 'But he lets his brother call all the shots.'

Sarah tutted. 'Don't let Diana hear you say that.'

Grace looked back at Joe, who was listening with a bemused look on his face.

A passing group of mercenaries gave the group a lasting stare. Grace studied the crests on their sleeves: a long spear set against a bronze shield emblazoned with an eight-pointed star. She felt their gaze moving over her body. One of them mumbled to his friend. They broke into laughter and walked on.

Grace breathed deeply, trying to quell that old feeling that arose whenever boys laughed and stared. 'Are they always this unfriendly?'

Sarah shrugged. 'Don't let it get to you. Some of these guys think they're God's gift to women. Comes from fighting hand-to-hand with ghoulies. But people like us value mind over muscle.' They stopped at a glass sliding door.

'Ghoulies? That's what you call them?' Grace noted the derisive tone. Perhaps they were talking about different monsters here.

Sarah slid the door open. A rush of cool air hit their cheeks; in the distance Grace could see a blur of movement among the trees.

The red-headed girl, Maya, jogged past. 'You're late.'

Sarah rolled her eyes. 'That's Diana's assistant.'

Maya shot a look back. 'I'm a mercenary, actually. Try to keep up.'

Grace watched the girl disappear into the trees. 'Yeah, we've met.'

A Greek-style amphitheatre lay ahead, with six rows of grassed levels. Maya was sitting in the back row beside two other mercenaries. Both had cropped hair, like marines. One blond, one dark. The blond boy glanced up, gave the newcomers a once-over and looked back at his teammate. Grace noticed he wore the standard white t-shirt, but the front was emblazoned with *SERB PRIDE*.

The place was packed with people in white shirts. Ahead, a boy stood and made a joke, then he ducked down when someone threw a drink can at him. At the front, five young guys and two girls were standing in conversation. Grace gulped against the rising wave of nerves. But then again – with a closer look – this gathering resembled nothing more than a school assembly. This wasn't an army. They were just kids.

'Sit here,' Sarah said. They took their seats behind Maya and the two other mercenaries.

'Quiet!' One of the leaders stepped forward and stared out into the group.

'That's Ivan,' whispered Sarah. 'He's our squad leader. Hopefully you've both been assigned to him if Lucius knows what he's doing.'

Ivan ran his gaze along the crowd and began to take rollcall.

Grace scanned his face. Pale, with short, dark hair. She couldn't see his crest, but there was something about him that made her feel compelled to stare, as though she was drawn to him . . .

'Is he a telepath?'

Seth snorted. 'Hell, no. He's a merc. Hardcore one, too.' He looked at Grace. 'Why'd you think that?'

'Never mind.'

She continued to stare, mesmerised by his voice and the eyes that seemed to speak to whomever he looked at. And then Seth was nudging her arm. 'You're up.'

'Callahan, Grace,' Ivan repeated.

She raised her hand. 'Here.'

Ivan stared at her for a moment before looking down at his list again. 'Callahan, Joseph.'

When rollcall was over, the two mercenaries next to Maya turned and looked at Grace and Joe. 'You two are with us,' the blond boy said. 'Move it.' He cast a long look at Grace as he hoisted a large black bag over his shoulder and began to move up the stairs, closely followed by Maya.

'That's Armin,' Sarah said. 'Sorry about his attitude, but that's grunts for you.'

Armin glanced back. 'Shut up, girl. When was the last time you killed a ghoulie?'

The dark-haired boy coughed. 'Ahem.'

Sarah sighed. 'Grace, meet my stepbrother, Malcolm.' She pressed her lips together, struggling not to laugh at Seth, who was pulling faces.

Malcolm reached across, but didn't wait for Grace to accept his handshake. Rather, he grabbed her hand and shook hard. 'I'm Malcolm Penbury. You'll answer to me whenever Ivan's not here.'

'Ivan's always here,' Sarah said. 'So you won't have to answer to him often.'

Grace pulled her hand away. 'Okay then.' Seth was pretending to gag, shoving his forefinger down his throat. Sarah broke into laughter.

Grace began to climb the stairs. Malcolm fell into step next to her. 'So what do you have to offer us, Grace? What's your motivation for wanting to join up?'

'My parents were murdered by demons. I want to find the ones who did it, and kill them.'

'Yes.' Maya threw her a look over her shoulder. 'As you say in English, join the club.'

'It's true,' said Sarah. 'Everyone here has lost family that way. Well, except for Malcolm. He's still lucky enough to have his dad.' She gave Grace a meaningful look. 'You've met Marcus already, haven't you?'

'Yep.' Grace kept her tone friendly. She could feel Malcolm's eyes burning into her face.

The group moved into a small clearing surrounded by trees with climbing holds and ropes. Armin dropped the bag and crouched next to it, opening the zipper. He began to unload weapons and ammunition.

Joe wandered across. 'Tasers?'

Armin gave Joe an appreciative smile. 'Our training program is going to be totally different now you're here. We stun them, you throw them into a rift.'

'Neat.' Joe picked up a handgun and took aim.

'Don't you point that thing at me,' said Grace.

'Yeah, watch out,' said Sarah. 'Accidents do happen.'

'Yes, they do!' Maya snapped. She turned her gaze on Grace. 'You and your brother are replacements.' She tilted her head, eyes hard through her bright red fringe. 'A mentally unstable telepath got two of our team killed.' With a jaunty flick of her wrist, she loaded yellow cartridges into a handgun.

Sarah glared at Maya. 'It wasn't her fault.'

'Yes, it was. She was incompetent, arrogant and foolish.'

Sarah's eyes narrowed. 'She's not here to defend herself, Maya.'

'She's where she belongs now.'

'Shut up! You've got no idea!'

Maya just shrugged.

Grace stared at Sarah. 'Who's she talking about?'

Trembling with anger, Sarah watched Maya turn to the other mercenaries.

Grace touched Sarah's arm. 'Hey, are you okay?'

Sarah's face was flushed, her eyes ablaze. 'I'm fine.' She closed her eyes and breathed. 'Everything's fine.'

Making a mental note to find out who this disgraced telepath was, Grace reached out and touched the trunk of a nearby tree, where various hand and foot holds jutted out in an uneven pattern like giant wads of chewing gum, squashed and prodded into different shapes. She reached out and squeezed one between her thumb and forefinger. It felt reassuringly stable – and comfortable.

Sarah peered up. 'Have you climbed before?'

Grace lodged her foot into a lower hold and lifted off. Her foot came to rest on another hold. 'No.' She glanced up – another hold was within reach. She could do this. Stretching, she pulled herself up.

With fluid moves, she climbed higher, the pain in her injured ankle eclipsed by her desire to reach the top.

'You're not supposed to do that without a harness.'

'Oh.' Grace looked down and gave Sarah a half-smile. 'Bit late now.' She pushed further.

Sarah winced. 'Grace, climb down now.'

For the first time in months, Grace's stomach felt light.

Just a little bit further. The next handhold seemed higher but not beyond her reach. She could see above the tops of some smaller trees. She swung her leg up and stretched across to grab one of the handholds. Beyond, the peak of one of the cliff towers came into view. She stopped and gazed out at the ocean.

A quick glance down confirmed the awful truth – her enthusiastic climb had brought her much higher than she'd intended. Sarah stared up, pressing her palm against her stomach, her face creased with worry. Maya wore a smirk.

'Climb down, Grace!' Joe scowled.

Malcolm stood at the foot of the tree. 'I'll go up and get her.'

'No!' Grace swayed, struggling to climb down, her knees scraping against the trunk as she slid, her fingers tearing at the bark. 'I can get down myself!' She managed to get a handhold – phew. But she missed the foothold and her good foot was hanging, leaving all the weight on her hands.

Armin was staring up at the tree with a predatory grin, juggling a softball in his hand. The smile dropped, and he hurled the ball at Grace.

'Score! A direct hit!'

Grace's arms became heavy. Her fingers slipped away.

With a thump, she landed. A jarring pain hit her back. She lay her head back on the wet grass, closed her eyes and groaned.

Three, two, one – and she would magically teleport to anywhere but here.

She felt a warm hand on her arm. 'Are you all right?' She opened her eyes and caught her breath.

It was him. Ivan.

He peered down at her, frowning with concern. He had clear, near-perfect skin – apart from a small scar on his right cheek. Light blue eyes, crystal cool, but shining with an inner warmth that instantly made her feel at ease, cared for.

He smelled nice – a mix of the healthy male scent and light aftershave. And boy, was he ripped. Not obscenely, his muscles weren't bursting through his sleeves, but just enough to create an impression of lithe, gymnast-like strength.

'I'm okay.' She sat up.

Ivan gave her his hand and helped her up. His hand was warm and solid – like the rest of him. She hadn't really noticed this during rollcall, but he towered above everyone else – even Joe. She wiped the wet grass off her jeans, hoping her blush wasn't too obvious.

Sarah glared at Armin. 'You're a dickhead.' She lunged across and grabbed the softball from his hand.

Armin shrugged. 'What? She made a safe landing.' Grinning, he snatched the ball back, twirling it in one hand. 'We have initiations around here. You have to prove yourself before you can call yourself a mercenary.'

Sarah's cheeks flushed red. 'By having her neck broken? You stupid –'

Malcolm grunted. 'Why so touchy, Sarah? Off your meds?'

Seth glared at him. 'Shut up, Malcolm.'

'I'm okay, Sarah.' Grace looked at Ivan, who was speaking to Seth in a low voice. 'Who is he, anyway?'

'Ivan Konstantinov. He used to be with Spetsnaz – the Russian special forces. Lucius brought him in specially to train us, and he liked it so much that he stayed on. He's only twenty-one, but there are some stories about him.' She lowered her voice. 'His nickname is Ivan the Terrible. Apparently he killed a Level Twenty-two, all by himself.'

'Really?' Grace cleared her throat. 'I don't remember seeing him at the funeral.' She watched Ivan lead an attentive Joe past the row of climbing trees, pointing upwards.

'He was there. We all were.' Sarah took a deep breath. 'Whatever you do, don't get him angry. He's friendly nearly all of the time, but if you piss him off, he's all business.'

A whistle caught Grace's attention. Maya was watching her, with an expectant look on her face. 'If you want to join our team, you have to learn to handle a firearm.'

Grace lifted her chin. 'Doesn't sound too hard to me.'

'Well, there's not much else that you can do, is there?' Armin said. 'But your brother, on the other hand.' He whistled. 'Great potential.'

'Yes.' Maya nodded. 'All she's done so far is fall out of a tree.' She grinned.

Grace narrowed her eyes. 'I wouldn't have if you hadn't thrown that ball, you moron.'

Maya's smile dropped. 'Don't you speak to him like that.'

'Right.' Ivan's voice snapped through the air. 'All of you – sit down.'

Grace lowered herself to the grass and crossed her legs. Sarah touched her arm. 'Don't let them get to you, Grace. Diana told us about your gift. You're going to kick their butts. They'll never be able to do what we can.'

'No.' Maya gave Sarah a sarcastic smile. 'But then again, neither will we go insane and rot away in a padded cell.'

Sarah flinched. 'Shut up.'

Grace pointed at Maya. 'You know what? You talk too much.' She turned back to Sarah, whose face was red. 'Who is she talking about?'

'Someone who used to work here. Sit down.'

'What is wrong with them?'

'They're mercenaries, Grace. Arrogance comes with the territory.' Sarah tucked her knees up to her chest. 'I just ignore it. Most of the time I'm on the radio, away from the action.' Her eyes grew dim, staring into the nothingness.

Ivan ran his gaze along the group. 'Our training objectives have changed, given the new dynamics of the group.' Grace watched his lips move, noting the strange way he pronounced certain words; how formal his speech seemed compared to the rest of them. He seemed to sense her thoughts and gave her an extra-long look before turning to the mercenaries. 'You are to spend the morning in a live-fire simulation, then we'll meet up with these two for a combined exercise.'

Armin pointed to Grace. 'What about her? Will she receive any arms training? We're not about to put our lives in the hands of another incompetent psychic.'

Ivan threw him a hard look. 'Jelavic – to me. The rest of you – to the arena.'

Armin stepped towards Ivan. Maya gave Armin a reluctant look before disappearing into the trees. Grace couldn't hear what they were saying, but Ivan's tone was firm, his eyes fixed on his subordinate's face. Armin shook his head once. Ivan nodded towards the forest; Armin jogged away without giving Grace a glance.

Ivan watched her for a few seconds and then glanced at Sarah. 'Okay. Sanderson – you take Grace with you. Do some tests, let me know how she goes.'

TWELVE

GRACE HURRIED TO keep up with Sarah's long-legged stride as they passed the Residence. A wave of embarrassment hit as she thought about her ungracious fall from the tree. She looked up at the blonde girl. 'I don't usually do things like that. I don't know what came over me, really.'

Sarah smiled. 'You're grieving, and now you have to accept big changes in your life. It's normal to act differently at times like these.'

Grace nodded. She took a moment to study Sarah's face. This girl seemed so wise. She had a calmness about her that Grace had only seen in much older people. 'How old is everyone, anyway? I felt like I was the youngest there.'

'You are. You're seventeen, right? And Joe's eighteen?'

Grace nodded.

'Thought so. Armin and Maya are nineteen, Seth and Malcolm are both twenty-one, and I'm nineteen.' Sarah slowed her pace. 'Sorry. I tend to gallop along . . . I already told you our fearless leader is twenty-one – although he seems about a decade older. He's impressive, isn't he?'

Grace looked down, hoping that Sarah wouldn't notice the blush forming on her cheek. 'Yeah, he's good.'

Sarah smiled. 'Most of the girls here think he's pretty cute.'

Grace kept her tone casual. 'Does he have a girlfriend?'

'No. There's one girl who likes to think of herself as his chick. But he's never really shown any affection towards her in public, despite her efforts.' Sarah pushed her hands into her pockets. 'Your brother's nice-looking.'

Grace made a puking sound. 'Whatever you think.'

Sarah laughed. 'You'll settle in fine here, Grace. Just ignore Armin and Maya. They're like two lost souls who found each other, being from the same part of the world and all. People tend to hang out with their own kind, don't they?'

'They're just so unfriendly.'

'They're like that with everyone. Don't take it personally. I try not to. It's better that way. They are very good mercenaries, and if they get to like you, you will have their loyalty for life. At least they don't try to pull rank all the time, unlike my stepbrother.'

Grace stared into the forest. It was true – Malcolm had been out to show his authority from the moment they met. 'Why does he do that?'

Sarah smirked. 'Out of desperation. He wants to prove to everyone that he is worthy of being Ivan's second-in-charge – and not because his dad gave him the position. I think Marcus is disappointed, though!'

121

Grace grinned at Sarah's singsong voice. 'So, Marcus is your stepdad.'

'Right.' Sarah raised her eyebrows, grimacing.

'What about your mum?'

Sarah looked away. 'She died when I was five.' She shoved her hands into her pockets.

'I'm sorry,' said Grace.

'It's okay. I feel like I'm past the worst of it. I'm over eighteen and don't have to do what Marcus says anymore.'

'He seems very . . . controlling.'

'Yeah. Lucius is the one who's supposed to be in charge of us. But he always ends up doing what Marcus wants. I suppose it's because Marcus is the older brother, he thinks he's the boss.'

'I wouldn't let Joe boss me like that.'

Sarah glanced down at Grace's foot. 'How's your ankle healing up?'

'It's okay . . . just twinges every now and then.'

They stopped next to the light blue picket fence. Sarah swung open the gate and gestured for Grace to go ahead. 'Welcome to my veggie garden.'

'Yeah, Diana showed us this morning.' Grace stepped around an overflowing bag of pebbles and inhaled the rose fragrance. 'It's really nice.' Rows of dark ivy, littered with white flowers, crawled up the walls that overlooked the beds of lettuce, cabbage and carrot.

Sarah pointed to a chicken-wire barricade in the corner of the garden. 'And that is Snowflake.' A large white rabbit sniffed the air and then plunged its face into a bed of leafy greens. Sarah wandered across to crouch in front of the hutch.

She reached over and scratched the rabbit's chin. 'Been enjoying a nice feed?'

Grace sank to her knees and pressed her finger through the wire. The rabbit ambled across and sniffed it.

'Is this your rabbit?'

'Snowflake's one of the residents.'

'Does she live here? In this garden?'

'She lives in the hobby farm. Snowflake drew the short straw today; the others are snuggled up together.' Sarah stood up. 'Now – look at her, Grace. That rabbit's got a mind of her own, hasn't she?'

'Yes.'

'And do you think you can teach her to follow instructions?'

Grace glanced at the rabbit. 'I guess she could be trained.'

'How about making her follow instructions . . . without saying a word or even moving your arms?'

Grace thought of Joe, hearing her on the other side of the bedroom wall. 'I suppose it's possible.'

With a tilt of her head, Sarah turned to the rabbit. 'I'm going to tell Snowflake to walk to the right-hand wall.'

'Right.' Grace stood up and folded her arms. Her eyes darted between Sarah, whose own eyes were deep with concentration, and the suddenly still rabbit.

Snowflake turned and plodded towards the wall.

Sarah turned to look at Grace.

Grace shrugged. 'Maybe she decided to move on her own.' She squinted at the dark corner where the rabbit chewed a lettuce leaf. 'That's where the food is. A coincidence – she happened to be hungry.'

'Mmm. Yeah.' Sarah grinned. 'Coincidence.'

Grace scowled. 'Are you making fun of me?' Burning anger spiralled up from her stomach. It receded, she slumped; her arms felt as if someone had attached weights to her fingers.

'I think I'm going to sit down.' She slid into a plastic chair.

'Okay,' said Sarah.

'I feel so tired.' Grace closed her eyes. She began to drift into a warm darkness.

Wake up!

Grace's eyes flew open.

Sarah watched her with a small grin. 'You okay?'

'That felt strange.'

Sarah crouched in front of Grace and rested her hands on the armrests. 'I was able to get inside your head just then. I inspired anger and then fatigue. Finally, I told you to wake up. And I never spoke a word.' She pointed to her head. 'The element of surprise. You didn't see me coming.' Nodding in the direction of the hutch, she stood up. 'Why don't you try?'

Crouching, Grace laced her fingers in the chicken wire.

A picture – that's what she needed. Yes . . . that was it. An image to plant in her mind.

Snowflake looked up, stared for a moment, and turned. She plodded steadily towards the hutch. Without slowing her pace, she proceeded inside.

Grace let out a long breath and stared at the hutch. 'Unbelievable.' If only she'd been able to do that to Jesse Tyler.

'Grace, it took me three days of practice to learn that. You've done it on your first day.' Sarah pressed her hand to her forehead. 'I can't believe it. Ivan has got to see this.' With an excited gleam in her eye, Sarah stood up. 'What are the others going to say? No-one's ever been that fast . . . I can just see their faces now! Come on. There are still more tests to do.'

Bolstered by the praise, Grace followed Sarah out of the garden and on to the gravel path that led them back to the Residence. They entered the double green doors and continued down the warm yellow passageway, past the empty recreation rooms and the large kitchen, where the mid-morning sun reflected off the stainless steel benchtop.

'So what now? More animals?' Grace lifted her chin and took a deep breath, savouring the thrill of adrenaline, the confidence surge. She could do anything . . . anything at all.

They reached a door at the corridor's end. Sarah opened it; three people looked up. 'Morning,' they echoed.

Nerves needled up Grace's spine. 'Humans? Real people?'

'You forget – demons were human once,' Sarah whispered. 'They still retain some aspect of their humanity. This is the closest simulation we can provide. Unless you want to go to the asylum on your first day of training?'

Grace shivered. 'No, thanks.'

Sarah held up three fingers. 'You'll do three simple tests in here. Subject number one has three cups of water in front of her. Using telepathy, tell her to drink them in a particular order.'

Grace nodded. 'Not too different to Snowflake, right?'

'Then, with subject number two, plant some words in his head. The exact words you want him to say. Anything – just try not to humiliate him. He's doing us a favour.

'The third and final test is open to you. Do *not* give subject number three a command. Instead, try to plant an idea in his head. That he has an uncontrollable itch on his chin. That he has an irresistible urge to dance the samba.' They both giggled. 'This guy's a good sport, so he won't mind. The point here is that you create a desire that he cannot resist. That's the key.

'Oh, and you should know that Lucius and Diana are watching.' Sarah pointed to a camera hanging over the door. 'So do the best you can, okay?'

Sarah stepped out of the room and walked across the hallway. She knocked once and entered the room. Diana and Lucius were sitting at the desk, watching the monitor.

'Looks promising,' Sarah said. 'Snowflake was no challenge at all.'

'Yes, well we'll see how she goes with human minds,' said Diana. 'She must learn to use the gift properly.'

'Look!' Sarah leaned closer to the monitor. 'She's already done the first test!'

The first test subject raised a cup to her mouth, then she put it down. With slow, purposeful movements, she drank the other two – her eyes never leaving Grace.

'I can't hear a thing.' Lucius reached over and turned up the volume. A crackling hiss resonated through the speaker, as the second test subject, a young man with dark sideburns and Manchester United football t-shirt, stared at Grace with calm eyes and said, 'Chelsea are the best team in the league. They will win the premiership this year, for sure.'

Sarah laughed. 'Nice one.' She leaned forward, elbows on

knees. 'Okay. Number three is the critical one. If she can't do it, she won't stand a chance in the kill room.'

The young man sat quietly for several seconds.

'Nothing's happening,' Diana muttered.

'Quiet!' Lucius leaned forward. 'He pointed to the screen, where the third test subject was staring up at the roof, an alarmed look on his face. Next, he jumped out of his chair and crawled underneath the table.

'Looks as if she's done something,' Diana said.

Grace looked up at the camera. 'Finished!' She gave a thumbs-up. The third subject was peering up from the edge of the table, eyes darting back and forth. Grace reached out a hand. 'It's okay. You're safe. It was just an illusion.'

The man smiled. 'Oh.' With an embarrassed smile, he got up and slid into his chair. 'You really got me there.'

The door burst open. Sarah walked in, closely shadowed by Diana and Lucius, who pushed forward. He reached out and patted her back. 'Well done, Callahan.'

Diana nodded towards Subject Three. 'What did you tell poor Adam here? That there was a giant spider on the roof?'

The man glanced up with a smile. 'Very funny, Diana. No, for the life of me, I would have sworn that a bomb was falling on the building. Felt like I'd travelled back in time to the Blitz.'

'Well.' Lucius took a deep breath. 'I think Grace is ready to move on to full-scale training.' He shot a look at Diana. 'She has potential.'

'She must be given time to develop properly. Sarah, I'm trusting you to make sure that happens.' Diana glanced at the three test subjects. 'Shall we break for coffee?'

She ushered the visitors from the room. Lucius was the last to leave. He gave Grace a wink as he closed the door.

Sarah leaned on the table edge. 'You got off to a great start there, Grace. What you just did is known as "telepathic influence". Masking and influence are the two major skills that a telepath needs in this job.'

'What's the masking part?'

'Making sure your enemy doesn't know you're there. Creating an illusion. You'll get the chance – sooner than you think.'

Grace raised her eyebrows. 'So, what now?' She stretched her arms in front and smiled.

Sarah bit her finger nail. 'I wasn't planning to do this, but I want you to try a telepathic assault before this afternoon's exercise. I'd rather not let you in there with them until you can do it.'

'In where?'

'The kill room.'

'What the hell is that?'

'A training room . . . Look, I want you to try something. Imagine giving me a bad headache. Just like you told Snow-flake to go into her hutch. Go on!'

'I don't know.'

'Don't worry, I can take it! Come on. Do it. No . . . don't close your eyes. Look at my forehead. Think of the kind of pain you want me to feel. A sharp attack of pain, like a really bad migraine.'

Staring at Sarah's forehead, Grace imagined a hot white bolt of pain . . . digging. She broke off, closing her eyes. 'I really don't want to.'

Sarah sighed. 'Focus, Grace. You need to go on the offensive. They won't be expecting this.'

Grace took a deep breath. Okay. She had to hurt her. Past the skull and into the brain.

Suddenly, Sarah's face stiffened. Her hand shot out. 'Whoa!' She breathed heavily, her hand pressed against her heart. 'You're *good*.' She touched her forehead. 'Wow, that really burned.'

'Sorry.'

'No, don't be.' Sarah rested her hand on the doorknob. 'It's great! At last, someone I can work with.' She opened the door. 'Come on. I want to show Ivan what you can do.'

THIRTEEN

IN THE MIDDLE of the forest lay a sunken arena, surrounded by three rows of grass ledges. Above, Joe and Ivan were standing on a metal walkway from which observers could watch the action below.

Grace touched her forehead, imagining the burn Sarah had felt. 'Have you ever used that on anyone? A demon, or –'

Sarah kept walking. 'A human. Someone here. I'd rather not say who.'

'What happened?'

'He was beating someone up, someone I cared about.' Sarah pushed aside a large branch. 'This is the mercenaries' turf. It used to be an outdoor theatre.' She gestured for Grace to go ahead.

Armin glanced up. 'Back already?' He raised his eyebrows at Sarah.

Grace looked up at Joe, who was hanging his arms over the walkway railing like a monkey. Ivan peered down at Sarah. 'How did she do?'

'One hundred per cent pass. No problems at all!'

'So?' Maya stood up. 'She's yet to impress *us*.'

Sarah looked around at the group. 'You're going to pee your pants.'

The mercenaries exploded into laughter – except Malcolm, who stood rigid, arms behind his back. It was obvious he was trying to give off the aura of leadership. Grace's eyes flicked from him to Ivan, who was leaning over the railing. Comfortable, relaxed – and yet so in control.

'Yeah, right!' Armin tugged a strand of Sarah's hair. 'She's going to put me flat on my back!'

'Get away, you loser.'

Seth frowned. 'Why write her off so quickly?'

Armin threw his arms up. 'It'll be a waste of time! We should give her weapons training instead!'

Joe slid down the ladder and strode towards Armin. 'What are you so scared of? That she'll be better than you?'

Armin scowled. 'No. Her witchcraft won't work on me.'

Joe stared at him. 'Perhaps mine will.'

Tension filled the air as Armin and Joe eyed each other.

Grace tore her gaze away to see Ivan drop down the last ladder rung and jog across. 'All right, enough. Back away, both of you.'

He stood firm. Slowly, both boys took a reluctant step back.

Ivan glanced at his watch. 'It's twelve-thirty. Break for lunch, then meet back at the training room.'

* * *

GRACE CHEWED SLOWLY on her sandwich and stared at the table, trying to ignore the scornful stares coming from the mercenaries' table. They'd come in first and their table had filled up quickly. Grace glanced around the packed cafeteria. As Sarah had said, 'It stinks of bravado in here.'

Although Grace was relieved that she didn't have to join them, it had left a cold feeling in her chest to see Joe sitting with the mercenaries. Especially after how Armin had acted towards her. But then again, Joe seemed to be engrossed in everything that Ivan was saying.

Ivan.

A warm feeling ran through her body.

He looked over – Grace felt the heat rising in her cheeks. He'd caught her staring at him. A quiver ran through her insides.

A girl sauntered across and straddled the bench next to Ivan, facing him.

'She's the one I was telling you about,' Sarah said.

The girl wore a mercenary crest and looked very fit. Grace felt a stab of envy as the girl flicked her long dark hair over her shoulders and sent a sweeping look around the room. Her gaze stopped on Grace for a few seconds. Grace met her stare. The girl grimaced, as though she'd stepped in something foul, and placed a hand on Ivan's back. He leaned closer as she whispered something in his ear.

Grace tore her eyes away and yanked the straw from her drink bottle, taking a long gulp of water. She fixed her eyes on Sarah. 'You didn't tell me she was so gorgeous.'

'I don't see much beauty in her. She's not a very nice person.'

Grace slammed the bottle down. 'We're pretty outnumbered, aren't we?'

'There are over forty mercs and twelve engineers, but only two of us. There aren't many with our gift, Grace. Don't know why. I was pretty happy to hear there was a new telepath coming, let me tell you.'

'They don't seem to like us much.' Anger simmered in Grace's stomach. She peered over at Armin. What a rude, horrible rodent.

'I wouldn't say it's dislike. Rather, ignorance. Mercs respect firepower over mindpower. And some are superstitious, like Armin. You know – using the word witchcraft. Mercs don't understand the nature of our gift. They have lots of names for us: 'psychic', 'clairvoyant', even 'hippy'. It's intended as an insult, but I don't pay any attention. I've even been called a fortune teller before.' She smiled, leaning her chin on her hand. 'I wish there were more of us. We could team up and annihilate the demon population.'

'Yeah!' Grace grinned. 'That'd be so cool.'

'I've never had the chance to really get out there. I exist on the fringes, until Lucius needs me for something special. They rely on their weaponry too much, in my opinion. I've only been on five missions.'

'Really?' Grace's eyes shone. 'What kind?'

'Low-key. Small stuff. Everyone's so new and inexperi-enced. Thank God for Ivan. I think he'll really try to exploit your gift.' She looked up and smiled at Grace's confused expression. 'In a good way, don't worry!'

Sarah wrapped up the remains of her kebab and pushed it aside. 'In about twenty minutes, Ivan's going to throw you

133

into a survival situation. He needs to see if you can use your skills to repel attacks by the mercs.'

'Okay.'

Sarah raised her eyebrows. 'Ever been tasered?'

'Of course not!'

'That's what you'll be trying to avoid.' Sarah watched her closely. 'You'll use masking to get past them. If you can, use the telepathic assault. Remember?' She pointed to her forehead. 'Give 'em pain! Oh, and a word to the wise: don't try to give them any commands – don't *tell* them to do something. You know.' She pointed to the side of her head. 'In here. It doesn't work on them. They're too well-trained against that.'

'Okay.' Grace flinched, sensing a prickling stare from the other side of the room. Sure enough, Armin and Maya were looking at her. She muttered something; he broke into high-pitched laughter. Even the girl sitting next to Ivan looked around, smirking.

Grace ground her teeth.

Sarah leaned closer. 'Do you understand what I just said?'

Seething, Grace watched Armin take a swig of his drink. He banged his fist on the table, laughing hard. She clenched her jaw and stared out the window. She was going to sort him out. Right now. She tuned out everything in front of her – the reflection of the scattered chairs and tables in the window, the bulky, swaying trees, the hint of ocean spray at the top of the cliffs.

She planted the words in his head. *I'm a little teapot. It's a dance we always do.*

Definitely not a command.

The noise alerted everyone first. It was the scraping of Maya's chair. She stood up, eyes wide with confusion. 'Baby! What are you doing?'

Armin had climbed on top of the table and was now performing a dance. His left hand was made into a fist, planted firmly against his hip and his right arm was extended in a very silly angle. 'Here is my handle, here is my spout!' He leaned sideways, eyes blank, hand pouring tea into a giant, invisible cup. Coarse laughter echoed through the room.

Maya clawed at his leg. 'Get down!'

Armin grinned. 'It's what we always do!' Wildly, he shook his head, still pouring. 'Come on! Get up here.'

Grace caught Ivan staring across at her. He wasn't smiling.

Her face dropped. She knew he could tell it was her.

He shook his head at her – a single, sharp movement – and then turned back to the table.

Grace relaxed her thoughts, and as she did, Armin came out of his trance. Grace watched Ivan stand up and lean over the table. Shaking, Armin turned and looked at Grace. The mercenaries followed his stare. Armin's face turned bright pink. Malcolm was reaching over, trying to calm Maya, who was reared up like a wildcat, straining to lunge across the room and attack.

Grace grinned. She lifted her hand and gave them a little wave. 'My witchcraft seems to work just fine.'

'You bitch!'

'Sit down, Maya,' said Ivan.

Heart pounding, Grace turned back to her table. She grabbed the bottle and squeezed it.

Sarah pressed her hand to her heart. Eyes wide, she shook her head. 'You're asking for trouble.'

'Grace.'

She looked across to see Ivan striding towards her. The mercenaries were standing up and making their way towards the exit. Joe gave her a disapproving glare.

Ivan stopped next to the table.

Grace drew a deep breath and lifted her chin.

Ivan looked at Sarah. 'Go on ahead, Sanderson.'

Nodding, Sarah walked away. She threw Grace an apologetic smile before disappearing through the door.

Ivan leaned against the wall, arms folded.

Grace kept her gaze locked on his eyes, fighting the urge to dip down and stare at the taut muscle in his arms.

She smiled. 'Something wrong?'

'Why did you do that?'

'Do what?'

'The teapot dance.'

She shrugged. 'How do you know it was me?'

'Don't be – how do they put it in English? Coy.'

'What do you mean?'

'You did that to Jelavic. You got inside his head. I've never seen that kind of thing before. Although, I wouldn't expect any of my team to behave so badly.'

Her eyes narrowed. No way. Armin deserved it, and she wasn't going to take this. No more. Grace was a different person now.

'Are you criticising me? What *did* you expect me to do, just sit here and take his crap? He insulted me, and I wanted payback.' She shrugged. 'It wasn't hard, anyway.' She took a sip of water, hoping he wouldn't notice the tremble in her fingers.

Ivan raised his eyebrows. 'Is that right?'

'It was too easy, really.'

'Good. Then you'll find my little test no challenge at all.'

* * *

GRACE STARED OUT across the kill room. The place was like a converted barn. The ground consisted of large slabs of concrete. A watchtower dominated the middle of the space. Several small walls acted as partitions – like parts of a crazy maze had been ripped out and dumped in various locations. Right in front of her, a small brick structure with steps led up to a small lookout.

'You'll go up against these four mercenaries.' Ivan nodded in the direction of the group, who were standing nearby. 'Armin and Maya you know; the other two are Stephanie and Patrick.'

Grace grimaced. Stephanie was the girl who'd cosied up to Ivan at lunchtime. 'Great,' she muttered.

'They will be armed with tasers and other non-lethal devices. You are to use your skill to evade them. You must reach the opposite wall and hit the red button. There are obstacles you must negotiate on your way to the other side. It will be dimly lit – but that shouldn't worry you, should it? Given the skill you showed us in the lunch room.'

Grace blinked – was there a touch of disdain in his voice?

'Do you have any questions?'

She shook her head.

He raised his eyebrows. 'Are you sure?'

Grace glanced around the room. Should she memorise it? Nah . . . she'd didn't need to worry about that. The teapot dance was just the beginning.

'I can see what's involved here.'

Ivan gestured for the door. She hadn't even walked the room. 'Fine. Go outside and wait for me to call you.'

Grace blinked as the sunlight hit her eyes. Her eyes adjusted; gradually Sarah's outline became less of a dark blur.

'Did you take a good look? Know where to go?'

'Yeah, good enough.'

'Look.' Sarah pointed to a glass cabinet. Inside were black shotguns lined with yellow stripes and rows of matching cartridges. 'See those parts? They're for a taser shotgun. That's what they'll be using in there.'

Grace stared at the guns. She rubbed her arms – a prickling sensation was running up and down her flesh. Her stomach churned. She'd seen taser attacks on TV. 'Hopefully they won't get to hit me.'

'It's time.' Armin stood in the doorway, his voice cold.

Sarah smiled. 'Good luck. You can kick butt, easy.'

Nodding, Grace entered a dark, unnerving silence.

'Wait here.' Armin walked off, quickly swallowed up by the darkness. Grace felt a tickle of adrenaline in her stomach. Then she giggled, picturing him dancing like a teapot. This was going to be easy.

Ivan's voice thundered over the speakers. 'Whenever you are ready, Grace.'

She stepped forward. She was glad she wore sneakers. Grace made her silent way forward and up the concrete steps. She crouched, aware that her top half must be visible to those far away – and peered down.

Nothing . . . no, wait – there was someone. A dark outline: poorly hidden behind one of the partition walls. A slight sheen of grey light reflected off the tip of a gun.

She lifted her hand, and without giving a command, planted an idea. *Tired . . . need to sleep now.* The mercenary leaned against the wall, head back. The gun slid from the hand and dangled by the strap.

She hoped that was Stephanie . . . or Armin. Mmm . . . which one would she rather hurt? She smiled as she passed the sleeping mercenary. Oh. It was just Patrick. She darted down the steps and turned the corner with a jaunty step.

Making her way forward, she could see the hulking outline of the watchtower. Ivan was up there. She flirted with the idea of giving him a cheeky wave. A few more steps . . . she could see the other wall now, and the platform where the red button was –

Something exploded.

A light filled the room, sharp and offensive. Her eyes stung – as though she'd walked into a bright day from a dark room. She could see nothing but the blinding white. She slammed her hands against her ears – a pointless attempt to stop the ringing inside. And the dizziness!

Stop them . . . a voice was screaming, echoing inside her brain; the ringing was cruelly persisting, her vision was slowly returning. A cloud of smoke hit her throat; she coughed, fought a rising panic.

Stop them – before they taser you!

She closed her eyes, ground her back teeth together.

Stay away!

Get back!

And the voices floated across to her like an owl's hoot – calm, but laced with very human taunting. 'No.'

Her heartbeat began to accelerate. Sweat dripped down her back.

Turn around!

Go to sleep!

'No.' Low, predatory laughter spread around her, behind her, beside her. Circling her. She found herself throwing her hand out in front – a pathetic display of self-defence against an attack that she could not anticipate, or even see.

But then, he came into view. The dark, dull outline of a mercenary, standing to the left. She couldn't see anyone else. Ahead, the dim red glow of the button – she only needed to dodge one more barrier and she'd be at the platform.

She stared at the mercenary. *Back away.*

He grinned. 'No. Don't you pay attention?'

And then she knew the voice, felt the malice. 'I told you. Your witchcraft won't work here.'

She didn't feel the bullet make contact with her body but watched the world tip sideways; her face slamming against the cold floor. The worst pain ever; each muscle shrinking, tightening. Her breath caught in her lungs. Impossible to breath, impossible to think.

Armin tilted his head and fired again.

This time the bullet hit her lower, near her belly button,

doubling the pain. She felt her mind begin to swim away as the earth started to spin.

The watchhouse door flew open. Ivan slid down the ladder, closely followed by Seth, Joe and Sarah.

Mixed emotions in the blur of voices – anger, concern, fear.

Then, a new lightness. She didn't understand at first . . . but she was lifting off, floating above her body. Yanked away from the pain. Her senses disrupted. Sound was muffled, the voices now beneath her – for she was lifting into the air. Like the half-world between waking and sleep, when she would stumble to the bathroom in the middle of the night.

Am I dead?

Help me!

She lifted a hand as the ceiling drew closer. This couldn't be happening. She passed through the ceiling and out into the open air. Normally there'd be a feeling of cold as the breeze washed over her.

Nothing.

Just numb.

Before, the sky had looked bleached, and bunched clouds had blocked out the sun. Now, it was lined in a brilliant yellow. The world was new, aglow – and she was floating through it, helpless. She shot a desperate look below her, but the trees blocked her view of the people she'd just left behind. She should touch something.

Flinging her hand out . . . counting on that prickly feeling. But nothing. Her fingers passed through the branch like air. A butterfly hovered in front of her. Its jewel colours shining in this strange, surreal light. She could even see its tiny eyes peering at her.

Oh, God – find some reality.

Soon . . . too soon, she was hovering above the hillside overlooking Renfield and the road which had brought them to this place.

Calm yourself, Grace.

How could she get back? She tried to picture the arena, the gravel driveway, her bedroom. The roses in Sarah's garden. Ivan's eyes.

Will I ever get back?

She couldn't feel her heartbeat. But she could picture where she wanted to be . . .

Up . . . she floated over the treetops, back towards signs of life. Down . . . through the roof and the darkened air of the kill room. Past the burning glow of the ceiling lights . . . she heard Ivan bark something at Seth and then saw him scoop her up, cradling her head against his chest. He ripped the bullets away from her body. Her face looked pale, dazed.

Joe knelt next to her. 'Grace?' He shook her arm.

She watched Seth pick up a radio and shout something into it.

She saw Maya and Stephanie come out of their hiding places and crouch nearby.

Shivering, she closed her eyes and breathed deeply, trying to ground herself, bury herself as deep as she could into her body so that she would never have to feel that again.

Armin grunted. 'That'll teach her.'

Joe grabbed Armin and slammed him against a wall. Instantly, Ivan's hand clamped on to Joe's shoulder.

'Joe,' he said. 'Stay calm.'

Seething, Joe released Armin and turned back to Grace. He crouched next to her and touched her shoulder. 'Can you hear me, sis?'

Seth glared at Armin. 'That was stupid of you. What the hell is your problem?'

Maya stepped forward. 'She deserved it. For what she did at lunchtime.'

Stephanie nodded. 'It was an immature display. She needed to be shown her place.'

'Grace? Can you hear me?'

Grace's heart was thumping; her breath moving through her throat in sharp bursts.

Her eyelids fluttered.

Ivan gazed down at her abdomen where the second bullet had hit. 'Do you feel okay?'

Grace nodded.

It was true. There was no residual pain. She struggled to get up, but Ivan slid his arm around her shoulders, supporting her. 'Don't rush it.'

'I'm all right, really.' She glanced up at Sarah. 'How long was I . . . unconscious for?'

'About ten seconds.'

'Is that all?'

Sarah leaned closer and whispered, 'Why didn't you use a telepathic assault? You could've laid him flat!'

'I . . . lost focus.'

Ivan looked at Armin. 'Who told you to double tap?'

Armin shrugged. 'It was an accident.'

'There are no accidents. Night duty for the rest of the week.'

Maya scowled. 'That's not fair! We've finally got time off together!' She slumped. 'Great. Here we go again. Another Little Miss Victim, getting us into trouble.'

'Come on, Maya,' said Malcolm. 'Leave it now. It's not worth the effort.' He touched her arm, but she jerked away from him. 'Stay out of it!'

Ivan nodded towards the door. 'All of you. Dismissed.'

The others moved away; Joe hesitated. 'You okay, Grace?'

'You too, Joe,' said Ivan. 'On your way.'

Stephanie lingered. 'Is that all you want from me, Ivan?'

He nodded. 'You can return to your squad now. Thank you for your help.'

'Oh, I'm always here for you, Ivan.' The girl gave Grace a jubilant smile and headed for the exit.

Ivan turned around. 'Stand up.'

Grace caught her breath at his sharp tone. Her legs began to tremble, but she forced herself to her feet. Of all the people she didn't want to anger . . . she folded her arms and stared at his chest. To raise her eyes to his? Too heavy . . . impossible.

'You were out of line there, Grace.'

She bit her lip.

'Look at me.'

She found herself caught again in his eyes, but this time he lashed her with an uncompromising glare. Holding her. A fish caught on a hook.

'You didn't take the exercise seriously. Assuming you would win, that your opponents were inferior. It was arrogant of you.'

'That's not fair! I was the one who got –'

'*I'm* speaking, Grace.'

She gasped and then shut her mouth. So this is what Sarah meant. He was all business. Her cheeks began to burn.

'If we were on a mission and you went in with that approach, your teammates could be killed. Because of you.'

Her cheeks burned a little more; his words were a slap in the face.

A tight, gulping sensation hit, and fresh tears stung her eyes. She blinked rapidly, staring at his boots.

Ivan drew closer. 'I know this is all new for you, but you need to learn respect for your teammates and for yourself. You compromised your own safety, which is just as bad as risking theirs.'

'I'm sorry,' she whispered.

'I'm not sure that you're ready for my squad – or for this job, for that matter.'

She gasped. 'That's not fair . . .' The wind wheezed out of her; he'd given her a verbal punch to the stomach. 'You haven't given me a chance. I just . . .' Her throat constricted. She had just lost her parents.

'Do you really want this? Do you really want to fight?'

Nodding, she cleared her throat. 'Yes.'

'I'm going to give you a chance.' He bent closer; compelling her to look at him. 'But you will either accept that I'll demote you to a junior squad, or you'll enlist in my boot camp.'

Her eyes flickered, her heart lifted, she looked into his face. A glimmer of humour. A ray of hope. 'What . . . you would train me?'

He shrugged. 'Why not? I have a vested interest in seeing you do well. To have a telepath, or should I say, a telepath who can exercise self-control, is a very valuable thing. But you need to be trained properly.'

'Just . . . just you and me?'

'Mmm.' He nodded. 'Unless you have a problem with that?'

She shook her head.

'Good. I'll see you tomorrow morning. Half-past six. Do not be late.'

FOURTEEN

GRACE SAT ON her bed, pressing her fists into the mattress. Sunset had arrived and stroked the treetops in a watercolour mist of gold, brown and green. The telltale signs came: the clenching in the throat, stinging in the eyes. Cramping in the stomach. Grace held back tears. Pounding music from the recreation room and happy, lilting voices closed in on her, making her feel all the more lonely. Dinner in thirty minutes . . . how could she face them all?

She squeezed the edge of the quilt as the dark anger swelled in her stomach and adrenaline crawled up her spine.

Her gaze drifted to her phone, still sitting on the bedside table. She picked it up and looked at the message from that morning. Should she? She stared at the dying light outside, weighing up the options. To hell with this. She was out of here.

She slid the phone into her pocket and made her way to Joe's room and pounded on his door.

Joe flung open the door. 'What's up?'

'Look at this.' Grace shoved the phone into his hand and kicked the door shut behind her.

Joe stared at the text message. 'Tonight only, huh?' He shrugged. 'We can't really go, can we?' He passed her the phone back.

'Joe, it's the VIP tent!' She slumped against the wall, her fingers tapping against the screen. 'Come on! I've had a crap day. That tasering really hurt.'

Joe sighed. 'Don't play the sympathy card.'

'Are you too scared to go?'

Joe smirked. 'As if.' He lay back on his bed, hands behind his head. 'I don't really give a toss about what they say.'

Grace jumped up. 'Good.' She grabbed his ankles and tried to pull him to the floor. 'Come on!'

'God, you're so angsty!' He shoved his phone into his pocket and picked up a hoodie top. 'All right, then.'

Grace grinned. 'Cool.'

'The bike's out the back.'

'What – it's here?'

He threw her a 'you idiot' look and pulled the hoodie over his head. 'Yeah, I insisted they bring it here. How else did you think we would get away?'

She shrugged. 'One of their bikes.'

'They'd track it in a heartbeat. They've got more tech here than friggin' NASA.'

* * *

INSIDE, A STEADY throng of recruits poured into the dining room, drawn by the spicy, stomach-rumbling smell of roast chicken. Joe wheeled his bike around the back of the Residence, closely shadowed by Grace. He crouched as they passed the kitchen window. 'I'm hungry. Go grab me something while I start the bike.'

'No! They'll see me.'

'They won't. The door's just there. Use your mind tricks.' He whirled his fingers at the side of his head.

'That's the loony sign, you idiot.'

'You know what I mean! Go on – just a chicken leg.'

She glanced around. 'You've got to be kidding me.'

'Come on, Grace. I said yes to the concert.'

'I haven't practised enough.'

'Grace. You made Armin think he was a teapot. You can do this.' Joe slid his helmet on. 'Hurry, now.'

She rolled her eyes. 'O-kay.' She clenched her teeth and edged her way along the darkened wall. Peering around, she glimpsed two women in white aprons and chequered hats, laying out trays of chicken pieces, roast vegetables, bread and jugs of juice on the counter that separated the kitchen from the dining area.

Three, two, one.

You are the only ones in this room. Keep working. She walked inside and slipped between the women, over to the counter. She tensed at an unwelcome worry: what if they were mercenaries? They would see through her trick.

But the women just turned and moved around the benchtop.

Grace breathed out and took hold of a chicken leg. As she turned, she caught a glimpse of Ivan walking into the dining room. That bitch, Stephanie, was on his tail; with burning envy Grace watched the girl flick her mane and flutter her eyelids as she took a seat next to Ivan.

Her heart thudded. A sudden longing to stay overcame her.

Maybe she should. But then again, he had been horrible to her today. She would show him that she didn't need him.

She darted out of the door into the safe blackness of the night.

'Here.' She thrust the piece at Joe.

'Great.' Joe tore into the leg; with his other hand rumpled through his pockets. 'Got any cash?'

'Yeah . . . about fifty.' Grace fitted her helmet.

Joe swallowed the last piece of meat. With a loud belch, he flung the bones away.

'Pig.'

Grinning, Joe gunned the engine.

As they approached the gate, Grace closed her eyes; calmed her mind. Now this was for real. She wasn't a naughty recruit stealing food this time. If they were caught . . .

She breathed out and looked up at the guard, who was staring down at her with a confused expression. She created a picture for him: a long, black car, Diana in the driver's seat – her voice in his ear.

Open the gate, please, Brutus. The visitors are leaving.

The man nodded. 'Right you are, Diana.' He pressed a button; the riders passed through the gate.

* * *

AS THEY RAMPED onto the highway, Grace considered the possibilities. What if guards detected them? She imagined voices, shouting inside the Renfield walls right now, alerted by the screeching alarm. Panicked people running through the halls, searching for the newly missing. A light shone in her peripheral vision; she peered around and noticed a pair of headlights trailing them. In a blinding moment of panic she wondered whether they'd been caught. Then the headlights turned off into a side road, and she took a deep breath of relief.

To their right lay the eternal hills: the dividing line between the City and the great outland beyond – the red desert. Gradually, the landscape morphed from grasslands to small farms and cottages sitting on blocks of rolling pastures and then to quaint towns, where by day the narrow streets were cluttered with food stalls, antique vendors and clothing racks. Past weatherboard cottages, their trimming rusted with age. People sat on their verandahs, rocking in creaky chairs, their old-world presence defying the modern pace all around them as the cars rushed past.

Finally, the neon glow of the City and the palm-lined boulevard that sat on the edge of Cold River. Jets of purple and yellow light emanated from the esplanade park that spanned the entire eastern bank of the river.

* * *

THE WELL-BUILT SECURITY guard stood in a passive, unobtrusive manner against the wall at the festival entry gates. For the past four hours, he'd been checking each likely suspect against the photograph of the siblings. His eyes were starting to ache. The photo was crumpled around the edges from being held too tightly. He threw a tired look at his colleague, who rolled his eyes in return.

But neither of them would move. Mr Jones didn't take failure well, and both guards had young families to worry about.

He yawned, stretched his shoulders and tipped his head back on the wall. These kids had better show up.

A young voice floated across from the ticket counter.

'I was told to quote number 6940.'

The ticket collector smiled. 'Yes, that's fine. Just scan your phone here.' She turned and gave the guard a brisk nod.

With a harsh beep, Grace Callahan's ID came up on screen.

Bingo! The guard turned his head towards the wall and pressed his finger to his earpiece. 'They're here, sir.'

* * *

THE LONG BLACK car pulled into the reserved bay behind the VIP tent. An usher rushed forward and opened the passenger doors.

Andromalius and Zagan stepped out. The usher shrunk back as Andromalius eyed him. 'Vodka.'

'Yes, sir.' The young man ran towards the tent, nearly tripping over a crate of glasses in his hurry.

A group of kitchen staff on a smoke break stopped talking and stared as a tall, tanned blonde alighted from the car. Haures caught her reflection and grimaced, hating the platinum hair and sunburned skin. It defied her self-concept as an intelligent, educated woman.

She screwed up her nose. 'I hate this look.'

Andromalius slid an arm around her waist. 'If the boy hadn't seen you on the road, you could've stayed a beautiful redhead.'

Haures shot him a horrified look. 'What – are you saying I don't look beautiful now?'

Andromalius pressed his mouth to her ear. 'So beautiful, the idea of having to share you is driving me crazy.'

Andras open the passenger door; Mammon stepped out and smoothed down his jacket. 'Come here, my children.' He gave Haures an appreciative once-over. 'You look superb. Joe isn't going to know what hit him.'

Haures smiled, but a thudding pain persisted in her head.

This shapeshift had taken nearly all her energy. She eyed off the usher, who hovered around the edge of the group, carrying a vodka bottle. Yes. She wanted some of that.

'Uh, sir?' The usher gestured to Andromalius.

Mammon sniffed, as though he'd stood in something.

'Give it here!' Andromalius yanked the bottle away. The usher stumbled, losing control of the tray.

Haures caught one of the shot glasses and thrust it in Andromalius's face. 'Fill me up, baby. I'm the one doing the work tonight.'

'Not too much, young lady. You need to stay in character.' Mammon cast a firm glance around the group. 'Remember, only tell them what they need to know.' He walked towards the marquee.

'Don't you want the other glasses?' The usher gulped. 'Never mind.' He backed away into the shadows.

Haures drank her shot and closed her eyes as her throat burned. She tossed the glass on to the grass and pressed her palms against Andromalius's chest. 'It's just a game, baby. You know I love you, and *only* you.'

'I still don't like it.'

'Don't make a fuss. We're on to a good thing here.' She squeezed his hand and led him into the marquee.

* * *

As Grace and Joe left the ticket office, a waiter met them. 'The VIP tent is this way.' With a pleasant smile, he gestured for them to go ahead.

The electronica beat and the mass of swaying bodies filled Grace with a sudden longing to see Ivan; to feel his hands on her waist, his chest against her back and warm voice in her ear. Yet, he was horrible to her. The urge dissolved as she recalled the coldness in his voice; the mockery she'd endured from the other mercenaries.

Stuff him. Stuff all of them.

She stepped inside the marquee, Joe close behind her. The ceiling was dotted with fairy lights, white chairs swathed in purple velvet were tucked under round tables topped with chocolate fountains. People stood in cosy groups or leaned against the several bars that lined the edge. In the middle, a sushi train ran around the edge of a circular bar. Purple and silver stars hung from the ceiling. Beneath their feet, a thick red carpet.

'Wow.' Grace blinked. 'This is really nice.'

'Time for a drink.' Joe walked up to the closest bar. 'Coke.'

The bartender smiled. 'Certainly, sir.' He gave Grace an enquiring look.

'Orange juice, please.'

Joe shot Grace a smile. 'Money?'

She reached into her purse and pulled out a fifty-dollar note.

With a warm smile, Mammon leaned on the bar next to Joe. 'Bring me a bottle of absinthe and five glasses.'

Joe raised his eyebrows. That must have been expensive.

Mammon gave the siblings a friendly nod. 'Hello.'

'Hi,' Joe said guardedly.

The bartender brought their drinks. 'Fifteen-fifty.'

Sighing, Joe passed him the money.

Mammon waved it away. 'It's on me.'

The bartender nodded and walked away.

Joe gave Mammon a long stare and then shrugged. 'Thanks.'

'No problem.' Smiling, Mammon took his seat.

'It's weird,' Joe muttered, scanning his eyes around the group. 'I think I recognise that guy.'

Grace sipped her juice. 'Why's that?'

'Can't remember.' With narrowed eyes, Joe scanned the group the man sat with. His gaze came to rest on the girl. His eyes drifted over her face, the gold locks draped over her shoulders, the extreme neckline. What a hottie.

Andras looked over, giving them his most persuasive smile. 'Join us?' He gave Joe a long look.

Grace nudged her brother. *No.*

Joe swatted her elbow away. 'Love to.'

Grace sighed.

Andras looked across. 'The invitation was for you, too.' His eyes were very blue, and as she stared at them she felt her apprehension ooze away.

Mammon patted the chair next to him. 'You can sit here, sweetheart. We don't bite.'

'Okay.' Grace sat down. Across the table, Joe was leaning into the girl, whispering in her ear.

The guy with the blue eyes leaned in. 'My name is Andras. Would you like another drink?' He glanced at her empty glass.

'I'll get one when I'm ready.'

Andras nodded and stroked his chin. 'That's probably wise of you. Or –' he gestured to the green bottle in the middle of the table – 'you can have what we're having.' He winked. 'Might see the green fairy, if you're lucky.' He paused. 'You are over eighteen, of course?'

Grace gave him a vigorous nod. 'Of course.'

Andras passed her a glass. She pressed it to her lips, closed her eyes and tipped the glass back. Her eyes burned, her stomach clenched. 'That's horrible.' She put down the glass. 'No offence.'

'None taken. It's not for everyone.'

Then – like a smooth, caressing wind – tranquil warmth flooded her body. All was good in the world.

Andras gave her a knowing smile. 'Feeling better?'

'Yeah.' Wide-eyed, Grace looked at the bottle. 'That's amazing. I feel great.' She slid the glass across to Andras. 'Can I have another one?'

She swallowed, flinching as the green liquid burned its way to her stomach. 'Oh,' she groaned. 'It's really strong, though.'

'Sometimes we add something sweet.' Andras lifted his hand; a waiter appeared. 'Lemonade.'

Grace cast a look around the table. The older man was watching her with an expression she couldn't decipher.

The other two guys were talking quietly – although one of them, the blond guy, kept glancing across at the pretty girl, who was engrossed in something Joe was saying.

Grace let her eyes travel down the girl's neckline. It was black lace, which normally she would have liked to wear herself, but her breasts were pushed up and out, and it looked as though her belly was fully on show. She laughed to herself, imagining Dad's reaction if she ever tried to go out looking like that. Sadness hit her. Dad was never going to see her go out again.

With a laugh, Joe slammed his fist on the table; Grace looked up in alarm. Red-cheeked, her brother looked around the table, his eyes falling on Mammon's face. He caught his breath, clicked his fingers. 'Hey! I know who you are! You're that rich guy.'

The man nodded. 'My name is Mammon Jones.'

Grace studied his face. 'I've seen you on TV.'

Mammon smiled. 'That happens.' He swallowed a shot of absinthe. 'Mmm. Lovely.' He put down the glass and relaxed back in his chair.

'I'm Joe. This is my sister, Grace.'

'Lovely to meet you both.'

One by one, Grace examined the men at the table. Black shirts, black pants. Standard uniform for most guys on a night out. But there was something different here. The smell of refined cologne. Well-kept hair. Expensive watches.

And that super-expensive drink. These weren't ordinary people. She looked at Mammon. 'What are you doing here?'

Joe laughed. 'Forgive my sister. She can be rude.'

'Shut up, Joe.' She could tell he was play acting.

Mammon smiled. 'It's all right. Nothing wrong with a bit of youthful curiosity. We're here because my company is a major sponsor.'

Now she knew why he leaned back in the chair like a man perfectly comfortable in his surroundings, as if he owned everything around him.

Come to think of it: they all had that look.

Andras rested his arm on the back of Grace's chair. 'Excuse me.' He reached across her, brushing his hand over her arm as he reached for the drink bottle.

'He may look like the consummate company man,' Andras murmured. 'But Mammon's hobby on the side is hunting monsters.'

Mammon tutted. 'Don't tease them.'

Grace shot looks between the pair. 'What did you say?'

'He's just joking.' Mammon waggled his finger at Andras.

Smiling, Andras turned away and took a drink.

'Wait . . .' said Grace. She threw a cautious look around the tent before leaning closer to Andras. 'What do you mean . . . monsters?'

Joe looked over.

Andras and Mammon swapped looks. 'Perhaps we shouldn't tell them.'

'Tell us,' Grace said.

'All right then,' Mammon said. He sat back in his seat and pulled out a cigar. 'There's no other way to put it. There are demons out there, and we hunt them.' He shrugged. 'You probably don't believe us.' He lit the cigar, releasing puffs of smoke into the air around his head.

158

Joe leaned closer. 'No, we do. We hunt them as well.'

Mammon blew out another waft of smoke and raised his eyebrows. 'Which outfit are you with?'

'One in the south,' said Grace. She shot Joe a cautionary look. *Don't tell them too much.*

'Ah – you're with the Renfield lot,' said Mammon, smiling.

Joe nodded. 'Yeah!'

The three younger guys chuckled quietly.

'What?' Joe looked around the table.

Mammon took another drink and crossed his legs. 'Let's just say that you won't find *us* getting bogged down in paperwork, or spending hours sitting around a conference table. Do they throw files at you, make you read irrelevant rubbish about a demon's criminal history?' He snorted. 'None of that for us. We just go in and get the job done.' He flicked his cigar ash on the ground. Andras's eyes twinkled as he poured another drink. 'What do you both do? Any special skills, or abilities?'

Grace glared at Joe. *Don't tell them.*

Mammon tightened his fingers around the glass. 'You don't have to reveal anything.'

'We're still learning,' Grace allowed.

'Mmm.' Mammon sighed. 'And that will be a lengthy, painful process.'

Grace couldn't help but nod, remembering the cramping pain as the taser hit.

Andras leaned forward, trapping her gaze again. 'What about your parents?'

'They died.'

'How?'

Joe clenched his fingers into a fist. 'Murdered.' His voice trembled. Grace looked down at her hands.

'Oh.' Haures stroked Joe's arm. 'That's horrible.'

'You need to punish those who did it.' Mammon stared at Joe. 'There's no justice, otherwise.'

Joe nodded. 'I'd love to, but I don't know how that will happen.'

'Mmm. Frustrating, not being able to take action.'

The group fell into silence.

Andras smiled at Grace. 'On a lighter note, would you like to dance?'

'No, thanks.'

'Grace is a bit shy that way,' said Joe, ignoring the fierce glare she gave him. He turned to Haures. 'Shall we?'

Smiling, she nodded. 'Sure.'

Grace gasped as Haures stood up. The black lace microdress was attached at Haures's belly button by a gold clasp, revealing nearly all of her hips. A thick black band sat just on her pelvis, from which hung a very short skirt.

'Some dress,' she muttered.

'Thanks.' Haures gave her a sweet smile. With a grin, Joe took her hand and walked towards the dance floor; his chest puffed out with pride as every pair of eyes in the room followed their movement.

* * *

'JOE?' IVAN KNOCKED on the bedroom door and waited for a few seconds. He pushed the door open and glanced around. 'Nothing.'

Lucius peered into the room. 'When did you see him last?'

'Just before dinner.' Ivan scanned the area for clues – a wallet, keys – anything to suggest Joe hadn't left the premises.

Diana rushed up the hallway. 'Grace isn't in her room.' She shot Ivan a desperate look. 'Do you think they're still on the grounds?'

Ivan shook his head. 'Probably not.'

'My God!' Diana pulled out her phone and paced out into the hallway.

Lucius folded his arms. 'They obviously got past Brutus and took off somewhere. Grace must have played a mind trick.'

Diana came rushing back. 'No signal from either of them.' She hit another number. 'Brutus! Did my niece and nephew approach the gate tonight?' Diana sighed and hung up. 'Well, he wouldn't remember if they did.' She rubbed her forehead.

Lucius nodded. 'That's what I was saying.'

'I'm going to check if Joe's bike is there.'

Lucius watched Diana rush away and then turned to Ivan. 'It doesn't matter if Grace comes back, but we need Joe.'

Ivan frowned. 'It would be better if they both returned, Lucius.'

'Yes – but Joe is the more vital of the pair. And they did leave of their own will, Ivan. All I'm saying is, if they get in touch, make sure Joe comes back.' Lucins rubbed his glasses against his shirt before replacing them on his face and making for the door.

GRACE SWAYED IN her chair, her feet tapping. 'Oh – I love this song!' Was she slurring? Uhhr . . . who cared. Across the tent, Joe was pressed close against the girl whose name Grace couldn't remember.

She pointed a shaky finger at Andras. 'Anthony. Right? That's you?'

Grinning, Andras poured her another drink. 'It's better with the lemonade, isn't it?'

'Yep.' She reached forward, drank the shot, then leaned her head back on the chair. The little stars on the ceiling were dancing.

'Do you have a boyfriend, Grace?'

She rolled her head his way. 'Nup.'

'That surprises me. You're a good-looking girl.'

'I had one – last year.' Her head rolled the other way. The room looked as though they were underwater – everything seemed tinged in a sweaty blur.

'And?'

'We broke up.'

'Why?' Andras passed her the glass. 'Drink up.'

'He told everyone in the school that I'd done dirty things with him. *Really* dirty things.'

'And had you?'

'No! I mean . . .' she waved her hand through the air, spilling green drops on her t-shirt. 'We played around, but I didn't want to go all the way. He told everyone we did.' Her head lolled sideways. 'He spread foul rumours about me all round school.'

Andras shook his head. 'What a bastard.'

One of the waiters approached the table. 'Excuse me, sir.' He gave Grace a stern look. 'That young lady has had more than enough to drink.'

Mammon looked up. 'You're fired.'

'I beg your pardon!'

'You can beg all you want but you're still fired.'

The waiter's mouth dropped open. 'Who do you think you are?'

'You mean, you don't know?' Andras raised an eyebrow. 'You should be sacked for that alone!'

The waiter shook his head and strode away.

Grace gasped. 'You fired him!' She slumped onto Andras's shoulder.

Mammon stood up and patted Andras's back. 'You'll have to take her to bed, my lad.'

From the dance floor, Joe glanced across at Grace, slumped in her chair, head flung back. 'Let's take a break.'

Haures nodded. 'Okay. But before we do . . .' She pressed her mouth against his, her tongue cool amidst the warm heat of her mouth. She broke the kiss slowly, her eyes never leaving his.

Joe smiled. 'That was great.'

'Come on,' Haures whispered. 'Dance with me some more.'

Joe glanced across again – Grace was still slumped against Andras. 'I need to check on my sister.' He squeezed her hand as they walked back to the table. 'I'd like to see you again, though.'

'Oh, I'm not letting you get away from me.'

Joe slid into Mammon's empty seat. He nudged Grace's arm. 'Hey! Wake up!'

'Uhh . . . leave me alone . . .'

Joe stared at the near-empty bottle. 'Friggin' hell, Grace! How much did you have?'

'Shut up, Joe.' Her head jerked towards him. 'You're drunk too.'

'No. I only had one of those.' He glared at Andras. 'How much did you give her?'

Andras shrugged. 'She was doing fine – I even watered it down with lemonade.'

'She doesn't need to drink much. And she didn't eat anything.' He glanced up – Mammon was now standing behind Andras's chair. 'I think it's time we went.'

Mammon nodded. 'No problem, Joe. No harm intended with Grace.'

'Yeah, well . . .' Joe gave Andras a threatening stare. 'He's been feeding that stuff to her non-stop.'

'I thought she could handle it. I'm sorry, Joe.' Andras helped Grace sit up. 'Can you walk, sweetheart?'

'Yeah.' Grace stood up and then stumbled. Andras caught her. 'Try to focus, Grace.' He looked at Joe. 'Where are you parked?'

'Over that way.' Joe pointed towards the river.

'We'll help you.' They guided Grace past the crowds and through the main gates. The security guard who'd identified Grace shook his head with a disapproving frown as she was led past.

Andras eased Grace on to the kerb. 'There you are.'

Joe kissed Haures again, his fingers stroking the soft skin on her waist. Sighing with regret, he watched her slide into the car.

Mammon reached out his hand. 'Next time we go on a hunt, I'll call you.' He shook Joe's hand, slipping a small mobile phone into his palm. 'This is for your use only.'

Joe nodded. He reached into his wallet and slid out the card the paramedic had given him. 'This is you, isn't it?' He narrowed his eyes. 'Vanguard Security. I guessed by the initials: M.H. Jones.'

'That's us.' Mammon smiled. 'People do admire our work.'

'One of our guys seemed to think you'd help us. That you'd get the job done, when Renfield wouldn't.'

'He was right.'

'I want to catch the guys who killed my parents.'

'We will. I *will* call you.' Mammon got into the car and closed the door.

As the car moved away, he gave an approving smile to his apprentices. 'Good work – especially you two.' He nodded to Andras and Haures.

'We should drive them home,' said Zagan.

Mammon shook his head. 'No. Go away leaving them wanting more. Leaving *him* wanting more.'

FIFTEEN

GRACE FLOPPED ON to her back, her head nestled in the grass. All around, people were flooding from the festival gates; their voices mingling with the sound of Joe trying to start the bike. She sat up, groaning. Burying her face in her hands didn't help – in the dark, her world still spun.

'Damn it!' Joe lowered the bike's kickstand.

'What's wrong?'

'What does it look like? We're gonna have to call Diana.' Joe pulled out his phone and stared at the screen. Perhaps he should try Mammon. Joe could see Haures again . . . maybe stay the night in the City. He chewed on his lip for a few seconds and took another look at Grace, sitting on the kerb.

Sighing, he scrolled through his contacts. 'Oh, no. I don't have Renfield's number.'

'I do.' Grace held up her phone. Joe grabbed it from her swaying arm and scrolled through the contacts. 'Ah, Ivan's number. I see you've already saved it.'

He raised a provocative eyebrow.

She peered at him. 'So what?'

'That was quick, that's all. You only met him today.'

'So?' Grace dropped her head back on the grass, watching the thin wisps of cloud move across the sky as Joe made the call.

* * *

IT WAS QUIET around the conference room table as Ivan slid his phone into his pocket. 'They're in the city. Joe asked me to come and pick them up.'

'You can't!' said Maya.

Ivan looked at Lucius. 'Specifically me. He doesn't want Diana to come.'

Seth grunted. 'That's because he knows she'll completely go off at him.'

'We'll manage,' Armin said.

'No!' Maya gave Ivan a pleading look. 'You said you'd help Armin with his mission tonight. You know it's important for his leadership training! Why do we have to bend to whatever Joe wants?'

'Because he's a Ferryman, Maya,' said Marcus from the doorway. He strolled in and took a seat next to Lucius. 'He's very powerful, and we need him on our team.'

Malcolm sat back and folded his arms. 'It'd be nice if you valued the rest of us in equal measures.'

Marcus gave him a scathing look. 'If you were a Ferryman, I would.'

Malcolm's face flushed. He swallowed hard and stared at the desk, his fingers balled into angry fists.

Armin squeezed Maya's hand. 'I can go. Have some faith in me, babe.'

Lucius shook his head. 'I'm not sure that you're ready, Armin. Perhaps we should wait.'

'Rubbish,' Marcus said. 'He's already shown the leadership necessary to manage his own team.' His gaze fell on Malcolm – and in his eyes, yet another unspoken rejection. Unlike you.

Lucius grabbed the mission file and flicked through it. 'This is a low-level job. Armin can handle it.'

Ivan looked at Armin. 'It's your call.'

Armin shrugged. 'I was due to lead my own team soon anyway, wasn't I? We've just jumped ahead a few months.' He smiled at Lucius. 'I'll do it.'

Marcus gave his brother a firm nod and Lucius stood up. 'Okay. I guess now is as good a time as any. Good luck.'

* * *

By the time the chopper arrived, the car park was empty and the last of the festival staff had left.

'Get up, Grace.' Joe nudged her with his foot.

'Leave me alone.' The dark, still place she wanted to be didn't involve any movement. 'Oh, God.' She opened one eye. 'We're not *flying* home.'

Ivan alighted from the chopper, alone. He stopped a few feet away and folded his arms. 'Have a good time?'

Joe grinned. 'Yeah, I did, actually.'

Ivan looked down at Grace's dishevelled hair and glassy eyes. 'Can you walk?'

Grace groaned. 'No . . .'

Ivan slid one arm around her waist and scooped up her legs with the other. She held her breath as his face dipped close to hers. Could he feel her heart pound through her shirt? Without any apparent stress, he lifted her. As she lay her head on his chest, she could hear his heart: slow and steady compared to the rapid drumming in hers. Ivan helped Grace into her seat and pulled the harness across her body. She peeked up at him; when she caught his eye, there was an amused glint.

'I think I've had too much to drink.'

'It would seem so. It is a shame that I wasn't there to keep an eye on you.'

'I wish you had been.' Her cheeks burned at the intensity of his stare. She savoured his closeness, the warmth of his hands as they brushed against her bare arms; the intimate tone in his voice. Inwardly, she cringed at the memory of that other guy's arm around her shoulders – Anthony, or whatever his name was.

How could she have compared him to Ivan?

* * *

THE MORNING LIGHT was peeking over the horizon when they landed. Ivan peered at the light coming from Lucius's office. 'That's strange. They're still up.'

Standing at the desk were Marcus, Lucius, Agatha and Diana. Ivan glanced between them and a television monitor, which was playing footage of mercenaries moving through a corridor.

Diana pressed her lips together. 'There was . . . an accident.'

'What?' Ivan sank into a chair. 'What happened?'

'Everything was going well,' said Lucius. 'They appre-hended the two targets. As we said, a low-level job. But then they went upstairs.'

'Watch,' Diana said.

The monitor was split into four screens: each listed a mercenary name at the bottom, allowing the viewer to see from a different point of view.

Grace stared as the team entered a large curved room. 'What is this place?' she whispered. People were kneeled, praying, at circular rows of red velvet seats.

They watched Armin grab a woman and shake her by the shoulder. 'Miss! Can you hear me?' She didn't look up – but just kept crying, her head hung.

'It's hopeless,' said the mercenary named Stevens. 'We're not getting out of here.'

'Quiet!' said Armin. 'We're leaving this room, now. Where's Jameson?'

'He's dead!'

Armin looked at Stevens, who pointed to the floor with a shaking hand. The camera revealed a body lying in a dark puddle of blood on the carpet. Grace turned her face away, sickened, as Armin took a close look at the wound.

'He's killed himself, man. Can't take it.'

'Shut up, Stevens!'

'I *can't!*'

Through Armin's camera, they watched the distraught mercenary plunge a knife into his neck.

'Stevens! Oh, God, no!' Armin lunged forward, grabbing his teammate as he fell. Blood spurted onto the camera and onto Armin's face.

'Forget it! He's gone!' cried Jackson, the other mercenary.

Armin began muttering a desperate prayer as he rested Stevens's body on the carpet.

Grace gasped. 'What's making them do this?'

Followed by his one remaining teammate, Armin moved into a corridor. He slammed a shaped charge against the wall. 'Take cover!' The wall exploded, dousing the cameras in grey dust. 'Come on!' They ran through the gap in the wall.

The next few seconds were blurry, the sound distorted.

An outline emerged from the dust.

'What is that?' Joe muttered.

Ivan frowned. 'Why aren't they firing?'

Jackson seemed to jerk – an erratic, swaying movement. Then, he fell. He was lying on the ground, on his side – but his camera was still live. The final seconds of film captured Armin suspended off the ground by an unseen force, his body twisted at a strange angle.

Grace caught her breath. A sick feeling of horror swamped her stomach. Something was squeezing him – like a rag.

There was a snapping sound and then a thump – as Armin hit the ground.

Lucius folded his arms. 'The video just runs from here. We don't see anything from this point. The demon just disappears. Doesn't try to take the cameras, or do anything with the bodies.' He turned and leaned on the table.

'He needed me there,' Ivan whispered.

Diana frowned. 'Then we'd be looking at five casualties instead of four! Even you, Ivan – with all your experience – you still might not have been able to handle this! Don't look at me like that! Such a level of telepathic influence – to control all of those people, including our boys, with all their training? It's got to be something big.'

'Level Twenty-two,' Lucius mused.

Ivan frowned. 'What about the guy outside – Briggs? Why didn't he respond?'

'We've had no contact from him. We're assuming he's dead too.'

'They were dealing with something different here,' Lucius said. 'Something well beyond what we're used to. Stronger than anything we've seen before.'

Ivan stared at the monitor. 'I should have gone with him.'

'No you shouldn't have!' Grace blurted. Her cheeks turned red as they all looked at her.

'Damn it!' Marcus pounded his fist on the table. 'Four of our best – gone! This is ridiculous! These were highly trained mercenaries! Why didn't they control their minds!'

Diana scowled. 'Don't you understand, Marcus? They were outclassed!'

'That's garbage. Obviously they weren't trained to deal with the pressure.'

'Not true,' Ivan said. 'Armin always showed commendable presence of mind. Obviously, the team didn't know what they were up against.'

Diana nodded at Ivan. 'That creature – whatever it was – was able to take out four well-trained men.' She slumped in her chair, hand over her eyes.

Marcus thumped his fist on the table. 'This should not have happened! The entire *sarsareh* community will find out.'

Diana looked up. 'What are you worried about, Marcus? The loss of life, or the damage to Renfield's reputation?'

'If you don't mind,' Ivan said, 'I have a team member to counsel.'

Grace felt a rush of guilt. Poor Maya. She looked at Joe. *It's our fault.*

Scowling, Joe shook his head. 'No, it's not.' He felt the others' eyes on him.

Diana frowned. 'What did you say?'

'Nothing,' he muttered.

Diana cast a knowing look at Grace. 'Don't do that. If you've got something to say, speak up.'

'Sorry,' Grace muttered.

Diana stood up. 'Both of you – off to bed.'

Joe stood up and walked out of the office.

Diana sighed. 'See Grace to her room, will you, Ivan?'

Ivan took Grace's hand. She mentally protested; she wasn't a child! But her body responded differently: the heat of his other hand against her back was sending tingles all over her skin. Even with everything that had happened . . . she couldn't ignore the reaction his touch provoked in her.

'Take it slowly, now.'

She looked up at him. 'I'm sorry about Armin.'

'It is not your fault.' He pushed open her bedroom door. 'Come on – get to bed.'

She stumbled across and fell onto the quilt. 'I'm good here. Just leave me.' She groaned, throwing her forearm over her eyes.

He stood, arms folded. 'The way you are feeling now is punishment for drinking like that.'

She looked up. 'Don't you have any sympathy? I bet you like to drink.'

'Yes. But I know how to handle my vodka.' He glanced at his watch. 'Now, if I were to hold you to our schedule, you would have to be up in forty-five minutes.'

'No!'

'Goodnight, Grace.'

'Ivan.'

'Yes, Grace?' He poked his head back inside.

'I'm never drinking again.'

* * *

MARCUS CLASPED HIS fingers together. He glanced between Agatha and Lucius. 'We need to keep a closer eye on Joe. We can't risk losing him to the outside world.'

Lucius removed his glasses, gave them a quick wipe and returned them to his face. 'We'll keep him busy. Ivan's going to train him personally. Joe seems to respond to him. I have great hopes for Joe and Grace. I believe that they can be of use, once their skills are channelled appropriately.'

'We know *that*.' Marcus leaned back on his chair, his fingers drumming the table.

Agatha leaned forward and clasped her chin. 'The girl is way too powerful. Once she realises what she can get away with, she might encourage him to leave.' She raised her eyes to Marcus. 'Perhaps we should take Joe into our care and train him specially.'

Lucius shook his head. 'Ivan can handle them.'

'He doesn't have the right experience.'

'You're very wrong, Agatha,' said Lucius. 'You don't know where Ivan's been. Real combat. Not the skirmishes that you were involved in, so many years ago.'

The woman narrowed her eyes. 'Watch yourself, Lucius.'

Marcus stroked his moustache. 'We need to entice Joe to commit to our side. The taste of freedom last night may have been all too tempting. It wouldn't hurt to give him some toys. A new car, at the very least.'

He leaned back in his chair, eyes scanning the ceiling. 'Kit him up with everything he needs. Give him a greater level of responsibility within the squad. Train him up quickly, get him on his first mission within the month. By the time he's felt the adrenaline rush, he won't want to go anywhere else.'

Lucius paused. 'That sounds a bit soon. We don't want anyone getting hurt.'

'If Ivan is as wonderful as you say he is, nobody should. Don't risk Joe on the tougher jobs – leave them to our top guys.'

Lucius folded his arms. 'You've got all of the top guys. Think you can release them so they can do some real work?'

Marcus ignored the comment. 'Send Joe out to clean up the suburbs. You know, small-time work. Exciting enough to a newcomer who doesn't know the difference.'

'So, they're to be rewarded, rather than punished,' Agatha said. 'Diana won't like it. Nor will his teammates.'

'You leave Diana to me. And his teammates will obey my wishes, or suffer the consequences.'

Lucius peered over his glasses. 'Even your own son?'

'Malcolm knows his place.'

'Does he?'

'Look! Joe's the prime concern here. Grace simply has to be kept compliant – and fully supportive of our actions concerning her brother. We want him to put Renfield on the map, don't we?'

With a tired sigh, Lucius pinched the bridge of his nose. 'Grace could be very useful to us as well. Don't write her off; she's very gifted.'

Marcus shrugged. 'As long as she's compliant, I don't care.'

Lucius crossed his arms. 'Grace won't be a problem. Ivan seems to be winning her over. As long as that remains the case, we can focus on Joe.'

SIXTEEN

SHE WOKE.

Her sleep-crusted eyelids peeled apart lash by lash. Her tongue felt glued to the roof of her mouth.

Focus returned to her eyes. The clock read twelve-thirty. Gradually, her other senses kicked in and she registered that someone else was in the room.

She jumped with the fright – but settled when she saw Diana sitting at the end of her bed. 'Ugh.' Grace peered at her aunt through one eye. 'If you've come to tell me off about the drinking, there's no need. I'm never doing it again.' She buried her face into the pillow. 'Oh, my head . . .'

Diana shrugged. 'Maybe you will, maybe you won't.'

Grace peeked out. 'Aren't you mad at me?'

'Not now. Last night: yes. But I blame your brother more.'

'Why? He didn't force the alcohol down my throat.' Her eyes searched the bedside table for water. Some kind of liquid . . . anything!

'We've decided to fast-track your training. You and Joe will have specialised tuition with Ivan with a view to taking on a squad position within a month.'

'What?' No word of punishment?

'Get a proper sleep tonight. Tomorrow morning, meet Ivan at the gym. I believe you and he agreed on a time.'

* * *

HALF-PAST SIX THE next morning Grace entered the double doors of the Renfield gymnasium. It was an airy space, with open beams stretching across a low ceiling, an array of weightlifting equipment on the left-hand wall, and directly ahead – a climbing wall. Grace felt a surge of embarrassment, remembering her first attempt to climb. Joe was leaning against the wall, arms folded; Ivan standing opposite. She paused, watching Joe.

'Hello.' She slipped her hoodie off and hung it on a large silver hook.

Ivan nodded. 'Morning, Grace.'

She found her eyes wandering . . . down – along the muscle that rippled down his upper arms. Coughing, she looked up – and into those eyes.

Ivan walked across to the middle of the room and pointed at a blue gym mat. 'Sit down, both of you.'

Grace planted herself in the middle of the mat; Joe sat on the edge with his elbows on his knees.

Ivan lowered into a crouch and looked at them both. 'We've decided that you both need some physical training.'

Grace blinked. 'I don't. I'm a telepath. And Joe's . . .'

Ivan raised a finger. 'So, if an enemy resists your power and threatens to overcome you physically, what do you do?'

Joe shrugged. 'Open a bigger rift.'

'And you, Grace? What would you do?'

'Shoot them?' Grace chuckled. She caught his serious gaze and stopped laughing. 'Well, I'd have a gun, wouldn't I?'

'And if your opponent was a stronger telepath than you and was able to steal your gun away? What then?'

She fell silent.

'Up you get,' said Ivan.

Sighing, she stood. Joe slid away a few feet so he was resting his back against the wall; an amused glimmer in his eye.

'Sometimes we must fight hand to hand,' said Ivan. 'You must be able to defend yourself using physical means.'

'I could use telepathy . . .'

'Mmm.' Ivan watched her closely. 'From your half-hour lesson with Sarah? You're a beginner, Grace.'

Grace narrowed her eyes. 'I can hurt you.' She pointed to her forehead. 'In here.'

'Okay,' Ivan said, smiling. 'Do your worst. Attack me.' He pressed his forefinger against her head. 'In here.'

She grimaced; his voice was falsely high, an obvious attempt to mimic her. Anger simmered in her gut. She watched him watching her, calm expectation on his face. Fine. He asked for it. She focused on his forehead . . . and white-hot pain.

Ivan's face twitched – but then he grabbed her left shoulder and slid his foot behind her ankle. She gasped as he slammed her to the ground, the shock trapping her breath. But there was no pain, just a sense of being overpowered, no chance of escape – his hold on her unbreakable, uncompromising.

He locked his ankles around hers and held his hand against her throat. 'You're dead.'

He rolled away and sprang to his feet.

She dragged herself up, her breaths coming in hollow gasps. 'You knocked the wind . . . out of me.'

'I'm not a demon. I'm just a human being. But I can overcome your telepathic attack with this simple move.'

'Okay, you're not a demon, but you're probably better than any of their bodyguards.'

Ivan shot her a dark look. 'How do you know that? There you go again, making dangerous assumptions.' He folded his arms. 'A lot of private security are former special forces from Russia.'

'What . . . working for demons?'

He sighed. 'Grace, the bodyguards don't know their bosses are demons. As far as they're concerned, it's just a bigger pay cheque.' He nodded. 'Again. But this time, I want you to sidestep me as I come forward.' He moved sideways to demonstrate. 'See?'

She nodded; Ivan lunged at her. She slid on her heel and moved sideways, dodging his attack.

'Good. Now, lift your arms as so and block me. Then lunge forward like this.' His hands cut through the air in a simulated slice through her shoulder. 'See?' He showed her again.

She threw a glance at Joe. 'Are you going to make him do this too?'

'Yes. Why? Do you want to see him get his arse kicked?

Now, I'm going to come at you from different directions. I want you to practise the three simple moves I've taught you. Dodge, block and strike.'

He sprang at her again, slamming one hand against her collarbone. A sudden pressure against her back as he shoved her backwards. She tipped onto her heels and then crashed down to the mat. All the while, his arms were locked around her torso.

'Ow.' The back of her head throbbed. She groaned as he pulled her to her feet. 'Stop, now,' she moaned.

'Again.'

Time and again he ran at her. Even when she came close, her flailing fingers couldn't touch him. Ivan was dodging around her like a boxer. For good measure he slapped her thigh, the cracking sound reverberating through the room.

She winced. 'Hey! Don't do that!'

'Why not? You left yourself open, Grace.'

The frustration built, presenting itself in the gradual tensing of her shoulders, the sick anger in her stomach and the burning in her eyes. She dodged him this time. Good. Then the lunge – her stomach rolled as he pulled her through the air. Once again she felt the familiar slam-down against the mat, her bones jarring from the impact. He locked his ankles around her calves, paused, and stared down at her. 'Infuriating, isn't it?'

She regarded him through sweat-soaked strands of hair. 'Yes.' Even through the misery and humiliation she couldn't help studying his face. That smooth skin, the small scar on his cheek. His eyes shone with a calm intelligence, but behind lay a savagery that would emerge when provoked.

Tiny curves formed a smile at the edge of his lips.

'Do you still think you can take me?'

'No.' Burning with shame, she looked away.

His voice softened. 'I'll teach you how to, Grace. You don't need to think that just because you are a woman, you cannot fight a man.' He rolled away. 'Okay. You can take a break. You're up, Joe.'

Grace sat down and curled her legs up to her chest. Had he noticed her staring? Could he tell what she'd been thinking?

'By the way, Grace – I did feel that.' Ivan pointed to his head. 'You are gifted. But you need to realise that once an enemy knows your strengths, then that enemy can also resist your telepathy.'

She smiled.

'Don't,' said Joe. 'You'll give her a big head.'

'What – are you jealous?' Grace gave him a critical once-over. 'Don't annoy me, Joe. Or you'll be sorry.'

Joe smirked. 'Whatever.'

Ivan turned to Joe. 'All right then. Let's see what *you* can do. I want you to open a rift. As quickly as you can. And I want you to try to get me inside it.'

Joe grinned. 'No problem.'

'Grace, go to the other side of the room.'

With a sigh, she got to her feet. 'Are you going to taser him?'

'No,' said Ivan.

Joe shrugged. 'It wouldn't matter if he did.'

Grace scowled. 'Spoken like one who's never been shot.'

Ivan gave her a curious stare. 'Why did you ask me that?'

'That gun.' She pointed to his belt.

'It's not a taser. But it's not lethal either.' He grinned, as though remembering a private joke.

Joe hesitated as he remembered the bony monster. 'I'll go in right after you,' he said. 'That way you won't get hurt.'

'Whatever you think best.' Ivan folded his arms.

Joe didn't focus on any particular spot, but soon a dark, swirling sphere appeared around Ivan's feet. The pull was immediately obvious – even the chain around Ivan's neck was straining, pulling towards the ground.

Ivan jumped up and grabbed one of the exposed beams. Hanging by one arm, he reached around and drew the gun from behind his back.

Grace gasped.

Ivan fired.

Joe stumbled backwards.

In the time it took for Grace to breathe in and out, the rift vanished. Joe was bending over, hands pressed to his face.

Grace threw an angry look at Ivan, still hanging from the beam. 'What have you done?' She grabbed Joe's shoulders and turned him around.

One furious blue eye glared at her through a smear of red paint. She knew he'd rather have been tasered than this.

She exploded into laughter. 'You should see your face!'

Ivan jumped down, threw the paintball gun on a table and grabbed a towel. 'Here.' He threw it to Joe and studied his face for a few seconds. 'You're angry, aren't you?'

Joe clenched his teeth as he wiped the paint away.

'You don't want to let that anger control you, Joe.'

'You don't know what it's like.'

'Oh, you think?' Ivan lifted his shirt and turned around slowly. A row of faded scars lay across his torso and back. 'In Spetsnaz, part of the training is to see how much pain each recruit can take. Either you learn to control your emotional responses, or you're out. When I joined up I was dangerously angry. But I learned to manage that. I don't recommend their methods – but I want you to realise that I understand where you're coming from.'

He pulled his shirt down and thumped Joe on the back. 'Don't feel ashamed. Either of you. This lesson will make you stronger. You must learn to control your emotions. Curb your arrogance. Remember: no matter how potent your gift is, you must be able to think calmly. You'll learn how to do this. Now, come with me.'

They approached a table wedged beneath one of the tall windows that lined the corridor. A group of mercenaries was clustered around it. To her discomfort, Grace noticed Maya sitting among them.

Maya looked up. 'You!' Red, swollen eyes darted between Grace and Joe. 'Who the hell do you think you are?' She stepped over the chair and lunged across.

Ivan took hold of her arms. 'Steady, Maya.'

She looked up at him, pleading. 'They ran off, like two stupid, selfish children! And now Armin is dead . . .'

'It is not their fault,' said Ivan. He gave her a kind but firm stare. 'They are not to blame.'

'That is true.' Maya rubbed the tears away and lifted her chin. '*You* are.'

Malcolm stepped towards Maya. 'Let her go, Ivan.'

'Stand aside, Penbury.'

Trembling, Maya stared up at Ivan. 'He was so eager to prove himself to you after you put him on night duty. He was too tired to handle this mission!'

'It wasn't a matter of fatigue; the whole team was killed. Nobody is to blame but the bad guys.'

'He only volunteered because he wanted you to respect him.' She gave him a scornful glare. 'You! Like you matter that much!' She jerked forward and spat on his shirt.

Someone gasped, the air became even more charged with tension.

But Ivan didn't waver. His voice was calm, his eyes compassionate. 'He always had my respect. And now it's greater than ever.'

'At my expense.' Maya slumped. 'Let me go.'

Malcolm released Maya, who turned and sat down at the table again. He stepped closer to Ivan. 'Anyway, why aren't these two under suspension?'

Ivan stiffened at his tone. 'It's not your concern, Penbury.'

'Yes, it is my concern.' Malcolm pointed at Grace. 'They snuck out of here to go God knows where; she used her mind powers to mess around with Brutus's head. Now we find out they're not being suspended!'

Ivan's voice was quiet but threatening. 'You're forgetting your place.'

'As your second-in-charge?' Malcolm threw up his hands. 'Oh, but then again – that's not the case. No, I've been usurped by our Ferryman here.'

His words echoed off the walls. A crowd of onlookers formed a loose circle around the scene.

Grace gave Joe a surprised look. 'Really?'

'For some reason, the powers-that-be have decided Joe should step in.' Malcolm smiled. 'No – I'm just a lowly team member, asking the same question everyone else is.'

'Either way, you're my subordinate and you will obey my instructions,' Ivan said. 'Back off.'

'It's all right,' Joe said. He held Malcolm's stare. 'You just weren't good enough for a leadership position. At least, your father didn't seem to think so.'

Malcolm sprung towards Joe. 'You prick, you!'

'Enough!' Ivan's voice boomed down the corridor. He stepped between the two boys. 'Both of you. Back away.' He watched as Malcolm moved backwards reluctantly.

Ivan cast an angry stare around the group. Grace found herself shrinking back, along with most of the watching crowd. She reached over, grabbing Joe's sleeve. 'Leave it!'

Ivan turned to Joe. 'Back off, I told you.'

With furious eyes pinned on Malcolm, Joe stepped back. 'Fine.' He raised his hands. 'I didn't start this crap.'

'We're not finished, Callahan.' Malcolm kicked over a chair and stalked away.

* * *

GRACE'S HEART WAS still hammering as she and Joe followed Ivan to the end of the hallway, past groups of faces: some shocked, others accusing.

Ivan yanked open the door and nodded for Grace and Joe to go in first.

'You both all right?'

'Yes.' Grace looked at Joe. 'You calm?'

He shrugged. 'Take a better man than him to bring *me* down.' He grinned at Ivan. 'Weapons?'

Ivan picked up a yellow and black gun. 'Taser shotgun. You're familiar with its effects, Grace.'

Grace cradled the gun. It was lighter than she'd expected. Her finger twitched, and she felt a thrill at the prospect of pulling the trigger.

'Gimme.' Joe snatched the gun from Grace. 'Dance.' He aimed at her feet.

Grace frowned. 'You don't know what you're doing, you idiot.'

'See this?' Ivan pointed to a picture on the wall. It was of a clay pot, cut open down the middle to reveal the inside. It was half full of purple liquid, and two copper cylinders ran down the centre. 'Our predecessors – the first *sarsareh* mercenaries in Mesopotamia – harnessed electricity to disable demon energy. This was known as a Baghdad Battery.'

He smiled. 'Of course, we have made some advances in weaponry since then. You may have heard of the scientist Nikola Tesla? He wanted to create a shield for the entire planet. His idea was to broadcast a protective shroud of electricity, flowing freely about the Earth's atmosphere; effectively guarding us from demon energy.'

'That'd be awesome,' said Grace.

Ivan nodded. 'A bonus would have been free electricity for the people. However, his capitalist banker realised there was no profit in this and shut the project down.'

He shrugged. 'Ah, such is life. Okay. Protective clothing. Both of you take your shoes off.' Ivan tapped in a security code and a sliding door opened. He pulled out what looked like two shiny wetsuits.

'Smart suits. The fluid inside the skin of the suit becomes a form of body armour when subjected to a magnetic field, which the suit generates itself.' He beckoned for them to come closer. Ivan pressed one up against Grace's body. 'That looks like a good fit, actually.'

He passed Joe a suit. Grace lifted her leg to step inside.

'Hold on, Grace.' Ivan walked over and took the suit from her. 'You need to strip off first.'

She searched his face; there was no hint of a smile or even any embarrassment on his part. Her mouth fell open. 'Oh . . .'

'You don't have to be naked – just take off your pants and t-shirt. If it makes you feel any better, you can go into the change room.' He pointed to a door in the corner.

Grace stepped inside and shut the door. She hung her t-shirt and pants on a hook and slid inside the suit, surprised by how easily it fit. No zips or velcro. The fabric stretched over her body but seemed to mould to her shape after she'd pulled it on.

'Comfy.'

Ivan turned back as Grace walked out of the changing room. 'Good.' He gave her an approving once-over. 'Fits well.'

She blushed; his eyes had lingered around her waist and hips.

Ivan turned and opened another cupboard.

Grace looked sideways at Joe. 'I bet those other mercenaries won't have anything this good,' she whispered.

'He's a billionaire, Grace. I'm sure their home base has a lot more tech.'

'You're not thinking of seeing them again, are you?'

Joe shrugged. 'Maybe.'

'I don't think –'

'Pay attention, Grace.' Joe nodded at Ivan, who was lifting a black shotgun from the cupboard. He pushed it into Grace's hands. 'Here.' He stood close behind her and lay his hands over hers, adjusting her hold.

She held her breath.

'The Maul IV. Rapid fire, double barrel, twelve gauge shotgun with harpoon attachment. This will be your weapon. Specially designed. Ever fired a gun before?'

She glanced back into his eyes. His hands were still over hers, the heat from his body close to her back. She gulped. 'No.'

'Usually, we take down a demon by using three stages of attack. First, we hit him with a combined taser and neuro-toxin bullet. The taser shocks him, disabling the demonic energy. That way he can't use telepathy or telekinesis. The neurotoxin puts him to sleep within seconds. Then we bring him to Renfield. Of course, some demons are very fast or very strong. I've seen them resist the neurotoxins before. The demons are evolving. There are times when we even have to resort to hand-to-hand fighting.'

'Nobody can say you're not committed,' said Grace. 'I mean, if you have to go through all that.'

Joe grinned. 'Am I going to put a lot of people out of work?'

Ivan shrugged. 'Probably not. We will just have to change the way we do things. You will always need a strong rank of bodyguards around you.' He looked at Grace. 'And your sister here will be able to use her power to influence leaders and decision makers into taking the right choices. The *sarsareh* have many roles to play in society, you know.'

Ivan led them into a large room. On the far wall stood a row of dummies. He flicked on the lights. 'Seth's been very busy getting this ready for you both.' He hit a switch and one of the dummies began to float across the room, suspended by a large metal hook. 'This is a silicone dummy. You're going to practise on this before you try to harpoon a real demon.'

'Let's go!' Joe said.

Grace tilted her head. 'So, does this mean we can go on missions soon?'

'Perhaps. Right now, my concern is that you master your skills and that you are never defenceless against a demon attack. Hence, the suit.'

'Well, it feels good,' Grace said. 'Better than going out in jeans and a t-shirt.'

'Yes, just a little bit.' With a hint of a smile, Ivan took another shotgun from the cupboard and passed it to Joe.

'Cool,' said Joe. He aimed the gun at the dummy.

Ivan nodded. 'Hit it.'

Joe fired. There was a whipping sound; the dummy jolted backward. It swung back and forth, its chest impaled by a silver x-shaped claw.

'Yeah!' Joe whistled. 'What a shot.' He gave Grace a triumphant grin.

'That's your harpoon,' Ivan said. 'As you can see, it drives straight through the torso and doubles back in a cross shape, impaling your target.' A long silver cord connected the harpoon to the gun.

'That alone won't kill a demon. But, if you were to aim the gun at a rift and fire again, the cord would detach and hurl the demon inside at high speed. The harpoon is strong; its cord is made of diamond wire.'

Joe aimed to the left and fired a second time.

The dummy tore away from the ceiling, hit the ground and rolled a few times, finally coming to rest on its back.

'Cool!' said Joe.

Ivan nodded at Grace. 'Your turn.' She lifted her gun and took aim but froze as Ivan stood close behind her again. The heat of his breath on her neck; her hands wobbled in unison with her knees.

Ivan slid his hands over hers and helped her take aim. 'Ready?'

She pulled the trigger, heard the diamond cord whoosh through the air and only registered movement as the harpoon slammed into the second dummy.

'Whoa. That was fast.'

Exhilarated, she fired again. The dummy broke away and slammed to the ground.

'Ha! Mine went further than yours.'

'We'll see about that.' Joe lunged over and yanked the gun away. 'Best out of five.'

* * *

JOE WATCHED IVAN put the weapon back in the cabinet. 'Rematch,' he said.

Smiling, Grace shook her head. 'I won, fair and square.'

With Ivan's help, of course – at least for the first two shots. Her hands tingled at the memory of his fingers pressed against hers.

Joe looked at Ivan. 'When are we going on a real mission?'

'Within the month.' Ivan locked the cabinet and turned around. 'For that to happen, you'll both need intensive training. We intend for you two to work in a team. Ultimately, we'd like to see Grace at such a level that she won't need the harpoon gun; that she can use her telepathy to compel the demon to enter a rift. Are you prepared to listen to me so that I can help you?'

'Of course!' Grace said. She bit her lip, embarrassed by the gushing in her voice.

Joe nodded.

Grace followed Ivan back into the corridor. 'How can we practise that, though? Dummies don't fight back.'

Ivan grinned. 'No, they don't.' He closed the door. 'Well, you're in the right place. We have several demons in custody – many of whom are telepathic. Are you ready to show us what you're capable of?'

SEVENTEEN

'WELL, HAPPY BIRTHDAY.' Grace stared into her reflection. No-nonsense hair, pulled back in a bun. Steely look in the eyes. Shoulders squared, chin up. 'Licenced to kill.' Her mouth turned up at the little joke, but her stomach knotted with apprehension.

She turned her arm sideways, admiring the new crest on her t-shirt: the psychic's eye sitting on top of the red spear. Ivan's way of telling her she was one of them now. Not just a telepath but a mercenary, too.

Or, she would be. After this, her first mission. She swallowed, wincing at the needling sensation, a razor blade down her throat. Her head felt full, she battled dizziness. She coughed into a tissue and threw it away in a hurry.

Why, oh why did she have to get sick now?

And why not during the month before? The past four weeks had been nothing more than a long role-playing exercise – she'd never been in real danger with Ivan ready at her side, his gun trained on whichever demon she was 'fighting'.

Her first victim was incredibly easy.

'This individual has confessed to several acts of shocking violence, including disfigurement, stabbings, and murder.' Ivan had looked up from the file and nodded. 'Just remember – don't underestimate him. He has physical strength and speed on his side.'

True – but a weakling against her power of suggestion. *Lay on the floor, arms above your head, face-down.* It had only taken her seconds to control him.

The telepaths were another matter.

The first one . . . standing in the middle of the room, staring at Grace; she'd counted to ten, trying to compel him to walk to the back wall. Eleven . . . twelve . . . then, a memory wash-out. Next, her hands were pressed against cold stone. Her forehead ached, as though she'd been smashing it against something . . . she looked at the wall and the stamp of blood she'd left there.

There'd been a thump as the demon collapsed in a convulsive fit, mouth contorted in a silent scream as Ivan pummelled him with neurotoxin bullets.

Her cheeks burning, Grace had shaken her head. 'I didn't even feel him take over me.' She'd reached up and touched the tender swelling on her forehead.

Ivan had taken her by the shoulders; his voice calm, reassuring. 'Don't waste time on self-doubt. You've learned something here. We're here to back you up. See how important the weapons are, Grace? They inhibit the demonic power and give you a chance to take control of the mind. It's called being prepared. Taking no chances. Although, eventually you won't need taser back-up.

You're going to learn to hit them quickly, before they even know you're there.'

And then, yesterday.

The morbid high of it all. Controlling the demon, compelling him to walk towards Joe's rift, into the dark, cloudy death and whatever else waited there.

It made her shiver.

She stared at the stranger in the mirror and imagined what it would be like if none of this had happened. What would she be doing today?

Dinner with Mum, Dad and Joe?

Her first legal glass of champagne?

Her gaze fell on the water park photo. Two best friends with sunburnt noses, broad grins and messy hair at the most innocent time of their lives. She sighed. 'You're probably better off where you are, Allie. There are monsters out here.'

She drew three long breaths and made her way towards the conference room.

* * *

JOE SLUMPED BACK in his seat, arms folded. Lucius's voice was a low hum in the background, punctuated by occasional questions from Diana.

His mind rolled back to that night in the City. His lips on Haures's neck . . . the warm feel of her body pressed against him.

'Joe!' Ivan passed him a file. 'You need to read this.'

Joe cringed as he turned the pages, remembering what Mammon had said about paperwork and boring meetings. 'The whole thing?'

Diana looked up. 'It's important, Joe.'

'Okay.' Lucius stood at the head of the table. 'James Michael Allen, twenty-three. Level Thirteen demon. Suspected of murdering an elderly man in his home six months ago. The police couldn't find any evidence to press charges, but our sources traced the demonic energy to him.'

Grace gasped. 'That's horrible!'

Lucius gave her a grim smile. 'Allen's latest hobby is pushing drugs to school children.'

'You're kidding.' Joe stared at the file. 'Which drugs?'

'Methamphetamine.'

Grace shuddered, remembering the stomach-turning slide show from health class. She coughed, bringing a rattling sound in her chest.

'You don't sound well,' said Sarah.

Diana peered over at her niece. 'Perhaps you should stay home.'

'I'll be fine.' Grace threw a tissue into the bin.

Lucius flicked through his file. 'We suspect Allen's operation is backed by his family, given that they are based out of a suburban residence. Allen's known associates include his cousin, Travis Tyler, who was released from jail earlier this year.'

Grace narrowed her eyes as the name struck a bell. 'Is he gifted? I mean – do they have powers, like us?'

'No. These guys tend to rely on weapons. As you know, when they develop unusual skills such as telepathy, it takes a catalyst of some kind.'

'Like a gift from a high demon,' nodded Diana.

Lucius shrugged. 'Perhaps. Anyway, we haven't seen them exert any supernatural force. Not to say you shouldn't be prepared, regardless.'

'I'll just throw 'em in a rift,' Joe said. He leaned back in his chair.

Grace looked at Diana. 'Do the police know about us? If these guys suddenly disappear . . .'

'It will be an unsolved mystery. But you must be discreet.' Diana paused. 'Joe, I'm talking to you. Remember, to the UnSighted these filth look like ordinary humans. So when you open a rift I want you to do as little damage as possible.'

'Why not put them into the asylum?'

'We can't take in every demon we apprehend, Grace,' said Lucius. 'Most of our inmates are low-level offenders, anyway.'

Malcolm gave Grace a scathing look. 'If you have a problem with the way we do things, perhaps you shouldn't come along.'

'Malcolm,' said Marcus. 'Behave yourself.'

His son flinched.

Lucius closed his file. 'These guys need putting away – permanently. We believe they are also recruiting at local schools, so their activities will expand if we don't do something now.'

Ivan looked around his team. 'We have a very simple, straightforward plan. Grace, you're going to mask our presence, with support from Sarah. There are only five of them, so it will be a matter of opening a rift and getting them inside quickly. But you and Joe will have Malcolm, Sarah and me backing you up, just in case.'

'I think you should bring more support,' said Marcus.

'No,' Lucius said. 'We need to be discreet.'

'I disagree.' Marcus looked at Diana. 'Organise an extra squad to go along. For Joe's protection.'

Diana looked at Lucius, who shrugged. 'All right, then.' He folded his arms and stared at the ceiling.

With a nod, Diana got up and left the room.

Seth gave Ivan a frustrated look; Ivan gave Lucius a diplomatic smile. 'I guess it's safer that way.'

Ivan stood up. 'Let's move.'

EIGHTEEN

IVAN LED THE team past the kitchen and into a narrow, bleakly lit stairwell. Another squad of mercenaries met them at the top of the stairs. Malcolm nodded to one of them. 'Sounds like we've been demoted to bodyguard work,' he muttered, taking two steps at a time.

'Well, let's hope the Callahans are worth it,' his friend replied.

They reached the end of the stairs, and Ivan flicked on the lights, filling the basement with a fluorescent glow. Several vehicles, jeeps mostly, were nestled close to the walls, but two cars sat ready in the middle of the car park.

'This is your graduation present,' said Ivan.

'You're kidding.' Joe stared at the car. 'For me?'

Grace kept her face calm despite the indignant lump in her throat. 'It's not *his* birthday,' she muttered.

'Wow.' Malcolm gritted his teeth. 'That's really something.'

Sarah looked at him. 'What's *your* problem? I seem to recall your father giving you a Mercedes when you made the team.'

'Several months afterwards,' Malcolm said. 'And it was second-hand.'

'Well,' Sarah said, 'we've got more money now. So suck it up, princess.' She rolled her eyes.

'Get in.' Ivan opened the driver's door. 'Let me show you what she can do. I'll drive there, you can drive back.'

Grace ran her finger over the roof. The car looked familiar – from Joe's bedroom posters. 'This is a Mustang, right?'

'Yeah!' Joe jumped into the front passenger seat and ran his fingers over the dashboard.

'Imported from the US just last month.' Ivan touched a screen next to the steering wheel; the dashboard came to life in an array of green lights. 'Step out for a minute.'

The basement was bathed in a strange blue glow. 'See the incantations?' Beneath the paintwork were rows of blue script from front to back. 'Demon repellent. If there was a ghoulie in the room right now, he'd be looking for the nearest exit – but not knowing why.' Ivan looked at Grace. 'Almost telepathic in power.'

'But not as good as me,' she said.

'Can you sit in the middle?' Sarah whispered. 'I don't want to sit next to Malcolm.'

'Sure.' Grace slid into the back seat. As Sarah entered the car, Grace gave her a sideways glance. Sarah's brow was sweaty; her eyes glazed. Her mouth tense. 'Are you okay?'

Sarah looked away. 'I feel a little low today.'

Ivan peered into the rear-vision mirror. 'Can you handle this, Sarah?'

She scowled. 'Yes, Ivan. I'll be fine.' She ground her teeth at his indiscreet questioning.

Grace frowned at the strain in Sarah's voice. 'You okay?'

Malcolm slammed his door shut, turned, and smirked at his stepsister. 'Off the meds, are we? Tut, tut. Remember, you're a soldier. Don't get all weepy, now.'

'Go to hell.' Tight-jawed, Sarah stared out the window.

Ivan turned in the driver's seat and gave Malcolm a hard stare. 'Do not agitate my team. Understand?'

Malcolm shrugged. '*I'm* part of your team.'

Ivan stared at him. 'Then act it.'

Malcolm locked eyes with Ivan as long as he could and then broke away. 'Fine,' he muttered, slumping in his seat.

Grace stared at Sarah's profile. She didn't want to pry, but . . . 'Are you okay?'

'Forget it for now. Please.' Sarah drew a deep breath, folded her arms and stared out the window.

The engine growled as Ivan revved the accelerator. He poked his head out the window and peered at the other mercenaries in the jeep.

'Got the coordinates? Good.' He revved the engine and winked at Joe. 'Because they're not going to be able to keep up with us.'

Malcolm rolled his eyes.

With a squeal, the Mustang sped out on to the driveway and through the gates.

* * *

ADRENALINE SHOT UP Grace's spine as Ivan gunned the car past a truck before smoothly weaving it back into the traffic.

201

She felt a primal thrill at how confidently he handled the car.

The hair on the back of his head was starting to grow out a little. He hadn't shaved – perhaps he was growing facial hair – but it gave a rough edge to his face that she found sexy.

'About ninety minutes,' she heard him say. Joe was fiddling with the radio. Malcolm had turned his body away; Sarah was leaning back, eyes closed.

Grace rested her head on the seat and watched the countryside pass by – rambling green pastures broken up by the occasional house or the red flash of a tractor. Eventually they hit the clustered depression of the outer suburbs. Crossing a railway line, they moved on to a narrow, potholed road where asbestos fences, stained brown by bore water, separated decaying weatherboard houses from one another. Kids gathered in groups on the pavement. As the cars passed, they watched with hard, defiant faces.

Thank God they never had to live here.

They turned right and sped north on the freeway. To the left, the City's skyscrapers gleamed in the afternoon sun.

After another half-hour, they turned on to the major road that led all the way to the City's northern limits.

She stared at Ivan's neck. The heat and warmth of his body on hers during those early days of physical training – she missed it. When would she get a chance to touch him again? Her head grew light as she descended into another fantasy . . .

The skin on the back of his neck was warm as she ran her fingers through his hair. He grabbed her with one arm and yanked her around so she was facing him and pulled her close. His stubble rubbed against her neck, leaving a red glow on her skin. Then, he tilted his head and started kissing her . . .

'Grace!' Joe was looking at her.

She jolted. 'What!' With a grimace, she glanced at the mirror, where Ivan was watching her. Was there a glint of something in his eyes? Could he tell? Her hand flew up to her neck as a flush ran across her face.

'Look!' Joe pointed to the right as they turned on to a side street. 'Our house.'

Two family cars now sat in the driveway. The lawn was obsessively trimmed; trendy wooden blinds hung in the window. Two bikes lay on the grass; a fresh white letterbox sat on the lawn's edge.

'Sorry,' Ivan said. 'I was following the satnav.' He looked at Grace in the mirror again. 'I did not realise we would go past your old home.'

'It's okay,' Grace whispered. The same images came to mind – pictures of that final, awful night that moving three hundred kilometres away couldn't erase. But seeing the house made them even more raw, more visceral. She turned away as drips of rain hit the windscreen.

Sarah gave her a sympathetic smile.

A few minutes later, Ivan slowed the car. 'We're here.'

They pulled over at the edge of a crossroad. 'The brown duplex,' Ivan said. 'With the grey roller-door.' He unbuckled his seat belt. 'They're in the garage.'

A boy was standing across the road from the house. He peered around before pressing something into another boy's hand. The first boy was the taller of the two and his hoodie covered his face. He nodded; the second boy walked away.

Then the first boy turned and looked in their direction.

'Uh oh,' Sarah said.

Grace gripped the driver's headrest. 'Hang on . . . I know him!'

Joe squinted. 'Who is he?'

'Jesse Tyler!'

'Put him off, Grace,' Ivan said sharply. 'We don't need any unwanted attention.'

Grace stared at the boy's forehead, pummelling him with go-away messages. *Nobody's here. The car is empty.* The boy stared for another few seconds, then he shrugged and turned in the direction of the duplex.

'Good girl,' Ivan said. He nodded in the rear-view mirror as the jeep pulled up behind. 'Okay. Our back-up's here but they're not getting out of the car unless I signal them.'

'Jesse's got a terrible family life,' said Grace. She closed her eyes, flinching at the memory of tapping into his mind, feeling the burn of the belt as his father lashed him.

When she opened her eyes, everyone was looking at her. Joe frowned. 'You're not feeling sorry for him, are you?'

'Perhaps he can be turned around.'

Malcolm made a hissing sound. 'Don't be stupid!'

'Grace.' Ivan tapped the touchscreen. 'Here's his rap sheet. Want to know how many violent crimes he's committed?'

She shrugged. 'I just know that he's had it rough.'

'Tough. He's a target. You just saw him dealing to a child!' Ivan tapped the touchscreen again. 'Scanning for infra-red.' An image of the garage appeared, lit up in fluorescence. Ivan pointed to the pink shapes, moving around the building. 'Our targets. Five of them, as we predicted – including your friend.'

He looked at Grace. 'So, what are your orders?'

'Mask our presence continually.'

'That's right. And why must you do that?'

'There'll be less resistance that way.'

'That's all you need to do.' He gave her a hard stare until she nodded.

'Joe, you open a rift in the middle of the room. We will get them inside. That way there's no confusion. Grace, once more: what are your orders?'

'Masking our presence from the second we leave the car.'

'And?'

'Nothing else.'

'Good. Let's move.'

Ivan led the group. Sarah was next; Malcolm trailed behind Grace and Joe. All armed with harpoon shotguns, all creeping on their toes along the spookily quiet street.

Grace drew a long breath, her heart thumping as they crossed the road. From a distance she focused on the garage, sending ripples of telepathic energy into the place. *Nobody is here. The street is empty.*

Ivan looked back. 'Are you going to be able to handle this boy, Grace?'

She nodded.

Ivan yanked up the roller-door; Grace doubled her concentration.

It was a small room – a false front – another roller-door separated them from the inner sanctum.

The boy turned around with a start, but broke into a mocking smile. 'Grace Callahan. Back for some more, eh?' His demonic Shadow looked thicker, murkier than before. 'You must be one of them bitches that like a bit of rough.'

Grace breathed out, relieved. The masking had worked – Jesse Tyler had no idea that four mercenaries were standing next to her. Couldn't see them or hear them.

Oh, but she could feel the demons. The nausea burned its way up her throat, bile forced up by her clenching stomach. Cold fingers seemed to be pressing on her spine. It appeared as though her reaction to demonic energy was getting stronger, more intense.

She swallowed hard and stared at Jesse.

'Grace, why have you revealed yourself?' Ivan looked at Sarah. 'Sanderson, give her some cover.'

'I can't,' said Sarah with a strained voice. 'She's blocking me.' She pressed her hand to her forehead. 'Grace, stop it!'

But Grace raised her hand. 'Look, Jesse. I know that you're dealing. But you don't have to do any of that. I can help you.'

Joe groaned. 'Oh, Grace!'

Inside, the demon Travis Tyler was sitting at a table, playing cards with the others. He glanced across at the security monitor, where his little brother was talking to some chick. He watched for a few seconds and then turned back to his cards.

Malcolm ground his teeth. 'I knew this would happen!' He eyed Jesse through his gun sight. 'I'll just take him out now.'

'You stand firm, Penbury,' Ivan said.

Jesse spat on the ground near Grace's feet. 'You think I'm *unhappy?*'

Grace held her ground. 'Surely you are! But I can help you. Or you'll have to accept what happens. You're in trouble, Jesse.'

Frost began to spread down his legs, pooling around his feet and crawling across the concrete.

Ivan stepped closer to her. 'You didn't read his rap sheet, Grace. Burglary, aggravated assault – oh, one of his victims was an eighty-one-year-old woman. Do you want me to go on? People have tried to rehabilitate him. He's rejected it every time! He wants to do evil!'

Sarah watched the frost climb up the walls. 'Uh, guys, we'd better do something – quick!'

Jesse smirked at Grace. 'I like my life. I like what I do. Nobody can stop me.'

'I will, Jesse.'

'Ha!' He whipped a knife from his pocket and plunged towards her, the blade cutting through the air.

Grace stumbled away. She broke concentration; Jesse's mouth fell open as four people appeared out of nowhere.

'Travis!' A gang member pointed to the TV monitor. 'Company!'

The gang jumped to their feet, smashing over the table, spilling cola all over the playing cards. In their haste none of them saw the rift forming in the front room.

'Back-up!' Ivan shouted. The other mercenaries flew out of the jeep and pounded down the street.

Joe's eyes were deep in concentration.

Ivan ran forward and kicked Jesse in the stomach. The knife fell as the boy stumbled backwards, vanishing inside the rift.

With panicked breaths, Joe closed it.

For a moment there was silence.

Ivan stepped in front of Grace, gun trained on the roller-door. It hurled upwards, and in the gap stood five men, pointing their guns.

Grace felt her eyes drawn to Travis, who was watching her with a furious scowl, teeth bared, eyes enraged. His anger seemed to animate his Shadow – it looked to be tearing off his skin, trying to grab at her.

A torrent of bullets flew through the air.

Grace caught her breath and closed her eyes, waiting for the impact.

Joe shot up his arms – and a bigger rift exploded, swallowing the bullets, consuming the demons, leaving them standing in the middle of something that they couldn't comprehend.

A wind came.

It converged in the centre of the rift with a devastating boom, a clash of light and sound – and in a rush of thunder the demons were gone.

Too fast. The lightning subsided into small slivers once more. Inside, the rift resembled a low-level tornado. Then it vanished. Joe slumped, arms hanging forward; exhaustion weighing his limbs down.

Ivan looked at the ceiling. Only the back wall was left standing. The two side walls had collapsed, leaving jagged columns of brick at either side.

The roof was gone.

'Run!' He grabbed Grace's arm and pulled her towards the street. A deafening boom sounded; a dust cloud erupted. Ivan's fingers were still pressed into Grace's arm as the group formed a loose circle on the other side of the street. They watched the dust subside in shock.

'God,' said Joe.

The ground was blasted out, leaving a crater where the garage had stood.

'I did this,' Joe whispered.

Ivan released Grace's arm. He nodded at Sarah. 'See to those neighbours.'

Sarah turned and swept a look around the surrounding homes. People rushed out to the street and gathered in herds. Some clustered together in gossip groups; others shot curious looks at the strangers standing opposite the wreckage.

No looks of sympathy. No tears.

'They must have blown themselves up.'

'They were cooking drugs . . .'

'Couldn't have happened to nicer people,' said one man. 'Good riddance!'

'Shut up!' his wife hissed. 'They have friends around here, you know!'

Taking a deep breath, Sarah blanketed their minds with a calming direction. *Go inside. A gas leak. Nothing exciting.* Calm restored, the people turned and went back into their houses.

Ivan dialled Diana's number. 'Hi. Yes, all done. A bit messy, though.' He grinned. 'To be expected, I guess. We will need full demolition as soon as they can get here. The neighbours are under control, but someone will need to do a follow-up. Yes. We're on our way back now.'

Ivan pocketed the phone. 'Let's move.' As the other mercenaries headed off, he grabbed Grace's arm. 'Not you. I need a word with you.'

Malcolm was last to go; he shot an approving glance back, nodding. 'Give her the boot, Ivan.'

Ivan's voice was hard, his eyes cold. 'You deserve a reprimand, Grace. You just went ahead and did what you wanted to do. Again, you were arrogant.'

Grace fought the urge to shrink away. She lifted her chin in a small show of defiance. 'We were lucky,' Ivan added. 'That boy wasn't highly gifted. If he had been telepathic or very fast, we could have been looking at a very different outcome.'

'But . . . everything worked out, didn't it?'

'You disobeyed my orders and put your team at risk.'

'I'm sorry,' she whispered.

'No. This is your last chance. If you do this again, I'm kicking you off my squad.'

She gasped. 'People make mistakes!'

'Three strikes, and you're gone.'

She flinched at his heartless tone. 'That first time doesn't count! That was training!'

'You've been warned, Grace.' Ivan released her arm and headed towards the car. Grace ran to catch up with him, her eyes pleading. 'What if he could have been helped? He was forced into this life by his brothers —'

Ivan stopped and turned to her. 'Stop it! Stop thinking! It's not your place to think! You were told at the start that this is what we do! If you can't follow instructions, you have no future in this job.' Shaking his head, he walked away.

NINETEEN

Joe rested his head against the pillow, watching the trees swaying outside his window. It had been a silent, shocked trip home; his mind consumed by the devastation he'd just brought to that house, to those demons.

He had no idea . . . no idea at all.

He rolled over onto his side and turned his thoughts to more pleasing matters. Running his fingers along Haures's cheek and the softness he would find there. Winding her silky hair around his fingertips, pulling her face close to his and tasting the sweetness of her lips . . .

Something buzzed on the bedside table. Jolted, he rummaged around until his fingers landed on a small, cold shape.

Sitting up, he pressed the phone to his ear. 'Ah . . . hello?'

'Good evening, Joe. This is Mammon Jones.'

Joe sat up. 'Hi!' He ran his fingers through his hair. 'Ah – how are things?'

'We're going on a mission tonight. Would you like to come along?'

'Sure! Definitely!'

'I'll give you directions for a place to meet. Wait there for my car, and I'll fill you in then.'

TWENTY

GULPING WATER, GRACE cringed as pain sliced through her throat. Diana was perched on the edge of her bed. She reached over and pressed her hand to Grace's forehead. 'You're quite warm, dear. You should put on your pyjamas – the fabric will breathe better.'

Grace fell back on her pillow. 'I can't be bothered.' She struggled to draw a deep breath. Her lungs felt as if they were full of sawdust. 'Hope it's not the flu.'

Diana held out two painkillers and watched Grace take another mouthful of water. 'It's just a bad cold. Get some sleep and you'll feel better.'

'Thanks.'

With a mounting sense of loneliness, Grace watched her aunt leave the room. She was not going to feel better. Ivan hated her.

A few minutes later, a thump sounded at the door. Joe flew in. 'Grace!'

'What is it?' She sat up, wide-eyed.

'I need your help.'

'With what?'

Joe held up Mammon's phone. 'They called me.'

'Who?'

'Those mercenaries. From the festival? Remember, Absinthe Girl?'

'Ugh.' Grace lay back on the pillow. 'Don't mention that. I don't want to think about that night.'

'They've invited me to go on a mission with them. I want to, but I need you to sneak me out of here.'

'No.'

'Grace, come on!'

'Why? We just came back from a mission. You really made an impact there. Isn't that enough?' She coughed and took a drink of water. 'I feel like death warmed up. Anyway, I don't want to do that to Brutus again. You don't know what it's like when someone messes with your mind.'

'I really want to go.'

She studied his face, noting the pink flush around his neck and chin, the feverish glint in his eyes. '*Oh.* I know why you're so desperate.'

'Look – if we swapped places, and you wanted to go and see Ivan, I'd help you.'

Her smile dropped. 'What makes you think I'd want to see *him*?'

Joe sighed. 'Grace. It's obvious!'

'Not to him!' Cringing, she shook her head. She hoped he hadn't noticed. Especially now . . .

'Look – if you help me, I won't say anything to him.'

A horrified expression crossed her face. 'You would do that?'

He shrugged. 'The guy has a right to know, doesn't he?'

She narrowed her eyes. 'That's blackmail, Joe.'

'Just help me get out.' He glanced at the wall clock. 'It's half-six now. I'll try to get back by midnight.'

Sighing, she got out of bed, shuffling into her slippers and robe. 'Just this time, Joe. And never again.'

* * *

TEN MINUTES LATER, a firm knock sounded on her bedroom door. Grace jumped. She'd only just sat down on the bed. Her slippers were covered in wet grass. Panicked, she shook them off. Surely they hadn't noticed he'd gone.

To be safe this time, she'd put Brutus into a trance at a distance, rather than waiting until they were under his nose. 'Remember, back by midnight!' Joe had given her a thumbs-up as he ran through the Renfield gates and into the darkness.

Grace looked at the door. 'Who is it?'

Ivan poked his head in. 'May I come in?'

'Sure.' Apprehensively, she watched him cross the room carrying a bowl and spoon. 'What's that?'

'A remedy.' Ivan reached past her, sending a tingle across her skin as his hand brushed her arm. He placed a pillow in her lap and lifted the bowl onto the pillow.

She watched him, bemused. 'Aren't you mad at me?'

Ivan handed her the spoon. 'I was too hard on you earlier. I don't like losing my temper. I just don't want anyone to get hurt under my command. Especially you.'

215

Her heart began to pound. He trapped her with his eyes; liquid warmth again, the way they were when she'd fallen from the tree and looked up to see him leaning over her.

'May I sit down?'

'Sure.' Grace slid sideways to make room. She felt comforted by the welcome weight of his body as he sat, the way he rested his leg close to hers.

She took a deep breath, inhaling the spices. 'Yummy,' she breathed. 'I like tomato soup.'

'It's Borscht. Traditional Russian recipe.'

She glanced up and smiled at his proud expression. 'You made it?'

'Yes. It's about the only thing I know how to cook well.' He smiled in a matter-of-fact way.

She couldn't help but grin. 'You're a strange guy. I mean, in a good way. Not many guys I know would bring me soup like this.'

'It's my mother's fault.' He laughed. 'She made me this way.' He watched her take a spoonful.

'You don't like it.'

'No, I do. It just feels like I'm swallowing razor blades. It's yummy, honest.' She took a rattling breath. 'Did your mum teach you to cook?'

'Yes.'

'Do you see her often?'

'She lives in London with my sister.'

'Oh. That's a shame. Do you ever visit them?'

He shook his head. 'Not lately.'

'What about your dad?'

'He was murdered.'

Grace's eyes dropped. 'I'm sorry.' She took another mouthful of soup.

'Don't be.' He gave her a quizzical look. 'It is not your fault.'

She shrugged. 'It's a way of saying I feel sad for what has happened to you. Sorry is shorter and easier – I guess.' She reached across for her water bottle. 'Whoops.' She froze as soup tipped over the edge of the bowl, staining the pillow.

'Here.' Ivan passed her the bottle, his fingers brushing against hers. 'My father was a university professor in Moscow. I had a privileged life. Private tutoring, lots of travelling. By the time I was six I could speak fluent English – better than most adults. Everything was going well until my uncle was murdered. A journalist – he was investigating government corruption.'

'They killed him because of that?'

'They killed him because, along with my father, he was a member of a dissident organisation that held regular protests against the government. They were becoming too powerful, and the authorities couldn't have that. To them, my uncle was dangerous. He had charisma and the ability to charm people. In their paranoia, they thought he would overthrow their government and take power.' He chuckled, shaking his head.

'Surely the people knew what was going on?'

His face grew serious. 'Yes – but the government pro-paganda made sure people saw my uncle as a madman. They didn't just murder him, they assassinated his character.'

'And your dad?' Dread filled her as she imagined what he would say.

'After the police linked him to my uncle's dissident activities, they went after him.'

'Couldn't he have found protection – from someone in power?'

He smiled, watching her bring the spoon to her mouth. 'This wasn't the West, Grace. They came in the night, when he was working late, and shot him at his desk.'

Grace watched his face. He didn't falter, his voice didn't tremble. She guessed it was several years ago.

'Mother, Tatiana – that's my sister – and I moved out to the country. Then I joined Spetsnaz.'

'This might sound strange, but you don't seem like the military type. Not totally.' Her gaze dropped. She could feel his eyes burning into her.

'That's the first time anyone's said that to me.'

'Okay, so maybe I'm thinking of the stereotype.' She ran the spoon along the bottom of the bowl. 'But you seem different, somehow.'

'Well, I never intended to enter the army. I joined Spetsnaz because someone I trusted lied to me about who murdered my father. I killed innocent men because I thought they were linked to his murder.' His eyes drifted to the window. 'I still carry the guilt.'

'That's it! That's what makes you special.'

He looked over. 'What's that?'

'You have a conscience. You didn't like what you had to do in the special forces.'

'Mmm.' He shrugged. 'Perhaps. I would have left eventually, but finding out that this so-called ally of my father's was a demon certainly sped up the process.'

Grace's voice tightened. 'He had your father killed.'

'He betrayed me.'

'Did you —?'

'Yes. I killed him. How ironic for him: the training he helped me acquire in turn enabled me to destroy him.' He laughed — a bitter, sharp sound.

'When was this?' Grace scooped up the last of the soup.

'Three years ago. I'd just turned eighteen when the Sight developed.'

She put the spoon down. 'Was that when you killed —?'

He nodded. 'A Level Twenty-two? Yes.'

'Wow.'

'I know it sounds glorious, but I don't really feel any pride over it. I would rather relinquish the Sight and have my father back.'

Grace pictured Mum and Dad, climbing up the basement ladder. Their dead hands . . .

'How do you get over it?' Her bottom lip trembled.

'Time.' He sighed. 'And distractions.'

She fought the urge to lean over and stroke his hair.

She wished he would reach across and touch hers.

'I feel a bit better now. The soup was great.' She passed him the bowl; he placed it on the table. 'Good.'

She loved his smile. Uplifting, like a sunbeam on a cloudy day. 'You don't have to go, do you? I don't feel like staying in bed alone.'

Ivan raised an eyebrow.

'I didn't mean it to sound like that!' She felt her cheeks grow hot.

He stood up. 'You do need to rest.'

'The soup and painkillers have helped.' She didn't want him to go.

Ivan glanced around the room. 'Ah.' He bent down to pick up Grace's violin. 'You play music.'

She nodded.

'So do I.'

'What instrument?'

'Balalaika.'

'I've never heard one.'

'Well, then – want to come for a walk?' Ivan slung the case over his shoulder and reached out his hand. Grace took it and slid out of bed. She threw on a hoodie, slid her feet into her slippers and followed him along the corridor, then up a flight of stairs. Below were the sounds of cutlery crashing against plates as hungry recruits stormed the dining room.

'Ratatouille is on the menu tonight,' Ivan said with a grimace. 'Not very nice. You can tell Joe that you had some real Russian soup. Better than the slop he'll be eating right now.'

'Ah . . . yeah,' she muttered, scratching her neck.

Ivan pushed open a light green set of double doors. 'This is the senior wing,' he said.

'These rooms are huge!'

'You should get an upgrade in a few months.' Ivan pushed open his door. 'After you.' Grace stepped inside; Ivan walked past and pulled the curtains open.

'Welcome to my humble home.' Ivan crossed the room and pulled open his wardrobe door.

'Wow. Awesome view!' Grace gazed across to the cliffs, where the moonlight shone on the top of the rocky towers. Her gaze dropped to a bookshelf next to the window. Some authors she recognised from Lit class: Tolstoy, Dostoevsky and the playwright Chekhov. Above his bed hung a large Russian flag.

She turned to see Ivan standing close to her. In his arms was a black-lacquered instrument that resembled a guitar but with a triangular shape to the body.

'That's really nice.'

He nodded. 'It was my father's. I thought we might play together, Grace. You wouldn't happen to know any Russian music?'

'Um . . . Tchaikovsky?'

'No folk songs?'

'Only Irish.' A sudden twinge of guilt. All those times she'd whinged at Dad for putting on 'Danny Boy'.

Ivan began to strum. 'This is *troika*,' he said. 'Why don't you try to play along with me?'

Grace watched his fingers moving. 'Do you have the sheet music?'

'No.' His eyes were misty with a faraway look. 'I learned this by heart when I was a small child. Can you play by ear?'

'I can try.' She took her violin from her case. 'You're good,' she added, watching his fingers move.

'Thank you.'

She sat down and began to tighten the bow. Her eyes flickered back to the bookshelf, where a large, silver photograph frame held a prominent position. A tall blonde woman stood, her hand resting on an armchair where a moustached man sat. Both wore stern expressions, but there was a gentleness in the mother's eyes. Grace pointed to the boy in the picture, who was obviously trying to emulate his father's look. 'Little Ivan,' she said.

He shrugged. 'I don't remember that photo being taken.'

'You were a sweet little boy.' She ran rosin along the bow. 'I don't know what happened.' She grinned.

Ivan smiled but kept strumming. 'The picture on the right is my younger sister Tatiana, with her English boyfriend.' His voice sounded tight.

Grace placed her bow across the strings, positioning her head into the violin's chin rest. 'You don't like him?'

'I don't know the guy. But I've had good cause in the past to dislike her boyfriends.'

Grace tilted her head and listened as Ivan played a few more bars. She began to slide the bow across the strings and eventually settled into a steady rhythm.

Ivan nodded. 'Good. You play well, Grace.'

'Thanks.'

'I'll teach you some Russian, you can teach me some Irish. Then we'll blow them all away next time there's a party.'

TWENTY-ONE

JOE RAN ALONG the forest edge, his calves aching. Where were they? His eyes darted along the road, desperate to catch a glimpse of a vehicle.

Then, a pair of lights beamed in his direction. Haures leaned out of the back window. 'Here, Joe!' She pushed open the door and he slid into the back seat next to her. Andras hit the accelerator and the car sped towards the highway.

'Hi.' Haures slid over so she was nestled against him. She looked even more beautiful tonight, her blonde hair tied back so her curls cascaded down her back, her curves nicely wrapped in a black t-shirt and jeans.

'Hi.' He took her face in his hands and kissed her. 'I missed you.'

'I missed you more,' she whispered.

He looked at Mammon, who was sitting in the front passenger seat. 'What's the mission?'

'I'll tell you everything when we get to the apartment.' He raised his hand. 'Don't worry! It won't be a long, dull briefing. Just a chance to get our weapons, run through our plans and hit them hard.'

As they cruised onto the highway, Joe sat back and pulled Haures close to him. They stared at the roadside trees and their ghostlike trunks, lit up by the headlights then subsiding into the darkness. The car gained speed and the trees became one long, pale blur.

* * *

THEY PULLED INTO a car park deep below the City towers. Andras swiped a card; the lift doors opened.

Mammon's voice echoed from behind. 'I think, after this, Joe would like to spend some time on the yacht.'

Joe smiled and squeezed Haures's waist. 'Sure, why not?'

Andras grinned. 'You haven't seen his yacht. You'd be saying a hell of a lot more then.'

The lift doors opened. They walked into a spacious corridor, where silver marble columns shimmered under ultra-modern candelabra. Giant white beams separated Japanese-style ceiling windows and a gold-lined staircase sat at the corridor's end. Haures led Joe towards the stairs. 'This way.'

'Whoa.' Joe whistled. 'Nice.'

'This whole floor is ours,' Haures said. 'Mammon has parties here sometimes. Last time we decorated it as a winter wonderland.' She nuzzled Joe's neck. 'I wore an ice bikini.'

He smiled. 'What happened when it melted?'

She giggled. 'That's for me to know and you to find out.' They climbed the stairs and Haures pushed open the apartment door.

In the entrance hall, an illuminated wall fountain oozed gentle streams of water; its frosted glass background featured a wolf's head. The entire floor was beige marble, except the dark, polished wood surrounding the oversized fireplace. Purple neon highlighted the wall behind the bar, where several rows of expensive drinks sat in meticulous order. A long cream sofa took up the centre of the room, where Andromalius and Zagan sat. A ninety-degree floor-to-ceiling window looked over the cityscape and river beyond.

Joe shook his head, grinning. 'You're ridiculously rich.'

Mammon smiled. 'Is that a compliment?' He touched his chest with a mock look of hurt. 'I do try to help those in need, Joe. I've been looking for someone to head up my foundation. A young person with drive, energy – and most importantly, compassion.'

'You want to talk to Grace, then. She's the one with the bleeding heart.' Joe stretched his arms and yawned. 'No, don't get me wrong. I could get used to this.'

'Let's have a drink,' said Haures.

Mammon wagged his finger. 'We're working, young lady.'

Andromalius entered a security code and flung open a large cupboard door. He pulled out a shotgun.

'Whoa.' Joe took a step back. 'You've got more guns than Renfield.'

'That can't be true,' Mammon said.

'Well,' Joe shrugged. 'More than I've been allowed to see, anyway.'

'Still keeping you on a tight leash?' Mammon sighed. 'Have you been on any real missions yet?'

'Yeah! Today, actually. Some drug dealers . . . in the suburbs.' He looked around for their reactions. Mammon and Andras wore matching smirks; Zagan shook his head. Andromalius pulled out a box of bullets and scoffed. 'Sounds *real* exciting.'

Only Haures gave him an encouraging smile. 'That's better than nothing, I guess.'

'What'd they give you?' Andromalius began loading the shotgun.

'Huh?' Joe watched the cartridges slide into the magazine.

'Weapons-wise.'

'Oh – a combined taser/neurotoxin gun.'

'No live rounds?'

'Oh, yeah. Of course.' Joe lifted his chin. 'I don't really need them, though. I've got something better.'

'What's that?' Mammon raised an eyebrow.

Joe took a seat at the table and knocked on the wood. 'Put something in the middle here and I'll show you. Something you don't care about losing.' He sat back in his chair and waited.

Mammon leaned on his table, eyes glinting with anticipation. 'Your watch, Zagan.'

The young demon scowled. 'Do I have to?'

Mammon looked at him.

With a hiss, Zagan threw his watch on to the table. 'Feel like I've just been screwed in a poker game,' he muttered.

Joe lifted his palms – and concentrated.

Haures gasped, staring at the small cloud that appeared on the tabletop. 'What *is* that?'

'Have to be careful,' Joe said, holding his hands steady. 'It'll damage your table.' He relaxed, and the rift vanished – along with Zagan's watch.

The others exchanged glances. 'Impressive!' Mammon said.

'Imagine what I can do to demons,' Joe said. 'Not that I have to imagine. I did that today. Left one hell of a mess, though.' He scratched his head.

'Who cares?' said Mammon. 'That's amazing.'

'You're something else, Joe.' Haures leaned on her chin and stared at him.

Joe sat back in his chair, basking. 'Yeah. It's a pretty cool gift. But I haven't really taken it out for a spin yet – if you know what I mean.'

'Well, you'll get your chance tonight.' Mammon sat down. 'I'm going to get straight to the point here, Joe. It's taken us a few weeks, but we've found the demons who killed your parents.'

Joe went pale. 'What?'

'We're going to take them down tonight,' said Andras.

'Let's go now!' said Joe. Tense-faced, he jumped up.

Mammon smiled. 'Good. Keep hold of that anger, Joe. Maintain the rage. Trust me, it'll help you.' He looked around the group. 'Let's do it.'

'We can go on foot,' Andras said. 'The target is only a few streets away.' He pointed to the weapons cupboard. 'Choose your gun, Joe. May I suggest the Magnum?'

Joe strapped on a holster and took the gun from Andras. 'Awesome.'

'Not that you'll really need it, after what you just showed us.' Mammon clapped Joe on the shoulder and led him towards the lifts.

* * *

THEY MOVED THROUGH the entertainment district, where paper lanterns hung in golden symmetry, casting a sultry glow. Purple, red and blue lights shone along the pavement in alternating streaks. Low storm clouds combined with the stench of cigarettes, rotting food and beer brought a trapping humidity to the air.

Joe rubbed his sleeve over his forehead. He sighed, relieved at the sudden jet of cool air from a restaurant door. People jostled past him, chasing, hunting – fuelled by an unseen energy that prickled at their skin, filling them with a primal frustration.

But the high demon moved among the pack with the calmness of a veteran gamekeeper.

They wandered past a sports bar, where country tunes blasted through the doors and bouncers stood against yellow walls streaked in neon light. Working girls dotted the pavement, all flesh and enticing stares.

One girl turned towards Joe and gave him a seductive flick of her long pale hair. His eyes ran over her body: from the black leather skirt barely skimming her backside to the face slathered in make-up, and the large, unfocused eyes.

He felt nauseous. How old was she? For a second, he imagined Grace standing there, selling her body . . . the idea was simply too much. A powerful urge to protect this girl kicked in.

'Hi,' she said, stumbling towards him in a lofty pair of red shiny heels that matched her elastic top. Joe lunged forward and grabbed her by the elbows. 'You okay?' Gently, he released her.

From the shadows a man emerged, grabbed the girl's arm and pushed her towards Joe. 'Oi! No walking away, sunshine. You touch it, you buy it.'

Joe wrinkled his nose: the man stank of stale tobacco, sweat and one too many shots of whisky.

Mammon turned to the pimp. 'He's not interested. This is immoral, anyway! You ought to be arrested.' He looked the man over with a disgusted frown.

The pimp scowled. 'Not your problem, mate. He touched her, he pays. Or you can pay.' He shrugged. 'I'm not particular.'

Mammon stared at him. And in those dark, shimmering eyes, the pimp saw something. The promise of danger – no, worse. A room with no doors in a dark place. For millennia.

The pimp swallowed and wiped a strand of hair away from his forehead. 'Okay, okay.' He lifted his hands in defence, releasing the girl's arm and blending into the shadows.

A frown passed over Joe's face.

Haures squeezed his arm. 'What's wrong?'

'I'm surprised, that's all. I thought that guy would be a demon for sure.'

Andras shook his head. 'Most demons use humans for their more mundane jobs.'

They turned a corner, into a darker road where rows of cottages lent an unexpected suburban aspect to the otherwise seedy surrounds.

'In here.' They took shelter in a lane.

'Now, listen carefully. There are six guys in there – all demons. You go in and open a rift straight away. We'll back you up.'

Joe shrugged. 'Okay.' He held up his hand as the others began to move. 'I have to be careful with this. I don't want to take out any other buildings.'

'You won't!' Mammon thumped Joe's back. 'You're in control, Joe.'

They moved on to a darkened step, where light poured through a stained-glass circle on a dark front door. Joe peered sideways – a random thought about the neat state of the gardens flashing through his mind – and then Andromalius pushed the door open.

Calmly, they walked inside.

TWENTY-TWO

'YOU'RE A GOD, Joe!' Mammon lifted a champagne glass in a toast. 'Nothing I've ever seen comes close to what you did tonight.'

'Thanks.' Joe leaned back on the sofa, a cold drink nestled in his hand. Haures curled her legs up next to him, her hand resting on his thigh. He reflected on the past hour – the surprised look of the occupants in that gloomy little cottage – the last gasp squeezed from their lips before the rift consumed them.

All too easy.

The flash and boom of gunfire behind him. Unexpected. He hadn't seen the shooting take place – his eyes were pinned on his rift, in the middle of the house. The deep, rich satisfaction of the kill was pulsing through his veins.

He frowned. But the gunfire . . . That wasn't part of the plan. He looked at Mammon. 'Who were the other people in the house? I didn't expect to see them there.'

Mammon put down his glass. He sat back and gave Joe a long look. 'Does it matter?'

'They weren't demons. Why did you have to shoot them?'

'They were still involved in your parents' murders, Joe. We did our research carefully.' Mammon leaned forward, stroking his fingers on the cool wood of the coffee table. 'Now, if Renfield had been involved, they would've let those humans go. Or, worse, given them to the police. You'd have no satisfaction there. And as for the demons? Apprehended, taken to Renfield for questioning . . .'

He sighed. 'They would have lived on, only a stone's throw from where you sleep. Taunting you by sucking air when you could have seen them dead. Would you have preferred that?'

'No.'

'I didn't think so.' Mammon stood up. 'See how we do things, Joe? Imagine what we could achieve together. You've just executed six deserving criminals, in the way that only you can. Flawless.' He slid his hands into his pockets, jingling his coins.

'It did feel good.' Joe cast a triumphant look around the group. 'Real good!'

'Mmm,' Mammon nodded. 'I can see it in your eyes.' They could all see it – the red glow that lingered in his eyes; the mark of the Ferryman who'd begun to give himself over to his dark power.

'Tonight, you've crossed into a new world, Joe. And it can only get better.'

'Halphas!' Andras waved the empty bottle.

Joe watched as an old man shuffled in with a tray. 'Would you like another champagne, sir?'

'No,' Joe said.

'Well. Shall we?' Mammon looked at Joe. 'To the yacht?'

Haures squeezed Joe's hands. 'Yes! Come on!'

'I can't.' Joe looked at the clock near the bar. 'I have to get back.'

'Aw!' Haures pouted. She slumped back in the sofa.

Joe gave her an apologetic smile. He took her hand and stroked it. 'I promised my sister I'd come back by twelve. She helped me sneak out tonight.' He looked up and was met with a round of curious stares. 'She's telepathic.'

'Really?' Mammon gave Andromalius a meaningful look. 'Mind-reader?'

'No. But she can make people think what she wants them to think.'

'Interesting,' Mammon said. 'We can recruit her, too. I'm sure she's frustrated by the control that Renfield imposes on her.'

Smiling, Joe shook his head. 'Only if she can bring Ivan with her, and I don't think that's going to happen.'

Haures stared into Joe's eyes. 'I really want to see you again.'

'Me too.' He stroked her cheek.

'How about tomorrow night? We'll come and pick you up again.' She looked up at Mammon. 'Is that okay, boss?'

'Definitely. Joe, you can leave Renfield tomorrow night and join us for good. We'll celebrate with a little cruise up the coast.'

Joe nodded. 'I'd love to.'

'Good.' Mammon nodded at Andras, who stood waiting near the door, dangling car keys from his fingers.

Mammon shook Joe's hand. 'Until tomorrow night, then.'

233

TWENTY-THREE

GRACE OPENED ONE eye, squinted at the clock and rolled over.

Three firm knocks sounded.

'I'm asleep,' she groaned. 'Go away!'

Joe poked his head in. 'It's just me.'

'What do you *want*?' She pressed her face into the pillow.

'I need to talk to you about last night.' He sat down on the armchair and ran his fingers through his hair.

Grimacing, Grace sat up. She fumbled for a tissue. Her sinuses felt packed with concrete; her throat with sandpaper. 'It's eleven-thirty,' said Joe, 'I'm surprised Ivan hasn't dragged you out for training.'

'Training's over, numbnuts.' She ignored his provocative grin and took a sip of water. 'Anyway, I was out saving you from trouble in the middle of the night. I'm tired!'

Joe had a gleam in his eye. 'Mammon has asked us to join his team.'

Grace blinked. 'Us?'

He shrugged. 'I told him you wouldn't go unless a certain Russian came along too.'

'That's never going to happen.' Grace swung her legs over the edge of the bed. 'What did you say?' With a yawn, she scanned the room for her bathrobe.

'I told them I was interested.'

'Because of that girl?'

'Not just that. They seem very . . . effective.'

'How would you know that?' Grace pulled on her robe and slid her feet into her slippers.

Joe's eyes glimmered. 'Last night we killed the guys who murdered Mum and Dad.'

Grace froze halfway through tying her robe. 'You did what?'

'It was them! Mammon tracked them down.' Joe drew a deep, excited breath.

Grace sank on to the bed, her face pale. 'Sarah and Seth have been trying for ages. Now you tell me Mammon found them overnight?'

'Not overnight, Grace. It took them about a month.'

'Yet, Sarah said there were no clues out there, whatsoever. They'd pretty much stopped searching.'

Bemused, Grace stared at the golden weave on her bedspread. That was it. They were gone. She ran her finger over the pattern. 'I don't know what to say.'

'Aren't you happy I got them?'

Grace looked up. Joe's face was twisted in anger, disappointment and contempt all at once.

'Don't look at me like that! Yeah. Of course I'm happy. I just didn't expect it to be this way.'

For a few moments they sat quietly, then Grace gave Joe a piercing look. 'Did you know you were going on that particular job when you left here last night?'

'They didn't tell me until we got to the City.'

'So why didn't you call me?' Grace jumped up with an incredulous glare. 'I could've come up! Didn't it occur to you that I'd want to see the bastards?'

'I didn't want you getting hurt.'

'No, you just wanted to control everything.'

He watched her head for the door. 'Where are you going?'

'To get some breakfast. You can tell Ivan about last night; spread the good news.'

'No.' He jumped up.

She frowned. 'Why not?'

'I don't want them to know. I just want us to leave here, Grace. Tonight.' He stood in the doorway, blocking her exit.

'I'm not going, Joe.' She tried to push past him, but he grabbed her arm.

'Grace! Please think about it.'

'No.' She struggled.

'Wait.' He squeezed her arm. 'I didn't mean to hurt your feelings. I just wanted to avenge Mum and Dad. I felt like it was my place to do it.' He stared away, into the expanse of the hallway.

She regarded him. His face was so childlike, so open. A wave of compassion hit her. Last night, just before he'd vanished out of the gate, she'd noticed that his eyes were shining red. She'd written it off as a reflection, a trick of the eyes. But now – the glow was even more pronounced.

'Your eyes are very red, Joe.'

He shrugged. 'I'm tired. Big night last night.' He raised his eyebrows. 'So? We all good, then?'

'Yeah,' she mumbled. 'We're good.'

Joe trudged away, towards the recreation room. Grace followed at a distance, her mind consumed by his revelations.

* * *

IVAN AND SARAH were making orange juice in the kitchenette. Seth was camped on the sofa, staring at his computer; Malcolm sat flicking through TV channels.

Ivan looked up from the counter. 'Ah, Joe. Good morning.'

'Hi.'

Grace padded across to the counter. She gave Ivan a smile. 'Hello.'

'Good morning,' said Ivan. He glanced at her rabbit slippers and matching bunny pyjamas. Smiling, he passed her a glass of juice.

Despite her worry, she felt a warm, tingling glow, starting from her toes and culminating in a bubbly feeling in her stomach. He was using that voice again, that deep, soft tone that was just for her. She let her eyes wander, taking in the stubble on his chin and the way his eyes twinkled under the kitchen lights.

'Are you feeling better?'

Grace shook her head. 'But the juice is nice.' She took a sip and leaned across the counter, watching Ivan cut orange halves and pass them to Sarah, who pressed them into the machine.

'Oh, that reminds me.' Sarah turned away from the bench and reached into a drawer. 'Here, I got these for you.' She passed Grace a white box of tablets. 'Cold and flu. They should help.'

'Thanks. That's really nice of you.' Grace slid the box into her pocket.

Joe swept past the counter, heading for the fridge.

'Morning,' said Sarah in a half-whisper. She gave him a shy look.

'Hi,' he said, without a glance.

Sarah's eyes clouded over. She bit her lip as she crushed another orange half.

Joe yanked a can of cola from the fridge and crashed on the sofa, kicking his feet up on to the table. His eyes wandered to the TV, where a blonde reporter was standing in front of a house. She looked like a bit like Haures – same hair, great body . . . He imagined touching her locks, feeling the soft waves give under his fingers. Absentmindedly, he watched images of police, clad in blue overalls, moving about behind the reporter.

Then it struck him. Oh no.

The reporter was standing in front of the cottage from last night.

'Residents of the inner-city suburb of Mettham are in shock this morning after eight people were found shot dead in a local backpacker hostel. Nearly all of the victims were exchange students who attended nearby Eastside Technical College.'

Sarah gasped. 'Exchange students. They come here because it's a safe place to visit, and this happens!'

'There is speculation that the shootings were linked to the Northern Raiders motorcycle club, whose members frequently stayed at the hostel. However, none of the victims have been identified as club members. Northern Raiders founder Mike Eberts cannot be contacted for comment. Eberts was recently acquitted on armed robbery charges, fuelling speculation that the murders were not an act of revenge, but a tragic case of mistaken identity.'

Joe stared at the image of the biker. He remembered his face from last night as he sent him to his death. But why did the students have to die? Surely they wouldn't talk . . . who would believe a story about a giant cloud that swallowed people alive?

Ivan put down the knife. 'How strange.'

Grace looked at him. 'What?'

'Eberts was on our hit list. Hobbs's team was scheduled to go up there tomorrow night.' He walked across to the sofa and leaned on the headrest. 'I wonder if another outfit beat us to it?'

A chill spread across the back of Joe's neck. He jumped up. 'Anyone want to play?' Hands shaking, he began to sort the pool balls into formation.

A sick feeling spread across Grace's chest as she watched Joe fumble with the billiard balls.

That was them! The people you killed!

He shot her a warning look. 'Leave it alone,' he whispered.

The reporter continued. *'Police have released a CCTV video, which shows what they believe to be the group behind the killings as they approach the scene.'*

Joe froze. Grace shot a look at the others. What would the others do if Joe's face came up on screen?

'However, due to the poor quality of the images, police do not hold up much hope that they will assist in identifying the suspects.'

Joe breathed out.

He remembered an old saying of Dad's: Sometimes the innocent have to be sacrificed for the greater good. It wasn't his fault.

He didn't pull the trigger.

He replaced the triangle over the hook and looked across at Ivan. 'Game?'

'Sure.' Ivan stood up and picked up a cue. He chalked the tip, took aim and broke. A coloured ball rebounded off the pocket and swung back into the middle.

Grace walked away from the counter and stood near the door. 'Joe, I need a word.'

'Later, Grace.'

Yes, now, or I'll keep rattling inside your head. We need to talk, Joe!

With a growl, Joe threw down the pool cue. 'Give me a minute, Ivan.' He stalked out to the corridor where Grace waited. 'What?'

'I'm going to ask you straight,' she whispered. 'Was that them?'

'Do you really think I would murder innocent people?'

'No.'

'So, you shouldn't have any questions for me.' His eyes flashed with anger as he turned back towards the room.

'Wait!' She grabbed his sleeve. 'I'm not accusing you of anything.' She watched him closely. 'But you *can* talk to me, Joe.'

'I don't know anything about those people! Now back off, Grace!'

Trembling, Grace watched him walk back to the pool table. He picked up the cue and took a shot.

Sarah caught her eye. 'Grace, how about we have a DVD marathon today? We don't have any jobs on, do we, boss?'

Ivan shook his head. 'Nothing as yet.'

Grace sniffed, fumbling in her pocket for a tissue. 'Sounds good. Just let me go have a shower first.' As she moved towards the bathroom, a great burden of worry settled on her shoulders, filling her with dread, and she knew it wouldn't shift until she found out the truth about last night.

Sarah waited until Grace had left the room and then sidled up next to Joe. 'I've organised a surprise for your sister. A belated birthday party. Tonight.' She leaned over the pool table and gave him her sweetest smile.

Joe watched Ivan take his shot. 'Oh, yeah.' He shrugged. 'Sounds all right.'

Sarah caught her breath. 'Oh.' Red-faced, she looked down. 'I just need you and Ivan to start the bonfire –'

'What time?'

'Sundown.' Sarah gave him a quizzical look. 'Why, got other plans?'

Joe shook his head. 'Nothing you need to worry about. Sure, I'll help Ivan start the fire.' He pushed the pool cue in front of her. 'Excuse me. You're in my way, and I need to take my shot.'

* * *

As the credits for the third movie crawled up the screen, Grace watched the late afternoon shadows start to move across the window. She drew a long breath through her nose. The burn in her throat had disappeared; her head felt lighter. The tablets had done their work.

She glanced across at Sarah. Her friend's jaw was tight. She'd been fidgeting with the hem of her jumper the whole time and gazing out of the window at regular intervals. Grace did a quick scan around the now-abandoned rec room; the guys had gone off to play football on the oval a while ago.

She looked back at Sarah. 'Are you okay? I . . . feel as if something's not right.'

Sarah lifted her chin and breathed deeply. 'Does your brother . . .?' She sighed and hung her head. 'Never mind.'

Grace curled her legs up into her chest and rested her head on her arms. 'What's wrong?' She examined Sarah's lowered head.

'Nothing,' Sarah muttered, her cheeks aflame. 'It's just – maybe I got my signals mixed up. He seemed so friendly but now he's gone cold.'

'Oh.' Grace could feel it, hear it in Sarah's voice: the pain of unrequited love. 'I'm sorry. I think you and Joe would be great together.'

Sarah pulled together a smile. 'I don't know if he thinks that.'

'Sarah –'

'I don't really want to talk about it, Grace.'

'Okay.' Grace uncurled her legs and sat forward. She took a sip of water and was relieved to find that the liquid slid down without any pain. 'Thanks again for those tablets. They worked really well.'

'It was all part of the plan.'

Frowning, Grace watched her friend stand up. She cocked her head. 'What plan?'

'Come with me if you want to find out.' Sarah thrust out her hand.

'O-kay.' Smiling and frowning at the same time, Grace let Sarah help her up from the sofa. Her mind racing, she followed her friend down the hallway. 'What's going on?'

They stopped outside Sarah's room.

Grace bit her lip. 'Tell me what's happening!'

Sarah opened the door. With a mock frown, she waggled her finger. 'Patience!' She slid her arm up the wall, flicked on the light and stepped inside. 'Come in, but close your eyes.'

'Oh, come on!'

'Just close your eyes!'

Grace shut her eyes and sighed.

With a flourish, Sarah pushed opened the wardrobe door. 'Ta da!'

Grace's eyes flew open. 'What's that?'

'For you.'

Grace grinned and ran her fingers along an emerald-green halter top, which shimmered in the light. Silky, smooth and cool to the touch. Behind it was a pair of dark denim jeans – a row of rhinestone studs lined the pockets. A pair of silver wedges were tucked next to Sarah's sneakers and boots.

'And for the finishing touches . . .' Sarah held up a pair of diamante drop earrings. 'They're mine, but you can borrow them for the night.'

'They're gorgeous.' Grace took the jewels between her fingers. The light shimmered off the stones, revealing an intricate flower pattern. She lay them on the dressing table. 'But where are we going?'

Sarah winked. 'You'll see. Now let's get your hair and make-up done.' She bent down and slid a pink box out from beneath the dressing table.

'My make-up case!' said Grace.

'Yes,' Sarah admitted with a guilty smile. 'I had Joe go and get it for me. He was reluctant, but . . .' She sighed. 'He did it for you.'

Grace turned towards the door, finger raised. 'Well, he forgot the most important thing – my straightener.'

'No, don't iron your hair. It looks nice with the curls.'

Grace threw Sarah a sour look. 'No it doesn't.'

Sarah picked up a hairbrush. 'Yes, it does! And I'm not the only one who thinks so. Now, let's get started.'

TWENTY-FOUR

THIRTY MINUTES LATER, Grace followed Sarah out into the courtyard, where the evening gloom had settled into a silvery fog. 'Where are we going?'

'For a little walk.'

'It's so cold!'

Sarah gestured to the forest. 'Not for long. Come on.'

Grace followed Sarah along the misty path. 'Ooh!' A droplet spilled from a low branch on to her shoulder, leaving a cool trail down her back.

'Careful here. It's muddy.'

Grace rubbed her upper arms. Goosebumps had spread across the flesh, making her shiver. 'Seriously, where are we going, Sarah? We're nearly at the oval!'

'Stop here. Close your eyes.'

'Not again! Sarah –'

'Close them.' Grinning, Sarah pressed her hands over her friend's eyelids. She led her friend through a fringe of trees. Grace felt a surge of heat and –

'Open your eyes!'

The light hit Grace's face first, a blend of hot reds, yellows and purple. In the middle of the oval, a lively bonfire was sending small sparks into the air.

'Happy birthday!'

A crowd of happy faces greeted her. Everyone waved sparklers in the air, making patterns against the black night like golden snakes, whirling and circling.

Joe gave her a kiss. 'Didn't think we'd forget, did you, sis? Shame on you.'

Grace stared at Joe's face. His hair was dishevelled, his eyes seemed wild. 'You okay?'

'Yeah. Why wouldn't I be?' He walked away – an overconfident swagger that irritated her.

Seth leaned down and kissed Grace's cheek. 'Many happy returns.' He pressed a small felt bag into her hand. 'I could have given you something to represent my mother's side of the family, but then I imagine you would get lots of Western-style presents.' He grinned. 'This is a traditional gift from my father's side instead.'

'Thank you!' She fished into the bag and drew out a pair of gold earrings shaped like two golden tubes with a dark sphere at the bottom of each.

'Oh. They're lovely! So unusual.'

'From Nigeria,' Seth said.

'Thanks, Seth.' She gave him a hug and watched him walk away, merging into the crowd of strangers who were celebrating her coming of age. She had no idea about Seth's background. In fact, Grace barely knew anyone here, except Ivan and Sarah.

'My lovely niece.' Diana clasped Grace's shoulders. 'Happy birthday, sweetheart. Your mum and dad would've been so proud of you.'

'Thanks.'

'We old fogies are going to leave you alone. Behave, now.'

The music grew louder, filling the air with a primal drumbeat. Grace savoured the bonfire's warmth on her bare arms.

Then, there he was. Moving towards her with that strong, confident walk. Looking amazing in a deep blue t-shirt and black pants – the first time she'd seen him in civilian clothes.

Ivan's eyes locked on hers; she felt paralysed, unable to look anywhere else. Her heart began to beat harder as he stopped in front of her. His gaze flickered all over her body; she couldn't mistake the gleam in his eyes.

He shook his head. 'You look very beautiful.' He reached into his pocket, drawing out a small velvet box. 'Happy birthday.'

She lifted the lid. Tucked among small frills of red satin was a gold ring. Its top was flat and round – with a pale blue stone in its centre.

'Oh, wow.'

'It's a moonstone.'

Grace stared at the ring. It caught the firelight, revealing flecks of white throughout the stone. He touched the ring to her fingertip and held it there. With a smooth movement, he slid the ring onto her right ring finger. His gaze swept over her face and dropped to her neckline before flickering back up to meet her eyes.

She shook her head. 'I can't believe you would give me this.'

His eyes dug into her, searching. 'Why?'

She could only smile.

Ivan reached down and took her hand, leading her towards the bonfire. The beat slowed down as a love song started. He slid his hands around her waist, and she responded by looping hers around his neck.

She gasped as he lifted her off her feet so that she was looking down at him. Gently, he whirled her around until they'd turned full circle. She caught her breath, stunned. He lowered her, touching her body against his as her feet touched the ground.

'I didn't expect that.' She giggled as he lifted her again.

He looked up, holding her in the air.

'You're really strong,' she whispered.

Ivan just smiled, spun her around again, then lowered her so her feet were on top of his. His mouth enticed her, just within reach of her own lips. He pulled her to him and moved her slowly, swaying to the rhythm.

He rested his head against hers. Her heart pounded at the feel of his hands pressing her close against his chest.

* * *

IN THE KITCHEN, Maya grabbed a bottle and poured another messy glass. She closed her eyes and swallowed the shot, then she slammed the glass onto the benchtop. Her chest ached with grief at a sudden memory that forced itself into her consciousness like an unwelcome guest. Their last anniversary, when they'd spent the night drinking, dancing, holding each other.

There would be no more dancing. Her future had been stolen; she faced a life without the husband Armin would have been or the children they would have shared. In her watery vision she could make out the candle-like glow of the bonfire – its fiery peaks glowing over the treetops. 'To hell with this,' she whispered. She slid off the bar stool and stumbled out of the rec room.

* * *

GRACE SLID HER fingers to the nape of Ivan's neck, the rough edge of his hairline. The silken fabric of her top clung to her skin, warmed by his hands. She looked up; he returned the stare, running his gaze over the flush in her cheeks, her eyes twinkling in the golden light.

He cupped her face in his hands. This was it. He was finally going to kiss her.

But she gasped. Something was wrong. She saw a vivid picture of Joe's face, his eyes blazing with anger.

Ivan pulled back. 'What's the matter?'

Grace threw erratic glances around the crowd. 'Where's Joe?'

'What is it?' Ivan took her shoulders. 'Look at me, Grace.'

'Something's going to happen!'

'What?'

'I don't *know* what! Just something to do with Joe!'

Ivan took her hand and led her through the crowd. 'Come on. We'll find him.'

* * *

MALCOLM WAS HOVERING at the edge of the crowd, watching with a tight jaw and sullen eyes when Maya stalked past. 'Hey!' He grabbed her arm.

Grimacing, she jerked away from him. 'Leave me alone, Malcolm.'

'You nearly fell over then.'

'I said, leave me alone!'

The song ended, in the sudden quiet all ears turned to the drunken girl. Maya stood, her back stiff, her eyes fiery. 'Why do you bother me so much, Malcolm?'

He sighed. 'Why do you think?'

Her head wobbled back and forth – finally her eyes glinted with understanding. 'You?' She made a humphing sound. 'You can't love *me*!' She raised her finger and jabbed it into his chest. 'You're *nothing* compared to Armin!'

'Maya, Armin's gone.'

She gasped. 'Don't you say that!' She ripped her hands free and smacked his face. Malcolm staggered back, his eyes wide, shocked at the sudden sting on his cheek.

Maya gave him a cruel grin. 'Get lost, loser.'

'You hurtful bitch!' Malcolm grabbed the girl by the collar and dragged her back to him. He whirled her around and landed a sharp slap across her cheek. She fell to her knees, whimpering.

'Oh, God! Maya, I'm so sorry!' Malcolm reached down to help her up. Another hand clamped down on his forearm. He looked up; Joe glared at him, a red, violent glow in his eyes. 'Leave her alone, Penbury.'

'Shut the hell up, Joe.' Malcolm straightened his back and scowled at Joe. 'You've got some cheek stepping in here. You weren't there to help Armin. It's your fault he's dead.'

'Bullshit.'

Sarah dropped to her knees and put her arm around the sobbing Maya. She shook her head. 'That's not fair, Malcolm.'

'No-one asked you, Sarah.' Malcolm curled his fingers into fists.

Joe shook his head. 'Don't even try it, arsehole.'

Grace appeared at Joe's side. She touched his arm – his eyes were blisteringly red. He didn't acknowledge her but just stared at Malcolm; a murderous gaze.

'What's going on here?' Ivan said. He took a look at Maya and then nodded to a group of recruits. 'Johnson, Anderson – take Maya to her room.'

Grace peered into Joe's eyes. 'You okay?'

With a regretful frown, Malcolm watched the recruits lead Maya towards the Residence. He turned and pressed his finger into Joe's chest. 'It's about time you and I had it out.'

Ivan stepped between them. 'Penbury, go to your room, now.'

Malcolm smirked. 'You can't make me leave. Anyway, Ivan, why don't you tell Grace the truth?' He smiled at Grace's confused expression. 'Aw, it's tragic. Ivan's job is to keep you happy, so you don't cause any problems with their precious Ferryman. After all, Joe's the one they want. He's the one with the special power. They don't give a hoot about you, and neither does Ivan.'

Grace looked at Ivan. 'Is that true?' Her voice trembled.

'Of course not.' Ivan gave Malcolm a warning glare. 'He's just had too much to drink.'

'Not a drop, actually.'

Grace bit her nail as the nagging doubt developed, bringing a sick feeling to her stomach.

'You're just pissed off with the world, Penbury,' said Joe. 'What's the matter? Can't win Daddy's approval?'

Malcolm lunged forward and punched Joe in the face. Joe staggered back but recovered.

Ivan stepped between them. 'Enough!'

Joe dodged around Ivan. He seized Malcolm by the sleeves and smashed him with a headbutt.

Malcolm fell on his backside, his hands pressed against his forehead. His vision was dizzy, but he could still see Callahan's eye and the sliver of blood oozing from the rapidly forming bruise. 'Whatever problems I've got with my dad, at least I can be proud of him. Unlike you.'

Joe blinked. 'What the hell did you say?'

Malcolm looked up with a fierce grin. 'I know all about your father. Everyone knows. Daniel Callahan was a coward who ran away from his responsibilities.'

Instantly, a swirling rift materialised. This wasn't like the cloudy sphere Joe usually opened. This was an angry rift, borne of his fury and his sheer will to punish. Screeching and roaring, with angry clouds and erratic streaks of lightning flashing out from the core.

Ivan shot his arm out to protect Grace.

She lunged forward, struggling against his grip. 'What are you doing, Joe?'

In unison, the crowd surged back; all eyes locked on the rift and its magnetic pull, against which Malcolm was struggling. He was too close. Petrified, he watched as his pendant disappeared inside the cloud. He could feel his hair standing on end, his clothes beginning to tear away from his body.

Joe grabbed a tuft of Malcolm's hair and dragged him forward.

'Don't!' Grace screamed.

Malcolm went head-first into the rift. He struggled, digging his heels into the cold earth. His howls sent a chill up Grace's spine. The crowd watched in silent horror as his arms and legs twitched, as though an electric current was surging through him.

Inside the rift, Malcolm thought he saw something coming at him. He blinked – in the height of his panic, Malcolm's inner voice spoke: it's just a trick of the eyes.

But the lightning exploded again, and he saw dark shapes flying towards him.

They were Shadows. Racing for the rift opening. Racing to get out.

The first of them drew close and pressed an icy finger to Malcolm's forehead. The finger slid up and over the crown of his head, leaving a cold trail across his flesh. The finger began to burrow at the back of his skull. Frozen, Malcolm felt a dark energy start to push into him the way a sperm forces itself into an egg – taking his body, possessing him.

He screamed.

Ivan ran forward and grabbed Joe's arms. He yanked him backwards with an almighty wrench, also pulling Malcolm away in the process.

The rift dissolved into wispy ribbons of grey. After the monstrous noise, the air was ghostly quiet – except for Joe's deep breathing.

And Malcolm's twisted moans. He pulled his legs close to his chest. Tears gushed down his face as he began to rock backward and forward. 'A Shadow . . . grabbing at me . . . trying to take me over.' His eyes began a wild dance, to and fro. 'It was going to possess me.'

TWENTY-FIVE

RED-FACED, JOE STARED at Malcolm, who was cowering on the grass. 'Don't you ever talk about my father again.' With a brief look at Grace, he turned and headed towards the Residence.

Grace shivered, watching a group of mercenaries help Malcolm to his feet. What had he seen in there?

A few minutes later Diana arrived. 'Take Malcolm to sick bay.' She glanced around the crowd. 'What happened, exactly?'

A volley of voices responded. 'He was wasted. Stupid moron. Can't hold his drink.'

'No, he wasn't drunk. Well, maybe love-drunk.' Laughter rippled through the air.

Ivan took Grace's hand and slid his fingers under her chin, lifting it until she was looking at him. 'Nothing Malcolm said is true.' He kissed her cheek.

'Okay.' She gave him a weak smile.

He squeezed her hands and then turned to follow the medics, who carried the delirious Malcolm towards the sick bay.

* * *

JOE SCREECHED OUT on to the highway, his heart still pounding. He should have relished this, his first drive of the Mustang. The soft give of the leather seats, the responsiveness of the engine should have filled him with earthly joy.

He reached into his pocket and pulled out Mammon's phone. Behind him, Renfield's alarms must have been screaming. He chuckled, remembering Brutus's face at the guardhouse.

'Open the gate.'

The guard had given him an incredulous smirk. 'Oh, no, you don't. You need permission to leave.'

Joe had opened a small rift in the palm of his hand. 'I can make this grow to the size of a mountain in under a second. I'll throw you and all the other guards inside. Open the gate.'

Mammon answered the phone. 'On your way, Joe?'

'Where can I meet you? No, not your apartment – I'm in their car, and they'll track it. I don't want them coming after me.'

'Head to Southport. We'll meet you at Pier Twelve.'

'Okay.' Joe put down the phone and sped up.

* * *

GRACE WALKED ACROSS the driveway and towards the external doors of the Residence, where warm light flooded across the gravel.

Sarah touched her arm. 'Are you okay?'

'Not really. Things just seem to be getting worse.' Grace sighed. 'I can't believe what Malcolm said.'

'I wouldn't listen to him. He's a jerk.'

'It's awful, what happened.'

'It wasn't Joe's fault,' said Sarah. 'Malcolm shouldn't have provoked him like that.'

Excited voices murmured behind them. 'What a nut job! He should be put away for that.'

'I wouldn't trust him on a mission. What a friggin' temper!'

'Shut up!' Grace turned around and gave them an angry stare.

'Come on, Grace.' Sarah led her into the courtyard. The fountain released microsprays of water into the air, wetting the leaves of the olive trees that bordered the square. Grace slid on to a bench; Sarah took the seat opposite her.

'I don't know what's come over Joe,' said Grace. 'He's not himself.'

'He seems – arrogant.'

'He's always been a bit like that. But yeah, now more than usual. He thinks he's invincible.' Grace chewed on her nail. 'But he's still my brother. I don't want anything to happen to him.'

Sarah leaned her elbows on her knees, staring at the pavers. 'I know how you feel, you know.'

'Huh?'

'When people say bad things about someone you love.' Sarah looked up. 'I never told you that I have a sister.'

'I didn't know that.'

'She's telepathic too,' said Sarah. 'But she went wrong. Lucius and Diana say that she lost control of her power. Two mercenaries were killed . . . but it was an accident.'

Grace clicked her fingers. 'I get it! She was the one Maya was talking about.'

Sarah nodded. 'They love to badmouth her. But they wouldn't have dared when she was at her strongest. She was really gifted, like you.' She reached up and pulled a leaf from an overhanging olive branch.

She began to tear the leaf into rough strips. 'I saw how badly she struggled to control her mind. I wanted to keep her here, to help her. But *he* put her away. His own stepdaughter!'

'Marcus? Where did he put her?'

'Where do you think?' Sarah nodded in the direction of the asylum.

Grace gasped. 'But they keep demons there!'

'Yes, they do.'

Grace shivered. A human in that place! She pictured Joe in there, struggling against chains, mad-eyed. A bolt of adrenaline raced up her spine. 'Sarah! How can you be here like this, while your sister is stuck in there?'

Sarah flinched. 'Don't you judge me, Grace!'

'I'm sorry.'

'I tried so hard to do something. They wouldn't let me see her. I hung around that godforsaken place for hours. The guards came out and tried to bully me, but I held on. Eventually, Marcus threatened to throw me out of here if I didn't back off.'

Grace narrowed her eyes. 'When you told me you attacked someone here, you meant him.'

'I hit him with a telepathic assault,' Sarah said. 'He was beating her up. It drove me crazy.' She reached into her pocket and pulled out a small pill box. 'That's why I take these meds.'

'We could try to see her again. Lucius might let us –'

Sarah shook her head. 'No, Grace. It's too late. She's gone.'

'What do you mean?'

'I had to come off the meds a few days ago to help you with that mission.'

'And?'

Sarah shoved the box back into her pocket. 'The pills are inhibitors. They cut off my telepathy, stopping me from sensing things. When I first met you and told you that I couldn't read minds – well, that was a lie. I can. And the reason why I was upset on the mission was because I could sense Anna again. I could read her thoughts. And it was that day I realised she's not the Anna I know. Not anymore.'

She gave Grace a hard stare. 'When I said she was *gone*, I meant that she has degenerated.'

Grace's heart pounded. 'Oh, no. Not . . .'

'I've lost her, Grace. She's become one of *them*.'

TWENTY-SIX

JOE STEPPED OUT of the car and stared up at the dark blue boat – no, *ship* that floated off the pier, its great spotlight beaming over the harbour. 'No way.' He shook his head. 'That can't be it.'

Then he saw Haures's golden hair, whipping in the wind. 'Over here, Joe!' She waved to him from the gangway. He jogged across; she gasped as he drew near. 'Your eye!'

He jumped up on to the gangway, stopping just before her. Swooping down, he planted a long kiss on her mouth. 'It's nothing.'

She reached up and ran her finger over the bruise. 'Did you get into a fight?'

'It's over now.' He pulled her to him and they walked up the gangway. The crew were a flurry of white, casting away the ropes as the engine thundered to life, sending rippling vibrations along the walkway.

Haures led him towards the glass elevator in the main

cabin. After a few smooth seconds the doors opened on to a vast, luxurious sitting room. The wood-panelled ceiling was dotted with down lights, bringing out the subtle detail in the cream leather sofas and laying a soft glint on a giant, glass coffee table. On the far side, a mirrored wall set off rows of top-shelf liquor with sparkling detail; red leather bar stools were tucked under the bar's solid frame. The night lights of Border City twinkled through the giant windows that lined the room. Beyond, the dark seas lay in wait.

Joe shook his head. 'Unbelievable.'

'There's also a cinema, spa, gym and billiard room.'

'This is bigger than my old house!'

She ran circles around his shirt with her fingertip. 'The only room you really need to see is the bedroom.' She lifted her gaze; the look was soft but suggestive.

Joe's heart quickened.

'Ah, Joe!' Mammon slapped him on the shoulder. 'Fabulous to see you. Let's celebrate.' He sank onto the sofa and threw Halphas a glance. 'Drinks.'

Joe sat down, pulling Haures next to him. 'I'll have a Corona.'

'Diet Coke.' Haures stroked Joe's leg. Her eyes flickered up to his. Joe leaned over and pushed her hair aside, baring her neck. 'You were saying about the bedroom?' He pressed his mouth against her skin, tasting her, his imagination wandering . . .

Mammon watched with a smile.

The old servant appeared with a tray. 'Here you are, sir.' He smiled, handed Joe the beer, then hobbled across and lay a glass of whisky in front of his master.

'So.' Mammon's fingers tapped the leather. 'I gather that you are ready to join us?'

'Yeah. But I want my sister brought here.'

'Of course. Naturally.' Mammon took a sip of whisky. 'We will see to that tomorrow morning. We can even dock near Renfield, to make it faster.'

He swallowed the rest of the whisky; the old man refilled his glass.

Joe watched Mammon take his drink. Nervously, he ran his fingers over the edge of the sofa. 'About last night.'

'Yes?'

'We killed innocent people.'

Mammon leaned forward. 'Yes.'

Joe stared at him. 'That's all you have to say?'

'It comes with the job.'

'But . . . I feel guilty.'

'Who do you think you are, Joe? An ordinary mercenary? Or something greater?'

Joe shrugged. 'I don't feel as though I fit in with the others.'

Mammon snapped his fingers. 'Exactly! You're not the same. Whether or not you want to admit it, Joe, you are a destroyer. Your job is not to create or nurture. It's to do the job most people out there find distasteful. They'd rather hide behind their white picket fences.' He sat back and stroked the soft leather, savouring its texture. 'Ever seen *A Few Good Men*?'

'Yeah. My dad used to like it.' Joe pictured Dad, sitting in the recliner with a beer, rattling off the film's memorable lines.

Sadness welled in his gut.

Mammon narrowed his eyes; his voice intense. 'Remember the scene where Jack Nicholson is under cross-examination in court? What he says to defend his difficult but necessary role?'

'Yeah.' Joe took a gulp of beer.

'We need you on that wall, Joe. And part of being the vigilant defender – which is basically what *sarsareh* means – is to make tough choices. Unavoidably, we must sacrifice the innocent for the greater good.'

'Yeah,' Joe sighed. 'I guess you're right.'

Mammon clasped his hands and leaned forward. 'I know I am. But the good news is we won't need to do that in future. We can spare the innocent from further tragedies.'

'Why is that?'

'We believe that this fight will be over much faster if we use fire to fight fire.' He leaned forward, eyes glittering. 'You know we don't mess about, don't you?'

Joe nodded.

'Have you ever wondered where the demonic energy originates?'

'I know where it comes from.'

'Do you really? You've been taught that human beings just manifest the demonic energy, haven't you? That they *grow* it?' With smiling eyes, he pressed his hand to his lips as though to suppress a laugh. 'That's a very basic theory.'

He raised a finger. 'Let me fill you in on the truth. The energy doesn't just materialise out of thin air. These people summon it – subconsciously, of course. It attaches itself; it merges with the human to become one being. Perfect symbiosis, in many cases. So, where do you think the energy comes from?'

'Hell,' whispered Haures.

Mammon pressed his palms together. 'Imagine if you could open a rift and bring through the demonic energy in far greater quantities. Then, destroy it! That would put a stop to the dark entities that are seeping in. That way, we're cleaning house on a universal level – not just planet Earth.'

Joe nodded. 'That sounds like an awesome idea.' A chance to alleviate his guilt, to make amends for the innocent lives taken last night. He finished his drink and set the bottle down on the table. 'I would definitely be in.'

Mammon smiled. 'Excellent. Why don't we do it tonight? Wake up to a new world tomorrow.'

Joe shook his head. 'I'm a bit tired. It takes a lot of energy, you know.' His gaze turned to the smooth skin on Haures's shoulders and neck, her lips, full and sweet. *Energy I'd much rather use somewhere else*, he thought to himself.

'Fine.' Mammon leaned back and spread his arms on the sofa's headrest. 'Get some rest and we'll talk in the morning.' He gave Haures a sharp nod.

She stood up and reached down for Joe's hand. 'Come on. Let's go for a walk.'

* * *

As MAMMON WATCHED Joe walk out on to the deck, he felt a stirring at the back of his head – his essence was burning to get out and kick this boy around the room – to make him obey immediately. But, no. Slowly, gently. He was too close to frighten Joe off now.

* * *

IT WAS NEARLY two am when Haures stopped outside the guest cabin. Gently, she pressed her lips against Joe's mouth.

'Goodnight, then.'

Joe pouted. 'What – you're leaving me alone?'

She pinched his cheek. 'You need to rest for tomorrow. It's not every day that you save the world.'

Joe pulled her close, his hands caressing her back, his forehead pressed against hers. 'I want you,' he whispered.

She touched his lips with her fingertip. 'The feeling's mutual. Tell you what – we'll go away tomorrow night. Just the two of us. Mammon will want to reward you. Did you know that he has a private island in the Caribbean?'

'Sounds great,' Joe smiled.

'So . . .' Haures pulled her finger away. 'Sleep tight, and tomorrow night we'll be in our own bed.'

Joe tilted his head. 'You promise?'

She nodded and ran her finger down her chest, lingering between her breasts. 'You'll be well rewarded, Joe.'

'Okay.' He kissed her again, then he turned towards his cabin.

* * *

JOE FELT HIS body begin to relax and his limbs grow numb as sleep approached. As he drifted towards dreaming, a low voice was speaking in the distance – far away, as though it were in another room on Mammon's yacht.

Then, in the dark, a tiny white dot appeared. It grew into a shimmering circle of light. Strange, he didn't usually see stuff just as he was about to go to sleep . . .

The voice grew louder. 'Joe, wake up.'

He opened his eyes. The room was soaked in the light, but his eyes didn't sting. His pulse shot up as he realised: the light was a rift.

A figure stepped out of the white fog. 'Hello, Joe.'

Joe squinted. 'Who are you?' The man looked as though he was wearing some kind of robe . . . but the light flooded out so much detail. A sweet, burning scent came – like the incense candles that Mum used to buy.

'My name is Utu. I thought we could have a little walk.'

Joe breathed out, blinking. Of all the weird stuff that had been happening . . . But a resounding sense of calm seemed to overcome him. 'Okay.' He glanced out the window; nobody out there seemed to have noticed. Then again, it certainly was more gentle than the hellhole he'd shoved Malcolm's head into a few hours before. He grimaced as he remembered the boy's horrified face.

Utu turned towards the rift. 'You can enter.'

Joe paused. 'Are you sure?'

'You have nothing to fear, Ferryman.'

As Joe stepped inside, the insides were awash with the same landscapes he recognised in his own rifts: the grey, lightning-flecked clouds.

He heard a rush of wind.

Something was coming.

He could hear a tearing, screeching howl; could see several blurs of white coming at him like arrows – he closed his eyes in terror.

Then, silence.

'It's all right, Joe.' Utu's hand was warm on his arm.

Joe opened his eyes. The bony monster – no, make that

monsters – were suspended in the air around him. He counted at least twenty; they hung there, calm, quiet – even obedient – their monstrous, hollow eyes fixed on nothing in particular; those teeth not snapping. Just hanging . . . waiting.

'They're yours to control, Joe. Remember?'

'What are they?'

'Reavers. See the lightning?' Utu pointed to the surrounding clouds. 'It is a lot further away than you think. That lightning is actually the Reavers, travelling at high speed through the infinite space of the rift.'

'What are they?'

'Guardians of the rift. Consider them antibodies, whose purpose is to clean out any foreign bodies in here.'

'But *we* survive?'

'We're Ferrymen, Joe.' Utu gestured ahead, and a stone path appeared with calm water on each side. 'Shall we?'

TWENTY-SEVEN

GRACE WOKE AT dawn – the shafts of gloomy light peering through the curtains hit her face, dragging her from her dreamworld. She peeled apart her crusty eyelashes and rolled onto her side, hugging the pillow closer. A crushing depression hit as her mind replayed last night's drama.

Despite Ivan's reassurances something ached inside. Those things Malcolm had said . . . they sounded all too true – the bosses did want Joe, and by raining gifts on him, promoting him and feeding his ego, they'd shown where their priorities lay. She could just imagine Marcus sitting there, Malcolm at his side, discussing with Ivan the importance of her seduction. And all the while, he was probably seeing that girl, Stephanie. Or if not her, someone else.

Ivan probably didn't even care about Grace at all; he was told to make her happy. She stared at the window as new spatters of rain fell, blurring the outside into a mass of green, grey and white. Warm tears spilled from her eyes. She curled up into a ball and choked out a sob, her stomach contracting with the knifing pain at the thought that he'd betrayed her; and worse, the idea of a future without him.

* * *

JOE'S EYES SNAPPED open. He sat up, mouth open, eyes wide as he stared around his surroundings.

He was back at Renfield.

A memory poked through his mind – the last thing he recalled was standing on the deck, saying goodnight to Haures outside the guestroom. Then, as if floodgates had been smashed open, the whole memory spilled through.

The boat.

The blinding light.

Utu.

'I went into a rift last night.'

His hand flew up to his eye: no tenderness there. Catching his face in the mirror, he nodded in confirmation. The bruise was gone. Somehow it had healed while he was away.

He looked down – and saw that he was wearing a new amulet. He cradled it in his fingers, staring. It gave off a warm light and a calming energy. The chain was silver, and the amulet itself was a blue stone, inside which lay a small circle of wood.

Chunks of memories – things he had thought happened in a dream – began to come together as a reality. The old man – Utu – had given him this amulet. 'It will give you powerful protection against demons – far more than the pendant your father gave you.'

And then, he remembered the whole discussion.

The truth about Mammon.

The truth about himself – and how close he came. He shuddered. He needed to find the others.

Joe jumped out of bed, put on his jeans and t-shirt, then headed towards Grace's room.

TWENTY-EIGHT

'To hell with this.' Grace was tired of her thoughts going around in circles. It was time to find out for sure. Marching along the corridor, she ignored the groans from neighbouring rooms as she pounded the door. 'Ivan! Open up!'

He pulled the door open and gave her an alarmed once-over. 'Grace?' He peered at the dark circles under her eyes. 'Are you okay?'

'Why did you lie to me?'

He took her arm and pulled her into the room, kicking the door shut behind him. 'Malcolm is the liar, not me.'

How much Grace wanted to believe that! 'You knew I played the violin. You pretended it was a surprise when you saw it in my room.'

'That's not true. I didn't know.'

'What else did you know about me? Did you do your research? Find out you everything you'd need to know, so

271

that you could pretend to be interested? Fake being my friend, and –' The tears began to well; she forced them back.

He held her by the arms; she wrenched away. 'Don't. I don't want you to touch me.'

'Then why did you come here?' The calm in his voice irritated and unnerved her.

'Nothing I have said or done, none of it was a lie,' he said.

'I don't know. You could be lying to me right now.'

His eyes fell on the moonstone. 'I gave you the ring.'

She looked up. 'So?'

'My father gave that ring to my mother.' He held her hand, stroking her fingers. 'I wouldn't give it to just anybody.'

'What about that girl, Stephanie?' She bowed her head, squeezing her eyes until the tears would disappear.

Ivan cupped her chin, lifting it. The warmth sent a longing pain through her; the feeling was so close, just like last night.

His words were a whisper that caressed her face. 'I don't care for her. But I don't want to hurt her feelings. It's my fault; I should have told her.' He sighed. 'Yes, they wanted me to keep you happy. But I did that of my own free will. Not because they told me to, but because I care for you so much.'

She blinked. 'You do?'

He stroked her cheek with his forefinger. 'I like you more than you could ever know. I've wanted to be with you from the first day we met. When you looked up at me, after falling out of that tree, I had to restrain myself from pulling you into my arms.'

She blushed and lowered her head again. He slid his finger

under her chin and lifted her face to his. His eyes burned into her; she felt her legs quiver.

'With each step you've taken, with each day that's come to pass, I've grown to care about you even more.' He caressed her cheek.

Grace stared at him, tilting her head so her cheek rested in his palm. The anger was melting away now, and that warm feeling was spreading through her body. She knew she had a stupid, puppy-dog look on her face.

'Sometimes, when I've been angry with you about how you've handled a situation it's because I was so afraid that you would be taken from me,' Ivan said. 'I could not stand it.'

'You won't lose me,' she whispered. Her heart was pounding now.

Ivan slid his other hand around her waist and pulled her close, pressing her against him. She tilted her head back to look up at him. He bent his face towards hers, touching his lips to hers very gently at first. He pulled back for a moment, and she lost herself in the soft affection in his eyes.

Then he kissed her again – more deeply this time, his mouth warm and comforting, the pressure just right, his tongue poised at the edge of her mouth but just tickling, never pushing. His hand stroked her back in gentle circles. She slid her fingers behind his neck and caressed his hair. A longing for more flooded her, and she followed her instinct, pulling him closer, her mouth giving him a little more room, her tongue teasing his.

A sharp knock jolted them both. She groaned. Ivan rested his forehead against hers. 'What timing.' She blushed under his heated stare.

With a smile, he planted a tender kiss on her fingers before letting go.

'This had better be important.' Ivan opened the door.

Joe stumbled in. 'I need to talk to you both.' He stood in the middle of the room.

Grace stared at him. 'How did you know I was here?'

'Everyone knows you're here. You woke up half the Residence, apparently.'

'What is the matter?' Ivan shut the door and gave Joe an appraising look.

'Last night I went to see those mercenaries again.'

Ivan glanced from Joe to Grace. 'What mercenaries?'

'Mammon was pretending all along,' Joe said. 'He wanted me to open a rift for him. He's a *demon*, Grace! All of them are.'

'No, no. They can't be,' said Grace. 'They don't have Shadows. And I don't feel sick near them.'

'They can conceal their essences,' said Joe. 'Which explains why you don't get sick.'

'Who is Mammon?' demanded Ivan.

Grace frowned. 'How do you know all this, Joe?'

'Utu told me. Inside the rift.'

Ivan threw up his arms in frustration. 'What the hell is going on?'

'Sorry, Ivan.' Joe gave him an apologetic smile. 'I should have told you about all this.' Having caught his breath, he now began to pace around the room.

'At first I thought I was dreaming.' Joe reached under his shirt and pulled out the amulet.

'Wow.' Grace took the sapphire stone between her fingers. A small wedge of wood was encased within the stone. 'Is it real?'

Joe gave a vigorous nod.

'It gives out a great deal of energy,' said Ivan.

'Utu's a Ferryman, just like me. He came to warn me about Mammon. He told me a lot, Grace. There's so much to tell you!'

There was another knock at the door. The three looked towards the door and then back at each other.

Joe nodded. 'It might be Diana. We need to tell her everything.'

Grace swung open the door.

Malcolm stood in the doorway, his face sweaty and pale, his eyes distant. It was clear that the shock over last night hadn't left him. But something else shone in his eyes. A glint of emotion, something new.

Grace gasped. 'What are you doing here? You should be in hospital!'

Trancelike, Malcolm lifted his hand. The gun glinted in the early morning sun. He pointed it straight at Joe. 'They said that you'd come in here.'

Grace recognised the emotion. It was the kind she'd seen in adults whose innocence had been robbed at a young age through some savage act, leaving them with the disturbed, intimate knowledge of the darkness in the human soul.

He was going to murder her brother.

'No!' She lunged to the side, trying to grab Joe and pull him away. She felt Ivan move with her; his body blocking hers, his arms flailing to grab her.

'Stop!' Ivan's shout was drowned out by a thunderous boom as Malcolm pulled the trigger.

Then, an abrupt silence. Malcolm let his hand drop to his side, his face clenched with horror. He watched Grace lean over Ivan, who was slumped on his back next to her. 'Ivan?' Grace touched his face. Pale, lifeless eyes stared past her, at the ceiling. Blood gushed from his t-shirt, from the bullet that hit his heart.

TWENTY-NINE

THIS WAS A new terror, a sick wrenching she hadn't felt before. Even with Mum and Dad . . . Grace pressed her ear to Ivan's chest, where blood was now pumping from the wound, soaking his shirt. There was no sound, no movement in his lungs.

'I can't hear his heart!' Oh, God – no. No. This couldn't be happening.

Shaking, Malcolm dropped the gun. 'I didn't mean to shoot him.' He pointed a trembling finger at Joe. 'It was supposed to be you!'

A small crowd had gathered near the doorway. Grace threw a desperate glance backwards. 'Call the medics!'

A firm hand descended onto her shoulder. 'Grace, let me take him,' Joe urged.

She wrenched away, dislodging his hand. 'No! Get the medics!'

'Grace, get off him.' Joe shoved her aside forcefully. 'Get off him!' He slid his hands under Ivan's armpits.

A rift of white light began to form in the corner of the room. 'Leave him to me.' Joe began to drag Ivan into the rift, their bodies swallowed up by the blinding glow.

'Let us through!' The crowd parted, three medics burst into the room. 'Stop!'

'I'm coming with you!' Grace lunged forward and slid her hands under Ivan's chest. She felt the energy pull them inside. The last glimpse she had of Earth was of the shocked faces watching them disappear into the rift.

THIRTY

As THE SUN spread its early morning light over the ocean, Haures knocked on the guest cabin door. 'Joe?'

She pushed the door open and then stopped dead. Gasping, she pressed her hand against her chest.

In the middle of the room, between the bed and the far porthole, sat a crater. Her eyes flickered to the right, where something big had punched through the wall, exposing the port-side deck and the sun's rays shimmering on the water. Whatever had happened here, it had destroyed most of the floor, shredding the carpet and eating the floorboards below.

Haures sank on to the bed, her heart pounding. 'Where did you go?' she whispered. 'What did I do wrong?' She stared at the wrecked room for a few seconds before standing up. On her pitiful trudge back to her cabin she cast a desperate, indecisive look over the railing.

Jump now, or wait for the boss to punish her?

She entered her cabin and sat on the edge of the bed, staring through the porthole at the gentle waves that ran towards the shore.

'Coward.' As she glared at her reflection, her hair changed back into rich burgundy; her skin several shades paler. Her eyes transformed: baby blue turned green.

The door opened; Mammon breezed in. 'All ready for our big day?' He stood checking his watch. When he finally looked at her, his smile turned to a frown.

'Why have you shapeshifted?' He threw a tense look towards the ensuite. 'You'd better change back while Joe is in the shower.'

'There's no point,' she whispered. Shaking, she stared at the carpet. 'He didn't stay here last night.'

Mammon's voice trembled. 'What?' He turned to Andras, who was standing on the deck outside. 'Check the guestroom.'

'Yes, Master.' Andras jogged away, barking orders at nearby deckhands.

Mammon looked back to Haures. With a growl, he grabbed her hair and yanked her upwards so she was pressed against the wall. 'I told you to stay with him!'

She gasped and lifted her hands in a prayer-like gesture. 'I wanted to lead him on; make him believe that he would be rewarded after opening a rift for you. I . . . thought –'

'You don't have the right to think!' He smacked her face. She cried out as his fingers squeezed tighter around her neck.

Passing crewmen peered in but looked away again. Just the boss, playing with one of his girls.

Mammon lifted Haures higher so that her feet were hanging. She clutched at his hand, struggling to pull his fingers away. Fear stabbed at her. Was he going to throw her into the sea?

She was caught in his stare, terrified.

He swatted her hands away and then stabbed cold fingers into her belly.

She gasped – was he going to impale her stomach?

'You've disappointed me, Haures!' He threw her across the room. For a few, long seconds she was airborne until she smashed against the bed frame. Moaning, she rubbed her sore side.

'Hey!' Andromalius loomed in the doorway. 'Get your hands off her!'

Mammon stared, incredulous. He strode across and in a swift move, broke the young demon's neck. Andromalius collapsed on the floor.

'No!' Haures cried. She began to crawl across to her lover's body. Mammon turned towards her.

Andras's heart thudded loudly as he returned from checking the guestroom. He couldn't wait to tell the boss about his discovery. Andras stood in the doorway, arms folded. 'Joe's not on the yacht, Master.'

He glanced at Andromalius's prostrate form and whistled. Three crewmen jogged up to him. Andras nodded at the body. 'Throw it overboard.' He watched as Mammon bent over the sobbing girl.

'You're lucky,' Mammon murmured. 'I'm fond of you.' He reached down and stroked her cheek with the back of his forefinger. 'I am a patient man, and I will get what I want.

'But you owe me, Haures.'

He stood up.

'There's something you need to see, Master,' Andras said.

Mammon growled in his throat but nodded. He followed the young demon along the deck until they reached the guestroom. Andras opened the door.

Mammon stood, silently observing the wrecked room.

Rift damage.

He inhaled; the smell of incense lingered. An energy still filled the room – energy he'd felt centuries before.

The high demon's eyes glittered with recognition.

Mammon turned and gazed out at the horizon. A single, gutteral word escaped his throat.

'Utu.'

THIRTY-ONE

INSIDE THE RIFT, it was surprisingly calm. The universe didn't flash past like Grace imagined it would do. No galaxies, no stars. No blackness of space. Just this – the cloud, which was growing whiter and whiter as they moved on.

But then a wind came.

'Don't panic,' Joe said. He stopped and stared into the rift. Grace held Ivan closer, her hands trembling. She sensed that something was coming. Then she saw them: a pack of bony creatures hovering nearby.

'They won't hurt you!' Joe cast a commanding look around the rift; the Reavers turned and disappeared.

The glow grew brighter, eventually burning out all else until the lightning, even the clouds were bleached into a blurry fog of white light.

And then they were standing there. In a cottage, with the hint of a blue sky above and a green field rolling into infinity.

Carefully, Joe began to lower Ivan's body to the floor. Grace resisted, holding him tighter. 'What are you doing to him?'

'It's all right, Grace. We can put him here. Come on, help me.'

She knelt over Ivan, staring into his face. Her fingers stroked his cheek; she kissed him as a tear rolled down hers.

Nothing had changed. There was no spark in his eyes. Yet, he just looked like he was sleeping. In the distance, she thought she heard a voice say, 'It's already begun.'

Joe stood up and looked around. 'This is different from last time.'

'To what?' Grace looked up and realised he wasn't talking to her. He was looking at an old man, wearing deep blue robes, standing in the middle of the room. Behind him, a large brown chair set off an amber glow. The room smelled sweet – like the candles that Mum used to burn. They used to clog up Grace's sinuses. But this scent didn't. Intangible, smokeless in nature – the smell seemed to follow the strange little man as he walked closer.

'Hello again, Joe,' the little man said. 'Yes, it will be different now Grace is here. Collective minds, collective reality – remember? Although, your sister seems to be strongly influencing the illusion.'

'Hello, Utu. Yes, she's telepathic.'

'She must like cottages.'

'This is just like our grandmother's place. She died two years ago. Grace still misses her. She used to love visiting when we were small.'

Surprised by Joe's sudden insight, Grace could only nod. It was true – nothing had ever made her feel more safe than waking up in Gran's house to the smells of butter melting on toast and old-fashioned tea brewing in a pot. Wrapped up in a flannelette dressing gown, she would rush to Gran's old wooden table, her chair scraping on the black-and-white checkered linoleum floor as she took her place. Gran's wrinkled hands would still be warm from turning the pasties in her wood-fired oven. Joe sitting opposite, grinning with his jam-smeared teeth. The sound of horses whinnying outside the window. Oh, how she missed Gran.

The old man stepped forward and broke into her reverie. 'Ah, little sister. How brave you've been.' He glanced down at Ivan's body.

'Please.' Grace dropped to her knees. 'Please help him.'

Utu nodded. 'The healing has already begun.' He gestured behind him, to the kitchen table. 'Come and sit with me, both of you. Leave your friend there so he can rest.'

'But –'

Joe lowered his voice to a calming whisper. 'He's going to be okay, Grace.'

Utu smiled as he took his seat; deep wrinkles almost obscured his eyes.

Grace edged on to her chair. 'What is this place?'

'This is Utu's rift.'

Grace looked at Joe. 'Why does it look like –'

'Gran's old place? You're doing that.'

'Mmm.' Utu rested his chin on his hands. 'You are obviously a strong telepath, so your desires are controlling what we all see.' He leaned forward and winked. 'It's a little like your story, *The Wizard of Oz*. As if you have tapped your ruby slippers and thought of where you want to be. A normal psychic reaction to a moment of heightened trauma.'

'It's so hard to believe.'

'Humanity's weakness is its short-sightedness. Who was it – your William Shakespeare, I think. "There is more to heaven and hell than your philosophies dare dream of."'

Grace nodded. '*Hamlet*.' She let out a hysterical laugh. Here she was, in an interdimensional rift, discussing Shakespeare with a strange little man called Utu.

'He was a wise man. Recognised a demon when he saw one.' Utu smiled and leaned forward, ancient hands clasped. 'Now. Do you have any questions for me?'

Grace stared at Utu. 'You're human, aren't you?'

'Yes.' The old man spoke slowly. 'But my survival will be difficult for you to comprehend. It should be enough to say that I live somewhere in between worlds.'

She looked around. 'Inside a rift?'

'Yes. Somehow, the rift sustains my existence.' Utu picked up a lace doily and smiled, weaving his fingers through the fabric. 'Of course, my tastes are slightly different.'

Grace nodded. 'Why didn't you contact Joe earlier, if you knew all this was going on?' She shot an anxious look back at Ivan, and relief flooded her. He was breathing again.

'I don't have a crystal ball, little sister. I can only see so much, and my visions do not just appear when I want them to. The first time I saw your brother in a vision was when he lost his temper at your birthday party.'

Ashamed, Joe looked at his hands.

Utu sighed. 'I knew I had to get to him, that he would need my counsel. But that is not an easy feat. Forcing the rift from the other side takes a lot of energy, and so, I am tired. And then to discover that he was in the company of a high demon?' Utu shook his head. 'I am very glad I reached him in time.'

'A high demon?' Grace said. 'Mammon?'

'Yes. Although, I do not know him as Mammon Jones. I would not be able to recognise him.'

Utu lifted his hand and waved it across the air. 'But I can tell you who he was, and more importantly, what he did long ago.' A cloudy image appeared – a four-storey square building with cascading plants, overlooking a river where small boats with white patchwork quilts for sails loitered.

'The Hanging Gardens of Babylon,' said Grace.

Utu nodded. 'During my youth we had a Scourge. The demons – or dev'h, as we called them – were loose. Children were being snatched off the streets, thievery and corruption were rife. Mine was a luxurious city of riches and gold, but beneath the glamour there was evil. My brother Balthasar lost his daughter, his beautiful Nineveh. Abducted, enslaved, murdered. Only nine years of age. Balthasar approached me, along with a small group of neighbours – all victims of the Scourge. They sought answers – I could offer them little, although I knew all too well of the evil that had layered itself over my city.'

The image vanished and another materialised – an earthy-coloured tower with walkways snaking up its sides.

'Up the ziggurat they went. My contemporaries – men I'd studied and worshipped with – now surpassed me, taking the top positions in the priesthood. They did not seem overly concerned with battling the Scourge, but more with filling their pockets with gold. I sent Balthasar away so that I could meditate on the problem.'

He tapped his armrest. 'In this very chair, I sat in trance. On the seventh day, at dawn, I opened a gateway into another world. There was a man waiting at the edge of that rift. At first I thought he was an angel. He told me that henceforth I was no longer Utu but Ferryman. His name was Marduk. He told me he was my predecessor, just as I told you, Joe, that I am yours. Marduk gave me the Gift of the Eye. From that day on, I could see the true faces of the dev'h: thief, merchant – and even priest. He also told me that a powerful dev'h – not born of this world – was the influence that wrought a Scourge on my city.'

'Mammon,' said Grace.

Utu nodded.

'When I invited Balthasar into my home, along with his friends, we made plans to go after the high dev'h. I began to shadow the high priests all across the Empire.

'You may not know that Babylon means "Gateway of the Gods". Well, in the middle of the Syrian Desert there was a city called *Tarra Satana*. The Devil's Gate. Just outside of the town there was a temple that housed a sacred stone – a crystal that resonated to the sound of the Rift. You must understand this was much larger, much more powerful than anything I could summon. Three hundred years of acolytes praying around the crystal, surrounding it in dark vibrations, and the crystal remembered. It was here that I found the high dev'h, waiting on the steps that cascaded from the crystal's platform, surrounded by a host of my former colleagues – including my former teacher, a man I'd respected most greatly. To my eternal grief, my teacher was the man who opened the Dark Rift.'

'He was a Ferryman too?'

'No.' Utu raised a warning finger. 'Merely a Gatekeeper. Unlike you, he could not enter a rift – only open one, with the help of the high dev'h.'

He waved his hand again – an image of black clouds moving across a desert plain. 'The high dev'h looked at me and laughed, while his armies poured out of his Dark Rift and into freedom. He told me I was too late. I watched his hordes fly away to possess the people of Tarra Satana. I heard the screams across the sands and knew I could do nothing to save their lives.

'But I also knew what I could do. I opened my own rift beneath the feet of the high dev'h. As he fell inside I heard the sounds of his physical body being ripped apart.'

Joe grinned. 'The Reavers.'

Utu smiled. 'You have an amusing attachment to the creatures, Joe. The last thing I heard as I stumbled away was the cracking of the crystal as it hit the temple floor – it was toppled over by the collapse of the stairway. When the crystal broke, the Dark Rift collapsed in on itself and caused the earth to implode, burying the temple.

'Of course, that didn't save the innocent people of Tarra Satana. And if the high dev'h could bring that much damage to one city, imagine what he could do to the planet.'

Grace shuddered. 'What happened to that city?'

'I had to get rid of it. I couldn't allow other cities to be exposed. I knew that once the dev'h had finished with Tarra Satana, his minions would simply move on.' He bowed his head.

'I destroyed the city. In some way I feel that is why I am here. This is my purgatory. Punishment for killing the innocents of Tarra Satana.'

'But they were possessed!' Grace shook her head, frowning. 'You had to do something!'

Utu sighed. 'Killing a few to save many may sound like a logical choice. But every choice has consequences, like ripples on a pond.' He fell quiet, his eyes shadowed, head bowed.

'Anyway, that is where the *sarsareh* began. Balthasar's three sons became mercenaries, and we tried to eradicate as many demons as we could. Of course, it has been a long and hard battle. In a way, we've come full circle, with the high dev'h returning to try and take Earth once more.'

Utu lifted his head, staring at something behind Grace. 'Ah, now. There you see. All better.' Grace spun around in her seat. Ivan was standing up, staring at Utu. 'What's going on?'

She flew forward and hugged him. 'Do you feel okay?'

Ivan's eyes shone with a soft, loving gleam. He reached down and stroked her hair away from her eyes. 'I'm fine,' he whispered.

He looked over at Joe. 'Where are we?'

'Joe brought you through a rift,' said Grace. 'This is Utu. He's a Ferryman.'

Ivan offered his hand to Utu. 'I am honoured.' Then he pulled Joe into a bear hug, thumping his back. 'I owe you, my friend.'

With a grin, Joe nodded at Grace. 'I couldn't stick the idea of seeing her mope around every day 'cause you weren't there.'

Utu smiled. 'We've been talking about our encounters with Mammon – the high demon, who unfortunately seems to be on the loose again. He has been trying to get a hold of Joe.'

They returned to their seats.

Ivan listened, squeezing Grace's hand from time to time, as Utu told him the story of Tarra Satana.

Ivan nodded. 'Diana had a theory that a high demon was behind everything.' He looked at Joe. 'The bike accident, the truck's near-miss and your parents.'

'Oh, my God!' Grace's voice trembled. 'He was the one who killed Mum and Dad!'

'And I killed innocent people because he tricked me,' Joe whispered.

'You must not let the guilt take over, Joe,' Utu said.

Joe drew a deep breath and nodded. 'Mammon asked me to open a rift last night.'

'No!' Grace said. 'You didn't, did you?'

He threw her an angry look. 'Of course not!'

'What did he say it was for?' said Ivan. 'He cannot have given you the real reason.'

'He suggested we bring through demons from the hell world and kill them. To stop the demon Scourges once and for all.'

Ivan rubbed his forehead. 'He wants to bring through an army.' He drew a deep breath. 'I'm very, very glad you didn't help him, Joe.'

'There's more. Last night when I opened that rift and pushed Malcolm inside, I really wanted to kill him. Utu told me that I opened a Dark Rift.'

Grace and Ivan looked at Utu. The priest nodded. 'That's right.'

'Malcolm saw Shadows coming at him, remember?' Joe glanced around the group. 'That means that I came close to helping Mammon last night. His army would have gone through – and it would have been all my fault.'

'But you didn't,' said Grace, touching his arm. 'That's all that matters right now.'

'And we are all the wiser,' Ivan added. He folded his arms and sat back in his chair. 'We know that if you are angry, you bring on a dark, dangerous rift that links to the demon world.' His eyes twinkled as he considered the possibilities. 'While that could work to our advantage, we need to learn to harness that anger first.'

Utu nodded. 'Exactly.'

'But what are we going to do now?' Joe jumped up, his eyes shining with renewed vigour. 'I want to take Mammon down.' His eyes met Utu's. 'I know where to find him – and we could move now.'

Ivan held up his hand. 'You need some more practice with rift accuracy, my cookie cutter. Remember the garage?'

Joe grinned and scratched his head. 'I can make one hell of a mess, can't I?'

'Anyway, I daresay Mammon will have returned to land by now,' said Utu. 'This will take planning and a calm approach.'

'We can take him,' Joe said. 'I haven't seen him do anything special. Really, he's just a man when you think about it.'

'You know that's not true, Joe.' Grace looked at Utu. 'Is it?'

The old priest smiled. 'Mammon is not just a man, Joe. He hides his essence well. And that essence is deadly, if unleashed. He is dangerous, not just because of his capacity for physical violence – but because he has wrought a massive influence over the planet for many centuries. He has more followers than you can imagine. That is where the danger lies.'

'Can we really kill him? If he's been around that long?'

'Grace, there is no such thing as coincidence. You, Joe and Ivan found each other; now you form a powerful circle: Warrior, Seer, Ferryman. You will overcome the high demon. But you must be faithful in your abilities and ready to adapt, to change.' He held up two amulets and passed one to Grace, the second to Ivan.

Grace stared at her amulet. It was an emerald circle and, like Joe's, inside lay a small piece of wood.

Ivan held up his amulet and whistled. 'Diamond,' he said.

Utu smiled. 'Now you can all proudly claim that you have a significant piece of Utu's Chair.'

All three looked at him curiously.

Utu smiled. 'Back in the old days, during my early visits from Marduk, I would sit in this chair – made by my father from the wood of an olive tree. Marduk's presence always left residual power in the room, and the chair seemed to retain it the most. These amulets have great power – far more than your guardians' pendants. Theirs contain only small shards of this, the original wood.'

'Ferryman power,' Joe whispered.

Utu caught the glint in Joe's eye and gave him a stern look. 'Humility and temperance, Joseph.'

Joe's face turned red. 'Sorry.'

Grace ran her fingers over her amulet. 'Will there ever be a time when there aren't any demons on Earth?'

Utu gave her a long look. 'Consider this. Demonic energy exists over the world like an unseen blanket. It is everywhere. There is nowhere it cannot go. Where does it come from? Some say that humans generate it; others claim it seeps in from other dimensions. Slowly – and not necessarily through a rift. For as long as that energy is allowed to exist, for as long as humans draw it, attract it, and eventually absorb it – there Mammon will be.'

'But,' said Grace, 'if there's bad energy, surely there's good energy too.'

'True.'

'And if there are demons . . . '

'There must be angels?' Utu gave her a sad smile. 'I'm afraid not. At least, not the kind that you like to imagine. It would be wonderful, wouldn't it?'

'We can't expect any help? It's all up to us?' Grace's shoulders slumped. Exhaustion hit as she mulled over the prospect. They couldn't do it alone.

'There are some who will help. But human beings must change if they want to see the day when no more Scourges afflict the world.' Utu wrapped his robes around him.

'Now, you three need to go home. Safe journey – and may you win this fight and return to a life of peace and serenity.' He bowed.

'Till next time, then,' Joe added.

The old priest watched them move away. 'Oh . . . Joe?'

Joe turned his head. 'Yes?'

Utu's eyes twinkled. 'When you meet the high demon again, please give him my regards.'

THIRTY-TWO

THE YOUNG NURSE tipped a handful of pills into a plastic cup. 'Here you are.' She gave the patient a smile as he took the cup and swallowed its contents. 'And a chaser.' She passed him a glass of water. The patient took a sip; the glass hovered in his hand just below his chin. The nurse reached over and caught the glass just as it slipped from his fingers.

He stared off into the ocean, his eyes flat and dull.

How did he get here? When did he get here? He remembered firing at Callahan. Damn Ivan for getting in the way. It wasn't what he'd wanted.

No room for guilt.

The pills numbed things a little. But they couldn't stop the nightmares.

The nurse patted his shoulder as she moved away.

Malcolm's arms dropped to his sides. The tide was beginning its nightly invasion of the shore. Soon the pale sands would be sodden – and by morning, strewn with light green shards of seaweed and some stringy brown matter. There'd be shells, too. As a child, he'd loved the rare morning walks at the sea's edge. Especially collecting the shells, cuttlefish and other items cast over the sand by the relentless tides.

But there was no joy in this beach.

Hibiscus Retreat, on an island eighteen kilometres off the Border City coast. A mass of Bali-style bungalows, mini waterfalls and plunge pools. But Malcolm knew a loony bin when he saw one.

The doctor had advised him to expect an indefinite stay.

* * *

IT WAS ALMOST midnight when Sheree did her last round. Everyone was asleep – nice and calm for the handover. She passed Malcolm's room and gave an approving nod at his still figure. She walked on. A sudden gust of wind hit her back. She turned to see a flashing of light bounce off Malcolm's door.

She ran back into the room and fell to her knees with a terrified howl. She clamped her hands to her ears as the noise penetrated her eardrums, stinging them. The patient was lying flat on his back – she could not tell if he was awake, although surely he had to be – for the massive, black cloud hanging above his bed was emitting screeching sounds and flashing shards of blinding light, shaking the whole room.

* * *

MALCOLM.

He woke with a start, his eyes doing a wild scan of the room, sweat lining his brow.

Two men were standing by his bed, smiling in that false, manipulative way of psychiatrists.

With a deep breath, Malcolm lifted himself on his elbows and sat up. 'I was wondering when someone would come to see me.' He watched the men pull up two chairs – one on either side of him. The younger man sat closer, the older man must have been the note-taker.

'Sheree told you about my nightmare?' His eyes flickered up to the ceiling. But was it really a dream? 'The pills don't work. You'll have to up the dose.' He eyed the younger man with vague interest. 'You're well-dressed for a doctor. Did they drag you away from the theatre?'

Mammon smiled at Malcolm. 'Hello.'

Malcolm coughed and took a sip of water. 'Who are you guys?'

'I'm an interested friend,' said Mammon. 'I'm aware that you opened a rift tonight.'

'Who told you?'

Mammon nodded at Halphas. 'My associate here. He, too, is gifted.'

Halphas grinned at his Master's praise. 'You have an amazing power, Malcolm, and we want to help you use it.'

Malcolm tilted his head and gave Mammon an appraising stare. 'You know, if it weren't for the fact that you look perfectly normal to me, I would have sworn you were a demon.'

Mammon laughed. 'I'd like you to use your special talent to help me with an important project.'

'I'm not stupid, you know. I realise what you're talking about.'

Mammon clasped his hands in a prayer-like gesture. 'Of course. I apologise. You're a bright young man and you deserve a great opportunity. If you help me by opening a rift, I will make sure you get everything you want. Everything!'

Malcolm's gaze darted between the two men. 'You're not mercenaries.'

'No.'

He lay back on his pillow and examined his fingernails. 'Rifts are used for one thing – sending demons back to hell. Nobody in his right mind would try to reverse the process. So why are you asking me to? Unless . . .' He gave Mammon a long look. 'Unless you're a demon yourself.'

Mammon tutted. 'What a preposterous idea! I'm not a demon. I'm a being who likes this world. Do demons like humanity? I am nothing more than a man. A man who looks after his friends, Malcolm.'

Halphas nodded.

Malcolm smiled, wagging his finger at Mammon. 'The trouble with people is they underestimate my intelligence. So tell me: how *do* you hide your Shadow? You must be quite skilled.' He pressed his finger to his lips. 'Don't get me wrong, I don't have a problem with it. It's quite amazing, really.'

'I can offer you a prosperous future, Malcolm. Recognition and power beyond your imagining.'

'I'm not a Ferryman. I can't promise that I will be able to do it again. I don't know how it happened, to be honest. Maybe I dreamed it. But if it's real, when Joe pushed my head inside the rift, perhaps that triggered something.'

Mammon nodded. 'You opened a powerful rift. Its energy practically smashed into my yacht. I can help you to control the rift. All you need to do is get it going. You start the engine, I fuel it.'

Malcolm scowled. 'You don't understand. I didn't try to open the rift. It just occurred by itself. I was having a bad dream when it came.' He shrugged. 'I don't even know if I could do it again.'

Mammon leaned forward and clasped his fingers together. 'I'd like to give you the benefit of the doubt.' He glanced at Malcolm's bedside table, which was conspicuously bare of flowers and cards. 'You haven't had any visitors, have you? None of them have bothered to come and see you.'

Malcolm curled his lip. 'So?'

'Do you plan to go home to them?'

'In about a hundred years, when they let me go.' Malcolm rubbed his hands across his face.

'I can offer you immediate freedom. To walk out of this place and into a life of luxury, privilege and power you cannot yet comprehend.'

Malcolm looked at his mercenary shirt, hanging over a chair. That crest no longer meant anything to him. 'I only want one thing. To burn Renfield to its foundations and all the human vermin that live inside it.'

Mammon nodded, eyes flashing. 'Consider it done.'

'But I want my father to be kept alive.'

'Of course. Halphas, pack Malcolm's belongings.'

'Yes, Master.' The old man moved about the room, shoving Malcolm's clothes into a plastic, hospital-issued bag. With a cautious glance back at Mammon, he shoved the mercenary shirt inside the bag.

Malcolm slipped out of bed and threw on a t-shirt.

He slid his feet into a pair of flip-flops and smoothed down his hair. 'I'm ready. But how are we going to get out of here?'

'You leave that to me.'

Halphas stood at attention. 'All packed, Master.'

'Excellent.' Mammon smiled and gestured towards the door. 'Shall we?'

In silence, the trio walked from the room and into the night.

PART THREE

THIRTY-THREE

IVAN HAD AN amused twinkle in his eye as he watched Grace run her fingertips along his face, past the sandpapery stubble to the softer flesh of his neck. 'Think I need a shave?' The sofa creaked as he shifted his weight. She kicked off her shoes and snuggled closer. His t-shirt was soft, but she yearned to go further, to take if off and stroke the bare warmth of his chest.

And by the animal look in his eye, he felt the same way.

'I like touching your face.' Grace lay her head on his chest, soothed by the sound of his breathing, the firm thump of his heart.

Ivan rested his head back on the armrest; his fingers snaked up under her shirt. He stroked her back with the side of his thumb. 'I think I'm getting the better part of the deal.'

He slid his fingers under her chin and lifted it. 'You feel afraid.'

She nodded. 'How can you tell?'

'I just know.' He ran his finger down her cheek. 'Don't worry, little one. Nobody will ever hurt you while I'm alive.' He slid his fingers into the nape of her neck and pulled her face close in a long kiss.

A low tapping, and their lips broke apart. Grace laughed; Ivan groaned. 'Why does this keep happening?' With a frustrated smile, he eased Grace to the side and jumped up.

Diana was at the door. 'How are you feeling?'

'I'm fine.' Ivan opened the door wider. 'Come in.'

Diana stepped into the room but froze when she saw Grace lying on the couch. 'Oh.' She cast an accusing look back at Ivan.

Grace sat up. 'Hi, Diana.' Her cheeks began to flame with embarrassment.

'Hi.' Frowning, Diana sat down. She watched Ivan sink on to the sofa next to Grace and take her hand in his. Diana rubbed her forehead and sighed. 'So, you two are seeing each other now?'

'Uh-huh,' Grace nodded. She looked up at Ivan, who smiled.

Diana's eyes lowered to the amulets around their necks. 'What are those?'

'They're from the rift, from a friend we met.' Grace reached up and held her amulet between her thumb and forefinger.

'Utu,' Ivan added.

'Really?' Diana gasped. 'That's . . . amazing! He's the stuff of legends. You mean you actually met him?' She took a deep breath. 'Well, Joe did very well. Quick thinking on his part.'

'Indeed,' said Ivan.

Grace crossed her legs underneath her. 'What happened to Malcolm?'

'He was committed for treatment.' Diana leaned forward. 'But there's a problem. Somehow Malcolm has managed to escape.'

'How?' Ivan frowned. 'That's a secure facility.'

'I don't know what Marcus is more annoyed about,' said Diana. 'Having forked out all that money for treatment, or the fact that his son has gone AWOL.' She clasped her fingers together. 'Joking aside, Malcolm just walked out of there. There was no intervention from the guards – in fact, they did everything they could to help him get out.'

'Sounds like someone with telepathic power,' said Grace.

'Yes.' Diana gave Grace a long look. '*You* should know.'

Grace felt a pang of guilt. Poor Brutus.

'But that's not all,' added Diana. 'It's even worse. The night nurse reported seeing a large circular cloud above Malcolm's bed, about an hour before he disappeared.'

* * *

Malcolm chewed on a blade of grass and sat back on the day bed, his head comfortably wedged between two silk cushions. He clicked his fingers. Halphas ambled across, refilled Malcolm's glass, then backed away a few steps. Mammon had told him to stand by as the boy's servant; to tend to his whims. He rolled his eyes as Malcolm raised the glass in a mock toast.

'Thank you, my man.' Malcolm swallowed the contents in one gulp. He tossed the glass to the side and lay back, watching as the girl – he couldn't remember her name – applied the last few colours to the canvas.

'There.' She stood back and tilted her head before shooting him a glance. 'Want to see my landscape?' She wiggled her way over to him and dropped her hand. 'Let me help you up.'

Malcolm squinted. 'Can you stand just to the left? Ah, that's better.' He dropped his hand. 'In fact, can you bring the painting here? I can't be bothered moving.'

With a mock sigh, the girl ambled back to her canvas. Malcolm watched her move with an appreciative smile. The micro-bikini – yellow polka-dot, no less – wrapped her curves pleasingly. The dots nearly a precise match for the hair that streamed across her back and over her full breasts.

The girl lifted it from the easel. 'Oh! It's heavy! Are you sure you won't come over here?'

Halphas coughed. With a minute sway of his forefinger, he gestured for her to move.

She grunted as she lifted the painting.

Malcolm leaned on his side and rested his head on his palm. The canvas rested in front of him, supported by what's-her-name's knees. She'd captured Mammon's mansion well, he had to concede. The Greek columns were proportionate in size to the rest of the building, the balconies' fine wrought-iron patterns carefully detailed. She'd even caught the watermark crest that graced every window: the head of a wolf.

Yes, she'd captured the vastness that was his new home.

'What should I paint next? The indoor pool? The ceiling there is gorgeous! It'd be a challenge! Although, my neck will get stiff . . . what about the great hall? Oh, I know – the opium den!'

Malcolm nodded. 'Yeah. In fact, that's the one place I'd actually get off this bed for.' He rolled to his feet. 'Come on.'

'Hold on! I need my paints! And another canvas –'

Malcolm grabbed her arm and yanked her to him. 'You won't need them now, baby.' They walked towards the side entrance in an awkward stumble, her giggles piercing the air. He shot a look back. 'We won't require your services for the rest of the afternoon, Halphas.'

The old man watched the pair slip away. He gritted his teeth, swallowed his irritation at the boy's attitude, and moved across the grass towards the mansion. Passing through the marble splendour that was the great hall, Halphas paused to gaze up at the grand staircase.

'Here we go again,' he sighed.

During his servitude, Halphas had witnessed six attempts by Mammon to open a Dark Rift.

And six times Halphas had stopped him.

He did not wish to speculate on what his future would hold if Mammon ever found out.

The last boy – Jeremy – had come shockingly close. But then, Halphas had terrorised the lad, telling him how Mammon would wear his body out and bury him when he was done.

Halphas peered across the room and caught his reflection. He should have been dead so many years ago. The only gift Mammon ever gave him? An extraordinarily long life. Oh, the cruelty of it. He remembered Mammon's gifting words: 'You always said that the greatest gift you could ever have would be to serve *me* forever, Halphas.'

'Damn you,' he muttered. He limped on through the hall.

His service was a sham. He knew Mammon only kept him around because of his unique gift: to 'tune in' and detect rift activity on Earth, then locate the source.

If Halphas ever stopped providing this gift, Mammon would destroy him.

If a Dark Rift was opened tomorrow night, Mammon would destroy him.

There was only one choice. Now he had to enter the most dangerous stage of the game.

Sabotage.

He watched as yet another limousine pulled up outside the mansion. 'Fools,' he hissed. These Earthborn demons, these elite members of society, these pawns who were offering up their bodies. Hosts – for Mammon's allies to possess, once they were through the Dark Rift.

They would all just have to be disappointed.

For Halphas's life depended on Mammon's army never getting through.

THIRTY-FOUR

MAMMON SWEPT ASIDE the curtains that separated the opium den from the swimming pool enclosure. Seemingly irritated, he scanned the body lying face-first on the velvet settee.

'Ahem.'

Malcolm's face sprang up; bloated eyes battered the sleep away. 'Oh. Didn't see you there.'

Mammon sank on to the settee next to Malcolm. 'I take it you are comfortable here, in this house?' He crossed his legs; his fingers stroking the velvet.

'Yeah.' Malcolm sat up. 'Although I was expecting to find some actual opium here.'

Mammon tutted. 'Malcolm. Do you think I would permit drug abuse in this house? Anyway, it might stop you performing your duties for me.'

Malcolm blinked. 'Yeah.' He removed himself from the settee and stretched.

'You've rested this morning, and we have two more days

to perfect your technique.' Mammon stood up. 'So, you'll be happy to spend another day in rehearsal.' He strode across and slung his arm around Malcolm's shoulder. 'We have a lot to prepare for.'

Malcolm followed Mammon through the pool house. He gazed through the arched windows at the willow trees, which were shaking in the wind. The pool was immaculate in its stillness, reflecting the many Grecian statues that stood about its perimeter like silent watchmen.

They walked through a circular sitting room, where lemon-coloured curtains hugged the wall and a servant rubbed polish into a chandelier. The man was quick to lower his head as Mammon walked past.

Malcolm gave the cinema a longing glance as he passed it. He'd hoped to watch an action movie in there with the bikini girl this afternoon.

'Right.' Mammon stopped in the great hall. He gave Malcolm an encouraging smile. 'It's all up to you, my lad.'

Malcolm climbed to the top of the stairs, turned around and took a deep breath. 'I hope I can make it last today.'

'Practice makes perfect, my boy. Consider your prior failures as stepping stones to the reality of what you *will* achieve on the night.' Mammon leaned on the banister. 'Halphas!'

'I'm here, Master.' The old man hurried across the floor.

'Bear witness. Today, our Malcolm will open a perfect rift.'

'Right you are, Master.' Halphas stood a few feet back from Mammon and watched Malcolm squeeze his finger-nails into his sweaty palms. Inwardly, Halphas chuckled.

'Um . . .' Malcolm scratched his head. 'Won't they be able to track us doing this?'

'They?' Mammon said.

'Renfield. My old employer.'

Mammon smiled. 'This mansion is protected thanks to the electromagnetic fields built into the walls.'

'Really?' Malcolm ran his fingers over the white paint. 'What, like a Faraday cage, or something? Whoa. You're really serious about all this.'

'Yes.' Mammon clicked his fingers.

Halphas smiled. He knew Master's impatient gestures.

Malcolm dropped his hand and began stretching his arms in wide circles. 'Okay, so do you want me to try now?'

Mammon nodded. 'Absolutely.'

Minutes passed. As the sweat streamed down Malcolm's cheeks, Halphas imagined the high priests at Tarra Satana, chanting in the sand-swept temple. They wouldn't have perspired like this. The crystal would have done all of the work.

'That's it! There's the beginning!' Mammon ran up the stairs.

A tiny grey cloud hovered in the air, around eye level with Malcolm.

'Okay, careful now!' Mammon edged sideways, careful not to touch the newborn rift, and stood next to the boy.

'Right. Let's make it bigger . . . excellent. Now, we wait to see what appears. My associates will be jostling one another – it will be amusing to see who wins the race.' Mammon's eyes, birdlike in their intensity – fixed on the cloud as it began to bulge, like a hand was pressing against the inside.

Then, the rift gave birth. A creature slipped out, falling onto the tiles in a decaying heap of bone and grey flesh.

Slit-like eyes, the irises a dull white with a red pupil. Webbed fingers and toes reminiscent of an infant that did not develop fully while in its mother's womb; the grey skin of a reanimated corpse.

Malcolm panted. 'What *is* that?'

'Not from my dimension.' Mammon's face was twisted in disgust. 'We only move in pure, perfect Shadow. Halphas – bring me the Luger.'

The old man rifled through a small bureau drawer. 'Here you are, Master.'

Mammon snatched the pistol and pointed it at the creature on the floor. Shots rang out and the body jerked at the impact.

'I think it was already dead,' Malcolm said.

'Abomination.' Mammon lowered the gun. 'Get rid of it, Halphas.' He waved a white cloth in Malcolm's face. 'Clean up. You look terrible. No, I don't want the handkerchief back. Now, go and drink a glass of water and come back here straight after. This setback will not deter us. Smile! All will be well. Your predecessors never got this far.'

He turned back to Halphas. 'Do hurry up and remove that thing.'

* * *

HALPHAS DUMPED THE creature's body into the boot of the limousine. He peered into the kitchen: the boy was still guzzling water. Halphas pushed the door open and wandered over to where Malcolm was standing, propped up by the bench, glass in hand.

He stopped and studied the boy's pallid face. 'Well, that wasn't very successful, was it?'

Malcolm drained the glass and slammed it on to the benchtop. He eyed Halphas with an angry glare. '*You* couldn't do it.'

Halphas folded his arms. 'You do realise that Master won't keep you around, even if you do eventually succeed.'

Malcolm smirked. 'You're just jealous because he thinks I'm better than you.'

'I saw how much you perspired up there.' Halphas reached into the cupboard and selected a glass. He filled it with water and took a sip. Leaning on the benchtop, he gave the boy a smug smile. 'You don't know how much power is needed to open a Dark Rift. It's enough to kill a man stronger than you, even with Master's help.'

'I'm going to practise. By the time the ceremony comes around, I'll have perfected it. I've still got two days.'

'We'll see.' Halphas emptied his glass into the sink and walked out of the room.

Minutes later, he drove out of the mansion grounds and turned left on the highway, heading south. On the passenger seat, an invitation. In his pocket, a piece of the boy's old uniform.

If he wanted to stop Mammon this time, he was going to need help.

THIRTY-FIVE

'I HAVE NO doubt that Malcolm is in the company of a high demon.' Diana looked around the conference room, where a mix of reactions met her stare.

Lucius nodded. 'It would seem so.'

Marcus threw him an angry look. 'There is no proof of that.'

'From what Joe tells us, Mammon Jones is desperate to open a rift. Now we find that Malcolm has developed that ability and has since disappeared. It doesn't take much intelligence to piece this together!'

'Sarah hasn't picked up on any rift activity,' Agatha said.

Diana ran her fingers through her hair. 'No, but the one time we do may well be the one time that the world as we know it changes. We can't leave it too late!'

'Don't be melodramatic,' Marcus said.

Grace scowled. 'She's not. This is real.'

Marcus leaned back in his chair and settled a cold stare on Grace. She met his eyes for a few seconds and then turned her attention to Diana. Her heart pounded. Ivan rested his hand on her knee underneath the table. She could almost hear his voice: *Be calm, little one.*

'If we can prove that Mammon Jones is a legitimate target, other *sarsareh* orders will join us and provide support. He could be anywhere – we need our networks to help track him down.' Diana looked to her right. 'Sarah, you and Seth do the research. Find out what you can about any alleged criminal activities – not just on his part, but concerning those in his employ. I need answers by this afternoon. Get to work.' The team filtered out of the room. Diana stood up and looked at Lucius. 'Shall we?'

Marcus reached out and held Lucius's arm. 'Diana, I need a private word with my brother.'

Diana gave Lucius an enquiring look.

Lucius nodded. 'Go on. I'll meet you in the office.'

'Right.' She closed the door behind her. 'Ivan!' She hurried along the corridor to catch up; he, Grace and Joe were almost at the recreation room.

Grace looked at her aunt. 'What is it?'

'An administrative matter, dear. You and Joe go on ahead. Ivan will be with you in a moment.'

'Oh. Okay.' Grace shot a quick look at Ivan before following Joe down the corridor. Diana waited until they disappeared into the recreation room.

'About my niece.' She gave him a critical stare.

'Yes?' Ivan's face was open, his posture relaxed.

'Are you serious about her?'

'Yes. I am.'

'I have concerns.' Diana folded her arms and glanced around. 'About your relationship.' She held up her hand.

'Don't get me wrong: you're probably the one man here that I would want to see her with. You're honest, honourable and trustworthy.'

'Thank you.'

'But you're her commanding officer.' She began a slow walk towards the recreation room. 'Do you think that you might find it hard to treat her as a soldier?'

Ivan fell into step next to her. 'I have given this much thought, Diana. I am not going to give Grace any leeway as my subordinate. I have spoken with her already, and she understands this. I want her to be able to defend herself and be a good, strong fighter.'

'Right. Well, if that is true, I'm prepared to give this relationship my blessing. You do understand that I am standing in for her parents. She's young, impressionable and vulnerable.'

'I know.' A swell of protectiveness filled Ivan. 'And although I will train her to the best of my ability, remember this: nobody will hurt her while I'm alive, Diana.'

'I'm going to hold you to that.' But Diana nursed a secret, relieved smile as she headed towards the office.

* * *

IN THE CONFERENCE room, Lucius edged away from his brother's grip. 'What is it?'

'We're not going to send Joe on this mission.'

Lucius scowled. 'You can't be serious!'

'We need him for more important work.'

'I hate to break this to you, Marcus, but this mission is probably the most important thing Joe will ever do.'

Marcus drew a deep breath and fixed his eyes on Lucius. 'You are not going to send him, and that's my final word.'

Lucius stared at him for a few seconds. 'Is that right?' Shaking his head, he stood up and walked out of the room.

* * *

SARAH RAN DOWN the corridor, a computer tablet wedged under her arm. She knocked once on the office door and burst in. Lucius was sitting opposite Diana. Both wore tense expressions.

'I've looked into Jones's history.'

Diana looked over. 'And?'

Sarah chewed her lip. 'Mammon Jones is as clean as a whistle. No criminal record; no allegations against him personally.'

'Oh. Well, that's no help, then.'

'But, plenty of people working under him have been implicated in a range of crimes, including drug-trafficking in South America and Asia, and people-smuggling. There have been rumours of involvement in Eastern European slave trading and illegal arms sales in Africa.' Sarah rolled her eyes. 'Of course, none of this can be proven. Nobody's ever been able to lay charges. Jones must have the best lawyers in the universe. He even sued a police department for making allegations against one of his company directors.'

'Any word on Mr Jones's whereabouts?'

Sarah's face fell. 'We can't seem to track him. He's not on his yacht, or in his apartment in the City. They are the only residences he owns here.'

'Well, the only ones registered under his name,' said Lucius.

'There's been no sign that he's left Border City,' Sarah added. 'His plane is still at the airport.'

'He does have a huge jet,' Lucius said. 'Enough to carry hundreds of demons.'

Sarah coughed. 'What do you want me to do now, Diana?'

'You and Seth meet with Ivan, Joe and Grace. They're in the rec room. Now that we've got some idea that he's still here, and you might be able to provide some intelligence to help them.'

She gave Sarah an encouraging nod. 'Dismissed.'

Diana watched the girl close the door and then looked back at Lucius. 'You were saying?'

He took a deep breath and set his jaw. 'I realise now that I haven't shown the leadership that you all deserve.'

Diana raised her eyebrows. 'Quitting?'

'It's time I set an example. Not just with my bad habits, but with how things are run here. This is a military facility, after all.'

'May I speak freely?'

'Of course.'

'Your brother runs this place, not you.'

Lucius met her gaze, but with a self-conscious glint in his eyes. 'That's a fair comment. But as of today, that changes. We're going to take back control. Marcus has kept too much information from us.'

Diana nodded. 'I've always been curious about the identity of our benefactors.'

'As have I. Not to mention the reason why he needs so many guards up there.'

'It was easy to turn a blind eye, or even to justify it,' said Diana. 'Given the nature of the inmate population.'

'He doesn't want me to send Joe on the mission.'

'That's absurd! Why on Earth?'

'Apparently there are more important jobs in line for Joe.' Lucius stood up. 'I don't know about you, but I am tired of being kept ignorant. I am going to confront my brother and acquire the information we need. I'm also going to bring the majority of his guard back to active service here.'

Diana raised her eyebrows. 'He won't like that.'

'We have bigger problems than him to worry about. We need as much manpower as possible if we're going to take down Mammon Jones.'

'Really, we're going to need some outside help.' Diana picked up the phone. She began to dial but then stopped and gave Lucius an enquiring look. 'Shall I?'

Lucius nodded. 'Do it.' He stood up. 'I will meet with you all when I come back from speaking with my brother.'

Diana pressed the phone to her ear. 'Hello, Jorge? We have a problem, and we need your assistance.'

* * *

IVAN LOOKED UP as Sarah walked in. 'Any news?'

'If it could be proven, Jones is actually a world-class criminal who gets his lackeys to carry out his evil deeds.'

'That doesn't come as a surprise.'

Ivan looked between Sarah and Seth. 'So we haven't had any luck in tracking his whereabouts?'

321

Seth shook his head. 'It's like he's disappeared into the Earth. We need to find a way to seek him out. Combing the city street by street, if we have to.'

'We don't have enough people for that,' Ivan said.

'Diana is going to organise some back-up from other *sarsareh*,' said Sarah.

'They may not come until we have a definite target. We need to find out where he's hiding.' Ivan sat back, frustrated. 'All the plans in the world don't count if we cannot identify his location!' Sarah pulled out her phone and started surfing news channels.

Diana walked in. 'Any progress?' She sat down and looked around the group. 'Where's Joe?'

Sarah looked up from her phone. 'He went to see Marcus.'

'What? Why?'

'Joe didn't say.'

Diana frowned. 'Well, Lucius is on his way up there, so we'll find out soon.' She glanced at Ivan. 'The good news is he's going to bring back some of the guards to help us with this job.'

Seth snorted. 'Good luck with that.' He threw down a piece of paper and sat back, arms folded.

Diana's voice was calm. 'What do you mean?'

He gave her a flat stare. 'Marcus won't let go of his guards.'

Diana sat up in her chair and gave him a hard look. 'Yes, he will.'

'Nope.' Smiling, Seth shook his head. 'Lucius won't be able to persuade him. He doesn't have the guts.'

'He's your commanding officer and you will show him respect.'

'Diana –'

'I mean it, Seth!'

He flinched. Diana never raised her voice. He took a sharp breath. 'I'm sorry. It's just . . . Ivan leads us more than Lucius does.'

'Regardless, it is not your place to question or criticise him like that.'

'Okay, okay! I'm sorry.'

'Right.' Breathing deeply, Diana pressed her palms together. 'What are you all thinking?'

Grace raised her hand. 'I was about to suggest that I might be able to help. I could search for Malcolm – or even the high demon himself. I don't know if any of you can do it, except for you, Sarah. Maybe. I mean, I've only done it once, but I could try . . . we could practise.' She gave Sarah an enquiring look.

'What are you talking about?' Diana said.

'I think that I can leave my body.'

'You're kidding!' said Sarah. She looked down at her hands. 'Wow. I've never . . .'

Diana looked shocked. 'Since when?'

'My first day of training,' said Grace. She glanced at Ivan. 'When I got tasered. Like I said, I've only done it once. I probably would need some practise.'

Seth leaned back in his chair and stared at Grace. 'So, you're suggesting you leave your body and search through the spirit world for . . . what, exactly?'

'A sign. A signal.' She cast a look around the group, hoping for support.

Ivan shook his head. 'No. It sounds dangerous.'

'I agree,' Diana said. 'I will not allow that.'

Grace shrugged. An embarrassed blush filled her cheeks. 'At least I've got an idea! What do you all suggest?' She looked around the group; silence ensued.

Diana clasped her fingers. 'I've requested back-up from another outfit. When we put our surveillance resources together, we should be able to find a way to track Jones down.'

Seth frowned. 'You don't sound sure about that.'

Diana put on a brave smile. 'We will remain positive.'

* * *

'Do you think the boy will agree to assist us?' the Frenchman asked.

Marcus nodded – an emphatic bob of his head. 'Yes, of course. He is aching for power; I've seen it in his eyes.' He looked over to the door as it creaked open, Joe peered in.

'Ah, here you are! Come in, come in! Thanks for taking the time to get here. I'd like to introduce you to Monsieur Chevalier.'

Joe slid into the chair opposite Marcus. A small man with thin hair was sitting in the other visitor's chair. The man leaned over with a broad smile. Joe couldn't help but stare at the coffee stains on his teeth. 'It is a great honour to meet you, Joe.'

Joe reached over and shook his hand. 'Hi.'

'Please, call me Jacques.'

Joe peered around the room – a guard stood in each corner. Even in here they were armed. 'What's this about?'

Marcus gave Joe a calculating stare. 'It's time for you to start using your gift properly, Joe. You're a mercenary now.'

'Congratulations,' added Jacques.

Joe shrugged. 'I've already been on a mission.'

'Well, we have something far more important for you to consider. An opportunity for you to achieve greatness.'

Joe gave him a suspicious look. 'What are you talking about?'

Marcus looked at him. 'How would you like to see the whole demon population wiped out in a matter of days?'

Joe blinked. 'How are you going to do that?'

'We have some friends waiting on the other side. Good people who want to bring peace to the Earth. With your help, they will.'

Joe pressed his face into his hands, stifling a laugh. Deja vu. 'You've got to be kidding me,' he groaned.

'No,' Marcus said. 'I'm very serious.'

'This is why you wanted me to come and see you?' Joe looked up and sighed. 'So you could ask me to open a rift? Who exactly do you want to bring through?'

Jacques sat forward. 'Higher beings,' he said. 'Superior beings who will teach us how to live in peace and unity.'

Marcus nodded.

'Unity, huh? Look, you're not the first person to ask me to do this. Mammon promised me a magical peace, too.'

Marcus stared at him. 'This is completely different, Joe.'

'I'll bet you have a very particular idea of how the world should be, right?' Joe stood up. 'Everyone thinking the same way, following the same rules.'

Marcus stood. 'Would that be so bad? It would be for the good of humanity, Joe!'

'Yeah,' Joe scoffed. '*Your* definition of good.' He turned and walked towards the door.

'Joe,' Marcus called after him. 'You'll regret this.'

'No, I won't.' Without looking back, Joe closed the door behind him. As he stalked towards the entrance, he caught sight of Lucius walking towards him.

'What are you doing here, Joe?'

Joe glared. 'If you think you can try and talk me into it, don't waste your breath.'

Lucius frowned. 'What are you talking about?'

'You don't know?' Joe said. He nodded in the direction of Marcus's office. 'Ask your brother and his friend.' He headed towards the door.

* * *

LUCIUS PUSHED THE door open. Marcus was leaning over his desk, speaking in a quiet voice to his visitor. Lucius cleared his throat. 'I need to talk to you.' He glanced around the room and frowned. There were four guards inside. His gaze dropped to the firearms. This wasn't right.

Marcus looked up. 'Not now.'

Lucius closed the door. 'I'm afraid it will have to be now.' He shot Marcus's visitor a suspicious look. 'What is going on here? I just saw Joe in the entrance hall.'

Marcus sat back in his chair. 'Sit down.'

'No, I'll stand.' Lucius pressed his hands into the back of the guest chair.

The Frenchman stood up. 'Hello, Lucius. I'm Jacques Chevalier.'

Lucius nodded. 'Good afternoon.'

Marcus's eyes were pinned on Lucius's face. 'Jacques represents our benefactors.'

'Oh. Well, thank you. Marcus has never revealed your identity.' Lucius scratched his head.

Jacques stepped closer and smiled. 'Well, now my employers wish to take the next step in our agreement.' He clasped his hands and waited with a patient smile.

Lucius looked at him. 'And?'

Jacques lifted his hand in a dramatic flourish. 'They will bring peace to the Earth.'

Lucius stared at the Frenchman. 'Who are *they*?'

Marcus stood up. 'Our friends will come through our own rift. No demon will be able to compete with them.' He began a slow walk around the table, eventually stopping in front of his brother. 'We're talking about a solution for peace. A final, permanent end to the conflict on this planet.' He placed his hands on Lucius's shoulders.

Lucius frowned. 'That's why you wanted to see Joe.'

'Correct.'

'And he turned you down.'

'To his detriment. I was hoping you would be able to talk him around.'

Lucius took a step back; Marcus's hands dropped away. 'You realise that you and the high demon have virtually the same goal in mind.'

'Yes, except ours is noble and pure and divine! Damn you and your comparisons!'

'It's not going to happen, Marcus.' Lucius turned to the Frenchman. 'I'm sorry, Monsieur Chevalier – but we cannot assist your employers in this matter.'

Squaring his shoulders, Lucius looked back at Marcus. 'I need you to return twenty-five men from your guard for active duty.'

The Frenchman coughed and gave Marcus a meaningful look.

Marcus stared at Lucius for several seconds. When he finally spoke, his voice was quiet but laced with anger. 'You forget yourself. I am the one who keeps this facility running. Our benefactors have expectations and I need Joe to help fulfil them. So, you *are* going to persuade him.'

Lucius eyed him. 'I think *you* forget yourself, Marcus. I'm in command of this facility. Those mercenaries answer to me. Even these guards that you've commandeered for your own use.'

Marcus smiled. 'Don't put this to the test, little brother. You won't like the outcome.'

Lucius narrowed his eyes. 'Just what do you mean by that?' He took a step forward.

Two guards moved to Marcus's side – swift and silent.

'Stand down!' Lucius demanded furiously. The guards did not move.

Lucius's heart was pounding. 'Stand down!'

With a very slight movement of his chin, Marcus signalled for the guards to back off.

He nodded at Lucius. Yes, the guards were moving back. And yes – it was because Marcus told them to. 'You see, little brother? They are loyal to me and me alone.' He turned and walked back to his chair with slow, luxurious steps. 'You will convince Joe to help us. You will do this today. You will call off the mission that you are planning and assign all of your resources to helping us.'

'Otherwise,' the Frenchman added, 'my employers will no longer fund your operation.'

A guard swung the door open. Lucius stopped at the door and stared at the impenetrable face. 'I don't know who you are, but if I trained you, then you should remember where your real loyalty lies.'

* * *

THE MEETING ROOM was quiet. Diana sat on the phone; every face at the table watched the conversation with tense eyes.

'Outstanding,' Diana finally said. 'Thank you!' She put down the phone and smiled. 'My old friend Jorge is sending his entire battalion across.' She looked at her watch. 'They're based in the East, so they'll be here by sunset. Now, Ivan – I want you to assume command of the combined forces – theirs and ours.'

Ivan nodded; Grace snuck him a proud grin.

'Great,' said Seth. 'Now, if we can just find the high demon, we'll be set.' He shook his head as it slumped into his hands.

Diana patted his arm. 'Don't be negative, Seth. I'm sure you and Sarah can work with Jorge's people to find out where Jones is hiding.'

'Any updates?' said a voice from the doorway.

Lucius walked in, closely followed by Joe.

Diana stood up. 'Sir.'

Ivan followed suit, then Grace and Sarah.

'At last,' said Seth with a relieved smile.

'Thank you.' Lucius took a seat. 'I don't expect immediate, undying loyalty – but I do appreciate the gesture.'

Joe slid into a seat next to Sarah. 'Hi,' he whispered.

She smiled. 'Hi.'

Lucius looked at Diana. 'Progress?'

'Jorge's people are coming, but they won't be here until this evening.'

'Fine. We have enough on our plate in the meantime. We need to be prepared to move at short notice. We have a job, very close to home. I never dreamed that I would have to do this.' He looked at Ivan. 'I'm going to need you to lead a team into the asylum and take control.'

Ivan nodded.

Lucius looked at Sarah. 'Sanderson, will you start some coffee? It's going to be a long night.'

'Sure.' Sarah wandered over to the sideboard and flicked on the urn. She sat back down and listened as Lucius and Joe began unfolding the true story about Marcus.

* * *

A GENTLE KNOCK sounded, and a girl poked her head around the door. 'I'm sorry to interrupt you, Diana, but there's a package for you outside.'

'Right. I'll be there in a minute.'

'Hey! Listen to this!' Sarah scrolled down the page on her phone. 'It says here that lots of high-profile people have been flying in. From all over the world! Celebrities, politicians, merchants. It came to the media's attention when Emile

DeMarco, an infamous Colombian businessman, was questioned thoroughly by airport customs police.'

'Drug lord,' said Seth.

'They had to let him go, but his arrival sparked an interest in the media when the airport public relations mentioned that he was one of many rich, powerful guests flying in this week. And the society pages can't pin it down to any particular event. There's no great horse race, or ball, or anything at the moment to attract that many five-star travellers.'

'Mammon,' said Joe. 'He's going to use those people for their bodies. Kind of like possessing them.'

'Hosts,' said Sarah. She grimaced. 'How hideous.'

'We have got to find out where he is!' Diana sighed. 'Sanderson, contact the airport and see if you can find out where these people are staying. Oh, and while you're at it, can you have a quick look at that package?'

'Sure.' Sarah slipped out of the room. Lucius looked at Ivan. 'So, Captain, what are your thoughts?'

Grace sat back and watched the conversation between Diana, Lucius and Ivan. Something was different now. A new air of security, authority and confidence.

Sarah poked her head inside the door. 'Er, Lucius? Sorry . . . Colonel?'

Lucius looked up. 'What is it, Sanderson?'

'You need to see this.'

* * *

THE PACKAGE WAS a large lump wrapped in calico. Ivan took a pair of scissors and began to cut the fabric.

'Wait!' Grace stepped forward. 'It might be contaminated or something!'

Diana raised a calming hand. 'It's okay. Seth already scanned it.'

With precise, long cuts, Ivan opened the sack.

Joe's hand flew to his mouth. 'Phew!'

They all covered their mouths; Grace backed away as her stomach began to convulse. 'Smells like it's dying.'

Sarah grimaced. 'I think it's safe to say it's already dead. Poor bugger. Where the hell did it come from?'

'It's obviously not human.' Grace looked at Joe. 'Do you think it came through a rift?'

Joe shrugged. 'Couldn't have. The Reavers would have torn it apart.' He scratched the stubble on his chin. 'Unless it was already dead.'

On top of the corpse lay a small white card.

Lucius reached into his pocket and pulled out his glasses to read the card. 'It's an invitation for tomorrow night. To a 9 pm gathering at 100 Belgravia Lane, Chesterville. Black tie.' He looked at Seth. 'Did you see who delivered it?'

'A guy in a suit and hat. Couldn't make out the face. We've traced the car to a hire company.'

Ivan's eyes narrowed. 'Hang on.'

Underneath the leg of the creature, a small patch of white material stuck out. Beneath: the image of a spear.

Ivan lifted the patch and held it in the air. 'Malcolm.'

THIRTY-SIX

THE ROSY GLOW of dusk set off the rosebushes and lime-stone brick of the Residence, creating a calm, soothing atmosphere. Grace stood in the courtyard, watching the fountain's misty spray.

Mercenaries from the east were flooding the Residence with new faces. They all stared at her – and Joe, of course – and that old sense of isolation had kicked in again.

Her stomach was clenching with nervousness. Once again, she cast a look towards the asylum. Ivan was in there right now, backed up by the best, most experienced mercenaries available. She closed her eyes, trying to blot out the image of him, fighting to the death with one of those guards . . .

'You all right?' With a smile, Sarah handed Grace a mug of hot chocolate.

'Thanks.' Grace cupped her hands around the mug, letting its warmth spread through her fingers.

'Don't worry. Ivan should be back soon. They've taken the asylum.'

Grace felt a flood of relief. 'How do you know?'

'Diana just told me.'

'What about Marcus?'

'He's gone. So is Agatha. So are all the guards. They just ran away before anyone got there. Apparently Ivan couldn't believe how easy it was.'

'What – they all just left?'

'Marcus would've seen all these new mercenaries flooding in and panicked.' She raised her eyebrows. 'Not so brave after all, my stepfather.'

'Where do you think they've gone?'

Sarah shrugged. 'I asked Diana the same thing. Thought I could help with intel. But apparently they haven't taken Renfield vehicles, so we can't track them. Lord knows where they got the transport from.' She sipped from her mug. 'Things will be different around here now. Marcus always made sure the money came through. We'll have to find someone else to fund us.'

'Well,' Grace sighed. 'I'm sure Diana and Lucius will figure something out.' She glanced at the clock tower. 'I'm glad it was all over so quickly.'

'Plenty of time for cuddling before bedtime.' Sarah gave her a playful nudge.

Grace blushed.

Sarah took a sip of the warm chocolate liquid. 'Lucius knows he has lost his brother for good.'

'Hmm.'

Sarah studied Grace's face. 'You're very quiet.'

'I'm thinking about tomorrow night,' Grace said. 'I wanted revenge, but now the chance is here, I don't know how to feel.'

'Stick with Ivan and everything will be okay.'

Grace put down the mug and shoved her hands into her pockets. 'I feel a bit sick, really.'

Sarah peered over her shoulder and smiled. 'I think you'll feel better soon. Goodnight, Grace.'

'Oh . . . okay. Goodnight.' With a small frown, Grace watched her friend's abrupt departure.

She felt a sudden warmth on her back; a pair of hands slid around her waist. Ivan kissed her neck. 'Hello, little one.'

'I missed you,' she whispered, turning to face him. He squeezed her close, smothering her mouth in a warm, urgent kiss. Her fingers crept up his neck to stroke his hairline.

She loved the feel of his body against hers.

'Come.' He took her hand and led her past the recreation room, where several pairs of curious eyes watched them pass, up the stairs and into the senior wing. He pushed his bedroom door open and carried her inside. 'Over the threshold,' he joked.

Her body pressed against his as he lowered her to the ground, catching her mouth on the way down in a long, hot kiss.

He kicked the door shut. They stared at each other for a few seconds. Blushing, she began to pull his shirt up, eventually tugging it off his head. He looked as wonderful as she knew he would – a fine spray of hair set against lines of hard muscle. Smiling, he lunged forward and grabbed her, pulling her to him, one hand sliding down underneath her bottom, his other hand sliding between the buttons of her shirt.

She curled her leg around his waist, encouraging his hand to slide along her thigh.

Ivan pressed his fingers between the buttons and pulled the blouse off her back. A sudden cool hit her skin. He bent down and picked her up again, his arms tight around her thighs as he carried her towards the bed. She giggled – he tripped over something on the way and they crashed onto the mattress.

'Oops.' He sat behind her, his fingers at work undoing her bra.

Grace caught her breath.

Ivan stopped and rested his chin on her shoulder. 'Are you okay?'

She closed her eyes and nodded. 'Keep going.'

He pressed his mouth against her neck, nibbling the flesh there. She giggled. With a soft kiss on her shoulder, he unclipped the bra and pushed it aside.

She tensed.

Ivan stroked her upper arms. 'Sure you're okay?'

His voice was so tender it hurt. 'I'm fine.'

What if they broke up, or if he thought this was just some one-night stand? How would they live together in Renfield then?

His hands drifted to her ribcage. His thumbs stroked her soft skin. 'I don't want you to rush into anything, Grace.'

Oh . . . but she wanted him.

She leaned back on his chest, reached up and slid her arms around his neck. 'Touch me,' she whispered.

She didn't want to lose him. What if he died tomorrow?

Ivan groaned, sliding his hands forward. She tilted her head so her lips were tantalisingly close. He bent and kissed her, not holding back this time. When he pulled back, there were tears in her eyes.

He withdrew his hands and turned her around to face him. 'You are not ready for this.'

'Yes, I am.' Grace pushed forward and kissed him hard.

Ivan took hold of her shoulders, pushing her back. 'Something is wrong.'

'I'm okay.' Her cheeks were hot, her lips aching to kiss him again. But her stomach tumbled with nerves and her mind was racing.

'You're not.' He took her chin and lifted it. 'Why are you so nervous, hmm?'

Grace stared into his eyes. 'I've never done this before. I came close once, and my boyfriend at the time told everyone we'd done it. Made me sound like some kind of slut.'

Ivan stroked her cheek. 'Now that, I would never believe.' He pulled her into a hug, stroking her back in circles; his breath warm in her ear. 'After tomorrow night, why don't we go away for a few days? Hmm? Would you like that?'

Breathless, she nodded.

Ivan nuzzled her cheek. 'What are you thinking about?'

Grace looked up and stroked his face. 'You.'

'We'll have plenty of time.' He kissed her – long and deep – then tugged back the quilt and slid into bed, pulling her close so her cheek was resting against his chest and her head snuggled under his chin.

As she floated towards sleep, her worries fluttered away. There was only now – just the security of Ivan's arms around her, his breathing rhythmic, his heartbeat strong.

THIRTY-SEVEN

MID-AFTERNOON, THE MERCENARIES began to assemble outside the Residence, each joining his or her own squad. They sat or crouched on the grass, many shielding their eyes against the sunlight that beamed at them just over the roof. Two distinct colours marked the separation between the orders: the Renfield troops were in black, the visiting battalion in khaki. On the steps, Diana, Ivan and the visiting leader, Jorge, were deep in conversation.

Lucius's voice boomed out through two large speakers, calling out each mercenary's name.

'Here,' the voices responded.

Grace wound her hair around her fingers, securing it with a hair net. She drew two bobby pins from her pocket and slid them in.

'You'll need a tighter bun than that. Don't want anyone grabbing your hair, do you?' Sarah sat down next to Grace, her face pale. 'You really should cut it.'

Grace gave her a close look. 'You okay?'

Sarah returned a jittery, restless nod. 'I'm off the meds.'

'Oh, right. Of course. For the mission.'

Sarah closed her eyes and tilted her head back. 'Trying to tune Anna out. She's so agitated!' Sarah bit her lip and stared in the direction of the asylum. 'Lots of strangers in the place.'

'Does she sound . . . different, now that she's degen . . .' Grace paused as Sarah gave her a hard look.

'Now that she's become a demon? Is that what you wanted to say?'

'I didn't mean . . .'

'It's not your fault.' Sarah folded her arms and shrugged. 'I have to face it. But she's still my sister.'

'Of course she is.' There was a tense silence. Grace scanned the crowd. 'I haven't seen Joe yet.'

'He's there.' Sarah pointed to the steps. Joe had joined Ivan, and was looking out over the crowd. Grace waited for the customary smirk, but to her surprise, Joe had a serious, almost humble expression.

'Hello,' a voice said.

Maya sank on to the grass next to them. She gave Sarah a sharp nod.

'Hi . . . how are you?' Grace scanned Maya's face. 'I didn't think you'd be coming.'

Maya just gave her a grim smile. 'I need to apologise to you, Grace. I blamed you for Armin's death. That was not fair of me.'

'It's okay. I don't blame you for feeling like that.'

'Anyway,' said Maya. 'Shall we make a fresh start?'

'Sure.'

'When this is all over, we're going to track down the thing that killed Armin.'

'We'll help you,' Grace gave her a firm nod. 'Me and Joe, I mean.'

'Thank you.'

'All right! Listen up!' Lucius stood back, hands clasped behind his back. An eerie hush fell over the crowd.

'You've all had your squad briefing today, and I expect that you all committed your orders to memory. That's the easy part. What you must do now is commit yourselves to this mission, knowing that there will be sacrifices to be made.' Lucius looked around the crowd with a firm eye. 'Failure to act on our part will mean a catastrophic outcome for the human race. Remember, you are *sarsareh*. Your role is to be a vigilant defender, to take action when no-one else will. You will be going up against a vast number of demons, and you must be prepared for surprises. They will have powers that we cannot anticipate. We know that they are ever-evolving, and when in the company of a high demon, they are more powerful than ever.'

A nervous rumble ran through the crowd. 'Jesus,' someone muttered. 'We're in for a slaughter.'

Lucius raised his hand; the murmuring stopped. 'But we have our own secret weapon.' He looked sideways at Joe and then turned back to the crowd. 'This will not be an ordinary fight. We have the advantage. Follow your orders and have faith.'

Lucius leaned in close to Joe. 'Sorry to put the pressure on you, son.'

Joe shrugged. 'No problem.'

'Assemble in your squads.' Lucius nodded out at the crowd. 'And good luck to you all.'

THIRTY-EIGHT

THE TRANSPORTS MOVED in a convoy – a long, black procession that snaked past the farmlands and into the city limits. Grace stared out at the old houses, remembering them from the night she and Joe escaped Renfield. Tonight, no-one sat on rocking chairs, no children ran the streets. The houses seemed to be surrounded by a blue-grey haze. Was their absence an omen?

'Focus,' Ivan had taken her aside today, his eyes serious. 'Don't let anyone or anything distract you. If we can't take him from a distance, you must get to Malcolm and stop him. No matter what else is going on around you – even if the worst happens, you must get to Malcolm.'

'The worst,' she whispered to herself as she stared at the back of Ivan's head, 'would be to live without you.'

He was so still, so calm – as always. Then he turned his head to look at her. His eyes told her of his love in the soft, open way he gazed at her. Then he dipped his chin in a warm, reassuring nod.

Grace looked at the others. Joe presented a calm face, but the sliver of sweat on his forehead told her he was nervous. Sarah was leaning back, eyes closed. Maya was staring out at the river, her face hard.

They drove past the City centre, its towers gleaming in the moonlight, and along a riverside road that connected the metropolis to its most affluent suburbs. As they stopped at an intersection, Ivan looked across at Seth in the driver's seat. 'Drones on standby?'

Seth nodded. 'Ready to go.'

'Do it.'

They pulled into a grove, well-protected by large bushes, willow trees and boulders. Gradually, the other six transports pulled in behind them; each carried twenty mercenaries from both Renfield and the visiting battalion.

Seth pointed into the distance. 'That's it.' A mammoth limestone wall, broken up by four guardhouses at the front, ran around the boundary of the property, culminating in a stone arch through which a driveway ran. Vivid lights shone from behind the walls; their exterior was also dressed in garlands of fairy lights. To the right was what looked like a hastily constructed car park, crammed with luxury vehicles. A group of drivers were sitting on a tree log, sharing cigars.

Another vehicle pulled into the grove – a large, black truck. The driver ran around and pressed a button at the rear. A ramp descended; a group of mercenaries ran up and disappeared inside the trailer. They re-emerged, driving a small fleet of quadbikes down the ramp and out into the open.

'Cool,' said Joe.

Ivan jumped out of the car and stopped to stare at the mansion. Seth followed; the other squad leaders came across and joined them. Ivan nodded at Seth. 'Send in the Sentinel.'

'Yes, sir.' Seth turned away, pressed his earpiece and muttered a quiet command. Somewhere, in that dark sky, a small stealth drone was soaring over the mansion, stealing images of all that went on below.

In the car, Grace looked across at Sarah. She was sitting very still with her eyes closed, head slightly bent.

'You okay?'

Eyes still closed, Sarah held up her hand. 'Wait.' After a few more seconds, she opened her eyes and let out a long breath. 'Damn it.' She shot Grace a regretful smile. 'My telepathy doesn't seem to be working tonight.'

'Sanderson,' Ivan called.

Sarah slid out of the car. Grace followed her; together they stood at the fringes of the group.

'Yes, sir?'

Ivan stood aside to allow Sarah to step forward. 'Can you give me a situation report? From the inside?'

Sarah lingered nervously at the edge. She rubbed the back of her neck. 'No, sir. I'm sorry.' She looked away from the prickling stares of the squad leaders. 'I can't see a thing. It's really . . . cloudy.'

'Never mind. Do you think you can still use masking and influence?'

Sarah nodded.

'Good.' Ivan turned away and pulled out a handheld computer tablet. 'We're accessing the most up-to-date imaging right now. Evans, can you send a small group across to deal with those drivers? Shouldn't be hard. Remember: non-lethal fire.'

Five mercenaries armed with tranquilliser guns stole through the dark and took up their position in the bushes behind the drivers. 'Three, two, one.'

Hands flew to necks; one of the drivers gasped, turning towards the darkened bushes. But they all slumped forward within five seconds. Sarah backed away from the group and stood close to Grace. 'Boy, do I feel useless,' she muttered.

Grace looked at her friend. 'What's causing it?'

Sarah shrugged. 'I can't tune in to anyone, let alone the high demon himself. It's like trying to find a spark in a raging volcano. Really, we can't be sure of what we're dealing with.'

A fresh chill ran up Grace's back. She folded her arms and took a settling breath.

Sarah smiled. 'I can still feel *your* thoughts, Grace. Don't worry. We'll still be able to do our thing in there.'

Grace nodded.

'It's easier,' Sarah said. 'With masking, you're targeting a specific area. Not as hard as trying to tune in to read one or two minds among a crowd like this.'

'You're so calm,' Grace whispered. How Lucius had wasted Sarah's talent. How Sarah had wasted her own talent by taking those meds. What kind of rift would Joe open? What would happen in there? Her mind began to hurtle.

Ivan looked around the group of leaders. 'Right. Let's recap on our plan. First we take the external gatehouse with sniper fire. Next, our drones will neutralise the guards in the second gatehouse. Then we move in on the bikes . . .'

Grace's stomach fluttered as she watched him speak. Mesmerising, the way he engaged each of the other leaders, how his voice held a combination of calm, authority and anticipation. She glanced towards the mansion, her heart hammering.

She'd be all right, as long as she stayed with him.

'Sentinel imaging is in,' said Seth.

'Excellent.' Ivan drew the group's attention to the surveillance image of the mansion on the computer. 'Right. Several armed guards on both sides of the driveway between the first and second gates. See how many of them are patrolling the hedgerows? The first wave of bikes – snipers – will take those guards, then we'll use bikes to push through to the second gate, which we'll blast with C4.'

One of the leaders pointed to the other figures on screen who were dotted around the garden area behind the second gate. 'Guests?'

'Hosts,' Ivan replied. 'High-ranking Earthborns. For Mammon's army.' He glanced down at the screen. 'The imaging won't pick up the Shadows, but my money's on their being demons. We don't expect them to be armed with live rounds; not with so many guards around. Regardless, we will take precautions. Everything else looks as we anticipated, with a greater concentration of guards as we get closer to the mansion. There are more hosts inside as well.' Ivan pointed to the mansion. 'My guess is Jones and his immediate crew will be at the rear of the mansion.'

One of the visiting leaders cast Sarah and Grace a critical look. 'Isn't there a way to know that for sure? What's the point of having psychics if we can't use them?'

Sarah stared at him through narrowed eyes. 'There's major telepathic activity in there. And there are only two of us.' She pronounced each word slowly.

He shrugged. 'Surely you can overcome it.'

'You don't understand! It's not that simple.'

'Oh, yeah.' He folded his arms. 'Here we go. Complications, the "you don't understand" bit.' He grinned at his colleague. 'It's always like that with telepaths.'

'How would *you* know?' Grace said. 'I don't see any on your squad.'

'Enough!' Ivan's sharp tone put an end to the discussion.

'We have our plan.' He looked around the group. 'Now, are there any questions?'

'No, sir.'

'Good. Five minutes. Seth – send in the Night Ravens.'

Ivan turned back to the car and reached into the back seat. 'Here.' He slid a pair of night-vision glasses over Grace's head. 'You need to be ready to use these if they cut the lights.' He squeezed her shoulders with tight fingers. 'Stay close to me, remember?'

She nodded, heart racing. 'I will.' Even at this distance, her demon 'radar' – as Joe had begun to call it – was pinging hard; the bile threatened to spill over, her stomach tied in firm knots. Her face crumpled with fear. Doubtless, there was so many of them in there. With a shake of her head, she closed her eyes, took a breath and sampled the cool evening air. Breathe. Just breathe.

Ivan passed her a shotgun, his eyes scanning her face. They flared briefly with concern, but his tone remained business-like. There was no time for anything else now. 'Remember, you are to fire at will. Don't wait for my word, don't leave anything to chance. You have live rounds: use them.' He pointed to one of the quad bikes. 'Jump on the back. I'll be with you in a minute.'

He picked up a rifle and took position with the other snipers, deep within the bushes. He stared up into the black-ness where the Night Ravens – ten attack drones – were already flying across, silent killers homing in on the guards at the second gate.

Ivan's eyes drifted across to his mark: a man in the first guardhouse, who was staring out into the darkness.

On screen, the red dots flashed at a furious rate then vanished. Obliterated.

'A direct hit.' Seth's voice was crisp in Ivan's earpiece. 'Secondary guardhouses are down.'

'Fire,' Ivan said. He pulled the trigger.

The guards fell instantly. Ivan put down the rifle, ran across to the bike and started the engine. 'Hold on, Grace!'

The bikes swooped through the stone arch and along the driveway. Grace caught a glimpse of Joe riding nearby with Sarah on the back, her shotgun trained on the bushes.

Grace lifted her gun, her eyes searching for a target. Behind, a wave of riders were spreading out, following Ivan's lead into the right-hand side of the grounds.

Joe and Sarah veered left.

It was easier than she'd thought. The guards were slow to respond to their assault. When she made her first kill, it almost seemed anti-climactic.

Something nicked at her arm. She looked down to see a light scrape in the smart suit.

A guard ran alongside, barrel aimed at her head. She tensed, lifting her gun.

Ivan was faster – he blasted the guard with his shotgun, while steering the bike with his other hand.

Relief swamped her.

Ivan lowered his gun and pulled the bike up next to the gate. 'Grace, Sarah – masking.'

Grace concentrated. She could feel the energy coming from the other side of that gate – the blend of desire, anticipation and fear emanating from the hosts in a solid wave of psychic energy.

Demons, all.

Politicians joked with actors, businessmen made propositions to celebrities. Each one truly believing it. They all believed that they would still be in control of their bodies tomorrow morning, no matter what happened tonight.

The hosts were mindful, attentive. Privileged eyes cast regular glances towards the mansion, waiting for that moment when their beloved masters would soar across to them and take possession of their bodies with their majestic power. Grace concentrated harder, feeling Sarah's energy merge with hers.

Nobody is here. There are no other people – just you, waiting for the glorious honour to take place.

Now, the hosts stood, silent as cattle in the night.

Grace gave Ivan a nod. 'They're ready.'

'Blast the gates.'

Three mercenaries ran forward; each slammed a shaped charge against the intricate steel weavings. They took cover just as the gate blew, bursting shards of metal inwards.

The bikes began to move around the edge of the crowd, heading for the mansion's great door.

THIRTY-NINE

AT THE REAR of the mansion, in a warmly lit, circular room bordered by golden drapes and large bay windows, Halphas watched the scene develop. Mammon was standing directly behind Malcolm, his hand clamped on the boy's head. Malcolm was standing, but not of his own volition. Like a great puppetmaster, Mammon was keeping the boy upright – while also devoting his energy to the small rift that had emerged in front of the pair.

It had materialised strangely, its clouds seeping into the atmosphere as if by force.

Now, it began its rapid growth.

Mammon's fingers dug harder; frost oozing from his flesh as he strained, teeth clenched, dark eyes locked on the expanding rift.

Halphas peered at the three apprentices standing nearby. To the youngsters, it must have seemed that Malcolm was in a deep, painless trance.

But Halphas knew better.

Hours before, his Master had finally realised there was only one way to make Malcolm open a Dark Rift. Something that Halphas had known the day he'd met the boy.

Malcolm would have to walk through his own nightmare. To live inside the same dream he'd woken from, sweating, as the rift shuddered above his hospital bed.

And so Mammon had entered his mind and dragged him into the dark place where his fears lived; flinging him into the pit where his terror tore at him, trapping him in its tentacles, rolling him down into the well of his subconscious; a place from which he would never return.

And now, a Dark Rift was forming.

Halphas sank into a chair, groaning as his pelvis creaked. His gaze flickered to the door and his senses tingled. Joe was out there, in the darkness. No doubt he'd brought an army with him. A warm, secret satisfaction flooded Halphas as he stared at his master's back. Mammon had never known – Halphas could detect where each and every Ferryman was at any moment. Down to the square inch. He didn't need to tune in, or search for a Sign. The Signs came to him. Of course, that wasn't something Halphas was about to reveal. Too big a trump card.

The rift grew some more, and Halphas pictured the Shadows: pressing, pushing against the rift's inner walls, bursting to come through and claim their hosts, who were kneeling in neat rows along the floor. Halphas's eyes creased with worry as he watched the rift grow. But of course, if Joe didn't kill his master tonight, that was a card Halphas was very willing to play.

* * *

ANDRAS GLANCED AT the CCTV monitor. He gasped at the swarm of bikes that were making their way around the insensible crowd. 'Master! We have trouble outside!'

'What?' Mammon glared at him. 'Well, see to it, Andras!' With gritted teeth, he turned back and kept giving energy to the rift.

The cloud expanded.

Andras closed his eyes and began to join with the hosts downstairs. *Fight! Kill them all!* The demons jolted – yanked out of Grace's trance and turned on the intruders. They dropped their champagne glasses and tore off their fine clothes as they raged towards the bikes.

They pounced on the mercenaries. Supernatural strength oozed through well-manicured fingers, breaking necks, squeezing throats until they burst. Those who had the power to move objects sent a combined wave of telekinetic energy across, crashing into several of the bikes and sending them into a violent roll.

'Fire!' Ivan shouted.

Grace raised her shotgun and pulled the trigger. All around her, a tide of bullets hit the hosts. Some of them fell.

'Wait! Get back!' Joe roared. He shot up his arms – the air exploded into a giant ball of cloud, spewing shards of lightning and sending a thunderous boom into the air. Consuming the demons in a frantic, turbulent death.

Joe dropped his arms. The disturbed earth settled into a shallow crater. Joe gave a delirious grin. 'Cookie cutter.'

For a few seconds, the entire battalion stared at the Ferryman in silent awe.

Joe slumped. He rubbed his forehead. 'Whoa. That was intense.'

'Conserve your energy, Joe!' Ivan pushed the bike towards the building. As they rode past the hedgerows, two guards – both demons – stepped out of the greenery, swiping their arms across the bikes. Ivan swerved; Grace shot a look back just as Sarah blasted the pair to kingdom come.

They rode on towards the left-hand side of the mansion, where a giant garage was dwarfed by an airplane hangar, next to which a dark strip of tarmac ran from the lawns all the way to the edge of the river.

Another demon guard sprang out from behind a statue, his cold hand slamming against Grace's throat. She soared backwards, hitting the pavement with an agonised gasp as sharp pain dashed up her spine. In the distance, she saw the bike skid to a stop.

The demon seized her around the neck, and she was dragged off her feet. Her hands flew to her neck, but too late – his fingers had begun their death squeeze.

Then, his Shadow dissolved into nothingness. The demon lurched backwards, hands searching the back of his head for the neurotoxins that Ivan had just fired into him. Powerless, he staggered around.

Grace slumped to the ground, leaning on the statue's column. She watched in terrified fascination as Ivan pulled the demon towards him and plunged a knife into the side of its neck. Blood erupted from the wound. Ivan sank the knife into the guard's abdomen and then drew the blade up, rupturing the vital organs and slicing him open.

The demon fell in a puddle of blood, flesh and entrails.

With weak legs, Grace dragged herself up, using the column to help her. She stared at Ivan's face as he wiped his knife on the demon's shirt and put it back into its sheath.

'You okay?' His eyes were hard. Savage, even.

Trembling, she nodded. 'Ivan the Terrible,' she whispered.

But when he took her hand and helped her to her feet, his grasp was soothing, his voice gentle. 'Come on.'

The squads began to regroup at the side of the mansion, near the hangar. Grace settled on the ground, next to Sarah. For a time, they watched the grounds in vigilant silence. Mercenaries shot regular looks upwards, but no more guards appeared on the balcony.

Joe nodded to the airstrip. 'Bet he's planning a getaway straight after.'

'Good point, Joe,' said Ivan. 'Adams, go into that hangar and put a banana in the tailpipe.'

Grinning, the mercenary ran off, explosive in his hand.

Ivan watched as Evans, one of the squad leaders, approached with a grim expression.

'All accounted for?'

'We've had some casualties,' said Evans.

Ivan nodded, his eyes grim.

Grace looked up at him. 'We should be careful when we go inside. Someone in there interfered with our telepathy, big time.'

'If only we could get in there and have a sneaky look.' Bemused, Ivan scratched his chin.

'I could.'

Ivan's gaze fell on Grace. 'How?'

'You know . . . what I said at the meeting.'

'Not a good idea. We may need to move suddenly. Anyway, you're unpractised at that kind of thing.'

'But we don't really know what's in there, do we?'

Ivan stared at her. 'That's true,' he admitted.

'I might not even be able to do it. But it's worth a try. Nobody will know I'm there, and I can find out what we're really up against.'

Ivan knelt in front of her. 'Are you sure?'

With a deep breath, she nodded.

'All right. But don't waste time in there, Grace. In and out.'

A hush fell as she sat back, leaned against the wall and closed her eyes. 'I haven't practised very much.'

Ivan's voice was close. 'Just try. If you can't do it, we'll go in anyway.'

Grace focused – imagining the white room. She always visualised this room when she was trying to go to sleep, using it as a springboard into a calm, peaceful dream after a harrowing day of training. The white walls appeared more quickly this time.

She imagined sitting inside the room, crossing her legs on a feathery floor.

Minutes passed, and she opened her eyes. 'I need something to trigger it. Last time, it was tasering.'

A mercenary, overly eager, stepped forward and took aim at Grace.

'No!' Ivan shoved him away. 'Sanderson. Can you help?'

Grace looked at her friend. 'The psi-attack, Sarah. Do it to me.'

Sarah nodded. 'If you're sure.'

Grace closed her eyes again; Sarah focused on her forehead.

Something was battering at one of the white walls. It trembled, vibrating like the ground when an earthquake hit. Grace's fingernails began to dig into the ground. Heat spread through her forehead. It stung, as though a scar was being slowly burned into her skull. She clenched her teeth, struggled to endure it, and then the white walls were trembling, shaking.

They exploded into pieces and fell away into the blackness.

She was out.

She turned her consciousness towards the mansion. Straight through the solid front doors – doing this freaked her out just as much as that first, horrible time – and she tried to close her eyes.

Can't. Not in body, stupid.

The joke was a tactic to remain calm, to avoid the desperate, disconnected feeling that being out of her body brought on.

Into a large entrance hall. Above, a giant dome with gold patterns lent an elegant light to the twin staircases that graced the back wall, their marble steps swathed in red velvet. Giant terracotta pots lined the walls, their innards bursting with white lilies.

A quick count put the number of hosts in here at one hundred. The light sparkled off the multiple chandeliers – somehow, it seemed brighter than it would if she were in her body, looking through her eyes. The women's dresses shimmered like peacock feathers – a vibrant blend of red, gold and blue – while the men's white collars were luminescent.

They milled around an immense statue of a golden calf, nearly as tall as the landing above the staircases that wound their way along the circular walls. On the right-hand wall, a massive portrait of Mammon. Yuck.

Up the stairs and towards the rear room of the mansion. That guy – Anthony, or whatever – stood at the top of the staircase, staring down at the gaggle of hosts. She looked into his eyes and remembered the calming sensation she'd felt when he looked at her.

He was the one controlling the hosts. Messing with their telepathy.

She soared past Andras and through the final door. There was a strange, squelchy sensation and she realised she'd just passed through a throng of human guards, stationed at the exit. Now she knew the difference – there was a cool, neutral feeling when passing through wood.

It was a circular room – an elegant ballroom.

Malcolm was standing on a dais, three steps higher than the crowd; Mammon directly behind him. The high demon's energies seemed to be directed at the rift but also at keeping the boy entranced. Grace looked into Malcolm's face. Vacant eyes sat deep in his skull; she sensed all his energy had been squeezed out by Mammon and dumped into the rift.

Malcolm was in a standing coma.

Malcolm wasn't there anymore.

She looked at the rows of hosts, and outside, back in the safe gloom of the night, her body reacted – her stomach raging with nausea. Top-level ghoulies. They kneeled in rows on the parquetry floor, arms behind their backs, heads bowed. All men. Each had his own Shadow – of course – which pulsated with energy, striving to touch the essence of the High One himself.

Grace glanced around; a rough count estimated fifty of them. Plus Mammon, Malcolm, and two of the 'mercenaries': another guy and that girl whom Joe had liked.

'Behold!' Mammon shouted. 'The Dark Rift!'

Grace was spellbound. The Rift's tumbling whirlwind, its thunderclouds in turmoil were drawing all physical matter in. She watched the curtains pull and strain against their fixings.

A doorway into Hell.

Dark shapes – Shadows – began to emerge from the Rift's mouth and spew out into the air. Each of them bore a unique, bestial shape. Each moved with the urgency of a beast mid-hunt – shadowy limbs chasing down prey. The energy field reversed, and the curtains fell back into place as the dark forces flooded the room.

FORTY

MAMMON WATCHED GLEEFULLY as his Shadows spilled out of the Dark Rift. 'That's it, my generals! Assume your places!'

It was sickening – Grace watched the first Shadow home in on its chosen host and then loom above the back of his head for a few seconds, forming a tornado-like shape, the tail a fine point like a bee's stinger, poised to enter. The Shadow pushed inwards, its dark energy rippling behind the skin, invading face, neck and torso – bringing gasps of pain from the host.

The gasping stopped. Grace watched the host calmly stand up and pull a cigar from his pocket. He lit it, took a puff and smiled at Mammon. 'Good to be back.'

Mammon smiled. 'Good to have you here, Bathin.'

There was no more demonic gloom around the body; no sign that this was an Earthborn demon. This Shadow, this Hellborn thing seemed to have obliterated the consciousness of the host.

Bathin looked at Haures. 'Mammon, I see you're keeping the same calibre of company as always.' His eyes lingered on her cleavage. 'Perhaps she can provide me with my first sample . . . of many.'

Haures scowled. She stepped towards Bathin and shape-shifted into his image: a fifty-something man – pale, sweaty and balding. 'I don't know if you'll like what you see.'

Grace backed out as quickly as she could – through the mountain of human flesh at the door, the cold, flat mass of the wood – and fled back to the dark corner of the house, sinking into her body as quickly as she could.

Her eyes fluttered open. She sat forward and tried to jump up.

'Steady!' Ivan was crouching in front of her. He grabbed her by the arms. 'Just go slow now.'

'The Rift is open!'

'Then we don't have much time.' Ivan nodded at the other squad leaders. 'Be ready to move.'

Grace looked over at Joe, who was sitting nearby. 'It's mammoth! Out of control. Like the one you opened that night, on my birthday – but worse.'

Ivan glanced at the mansion. 'So, how many are there?'

'The entrance hall is full of hosts. And about fifty upstairs. And they're already coming through.'

'What, through the Rift? What did they look like?'

'Shadows. Just Shadows. And when they possess a body, the Shadow disappears completely. You just can't tell they're demons.' Her eyes darted to Joe.

'That girl is there as well.'

'Haures,' he said.

'There's another guy there, from the table that night.'

'Andras?' said Joe.

'I don't remember their names.'

'You know – the one who gave you the drinks that night, at the festival.'

'No, he's out on the balcony, controlling the hosts. Another guy. I don't know what he can do.'

'Okay, then.' Ivan stood up. 'We crack the door and go in firing.'

* * *

ANDRAS PEERED OVER the balcony, sweeping his gaze over the hosts assembled in the entrance hall. 'Get ready to attack,' he said. 'Your futures are at stake here, and you will lose your chance at power if you let these mercenaries win.'

But it was quiet. For fifteen minutes – nothing. No point in sending a patrol outside just so they could get chewed up by the Ferryman's rift. Andras shuddered at the thought. He turned and slipped back into the circular room, where Mammon's Shadows were still floating about their hosts' heads.

Mammon shot him a demanding look.

'The hosts downstairs are ready,' Andras said, with a slight nod of his head. 'If you hurry, your next wave of troops can take their bodies and win the fight far more easily.'

'There's a protocol to follow here, Andras. These are my generals.' Mammon waved to the Shadows that were flying out of the Rift. 'They take the more important hosts, then we move down to the lesser-ranking folk downstairs. We will make it in time. The mercenaries are delaying. I suspect they may retreat. At the very least, they seem to be waiting for something. Courage, most likely.' With a smirk, he looked back at the rift.

For the first time in his apprenticeship, Andras felt angry at his master. 'If we had our mind-reader, we'd know why,' he muttered.

The front door exploded, sending ripples of shockwaves through the walls. Andras burst out of the circular room and back onto the balcony. He drew in a sharp breath as a group of mercenaries flooded through the front entrance. Once again his hosts were acting like sheep, and the mercenaries were slicing through them.

For the first time, he saw why. That girl! She was the cause.

'Damn it!' He swept a powerful telepathic wave over the remaining hosts. It was as though he'd shoved a battery up their arses. They retaliated, throwing themselves against their attackers. The fighting began to move up the stairs. The mercenaries had produced riot shields and were deflecting the attacks neatly.

That bitch – Joe's sister – was standing in the doorway, eyes entranced – obviously sending out a telepathic wave, overriding Andras's power; the hosts became docile, sheep to the slaughter.

'I should have killed her that night. Zagan! Get out here!'

Haures tried to run, but Mammon grabbed her arm. Amidst the multiple Shadows that were now pouring out of the Rift, he looked more frightening than ever. She froze.

'You stay right here,' he said. 'You owe me, remember?'

Zagan jogged over next to Andras. He looked down at the scene. 'What the hell went wrong?'

'We've lost them!' Andras hissed. 'The girl, Grace! She's too strong!' He watched as the last of the hosts was impaled by a harpoon.

Zagan gave Andras an impassive look. 'Not good for you, huh?'

Andras grabbed Zagan by his jacket, spitting in his face. 'Throw something at them!' He turned and ran through a side door, which led to a staircase. It would take him down to the garage, to freedom.

Zagan watched him leave and then turned with a smile. He slammed his hand through the air; the giant statue swayed and crashed to the floor, bouncing spear-sized splinters of marble through the air. The last living host was stumbling about, harpoon wedged in his chest. A marble splinter shot into his skull, killing him.

The mercenary who'd fired the harpoon laughed.

Zagan twisted his hand and lashed it forward. A large chunk of marble smashed into the mercenary's face.

The demon lifted more lumps and began throwing them around the room. There was nowhere to run – hunks of marble crashed down on the floor right below the staircase, even behind it, where a row of mercenaries were hiding.

Ivan lifted his shotgun and fired, sending a harpoon straight at Zagan's heart. The demon deflected the shot with ease, sending the harpoon spiralling down to the ground.

'Okay then,' Ivan snarled, flicking to live rounds. 'Cop this!'

Bullets rained through the air but then swept upwards, met by a tidal wave of telekinetic energy. They soared to the ceiling, losing energy as they climbed, then they bounced off the plaster, rattling to the floor like pins.

Ivan lowered his gun. 'Impressive,' he admitted.

Zagan smiled. He picked up another boulder.

'Take cover!' Ivan grabbed Grace, both moving out of the way as another giant wedge of marble crashed on to the tiles.

They dodged out the front door; Joe followed.

'Now we're outside! This is no good.' Grace looked at Joe. 'When I tell you, in here . . .' she pointed to her head. 'Open a small rift right underneath, where the rubble is.'

She shot a look back at Ivan. 'I'll mask my way upstairs, until I'm right behind him. Otherwise, he'll crush us all.'

'That's risky,' Ivan said.

'It's the only way. He's going to keep throwing things at us. And the Dark Rift is still open!'

Ivan nodded. 'All right.'

'He won't know I'm coming. Just get ready, Joe.'

Zagan swooped his arms through the air and clapped his hands together, then he burst them apart at speed. Below, a pile of rubble lifted and slammed out in various directions, taking chunks out of the wall. Grace climbed the stairs, keeping a steady level of concentration.

So far, so good. She crept up to the top of the stairs, her steps silent on the velvet. But that wasn't going to be enough. She doubled her focus. If Zagan turned around, all he would see was an empty staircase.

He paused for a second. Grace's heart nearly stopped. But he just hung his arms over the balcony, grinning. 'Come out, come out! I know you're there, little telepath! Or did you run away?' He feigned a pout.

Grace stared at his back. 'I'm right here, you jackass.'

Now, Joe!

Grace planted her foot in Zagan's back. For good measure, she hit him with a telepathic assault. He gasped at the sudden, hot pain in his skull. Fingers grappling at his head, he tripped and stumbled into the railing, then fell over the edge. Desperate to regain control, he somersaulted towards the floor – straight into Joe's rift. Grace watched him disappear inside. Joe paused, cocked his ear. 'Listen!'

They all stood in silence, listening as the Reavers came and ripped the demon's body to pieces.

'That still amazes me,' said Joe, shaking his head.

The mercenaries peeled away from the walls, running towards Joe, smacking his back with congratulatory slaps.

Ivan's voice cut into the clamour. 'It's not over yet! Up we go!' He took the stairs two at a time and then caught Grace around the waist. 'Well done.'

He moved towards the door.

'We can't just go in there,' Grace said. 'Mammon will destroy us.' She looked at Ivan. 'Let me check it out again. I can reach Malcolm there.'

Disapproving murmurs abounded. 'We're so close,' said Joe. 'We can just go in, guns blazing.'

'Come on!' Grace shot him a disbelieving look. 'Any minute now, those things that have come through the Dark Rift are going to come through *that* wall and start looking for bodies to take! We need to close the Rift!'

'We can take the room.'

'The demons in there are different, Ivan. We don't know what they're capable of.'

'Okay. Sit down.' He crouched next to her. 'Give her some cover.' An entire squad of mercenaries took their places in a defensive circle around Grace.

Sarah poked her head through. 'Do you need me again?'

'I'm going to try to do it myself.'

Darkness first, then she pictured the catalyst that seemed to come first: the white walls. She didn't have time for this. Grace blasted through the walls.

Malcolm.

Grace floated through the doors, past the rows of hosts, some still kneeling in wait, others fully possessed and gazing into mirrors, admiring their new vessels. Calmly, she headed over to hover next to Malcolm.

But how to reach him? She saw Mammon – thankfully, unaware of her presence – and his fingers pressed into Malcolm's head in a vicious lock. Then, Grace knew it.

She had to become part of the nightmare.

She pressed her hand towards Malcolm's face and felt herself begin to fall. Tumbling through a dark, narrow space. It was dark, but then – abruptly, she was standing.

The first thing she noticed: her feet, grey and cold. Her jeans bunched up around her knees, her chest shaking with cold under a sheer t-shirt. But there was a sun – she could just see its outline in the whitewashed sky. She stared; her eyes didn't hurt. The sun only gave off a grey, cool light.

There was no warmth to be found. The air seemed thin and she could only draw shallow lungfuls. No wind. Trapped inside an airtight container.

Her feet were carrying her across hard sand. A spike of pain hit her left foot. She lifted it to find a broken seashell sticking into her flesh. Pulling it free, Grace watched as dark grey blood oozed from the wound.

To her left, peeling flagpoles with torn, wrinkled flags slumped at half-mast. Behind, faded funhouse buildings sat, their colours eaten by salt. At the northern end of the beach sat a hulking pier that looked ready to fall down. Its iron supports were flimsy, like matchsticks. Closer, a smaller metallic shape jutted strangely from the sand: a ferris wheel, crashed to the ground. A weak tide dribbled over its rusty railings.

No people anywhere. No seagulls. A smell in the air – smoke from distant fires. The water was riddled with rotting seaweed; it gave off the smell of a rancid pool, instead of the fresh, salty scent of a healthy sea.

Malcolm was in front of her, kneeling – barely leaving an imprint on the unforgiving sand. Grace descended to her knees, her hands flat on the beach.

Malcolm?

He didn't look at her.

Do you understand what's happening?

He drew shapes in the sand with a small, white tree branch. His eyes seemed to register that she was there. His whole body tensed.

Why are you here, Malcolm?

Can't get out. His voice tightened with terror – he twisted up his face and trembled. Tried to shake off the fear.

Where is this place? Why are you here?

He screwed up his face again, not from fear, but rather to show contempt for her not knowing where she was.

This is Blackpool. I was born a few miles from here. My mum used to bring me in summer.

Grace peered around at the bleak beach. *But it's not summer now . . .*

Yeah, I know. He took a shuddering breath.

Must get him to move, to do something.

Is this a bad dream for you, Malcolm? What is it in here that frightens you?

For the first time, he looked at her. *Aren't you afraid? Look around. Look at what you see. It's all gone.*

She's all gone.

He never brought me back here. I begged him to. He never took me anywhere. Just dragged me out to the end of the world. To that place.

Then she died. He didn't let me see her then, either.

Malcolm didn't look up, but he pointed up the beach to where a shadowed figure stood. The cold light dropped on Marcus's outline; his face eternally turned away from his son.

Grace crouched in front of him. *You mustn't want to stay here, Malcolm. Surely not.*

Malcolm looked at the horizon. *But I don't want to die.*

Now, the sun was dropping at a frightening speed. Night swept over the sand like a dark, unwelcome wind. Malcolm turned back to his drawing. But the stick dropped from his trembling fingers and he couldn't see in the dark. He hugged himself, rocking back and forth. *It'll get better, eventually. I just have to wait. He'll get what he wants – and then I'll be free. It'll be warm, and I can lie in the sun by the pool . . .*

Grace looked at his outline. *I don't think so. I think it will get dark and cold before summer comes. It's only the beginning.*

You'll have to wait a long time for the sun. Mammon will never let you be free, Malcolm.

He turned to her, his eyes devastatingly vulnerable.

I don't want to live in the dark.

No. Do you want to see her again?

His face began to crumple. *Oh, yes.*

Where it's warm?

Yes. Tears spilled from his cheeks, plopping onto the sand.

Suddenly, a new light began to shine on his face, bringing colour, accentuating the redness in his cheeks down to the capillaries, the tiny veins in his eyes, even the clear shimmer of his tears. It was a light in which nothing could hide, but it was warm, emanating from the southern edge of the beach.

Did she make that happen?

No. This was something far bigger than any illusion she could pull.

This was home.

The light was moving away, radiating across the ocean. Up until that point, it had flooded everything else in the vicinity, but now a red and white lighthouse revealed itself, sitting on a grassy plain that seemed to hover above the water.

Grace pointed to the lighthouse. *Go now, Malcolm.*

A woman was waiting there. Her hair was loose, flapping around her shoulders in a temperate wind. Slowly, Malcolm stood up. Without looking back at Grace, he walked towards the woman, leaving the grey, ruined memory behind.

Once again, the lighthouse's bright beam saturated the beach. Grace blinked and squinted – but she could not see anything. When the light subsided, she looked again – and Malcolm had disappeared.

FORTY-ONE

'No!' MAMMON'S ROAR shook the walls as his Dark Rift began to collapse. His fingers pressed deeper into Malcolm's skull, desperate to spark another connection, but the boy had gone limp. With a thump, his body hit the carpet.

Mammon threw his head back and howled. *'Why?'*

In the safe darkness of the corner, Halphas allowed himself a very small smile.

The high demon watched, almost tearful as the clouds evaporated, leaving nothing but a trashed room and a tense, almost embarrassed silence among his generals.

Then, they all heard it. The reason – gasped through dying lips. *'Grace. Thank you.'* A final breath escaped Malcolm's body, and then he was free.

'Damn you!' Mammon lunged at the boy, smashing his foot into Malcolm's ribcage, over and over. A cracking noise accompanied each kick.

'Mammon,' Bathin said, half-amused by the tantrum. 'He is dead!'

'I realise this, Bathin.' Panting, Mammon glared at the door.

Outside, Grace opened her eyes to see Ivan's face in front of her. Thank God. She was back. She gave him a weak smile. 'The Dark Rift is gone.'

'We know,' Joe said. 'It's quiet. Too quiet.'

Ivan helped Grace to her feet. 'Well done. Now, to get in there and finish this.'

'The door is locked,' Joe said.

Ivan took a charge and planted it on the door. 'Take cover!'

Mammon pointed to the window. 'Get to the helipad, all of you!'

As the generals clambered out of the nearest windows, Haures darted into the throng. Halphas was limping in front of her. 'Hurry up, old man!' She shoved him through a window. He landed on the outside roof with a thump, crawled to his feet and threw her an indignant look before hobbling after the others.

'Oh, no you don't!' Mammon snatched Haures's hair and yanked her back; she squealed. 'Not you. You lost Joe, now you owe me!'

The door exploded, leaving dust and plaster in its wake.

Ivan led the others, shotgun trained. Mammon stood in the middle of the room. Ivan pulled the trigger. 'Now, Joe!'

A ball of cloud exploded. Joe's brow was tense – the concentration painful as he directed the energy upwards.

Mammon stumbled around as the harpoon skewered his torso, the back end forming an X behind his spine. His eyes were wide, fixed on Joe as he tried to open his mouth to speak. But no sound came; he watched in silent horror as Ivan turned the gun, aimed it into Joe's rift, and hit the trigger a second time – a controlled, yet rapid firing.

The diamond wire shot into the cloud.

The wire grew taut, and they all knew the Reavers were on the other end. Mammon flew into the dark void, screaming in a strange, high-pitched tone.

Joe closed the rift. He breathed out, bending over, hands on knees. Sweat dribbled from his forehead on to the carpet.

Silent shock took the room for a few seconds.

Ivan lowered his gun. 'We did it.' He reached over and offered his hand to Joe. 'Congratulations.'

Grinning, Joe shook Ivan's hand. 'You too.' He blinked, and in the darkness his eyes replayed the memory. Among the clouds and lightning shards of his rift, had he caught a glimpse of red hair, a hint of ivory skin?

He blinked again, shaking his head.

A sharp cry shocked him. The crowd of mercenaries moved in, all eyes searching the room for the source.

Then, Grace stumbled forward from the shadows, hands pressed to her stomach. She stared down at the blood leaching between her fingers.

Ivan ran at Grace, grabbing her as she swayed. He looked into her glassy eyes and the truth hit him instantly. 'You'll be all right,' he whispered. His gaze dropped to the wound – the clean, precise cut that had somehow penetrated the smart suit. 'Medics! Now!'

Mammon stepped out into the light, his fingers gripping the handle of a short sword. Its dark grey blade glinted in the light, but its edges seemed dull due to the shadow that it carried – an aura of dark energy. He gave Joe a smile, then he slipped a fresh handkerchief from his pocket and began wiping away Grace's blood.

'Joe.' He chuckled. 'Did you really think that you had me?' He cast a triumphant glance at the girl, slumped in Ivan's arms. 'Don't waste your time there, boy. She'll be dead in a few minutes.'

Joe spun around to the other mercenaries. *'Kill him!'*

But Mammon arched his back, his body contorting, blending flesh with demonic essence – until he took the form of the Shadow Wolf.

Joe stared in terrible fascination at Mammon's mystical transformation: no longer human, but not all spirit, either.

The creature sounded a roar – rumbling like the peak of volcanic eruption – and the ground shook. Mercenaries pressed hands to ears; some fell to the carpet, writhing at the piercing pain in their eardrums. Then, the roaring stopped and the Shadow Wolf reared up – its head brushing against the ceiling. On four legs, it began a crashing run towards the exit – massive claws gripping the sword, which now looked so small; a child's toy.

'Fire!'

Bullets just fell through the ethereal body, smashing into the far wall. The Shadow Wolf plunged on – its path clear as mercenaries leapt aside in terror – and with one last howl, it shot through the exit to be swallowed up by the darkness outside, towards freedom.

In silent shock, the mercenaries lowered their guns. Trembling, sweaty faces glanced at each other.

In the middle of the room, Joe began a summoning, speaking under his breath. He stood: eyes open, hands spread. The room began to glow as a bright circle took form.

Ivan carried Grace across to a chair. He sat down and pulled her onto his lap. With a gentle hum, he began rocking her. Three medics swooped on them. Upon examining the wound, they swapped confused frowns. The lead medic shook his head. 'I don't understand how the blade got through her suit! We'll have to get her straight to surgery.'

'Well? Snap to it!' Ivan growled. *'Hurry up!'*

'No.' Joe's voice boomed from the centre of the room. 'Wait. We'll take her to Utu.'

'Well, do it then!'

Ivan looked down at Grace. She reached up and touched the stubble on his chin. 'Don't be angry.' Her voice was so weak.

'Just focus on me.' He didn't like the look on her face. Frighteningly calm. A look he'd seen before . . . in the dying. He remembered his promise to Diana, and a deep panic hit as he pressed his hand against the wound once more. 'We'll stop the bleeding,' he whispered. But her eyelids were sagging, her breaths becoming fainter. Her face was already too pale.

She tried to smile. 'I saw something . . .'

He bent his face closer. 'What was that, little one?'

'I saw it. I don't know how to tell you . . .' As she faded into darkness, her last thought was of the lighthouse and that brief, indescribable moment of peace.

Ivan's heart pounded as he traced his finger over her pulse point. She was still alive. His head snapped up. *'Hurry up, Joe!'*

The rift reached its peak – the light too intense to look into without squinting.

Next, Utu emerged and looked at Joe. 'Mammon?'

'He got away.'

Utu looked over the damage. 'But how many came through?'

'I think . . . about fifty.'

'Fifty.' Utu's voice echoed, his tone grave. 'And they would have been his best.' The old priest began a slow walk across the room. 'A major victory for him.' He shook his head gravely at Joe. 'You have no idea. Our struggle has just become infinitely harder.'

'Hey!' Ivan gave Utu an angry look. 'There are more important things than that right now! She needs healing – fast!'

Utu bent down and stared at Grace's wound. His eyes shone with solemn pity. 'This is a spirit-blade wound.'

'Can she be healed or not?' Ivan demanded.

'Yes, but . . .'

'Come on, then!' Ivan stood; Grace secure in his arms. He was already moving towards the rift, when Utu stepped into his way, his hand raised in warning. 'She *will* be healed, but she is already absorbing the spirit blade's energy. You must understand, you must be prepared for this . . . the future will be hard for her.'

'She wants to live,' Ivan said.

Joe nodded. 'We'll take our chances.'

Utu lowered his arm and bowed his head. 'As you wish.' He turned and led them into the rift.

ACKNOWLEDGEMENTS

THE FIRST PEOPLE I would like to thank are John and Linda: my think tank, support group and critical friends.

Of course, I want to thank my wonderful mum, who has always been calm, supportive and overwhelmingly positive about this book.

Thanks must go to Cristina Briones and Abigail Nathan for their excellent, spot-on suggestions and ability to see little things that were invisible to me.

J.B. Thomas was born in Perth in 1971. Adopted at a young age, she grew up in a beachside suburb with three brothers. Her father – a prominent Perth lawyer, and later, a district court judge – died when she was 14.

She was inspired to write The Ferryman Chronicles by speculating what life would be like if demons walked among ordinary (and not-so-ordinary) humans.

She is a fan of Sergei Lukyanenko (*Night Watch*), Cassandra Clare (*The Mortal Instruments*), and Suzanne Collins (*The Hunger Games*). She also is an admirer of Alan Moore (*V for Vendetta*, *Watchmen*) and enjoys shows such as *Supernatural*, *Being Human* and *Dexter*.

J.B. Thomas lives with her husband in Perth, where she teaches English. She is a longtime fan of Great Danes, and when she's not writing or reading, she watches films, walks her dog, George, and on occasion can be found playing online games.

Mammon is her first novel.